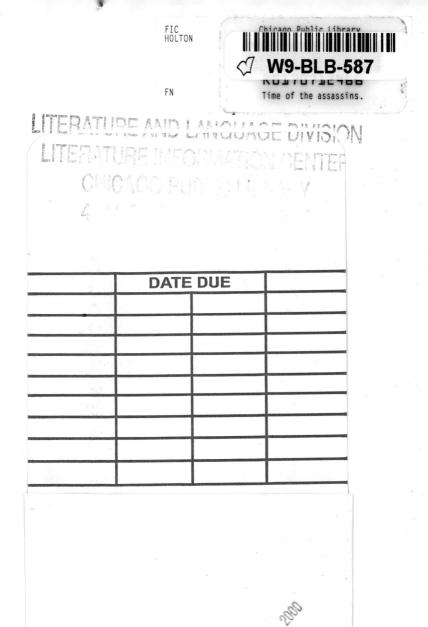

	DATE DUE		

TIME
OF THE
ASSASSINS

By Hugh Holton from Tom Doherty Associates

Presumed Dead
Chicago Blues
Windy City
Violent Crimes
Red Lightning
The Left Hand of God
Time of the Assassins

HUGH HOLTON

TIME
OF THE
ASSASSINS

A TOM DOHERTY ASSOCIATES BOOK

NEW YORK

TIME OF THE ASSASSINS

Copyright © 2000 by Hugh Holton

A Forge Book
Published by Tom Doherty Associates, LLC
175 Fifth Avenue
New York, NY 10010

www.tor.com

Forge® is a registered trademark of Tom Doherty Associates, LLC.

Library of Congress Cataloging-in-Publication Data

Holton, Hugh.
    Time of the assassins / Hugh Holton.—1st ed.
        p.   cm.
    "A Tom Doherty Associates book."
    ISBN 0-312-87333-6 (acid-free paper)
    1. Cole, Larry (Fictitious character)—Fiction.   2. Police—Illinois—Chicago—Fiction.   3. Chicago (Ill.)—Fiction.   4. Assassins—Fiction.
I. Title.
PS3558.O4373 T56 2000
813'.54—dc21   99-057469

First Edition: February 2000

Printed in the United States of America

0   9   8   7   6   5   4   3   2   1

Time of the Assassins *is dedicated*
to my grandson, Gabriel C. Cook,
born on August 16, 1999.

Acknowledgments

After thirty years as a Chicago police officer and ten years as a working novelist, I have been blessed to meet some of the best and most gifted members in both the fields of law enforcement and mystery writing. There is no way that I can acknowledge them all, but I will do the best that I can in the space allotted. Again, if I miss anyone, take heart. My next novel, *The Devil's Shadow,* will be published in 2001 and there will definitely be more acknowledgments.

To Commander Marienne Perry of the Second District, who brings knowledge, style, and charm to the task of being the top police boss in one of the highest crime per capita areas in the world. To Lieutenants Lilly Crump-Hales, Dave Bocian, Eugene Daly, and Don Kuchar. To Sergeants Prentiss Jackson, Rob Pet, Mark Thompson, Teresa Williams, Bill Callahan, and Patrice Mozee-Russell. To Sergeant Melvin Powell, who showed the politicians how to be an alderman during his brief stint at City Hall. To Sergeant Eugene Warling and Police Officer Joe Davenport, who taught me the power of the computer. And to some of the officers who get it done out on the mean streets of Chicago: Patrol Specialist David Cherry; Police Officers Gerald Sheppard, Rosavelia Del Rio, Dora Rogers, Mike Parker, Joe D. Parker, Tarita Preston, Laura Otto, Penny Nichols, Cynthia Womack, Claude Dunlap, Angela Pate, Maurice Willis, Steve Azzoli, Socrates Mabry, Lonnie Alston, Ronnie Taylor, Debora Howard, Alesia Morris, Michael Hayes, Sandy Ervin, Mike Ballard, B. J. Johnson, Chana Varnado, Teresa Williams, Benita Miller; and Police Aides Elaine Brown, Towana Lucas, Johnnie Smith, and Sharon Stokes.

I must always acknowledge the person who was singularly responsible for helping me become a published author, Mrs. Barbara D'Amato, President of Mystery Writers of America and winner of the Anthony, Edgar, and Carl Sandburg Awards for excellence in fiction. And to Barbara's family—husband Tony, sons Brian and Paul, daughter-in-law Cheryl, and grandkids, Emily and Adam Alexander D'Amato.

To Jeanne M. Damms and Mark Richard Zubro, who along with Barbara and myself, make up the Chicago Mystery Mob. Our motto: "We do drive by book signings." To Eileen Dreyer and Luci Zahray, who helped me with technical assistance, and Les Roberts, Jeremiah Healey, and Eleanor Taylor Bland, who always have encouraging words. And to all the members of the Midwest Chapters of Mystery Writers of America and Sisters In Crime.

—Hugh Holton, June 1999

In Memoriam

In memory of all of the police officers
who have given their lives in the line of duty, especially,

Michael A. Ceriale,

John C. Knight,

and

James H. Camp

of the

Chicago Police Department.

Cast of Characters

The Cops

LARRY COLE—Chief of Detectives of the Chicago Police Department.

BLACKIE SILVESTRI—a lieutenant on Cole's staff.

MANFRED WOLFGANG (MANNY) SHERLOCK—a sergeant on Cole's staff.

JUDY DANIELS—the Mistress of Disguise/High Priestess of Mayhem, a sergeant on Cole's staff.

JOE E. LEAK—Assistant Deputy Commissioner, New York Police Department.

TED WILLIS—Detective First Grade, New York Police Department.

FRANK AZZOLI—Detective First Grade, New York Police Department.

The Assassins

BARON ALAIN MARCUS CASIMIR VON RIANOCEK

CORNELIUS SHADE

HANNAH SPENCER

The C.I.A.

RICHARD "DICKIE" FAGAN—Deputy Director

PART

"But I don't want to be a detective."
—Larry Cole

1

Chicago, Illinois
DECEMBER 2, 1977
8:22 A.M.

Cleveland Emmett Barksdale, Sr., the senior partner in the LaSalle Street law firm of Barksdale and DeVito, P.C., was in his corner office in the fifteen-room, thirtieth-floor suite from which his corporate practice did business. On the desk in front of him were the morning editions of the *Wall Street Journal,* the *New York Times*, and the *Chicago Times-Herald.* It was a daily ritual for the senior partner to read each paper before the business day began. Also on top of the desk was a bone-china coffee service from which Barksdale poured himself cup after cup of strong black coffee, and a bowl-shaped brass ashtray into which the attorney dumped ashes and butts from the Marlboro cigarettes that he chain-smoked. Barksdale vowed to give up smoking as a New Year's resolution. However, the New Year was nearly a month away. Until then, he planned to continue feeding the nicotine poison into his body.

Barksdale and DeVito, P.C., had been founded by Cleve Barksdale and Joseph DeVito in 1959. Although listed as a corporate law firm, it did not accept clients "off the street," but had a select client list, which kept the firm on an annual retainer of $1 million per client. Seldom did attorneys from Barksdale and DeVito ever appear in any courtroom, and the work that they did for their clients was not clear to anyone outside of the firm. But they did perform valuable services. Very valuable services indeed.

On this winter morning, Cleve Barksdale was the sole surviving founding partner of the firm. Joseph DeVito had been shot to death during an invasion of his North Shore mansion in the summer of 1975. How the armed robbers managed to circumvent the alarm system and enter the house was a mystery. A fortune in jewelry, paintings, furs, and other valuables were taken, and a wall safe in DeVito's study had been blasted open. The safe's contents were known only to DeVito. Now, eighteen months later, the case remained unsolved.

Cleveland Emmett Barksdale, Sr. was a man of average height and weight. He had graying hair receding from a high widow's peak, signifying his sixty years. His features were as unremarkable as the rest of him, and he would easily go unnoticed in a crowd. However, this blandness of appearance had never held him back, instead; he had used it as an asset. Most people meeting Cleve Barksdale for the first time had a tendency to underestimate him, which was a serious mistake.

Barksdale finished reading the *New York Times* and picked up the *Times-Herald*. He only glanced at the national news section before turning to the Chicagoland local news. He liked to keep abreast of the events going on in his hometown—he was a graduate of the 1939 University of Chicago law-school class—even though most of these events were as far removed from his daily life had they occurred on another continent.

Taking a sip of coffee and lighting another cigarette with a gold Dunhill lighter, which had been a birthday present from his late partner, Barksdale's eyes fell on the lone photograph on his desk. The picture was of his grandson, Cleveland Emmett Barksdale, III. Unlike his grandfather, "Clevey," was anything but average. In the gold frame on his grandfather's desk, Clevey was wearing his brown and white football uniform bearing the number "57." He was a high-school sophomore playing linebacker on one of the best teams in the state. At the age of fifteen, he stood 6'4", weighed 255 muscular pounds and had a big, square-jawed face topped by a head of thick, dark brown hair. His grandfather thought that Clevey looked like a young Ernest Hemingway, and Cleve, Sr. had plans for him. Plans which would make Clevey a great deal more successful than Cleveland Emmett Barksdale, II, whom Cleve rarely thought about anymore with anything but disdain.

Barksdale was about to return to the newspaper when his secretary buzzed him on the intercom.

"Mr. Arcadio and Mr. Lima have arrived, sir."

"Thank you, Diana. Have them take a seat and I'll be with them shortly."

The two men waiting to see him had a 9:00 appointment. They were ten minutes early, but although they were the representatives of a man on his very exclusive client list, he did not plan to see them until the appointed hour. He went back to his newspaper, coffee, and cigarettes. Exactly twelve minutes later, he told his secretary to send the gentlemen in. By the time they walked through the door, the newspapers were gone and nothing but a manila folder was on the desk in front of Barksdale.

Francesco "Frankie" Arcadio entered Barksdale's office, followed by Tony Lima. Arcadio was the nephew and sole heir of Paul "the Rabbit" Arcadio, the reigning Chicago mob boss. Paul Arcadio was Barksdale and DeVito, P.C.'s most important client.

Frankie Arcadio was a tall, well-built man with blond hair and blue eyes. He was dressed in a custom-tailored, black double-breasted suit that didn't cost a cent less than $2,000. His white shirt was of Egyptian silk, and when he displayed his French cuffs, the embroidered monogram "F. A." was visible beside a pair of cuff links made from ancient Roman gold coins. His black shoes possessed a mirror shine and were also custom made. When he entered the office, he had a beige cashmere overcoat draped across his shoulders like a cape. Frankie pulled the coat off with a flourish and hung it across the back of one of the attorney's guest chairs before he sat down.

Frankie Arcadio was a sharp dresser and a handsome man, but the expensive trappings couldn't hide the fact that he was a hoodlum and a killer.

Tony Lima was an Arcadio Family soldier, whom Paul Arcadio had assigned personally as his nephew's driver and bodyguard. Lima was a little man with pinched features, who dressed like a cabdriver. If his appearance could be compared to an animal, he would best be described as a weasel. But Tony Lima was a very dangerous weasel.

Once they were seated, Frankie said sarcastically, "So what's up, Counselor? Uncle Paulie said you had an urgent matter to discuss with me and Tony."

Barksdale was all business: "Felix Albanese is about to turn state's evidence against your uncle and his organization."

Felix "Big Numbers" Albanese had been Paul Arcadio's bookkeeper and confidant for ten years.

Frankie and Lima exchanged questioning glances before erupting into long, loud laughter. While their guffaws echoed through his stately office, Cleve Barksdale remained stonily silent.

When Frankie finally managed to bring himself under control, he said, "That's bullshit, Counselor. Big Numbers ain't crazy."

Barksdale opened his center desk drawer and removed a compact tape recorder. Placing it on the desk blotter beside the manila file, he pressed the "play" button. There were a few seconds of silence, followed by the sound of a phone ringing. Then there was a click and:

"Hello," a deep male voice said.

"Okay, you got me. I'll testify, but you cops have got to protect me. If they find out, my life won't be worth spit and I'm scared to death of that crazy Frankie. That guy's a psycho."

The second voice possessed a distinctive nasal quality. When Frankie heard it, he jerked forward to sit on the edge of his seat and glare fiercely at the recorder.

"Don't worry, Felix," the deep voice said. *"I'll take care of everything. When are you coming in?"*

"At noon tomorrow. That will give me enough time to get the records you wanted together."

"I'll see you then and, Felix, don't disappoint me."

"I really don't have a choice, do I, Ryan?"

The tape ended.

"Sonofabitch," Frankie said softly. His eyes remained glued to the recorder as he repeated, "Sonofabitch."

Then he exploded. Leaping to his feet, his cashmere coat falling to the floor, Frankie jumped around the office screaming, "I'm going to kill that bastard! I'm going to gouge out his eyes and cut off his balls! I'm going to feed his ass through a meat grinder! I'm going to . . . !"

Throughout the tirade, Cleve Barksdale sat motionless, exuding a pronounced boredom at witnessing the mobster's antics. Tony Lima remained seated and made a couple of supportive comments that his boss didn't hear. Finally, Frankie ran out of gas and collapsed back into his chair. His cashmere coat remained on the floor. His face was flushed and he was breathing heavily. Slowly, he regained control and pointed at the recorder.

"Where did you get that tape?"

With the same calm manner and tone he had displayed since his visitors had entered the office, Barksdale said, "That information is between your uncle and me. The other voice was that of Chicago Police Department Chief of Detectives John T. Ryan. If Mr. Albanese does provide confidential information concerning your uncle's operation to the police, it could be quite damaging."

A cruel smile spread across Frankie's face. "Don't worry about Big Numbers. He ain't going to be talking to nobody after I get through with him."

Barksdale did not acknowledge this statement in any way. What the Arcadios did about Felix Albanese was not his concern. He had done his job. The Arcadio account would be billed a fee of $150,000 for his professional services.

2

Nineteenth District Tactical Officer Larry Cole was sitting in the waiting room of the law firm of Fitzgerald, Andrews, Andrews, and Cobb, which was located directly across the corridor from the suite of offices occupied by Barksdale and DeVito, P.C. Cole had accompanied his partner Blackie Silvestri, who was giving a deposition in a civil suit against the Chicago Police Department. Blackie had been notified that he would be required to give this deposition by Tactical Sergeant Wally Novak when they reported for duty at 8:00 A.M. Less than pleased over the interruption of their normal routine, Blackie had grumbled all the way from the Nineteenth District station until they reached the Loop.

"Three years ago, me and Hugh Cummings were working the night shift," Blackie said, as Cole drove from the parking lot in their new 1977 unmarked yellow Dodge police car. "We responded to a holdup alarm at the Fullerton and Halsted currency exchange. We pull up just as a heroin addict named Charlie Sparks comes running out the front door. It didn't take me and Hugh a great deal of effort to figure out what's going down, as Sparks has a gun in one hand and a cloth bag, with the currency exchange's logo on it, in the other hand. So before we could play, 'What's wrong with this picture,' Sparks fires a shot at us and jumps in an old rust-bucket Ford. The car is being driven by another addict named Sandra Green. They take off and we pursue."

Blackie paused for a moment to relight his twisted cigar. As smoke filled the car, Cole rolled the driver's side window down.

"You're going to give us a case of double pneumonia, kid," Blackie said, as frigid air blew into the car.

"It's either pneumonia or suffocation from breathing noxious fumes," Cole shot back.

"Nobody appreciates fine tobacco anymore," Blackie said.

"Finish your story," Cole said, flipping the heater on full blast against the chill of the below-freezing Chicago morning.

"Well, we chase the Ford a few blocks and this Sandra Green, who is driving the car, is high as a kite. She's driving like a maniac and we're trying to box her in with squad cars when she runs a red light at Sheridan and Belmont. The Ford is broadsided by a bus, flips over, and catches fire. Before we can do anything to save them, Sparks and Green are incinerated."

Cole frowned. "Two felons fleeing from the scene of a crime get killed in an auto accident. It seems simple enough to me. Why the lawsuit?"

Blackie's face contorted in a scowl. "Sandra Green was twenty-two years old when she died. She had accumulated a record of thirty-seven arrests with nine convictions and three prison terms since she turned seventeen. After she died, her mother, who hadn't seen the kid in two years, went to the Office of Professional Standards and accused me and Cummings of causing her daughter's death because we initiated the pursuit."

"That didn't go very far, did it?" Cole said, as he turned the police car onto Wells Street a block west of LaSalle.

"The Department found the complaint groundless, but Green's mother went to this"—Blackie consulted the deposition notice Sergeant Novak had given him—"Fitzgerald, Andrews, Andrews, and Cobb law firm, who filed a million-dollar wrongful-death lawsuit on behalf of the Green family."

Cole found a "no parking" zone and draped the microphone cord over the rearview mirror. This was done in case a traffic cop came along who was unable to do what any grammar-school kid was capable of; recognizing the unmarked vehicle as a police car.

After shutting off the engine, Cole asked his partner, "I don't see what good a lawsuit will do after the investigation was judged groundless."

Plugging the cigar stub into the corner of his mouth, Blackie said, "The city doesn't want to risk losing in litigation, so they'll probably offer a smaller out-of-court settlement."

As they got out of the car, Cole said, "Isn't that an admission of wrongdoing on the city's part?"

"According to the lawyers it doesn't, but they don't live in the real world anyway."

Larry Cole and Blackie Silvestri had been partners on the Nineteenth District street-crime tactical team since the death of Blackie's previous partner Hugh Cummings a year ago. During that period, the two men had become as close as brothers. Blackie was sixteen years older than his partner and still called Cole "kid." The bachelor officer had become the adopted son of Maria Silvestri, who demanded that he come to dinner at their house at least three times a week. Frequently Blackie brought Cole plastic containers filled with lasagna and spaghetti.

Larry Cole was 6'2" tall and weighed a muscular 200 pounds, which he maintained with weight training and jogging at least three miles every day. He had curly black hair, matinee-idol features and sported a thin mustache that Blackie joked made him look like a pimp. He was dressed in the casual civilian attire of the tactical cop in a white turtleneck sweater, black wool slacks and black boots. He wore a three-quarter length, fur-lined black leather coat against the early-winter chill of the Windy City. The tools of his trade were concealed at various locations around his body.

Cole carried a .45 caliber Colt Commander semiautomatic pistol in a shoulder holster and two seven round bullet clips containing .45 ammo in a pouch opposite the pistol. On his belt, concealed beneath the turtleneck, was a .38 caliber nickel-plated Detective

Special in a holster next to another bullet pouch containing a pair of speed loaders with twelve rounds of .38 caliber ammunition. In the inside pockets of his leather coat he carried a blackjack and a can of Mace. Strapped to his left calf was a serrated-edged six-inch blade hunting knife equipped with a compass. In a metal loop attached to his belt was a Kelite six-cell flashlight. He also carried two sets of Smith & Wesson handcuffs attached to his belt.

Cole did not take daily inventory of the items of mayhem he carried each day, but instead had learned from Blackie to use his weight to make sure he had everything. Today the weight felt right.

Blackie Silvestri was a heavyset man a couple of inches shorter than Cole. He had receding thick black hair and features that made him resemble a cross between the actors Sean Connery and Anthony Quinn. He was dressed in a very similar fashion to his partner, only his leather coat was brown, his turtleneck was black and the gun he carried in the shoulder holster beneath his coat was a six-inch barrel .357 magnum Colt Python revolver. This morning Blackie's weight also felt right.

Cole had been waiting in the law firm's reception area for thirty minutes. The receptionist, an attractive young woman, who was a bit too thin for Cole's taste, had offered the cop a cup of coffee. He had been forced to occupy his time with back issues of *Time* magazine. He hadn't possessed the foresight to retrieve one of his textbooks from his black 1974 Mustang parked in the station lot before they left. He was within nine semester hours of obtaining his bachelor's degree in public administration from Roosevelt University and had finals coming up in a couple of weeks. However, he wasn't going to be too hard on himself today. Yesterday he had received the results of the sergeant's exam, which had been given a couple of months ago. Cole had placed in the top 25 out of 8,000 officers taking the test. He would be promoted to sergeant in less than six months.

Cole looked up from the magazine and stared across the reception area at the opposite wall. "Sergeant Larry Cole," he thought to himself. It had a nice ring to it. He smiled.

Finishing the cup of tepid coffee, he stood up and walked over to the receptionist's desk. "Is there a men's room around here that I could use?"

She handed him a key attached to a green plastic tag. "It's down the hall, past the elevators right next to the entrance to Barksdale and DeVito, P.C."

"Thank you," Cole said and followed her directions.

A short time later, he was washing his hands when he heard a man's voice coming from the corridor. It was obvious that the speaker was angry. Suddenly Cole heard, "Big Numbers is a dead man. Let's head for his place now. We'll pick . . ." The voice trailed off as the speaker moved away from the washroom door down the corridor.

Cole replayed what he'd just heard in his mind. Someone was either planning a murder or possessed a gruesome sense of humor. The cop opened the door and stepped into the corridor.

There were two men waiting for the elevator. One was tall, blond, and elegantly dressed; the other looked like a weasel. The blond was punching the "down" button angrily. "C'mon," he said. "I haven't got all day."

Cole realized that his voice was the same one he'd heard through the washroom door. Then he recognized the man in the expensive black suit and cashmere coat. Frankie Arcadio and his uncle Paul Arcadio were frequently photographed by the media as they were reputedly involved in organized criminal activity in the Midwest. And now Cole knew that Frankie Arcadio was planning to kill someone called "Big Numbers."

The elevator came and the two men boarded without glancing in the cop's direction. When the doors closed, Cole rushed back to the law offices of Fitzgerald, Andrews, Andrews, and Cobb. The deposition was over, and Blackie had just returned to the reception area.

"I've got something," Cole said, fighting to keep the excitement out of his voice.

Blackie was still scowling after what he had experienced during the deposition, but he immediately picked up on his partner's urgency. Noticing that the receptionist was watching them, Blackie motioned for Cole to step out into the corridor.

Cole told Blackie what he'd overheard.

"Arcadio was talking about Felix 'Big Numbers' Albanese, the Rabbit's bookkeeper," Blackie said. The older cop had been raised around Mafia types. "Big Numbers lives in a Lake Shore Drive high-rise near Diversey. I bet that's where Arcadio and Lima are headed. Let's go, kid."

3

DECEMBER 2, 1977
10:15 A.M.

Frankie Arcadio and Tony Lima walked the rotund Felix "Big Numbers" Albanese off the elevator leading to the parking garage beneath the high-rise apartment building. The Mob accountant was trapped between the two men, and he was openly terrified at the prospect of what was in store for him.

"Can't you tell me what this is all about, Frankie?" Big Numbers pleaded.

"It's nothing, Felix," Frankie said, a cruel smile pasted on his face. "We just need to go someplace and discuss a few things."

"Look, if I could just talk to Mr. Arcadio, I'm sure I could straighten out any misunderstandings we might have."

"That won't be necessary," Frankie said. "I can take care of everything. Uncle Paulie is a very busy man."

They reached a metallic green 1978 Cadillac Eldorado with a white interior. This was Big Numbers Albanese's car.

"Get in behind the wheel, Felix," Frankie ordered. "You're going to give me a lift to our meeting place. Tony will follow in my car."

Big Numbers's bloated face was deathly pale. Sweat ran in rivulets down into his collar. "Jeez, Frankie, can't you tell me what this is all about?"

The mobster turned mean. "Get in the fucking car now, Felix."

Terrified, the bookkeeper did what he was told. As Frankie walked around to get into the passenger side of the Cadillac, he nodded to Tony Lima. Without a word, the bodyguard turned and headed for the exit from the garage. He'd parked Arcadio's Lincoln on the street a short distance away. Then he would tail Frankie and Big Numbers to a vacant warehouse on the West Side. Lima knew that this was going to be a one-way ride for Felix "Big Numbers" Albanese.

Once behind the wheel of his car the bookkeeper knew for a certainty that he was going to die. Perhaps he had known from the moment he'd opened his apartment door and saw Frankie and Lima standing out in the hall. He was crazy for thinking that he could outsmart the Arcadios, despite what that cop Ryan had promised him. Now he was going to pay the price with his life.

"Start the car, Felix," Frankie said.

Big Numbers grasped the steering wheel and came to a decision. Dead was indeed dead, but it would be infinitely better to die right here in this garage instead of letting Frankie take him to some isolated location where the psycho would open up Big Numbers's guts and make him watch them run out.

With a resolve he didn't think he was capable of mustering, Big Numbers said, "I ain't going nowhere, Frankie. Whatever you're going to do, you're going to have to do it right here."

Arcadio's face clouded with a depth of anger that revealed that he was truly insane. "Start the car right now, Felix."

Shutting his eyes against the terror infecting every limb of his body, he refused to move.

Arcadio pulled a nine-millimeter Browning semiautomatic handgun from a holster beneath his suit jacket and smashed the barrel into Albanese's face. Blood spurted from the bookkeeper's nose and he screamed.

Outside, Tony Lima opened the door of the Lincoln and was about to jump behind the wheel when he felt the barrel of a very large gun pressed against the base of his skull.

A voice he hadn't heard in a very long time said from behind him. "Freeze right where you are, Tony, and I won't make Gwen a widow."

Frankie Arcadio's bodyguard/driver stood stock-still as he was frisked quickly and expertly. A nine-millimeter Browning, the twin of the one Frankie Arcadio carried, was removed from Lima's belt.

"Aw, Tony, a parolee carrying a piece will get you sent back to the joint faster than mugging a judge."

Lima's arms were pulled behind his back and handcuff bracelets snapped on his wrists. Then he was spun around to face the two Nineteenth District tactical cops.

"Okay, Tony," Blackie said, "where's your boss?"

"I don't know what you're talking about, Blackie," Lima said, deadpan. "I'm currently unemployed."

A gunshot echoed from the garage. Cole ran for the driveway entrance. Blackie snatched the keys to the Lincoln from Lima's hand, shoved him face down on the backseat, locked the car, and followed his partner.

Cole stopped, pressed his back against the wall next to the ramp leading down and peered around the corner. The black cop pulled his .45 and jacked a round into the chamber. When Blackie caught up, he had his .357 magnum in his hand. They waited a tick before starting down the ramp into the subterranean garage.

The cops heard Frankie Arcadio before they saw him. He was whistling. The tune wasn't easily identifiable, because the mobster was having difficulty carrying it. It sounded a bit like "Harlem Nocturne," but Blackie and Cole weren't sure. Then, when the cops were halfway down the ramp, the well-dressed mobster strode into view.

Arcadio didn't see them. He was casually wiping blood from the housing of an automatic pistol with a white handkerchief. From the expression on his face, he appeared to be very, very pleased with himself.

The cops raised their guns. Blackie shouted, "Okay, Frankie, drop the gun and freeze!"

Arcadio's head came up with a jerk, and he looked quizzically at Cole and Blackie. For a long moment no one moved. Then Frankie turned his gun on them and fired. He managed to get off one round before Cole pumped four bullets into him and Blackie added an additional three rounds from the magnum. The mobster was knocked backward across the garage to bounce off the hood of a gray Buick. He fell to the concrete floor and lay motionless.

Cole trotted down the ramp and stood over the man he'd overheard plotting a murder outside a LaSalle Street law office. Now Arcadio's eyes were open in the stare of death, while blood began pooling beneath his body. Cole removed the Browning semiautomatic from the lifeless hand. Sticking the weapon in his belt, he noticed a Cadillac parked a short distance away. The interior of the driver's-side window was coated with blood. Cole walked over and examined it more closely.

The body of Big Numbers was upright behind the wheel. Arcadio had placed the barrel of his gun flush against the bookkeeper's right temple and pulled the trigger.

Making sure not to touch anything, Cole said, "This one's had it, too, Blackie."

When there was no response from his partner, Cole turned around. He saw Blackie sitting on the floor of the driveway where they'd been standing when they opened fire on Arcadio. Alarmed, Cole ran back across the garage.

Blackie turned fatigued eyes up to look at his partner. "He got me in the side, kid."

Cole looked down and saw a spreading bloodstain on Blackie's turtleneck. "Hang on, Blackie. I'll have an ambulance here in minutes."

Cole ran up the ramp leaving Blackie alone to stare across the garage at the man they had just killed.

4

DECEMBER 2, 1977
12:17 P.M.

Paul "the Rabbit" Arcadio called an emergency meeting of the top members of his organization. This meeting was held in his mansion on the lakefront in an unincorporated area north of Evanston. The principals arrived within five minutes of each other and were escorted to the study of the twenty-two-room house by Arthur Maggio, a thin, gaunt-faced man who was the Mafia boss's assistant.

The Rabbit relied on three men to help him run a criminal empire, which stretched geographically from the Canadian border to St. Louis, east to Cleveland and west to Kansas City. The Arcadio Family also had an interest in certain Las Vegas hotel/casinos, a major Hollywood movie studio and controlling interest in one of the most prestigious investment banking institutions in New York City. In Arcadio's study the three advisors took seats around a highly varnished conference table, which could seat twenty.

Salvatore Marino took a seat to the right of the large leather armchair at the head of the table. It was in this chair that the Rabbit would sit when he entered the room to convene the meeting. Marino was a jowly man with a huge midsection that not even his custom-tailored suits could hide and a luxurious head of thick salt-and-pepper hair. He employed a barber daily to keep his locks trimmed, shave his fleshy cheeks, and give him a massage. However, the tonsorial machinations did little good: Sal Marino was still a very ugly man. His features were bulbous and bloated, his face was pitted with the remnants of severe acne suffered during adolescence, and his eyes were dark, lifeless pools surrounded by fleshy lids above and enormous bags below. He had been a member of the Arcadio Crime Family all of his adult life, rising through the ranks from street soldier to underboss. After Frankie Arcadio, he was the next in line to succeed the Rabbit.

The second underboss was Antonio "Tuxedo Tony" DeLisa. At the age of forty-four, Tuxedo Tony was the youngest Mafia underboss in America. He'd gotten his nickname because he always wore dark clothing, mostly black, and habitually donned a black tuxedo whenever he went out after dark. DeLisa had risen so rapidly in the Arcadio Crime Family because he was a vicious killer who had no compunctions about murdering anyone who got in his way, be they friend or foe. It was rumored that even the Rabbit was afraid of DeLisa, and Arcadio kept a very close eye on this particular underboss.

The third member of Paul Arcadio's advisory circle was Cleve Barksdale.

The three men exchanged perfunctory greetings, but did not make small talk while they waited. Their business discouraged camaraderie because the day would probably come when they would have to kill one or both of the others. Also, as they were en route to the mansion, the thought had occurred to each of them that Arcadio's hasty summons could mean that today was that day.

The study door opened and Paul "the Rabbit" Arcadio entered. He was dressed in an immaculately pressed dark blue suit, red silk tie, and white shirt. His nephew's penchant for fine clothing had been developed by emulating the senior Arcadio. With long, athletic strides belying his seventy-five years, Arcadio crossed the study to take his seat at the head of the table.

Paul Arcadio was a tall, bald man with sharp features that made him resemble a hawk. His shoulders were still broad, indicating that prior to aging, he had possessed tremendous physical strength. The Rabbit displayed a powerful presence. It was a quality that accomplished actors and successful politicians exhibited: a combination of sex appeal, charisma, and machismo. Rabbit Arcadio also had another quality, which was apparent to the more discerning viewer. This was a man capable of extreme violence, a killer who enjoyed killing.

He got right to the point. "Big Numbers Albanese and my nephew Francesco are dead. Attorney Barksdale obtained information that the bookkeeper was about to turn over sensitive records concerning our operation to John Ryan, the Chicago Police Chief of Detectives. Big Numbers was also going to testify before a grand jury in exchange for immunity from prosecution. We learned of these plans, and my nephew and Tony Lima were dispatched to handle the situation. They were successful in ensuring that Big Numbers will never appear before a grand jury, but two Chicago cops gunned Frankie down. Tony Lima is under arrest. One of the cops involved is Blackie Silvestri."

The three men seated at the conference table noticed that Arcadio showed no emotion when discussing the death of his closest relative. Collectively, they speculated that Arcadio was not actually experiencing any feelings at all over the shooting of his heir. The Rabbit, whose nickname came from his ability as a youth to move very fast when he was running from the cops, was just that kind of man.

However, Marino, DeLisa, and Barksdale could sense a dangerous undercurrent in the Mafia boss's lack of emotion. They could only compare his cool outward facade to what would be experienced by someone stumbling accidentally into the lair of a dangerous wild animal.

"Silvestri's a smart cop," Arcadio said, maintaining the same casual tone. "In fact, he's probably smarter than your average nosy flatfoot out there." The Rabbit paused to give his next words greater impact. Now he leaned forward and said with a slight edge in his voice, "But he ain't psychic, so the question I have to ask is, how did he know about the hit on Big Numbers?"

Marino and DeLisa didn't respond because they didn't have to. In fact, at least for the time being, they were in the clear. They hadn't known about the hit on Big Numbers until after it had gone down and Silvestri had blown Frankie away. It was the attorney who was on the hot seat.

But Cleveland Emmett Barksdale, Sr. was as calm in appearance as Paul Arcadio in replying, "I disclosed the information regarding the contents on the tape and Felix Albanese's involvement with Chief John Ryan to only three people. You, Don Paolo"— Barksdale was one of the few people outside of the tabloids who used Arcadio's formal Mafia title—"your nephew Francesco, and Tony Lima, when they came to my office this morning."

Arcadio's dark eyes focused on the attorney like a pair of high-powered lasers. Marino's and DeLisa's gazes remained on him. Despite being under such close scrutiny by three of the most dangerous men in the United States underworld, Barksdale's relaxed demeanor did not alter.

"Perhaps a member of your firm could have come across the tape and leaked it to the cops for a price?" Arcadio stated.

"That is impossible, Don Paolo," the lawyer responded, maintaining rigid eye contact with the Mafia boss. "That tape hasn't been out of my possession since the instant I personally retrieved it from the surveillance location."

Arcadio nodded, but that simple gesture had an ominous quality. It was as if Paul Arcadio was pronouncing a sentence of death on the attorney.

"Perhaps you could give us some idea as to how Blackie Silvestri found out about this morning's plans?"

"I've given that some thought, Don Paolo," Barksdale said, "and it comes down to only one possibility."

"And that is?"

"Ryan had Silvestri guarding Mr. Albanese. I heard a news flash on the way here that one of the officers involved in the shoot-out with Francesco was also shot."

Arcadio again issued a solemn nod. "Silvestri was wounded, but not terminally. He is currently at University Hospital in serious, but stable condition. He is expected to remain there overnight for observation. I had my contacts in the police department check on Silvestri's and his partner's assignment. Silvestri works with a black officer named Larry Cole on the Nineteenth District tactical team. That is in the Chicago Police Department's uniformed or Patrol Division, as they call it. John Ryan is in charge of the detectives. Wouldn't it make more sense for Ryan, for confidentiality's sake, to have sent detectives to guard Big Numbers, as opposed to a high-profile, hot-tempered cop like Blackie Silvestri?"

A tension had developed in Paul Arcadio's study. Despite Barksdale's cool courtroom demeanor, it was obvious to his associates, Marino and DeLisa, that he was on trial. If the Rabbit came back with a finding of guilty, then the high-priced mouthpiece wouldn't live out the day.

Still composed, Barksdale responded, "I can't address the inner workings of the Chicago Police Department, but I'm certain we have the resources to find the answers to any outstanding questions you may have, Don Paolo."

Following Barksdale's response, a prolonged silence ensued during which no one moved. Finally Rabbit Arcadio broke the silence. "I plan to do just that, Counselor. As for right now I don't want anyone in the family doing anything to avenge my nephew's death or to involve the Chicago Police Department any deeper in our activities. Do I make myself clear?"

Each of the men seated around the conference table acknowledged the Mafia boss's order.

"Counselor, you and Antonio may go," Arcadio said. "Sal, remain here. I want to talk to you."

Barksdale and DeLisa walked out leaving Paul Arcadio and Salvatore Marino alone.

Cleve Barksdale rode back to the city in a chauffeur-driven black Cadillac limousine. The partition separating the driver and passenger compartments was closed. The attorney needed the solitude to enhance his formidable mental powers. Outwardly he appeared to be relaxed and enjoying the drive down Sheridan Road; however, internally he was under a great deal of stress.

The attorney knew that Rabbit Arcadio held him responsible for Frankie's death. He had given the best explanation he could as to how the cops had known about the execution of Felix Albanese and, if given enough time, he would find out exactly what had occurred. But Cleve Barksdale didn't have time.

Now the attorney came to a decision. At this very moment, Paul Arcadio was planning his murder. But Barksdale had come to the realization a long time ago that the knife cut both ways. It would not be a simple matter to eliminate a Mafia boss, but it was not unprecedented. Lucky Luciano had proven that on April 10, 1931, when he assassinated the heads of New York's Mafia families in one night. But Barksdale would have to do a great deal more than just eliminate the Rabbit. Before the limo reached the Loop, the attorney had formulated a plan. It was daring and would require everything to work on a precise schedule, but it could be done.

After returning to his office, Barksdale placed three calls. One was to a contact he had in Detective Division headquarters close to Chief John T. Ryan. The next was to a law firm on New York's Madison Avenue that provided the same service for their very special clients that Barksdale and DeVito, P.C., did for theirs. The final call was to Antonio "Tuxedo Tony" DeLisa.

5

L arry Cole was wading through a sea of paperwork. Following the shoot-out that morning, he had ridden to St. Joseph's Hospital in the ambulance with Blackie. The parking garage, where the shooting had occurred, had turned into an instant madhouse after Cole made the call to the Communications Center reporting an "Officer Shot" during a homicide investigation.

Marked police cars from the Nineteenth District, along with tactical cops and supervisors, had immediately raced to the scene. The streets near the apartment building where Big Numbers Albanese had lived and died became so clogged with police vehicles that the paramedics, responding to attend Blackie Silvestri, were forced to park a block away and push their portable stretcher down the sidewalk to reach the parking garage.

By the time they had stopped the bleeding, started an IV, and loaded the wounded cop onto the stretcher, the streets were packed with cops, reporters, mobile TV trucks, and hundreds of curious gawkers.

Cole walked beside the stretcher and helped the ambulance attendants load his wounded partner, who had never lost consciousness, into the back of the ambulance for the short ride to the emergency room.

Cole was pacing the floor of the hospital's waiting room when Commander Joseph Thomas O'Casey, the Nineteenth District police boss, and Tactical Sergeant Wally Novak arrived. O'Casey, who was nicknamed "the Leprechaun" because of his blue-eyed, cherubic appearance, was in full uniform with the gold oak leaves of his rank gleaming on the epaulets of his full-length blue coat.

"What happened, Larry?" the Leprechaun asked.

Cole told the commander everything in detail. Then the assistant deputy superintendent, who was the highest-ranking field officer in the city, arrived, followed by investigators from the Internal Affairs Division and the Office of Professional Standards. Cole was forced to tell the story over and over again until he began getting the distinct impression that he and Blackie were being accused of doing something wrong.

"Tell me, Officer Cole," a stony-faced Internal Affairs investigator with washed-out gray eyes said, "why was it necessary for you and Officer Silvestri to shoot the deceased suspect seven times?"

The question angered Cole, but he kept his cool and was about to respond when the Leprechaun stepped in.

They were in a narrow room reserved for police officers conducting investigations in the hospital. The room was equipped with an old desk, a couple of scarred straight-back chairs, and a rotary dial telephone. Cole occupied one of the chairs because he was the subject of the interrogation; O'Casey occupied the other because of his age and rank. Now the Nineteenth District Commander leaped to his feet, his ruddy complexion turning a shade darker.

"What's your name, Officer?" he asked the IAD investigator.

Startled by the commander's sudden aggressive posture, the investigator stiffened to attention and responded, "Agent Domanski, sir."

"When's the last time you worked the street as a regular cop?"

"I beg your pardon, Commander?"

O'Casey glowered and said, "When was the last time you were a real police officer, Domanski?"

"Eleven years ago, Commander, but I don't see—"

"Were you ever shot at?"

Domanski became uncomfortable. "No, sir."

"Did you ever fire a shot, other than on the pistol range?" O'Casey pressed.

"No, sir."

"Well, let's keep in mind that being shot at and forced to kill your assailant in self-defense is a very traumatic business, to say the least. I also want you to keep in mind that we're all supposed to be on the same side."

The interviews went a great deal easier after that.

A short time after the inquisition ended, Cole and the Leprechaun were allowed into the curtain-enclosed cubicle where Blackie was being treated. The doctor ordered the cops to be brief.

Frankie Arcadio's bullet had gone completely through Blackie's right side, but didn't hit anything vital. The big cop was lying on his back with his head propped up on one arm. He was bare chested, and thick hair covered his upper body. Cole was surprised that his partner was so muscular. With his clothes on, he looked much heavier. The wound was covered with white bandages.

"You look like you could get up and come back to work right now," Cole said, grinning.

"I could," Blackie frowned, "but the doc says I got to stay here for at least twenty-four hours."

"How are you feeling, Blackie?" the Leprechaun said with concern.

"Like a dumb cop who should have never let a lowlife like Frankie Arcadio get the drop on him."

"Don't be too hard on yourself," O'Casey said. "You and Cole acquitted yourselves with distinction today. I'm proud of you."

O'Casey became a bit misty-eyed.

Cole quickly in stepped. "Do you want me to call Maria for you?"

"Naw. I already did that, kid. Didn't want anybody else to tell her. She'd start thinking that this thing is a lot worse than it is." He patted his side just a bit too hard and winced in pain.

"Can I get you anything?" Cole asked, as he and O'Casey were about to leave.

"A cigar." Blackie mouthed the words to keep the straitlaced district commander from hearing him.

Cole mouthed back, "No."

Cole went to the station and started on the paperwork. Sergeant Novak permitted Cole to use the tactical supervisor's private office and typewriter. Cole prepared a lengthy case report detailing everything that had happened, from the moment he had overheard Frankie Arcadio planning to murder Felix Albanese, to Arcadio resisting arrest by shooting Blackie Silvestri. Then he typed up an arrest report on Tony Lima. Just as he was completing this report, two detectives, Riordan and Januszyk, from the chief of detectives' office, showed up.

"We're here to interrogate Tony Lima," said Riordan, a big, sour-faced cop.

Januszyk, who was a Riordan clone, added, "We don't expect him to tell us anything, but we got to try."

"You want to sit in on the interrogation?" Riordan asked.

"Sure," Cole responded enthusiastically.

But Januszyk was right. After they advised the little man of his rights, he refused to say anything other than "I want my lawyer."

Now, as the sky outside the police station at Addison and Halsted began to darken toward dusk, Cole finished the last report. Lima was going to be charged with first-degree murder; however, the detectives didn't think the charge would stick. Riordan and Januszyk told Cole that they would be lucky to get a reduction to criminal conspiracy, which carried a penalty of little more than a year in jail. An attorney named Frank Kirschstein from the law firm of Devito and Barksdale, P.C., had arrived at the station at 3:00 and demanded to see Lima. As soon as the attorney could get the case before a judge, the weasel was going to post bail and be back on the street. So much for justice.

Cole leaned back in Sergeant Novak's rickety desk chair and was just about to begin proofreading his reports when something occurred to him. He recalled being in the washroom that morning when he'd heard Frankie talking loudly out in the corridor, threatening to kill Big Numbers. Cole surmised that the mobster had recently discovered something about Big Numbers which had marked him for death. But where would the killer have obtained this information?

Lima's lawyer's card was lying on the desk next to the typewriter. Cole picked it up. "Frank Kirschstein—Attorney at Law—Barksdale and DeVito, P.C." This law firm was on the same floor as the Fitzgerald, Andrews, Andrews, and Cobb law firm, where Blackie had given the deposition that morning. There were only two suites of offices on that floor and Cole was certain that Frankie and Lima had come out of Barksdale and DeVito, P.C. The probability that the Mob hit man had received the information leading to the Arcadio bookkeeper's murder in that law office was high enough to be nearly a certainty. The problem facing Cole was, how was he going to prove it?

Sergeant Novak came into the office. "How's it going?"

The young cop sighed and rubbed his hands across his face. "I just wrapped it up, Sarge." He handed over the reports.

Novak spent a few minutes reading them. "Good, Larry. The Leprechaun just got a call from Chief Ryan. He wants you to bring him copies of these reports."

"Now?"

"Yeah. But he's not at police headquarters. You're to take them to his apartment downtown in Marina Towers."

6

S o, is your team ready for the championship game, Clevey?"
Cleve Barksdale asked his grandson.

They were seated in the dining room of the attorney's twenty-room Beverly Hills mansion on the South West Side of Chicago. The two Barksdales reserved this time each day to spend together. The grandfather usually drank black coffee and smoked cigarettes. The grandson would have his after-school snack, which usually consisted of a bowl of hot soup, two or three lunch meat and cheese sandwiches on rye or pumpernickel bread, and a couple of slices of whatever pie or cake their housekeeper had in the pantry that day. The elder Barksdale marveled at his grandson's appetite. Despite his after-school meal, Clevey would be ready to eat dinner at 7:30. Yet there was not one ounce of fat on the young man's body.

Each morning he got up at 5:30 and worked out with weights before breakfast. After school there were two hours of football practice. Throughout every minute of the day, the younger Barksdale was in perpetual motion. He was either working out, studying, or eating. His grandfather could envision the day when this young man was going to accomplish something truly amazing.

Clevey swallowed a mouthful of apple pie, chased it with a hefty swallow of milk, and answered his grandfather's question. "We are ready to play the game right now, Granddad, but the coach wants us to take it easy. Not leave our best game on the practice field."

Cleve lit another cigarette and said, "I can understand that,

Clevey. That's been known to happen to boxers as well as football teams."

"It won't happen to us." The young man polished off the rest of his pie and milk. "May I be excused, sir? I've got to study for a geometry test."

The older Barksdale smiled. "You may be excused."

"I'll see you at dinner, Granddad," Clevey said, as he headed for his room. The maid would clear the remains of the young man's snack from the table.

"Oh, Clevey," Barksdale called.

Obediently, the young man stopped and turned around. "Yes, sir."

"I have to go out for a while. I may not be back for dinner."

Clevey frowned. They ate dinner together every night. However, the young man had learned never to question his grandfather about his law practice or his clients. "Yes, sir. Will you look in on me when you get home?"

"If it's not too late. You know you're going to have to be ready for the big game this weekend."

"Yes, sir."

Alone in the dining room, Barksdale's features hardened. He was taking a big gamble. If he won, he would survive; if he lost, he would lose everything, including his life.

7

The United Airlines flight from New York City landed at O'Hare Airport. One of the deplaning passengers was a tall rapier-thin man with aristocratic features and flowing brown hair hanging to his shoulders. He was dressed in a custom-tailored Edwardian suit and carried a worn black leather suitcase that had been all over the world.

A couple of stewardesses on the flight had speculated that the handsome passenger in first class was a famous male fashion model. One of them had come close to getting up the nerve to ask him, but something stopped her. Perhaps it was his imperious manner or the coldness in his gaze when she served the in-flight meal. So he was a mystery, and the curious flight attendants had no way of knowing how lucky they were that he remained so.

The handsome man exiting the United Airlines flight into the O'Hare terminal was as much of an aristocrat by heritage as he was in appearance. He was Baron Alain Marcus Casimir von Rianocek, formerly of the German state of Bavaria, who was currently a naturalized citizen of Argentina. He was the descendant of a line of nobility which could be traced back ten generations. At one time the von Rianoceks had been one of the wealthiest families in Europe. An unending series of wars, from the time of Napoleon to that of Hitler, had laid waste to not only the von Rianocek fortune, but also the family, resulting in the necessity for the reigning baron to take up residence in South America.

Now von Rianocek was the sole survivor of the royal line.

Despite his ancestral lands having been plundered by the Russians after World War II and a fortune in art works and jewelry vanishing behind the Iron Curtain, the baron managed to live very well in Argentina. Very well indeed. This was because of his unique occupation. Alain von Rianocek was an assassin.

This was not to confuse him with a hired killer. Von Rianocek, at the age of twenty-seven, was a specialist in the art of murder. His services were extremely costly, but nevertheless in great demand. Because of his unique calling, he was extremely careful. Although a number of international security and law enforcement agencies, such as the CIA, FBI, Interpol, the KGB, and Scotland Yard, knew of him, they had never been able to put a name or face to any of the dozen assassinations he was directly responsible for.

Now Alain Marcus Casimir von Rianocek was in Chicago to carry out his thirteenth assassination. The contract had been ordered by the Mafia and, as the assassin of royal blood understood from the briefing that he'd been given in New York, it was to take care of an internal problem.

Outside the airport terminal, Alain Rianocek caught a Yellow Cab and instructed the driver to take him to the Hyatt-Regency Hotel on Wacker Drive in downtown Chicago.

8

DECEMBER 2, 1977
6:17 P.M.

The black Lincoln Continental with the tinted windows pulled onto lower Wacker Drive. It entered a loading dock area and stopped. A wino, bundled against the cold in a threadbare overcoat, rags and discarded newspapers, was huddled in a corner of the platform leading into the lower level of an office building. He noticed the black car and knew instinctively that this vehicle meant trouble for him. Quickly, he began gathering up his belongings, which he carried in two shopping bags, and left the area.

The black Lincoln, its engine idling softly as exhaust fumes rose into the winter air, waited ominously.

Less than five minutes later, Cleve Barksdale's chauffeur-driven Cadillac pulled up beside the Lincoln. The attorney got out and walked over to the other car. The back door opened and Barksdale got in.

Tuxedo Tony DeLisa, clad in a black leather trench coat over a black tuxedo, sat in the backseat alone. Two broad-shouldered, battered-featured ex-pugs, who served as the underboss's bodyguards, occupied the front seat.

"Take a walk, boys," DeLisa ordered.

Without a word, the two men got out of the Lincoln and sauntered over to the loading dock, where they could keep the Tuxedo's vehicle in sight. Pulling up their coat collars and lighting cigarettes, they waited.

"The Rabbit's put out a contract on you, Counselor," DeLisa began. "He gave it to Sal Marino's people."

Cleve Barksdale displayed no visible reaction to this news. Actually, he would have been surprised if Arcadio had *not* ordered his death.

Before the lawyer could comment, DeLisa added, "The Rabbit's gone a little crazy over this thing with Frankie. He's also ordered a hit on that cop, Ryan."

Barksdale sighed. "That is a very serious mistake. We don't kill cops, no matter what the provocation. That will bring the entire law-enforcement apparatus down on us from the federal to the local level."

"You're right. The Rabbit is out of control. But I've discovered that the cops found out about the hit on Big Numbers because Silvestri's partner Cole heard Frankie talking about it in the corridor outside your office. They had some kind of business with the law firm across the hall from you. The black cop had gone to the bathroom. He could hear Frankie through the door, so our favorite mob-boss's nephew must have been talking pretty loud."

"Does Don Paolo know about this?" Barksdale asked.

"You think that will change anything? The Rabbit doesn't cancel hits. In fact, I'm surprised he hasn't put out a contract on Silvestri and Cole for whacking Frankie."

"Give him time and he will," Barksdale said.

"Isn't that what it all comes down to, Counselor?" DeLisa said with a cruel smile. "It's all a matter of time, whether it is yours or Rabbit Arcadio's."

"I think we're in agreement on that issue, Mr. DeLisa, or should I refer to you as 'Don Antonio'?"

"Save the Godfather bullshit, Barksdale!" DeLisa had turned ugly-mean in the blink of an eye. "If we don't carry this off just right, then our lives aren't going to be worth two cents. Paul Arcadio is a Mafia boss. The hit on him has got to be so clean that no one in the other families will ever know we're involved. We're also going to have to whack Sal Marino and anybody in the organization who's loyal to him. You're talking about a bloodbath, and you and I are going to be right in the middle of it."

Barksdale had remained motionless during DeLisa's speech. Now, with a studied calm, he said, "Paul Arcadio set these events in motion this morning when he sent that stupid nephew of his to get rid of Felix Albanese. And even though Frankie made a mess of things, the Don is still the one responsible. We can either sit back and let Arcadio and Sal Marino roll over us, or we can do something about it."

DeLisa laughed. "What are you going to do, Barksdale, sue the Rabbit?! We're talking about whacking guys out here! Blowing their fucking heads off, for chrissakes!"

"I know that, Mr. DeLisa," Barksdale said, his cheeks coloring slightly, as the only indication of the enormous stress he was under. "To that end, I have taken steps to ensure that Paul Arcadio will never see another sunrise." With that, the attorney got out of the car.

9

DECEMBER 2, 1977
7:20 P.M.

John Thomas Ryan had been a policeman for twenty-eight years. In the parlance of the street cop, he was a "policeman's policeman." To him, law enforcement was not a profession, but a divine calling. A lifelong quest for justice, which was to be achieved at any cost, be it legal or illegal by the standards of a misguided society. A war against the forces of evil that perpetrated criminal acts on the streets of Chicago, which Ryan fanatically believed to be his personal property.

The chief of detectives had a particular animosity toward the mob. To him they represented an aberration in the American way of life. Organized crime was a cancer eating away at the vital organs of a healthy, democratic society, where there was opportunity for every man to succeed. John T. Ryan saw himself as the surgeon who was going to cut out that disease.

To his peers and supporters, Ryan was known as tough and unorthodox; to his enemies and detractors, he was considered a brutal sadist.

He had been accused of beating confessions out of offenders in felony cases, and had the highest number of suspects killed by him, while resisting arrest, in CPD history. A former Marine and professional welterweight boxer, Ryan kept himself in good shape for a man of fifty-five, and could level anyone half his age and twice his size with one punch. Many, both friend and foe, thought of Ryan as a purely physical individual. But the chief of detectives was actually a very intelligent, well-educated man.

He had earned a master's degree in history from Northwestern University and had written a well-received, scholarly thesis on the history of the Chicago Police Department. His thesis contained an account of one of the darkest episodes in CPD annals. The Memorial Day 1937 labor demonstration, during which the police officers assigned to crowd control opened fire, killed ten and wounded ninety demonstrators, many of whom were shot in the back. This was a quietly forgotten episode in Windy City law-enforcement history.

Ryan had assembled an impressive personal library of biographies and analyses of historical events. He could also read, write, and speak French and German. In January, he planned to begin studying Japanese at the Berlitz language school on South Wabash Avenue.

In appearance Ryan fit the image of the tough, no-nonsense, two-fisted cop. He was 6'3" and weighed 240 pounds that were beginning to settle in his midsection. There was a strange oddity about Ryan's appearance. His features were very similar to those of Mob boss Rabbit Arcadio. A half-drunk, careless Arcadio Family soldier named Mikey Scalise once remarked within earshot of Ryan that the chief of detectives was the Rabbit's illegitimate son. For his foray into sarcasm, Scalise received a broken jaw, broken nose, and ruptured spleen from the fists of a very angry chief of detectives. However, this did not alter the resemblance between the cop and Arcadio.

Ryan lived in a twelfth-floor, three-room apartment in the tube-shaped, multistoried Marina Towers complex overlooking the Chicago River. His residence did not mirror the public personality of the man who lived there.

The apartment was furnished with expensive antiques that Ryan had picked up on his annual vacations to Western Europe, Asia, and the Middle East. The paintings on his walls and sculptures gracing end tables were worth $500,000. There were well-cared-for plants in every room. Ryan had the walls painted and the hardwood floors varnished every two years.

Then there were the books.

The allegedly brutal, tough, two-fisted chief of detectives was a voracious reader. Besides the texts on history and the biographies, he collected leather-bound first-edition reproductions of classical works of literature. Every room, with the exception of the two bathrooms, contained cases filled to capacity with hardcover volumes in their original dust jackets, which were protected by plastic sleeves. Twice a year, he was forced to make a substantial donation of books to the library and John T. Ryan's name was well known to librarians throughout the Illinois State Library system. And it was not because he was a cop.

Chief Ryan was an intelligent, cultured man, who had a difficult job, which he did with a passion bordering on the fanatic. He was also very cautious because, in his storied career, he had made a great many enemies. Guns were concealed in locations all over the apartment, and he never let anyone whom he hadn't checked out first into his private residence. His front and rear doors, as well as all the windows 120 feet above State Street, were hooked up to a state-of-the-art burglar-alarm system, and the locks securing the place were the best money could buy. John Ryan lived in a comfortable, expensively furnished, scholarly fortress. Tonight the Mafia was going to breach the security of that fortress.

The ugly, rotund Mob underboss Sal Marino sat with three of his men in a full-size, four-door dark blue Oldsmobile in the Marina Towers parking garage. They were parked in an aisle near a bank of elevators leading to the apartments above. They were waiting for the resident of the Marina Towers complex who leased space number 126. This resident was a CPA who occupied the apartment next door to Ryan's.

The cop and the accountant had a common rear area where their garbage cans were located. Since the accountant had moved in, he and Ryan had begun playing chess. The cop was an accomplished player, and his neighbor had been a local tournament champion in high school. Three times a week, they played intense games, and tonight a contest was scheduled.

The Mafia henchmen, under the supervision of underboss Sal Marino, had discovered this information after a lengthy covert surveillance of Ryan's life and habits conducted by a private-detective firm affiliated with Barksdale and DeVito, P.C.

Marino was sweating. This was an important job. An unprecedented job. A job that would put him in tight with the Rabbit and place him in line to be the next boss of the Chicago Mob.

The three men with him had been selected carefully. If the hit went down as planned, there would be a heavy backlash from the cops. The Chicago mob would lose a lot of revenue, and a number of its workers would be jailed on real or trumped-up charges to put pressure on the organization to give up the triggerman on the Ryan hit. The cop organizations would probably put up a reward. So it was a requirement that the shooters keep their mouths shut. With these guys, it was guaranteed.

A gray Ford Falcon pulled into the garage, cruised past the Olds, and entered space 126. A thin man, wearing horn-rimmed glasses, a gray homburg, and a gray overcoat over a gray suit, got out of the car and locked it. Carrying a black briefcase, he walked across the garage toward the elevator.

The four mobsters got out of the Oldsmobile and followed him.

10

L arry Cole turned the unmarked Dodge off Wacker Drive onto State Street and drove north. He pulled into the driveway of Marina Towers, parked in an area designated "loading zone," draped the microphone over the rearview mirror, and got out. He entered the lobby and crossed to the reception desk.

"I have a delivery for Chief John Ryan in apartment 12A."

A bald, black man with a pronounced Jamaican accent said, "I don't take no deliveries for nobody, man."

"I wasn't going to give it to you," Cole countered. "I'll deliver it myself."

"Not without clearance from the occupant in 12A, you won't."

It had been a long day for Cole and he was tired. He could flash his badge and throw his weight around. However, this was Chief Ryan's apartment building, and he didn't want to raise a ruckus with this guy. At least, not yet.

The receptionist picked up a phone and dialed the intercom number for 12A.

Cole waited.

The chief of detectives had cooked an early dinner consisting of a tossed salad, followed by a shrimp pasta dish with a creamy sauce. He had two glasses of Chablis with the meal.

After washing the dishes and cleaning up the kitchen, he poured a glass of sherry and went into his study. The chessboard was set up, and he was waiting for his next-door neighbor to come over for tonight's game.

Ryan sat down in a chair on the side of the board on which the black pieces were arranged and stared out his apartment windows at the lights of State Street far below. In his professional estimation, the day had been a disaster. When he got up that morning, he'd possessed the means to destroy Paul Arcadio and his entire organization. By noon it was all blown to hell.

Somehow the Mob had been tipped off to Big Numbers Albanese's getting ready to turn state's evidence against the Outfit. There was a bright side to what had gone down this morning, as two Nineteenth District tactical cops had nailed Frankie Arcadio after he'd killed Albanese. And even though the mobster's bodyguard, Tony Lima, was in custody, Ryan's case against Rabbit Arcadio was dead.

The chief of detectives placed his wineglass down on a coaster next to the chessboard. Ryan had seen cases go down the drain before, but he had wanted this one. He had wanted it bad.

The intercom phone from the lobby buzzed. Ryan got up and crossed the apartment to the instrument mounted on the wall next to his front door.

"Yes."

"There's a gentleman with a delivery for you," the Jamaican-accented receptionist said.

"Does the gentleman have a name?"

There was a pause, and then the receptionist replied, *"He says he's Officer Cole from the Nineteenth District."*

"Did you see his identification?"

"No, but he's a cop. I can tell about these things."

Ryan rolled his eyes. "Okay, send him up."

The chief of detectives had met Blackie Silvestri on the night his former partner Hugh Cummings had been killed a year ago. In Ryan's estimation, the tactical cop was one of the best there was.

Silvestri would make one helluva detective. Ryan made a mental note to recommend that the two cops receive a meritorious promotion to detective for what they'd done this morning.

There was a knock at the rear door. That would be his neighbor arriving for their chess game. John T. Ryan entered the kitchen and opened the back door.

11

DECEMBER 2, 1977
7:53 P.M.

Larry Cole rode alone in the elevator up to the twelfth floor. He stepped off into the corridor and consulted the directory for apartment 12A. He was just turning to walk down the hall when he heard the unmistakable sound of three gunshots. It was obvious that the sound had come from 12A. Drawing his gun, Cole moved toward the apartment door.

Coming up to it, he hesitated. Perhaps he'd been mistaken about the shots. They could have been . . . No, he'd heard gunshots, and they had come from inside the chief of detectives' apartment. Now he had to come up with an immediate course of action. Blackie had always said that the best way to deal with a difficult situation was to be firm and direct. With this in mind, Cole stepped to the side of the door to keep from being hit by any shots fired from inside, rapped heavily on the door frame, and announced, "Police! Open up!"

12

John T. Ryan was dead. When he opened the back door expecting his CPA neighbor, Sal Marino was standing in the doorway with a .357 magnum in his hand. The mobster had expected the tough cop to be more careful and had his men holding the accountant with a gun to his head in case Ryan demanded a verbal ID through the door. But, in the end, Ryan was just as stupid as any of the civilians he had spent his life protecting. Without hesitating, the Mafia underboss shot the chief of detectives three times.

With two of the henchmen holding the arms of the terrified accountant, Marino and the other Mob soldier began pulling the cop's body into the living room. Marino was about to dispatch the witness when the heavy knock came from the front door followed by, "Police! Open up!"

The four killers exchanged startled looks. Then Sal Marino turned toward the door and raised the magnum.

13

The three bullets punched a triangular pattern through the door, and one of them smashed a hall lamp halfway down the corridor. It was obvious to Cole that this wasn't Chief Ryan's way of greeting guests and that something inside apartment 12A was wrong.

Cole snatched his walkie-talkie from the pocket of his coat and keyed the mike. "19-66, emergency!"

He waited for a response, but none came. Then he realized that he hadn't heard any cross traffic on the frequency the Nineteenth District was assigned to since he'd left the station. Again he keyed the mike and checked the transmit light on top of the device. It didn't illuminate, which indicated that the battery was dead. Now it was between him and whoever was on the other side of the door of apartment 12A.

Returning the radio to his pocket, Cole pulled out his snub-nosed .38 to supplement the .45. Then he took aim at the door lock and fired two .45 caliber rounds, destroying the locking mechanism. Cole kicked the door open. Then a shooting war began.

14

A ttorney Frank Kirschstein had gotten bail set for Tony Lima in night court. Despite vociferous opposition for granting the mobster's release by the assistant state's attorney, Lima's police record, the fact that he was currently on parole, was arrested carrying an illegal weapon, and was a suspected accomplice in a homicide, the judge granted bail. Three years later, the judge would be indicted for taking bribes to fix cases. The questionable setting of bail in the case of *State of Illinois* v. *Anthony Lima* would be scrutinized carefully by the federal prosecutors handling the crooked judge's trial.

The bail was set at $100,000 cash, which was posted promptly by a bail bondsman with known affiliations to the Arcadio Family. A car was waiting outside the Criminal Courts Building to whisk Lima to the North Shore residence of Rabbit Arcadio.

The weasely little man was ushered into the Mafia don's study, where he met with Rabbit Arcadio for half an hour. When the meeting concluded, Lima left the mansion and got back into the car that had driven him from the Criminal Courts Building. He was headed for the Beverly Hills neighborhood on the South West Side of Chicago where Cleveland Emmett Barksdale, Esq., lived.

15

Arthur Maggio watched the car bearing Tony Lima pull away from the front of the mansion. The Mob boss's assistant was in the living room across the central alcove from Rabbit Arcadio's study. The lights in the immense, lavishly furnished room were out and had anyone entered, the gaunt Maggio would be concealed in the shadows. This sense of seeming invisibility gave him some degree of comfort. He was about to make an important decision which would have a tremendous impact on the rest of his life or lead to his sudden death.

In the darkness of Rabbit Arcadio's living room, Maggio could detect movement in the huge house. The Rabbit's wife Maggie, his sister-in-law Dorothy, who was the late Frankie's mother, and the Rabbit's elderly aunt, Peggy, were in the kitchen preparing food. Frankie Arcadio's wake was set for tomorrow night, with the funeral to follow the next morning. There would be people coming to the house for the next few days to pay their respects to Paul Arcadio. The women of the household, who would dress completely in black for the wake and funeral, were ensuring that there would be enough food and drink. Frankie would be buried in style.

The thumping made by the sound of running feet on the second floor was also audible. The Rabbit's surviving nephews, nieces, and grandchildren were up there playing. The kids ranged in age from twelve to four, and there were enough of them to make the children's rooms and the entire corridor a disaster area strewn with toys, clothing, and candy wrappers. When the women got through in the kitchen, they would bring some order out of the chaos raging upstairs. The maintenance crew that came in four times a week to clean the mansion, as well as sweep it for electronic-surveillance devices, would take care of the mess the children made.

Another noise joined the symphony of human sound pulsating through the North Shore mansion. A click sounded across the alcove, and the door to Rabbit Arcadio's study opened. The tall, sharp-faced Mafia don closed the door behind him and stepped into the cone of light shining from a ceiling fixture.

Maggio remained in the shadows and studied his boss.

Unaware that he was being observed, Arcadio's mask of confidence dissolved. Maggio witnessed the Don's transformation into a tired, grief-stricken old man. Maggio also noticed something else: Rabbit Arcadio was frightened.

If Arthur Maggio ever had any doubts as to where his allegiance was this night, they were erased.

Remaining in the dark, Maggio watched Paul Arcadio cross to the corridor leading back to the kitchen. The Chicago Mafia boss was going back to be with the women. Maggio had cast his lot with the men.

16

DECEMBER 2, 1977
8:02 P.M.

The emergency console in the Communications Center at Chicago Police Headquarters lit up. Officers assigned to answer these emergency calls began filling out buff-colored cards recording numerous citizen complaints of "Shots Fired" on the twelfth floor of the Marina Towers apartment building overlooking the Chicago River. The Eighteenth District field lieutenant responding to the call realized at the instant he heard the emergency transmission that Chief John T. Ryan lived in that building on that floor.

Sal Marino and his three henchmen had come to the Marina Towers apartment building to kill one man; possibly two. Each of them was armed, and had planned to use stealth and the element of surprise to carry out Rabbit Arcadio's contract on the chief of detectives. Their weapons were adequate for the task at hand: two .357 magnum revolvers, a .38 caliber snub-nosed revolver, and an Uzi submachine gun, which was to be used only as a last resort. None of them carried extra ammunition.

Initially, when they realized that the black cop was alone, they figured collectively that they could make quick work of him, whack the accountant, who was the only witness to Ryan's execution, and get the hell out of there.

They planned to dump the weapons in the Chicago River. Then they would split up, with Marino and one soldier driving to Milwaukee. There they would catch a midnight flight to Mexico City. The other two would drive to St. Louis and would take an early-morning flight to New York en route to London. It would be a year, possibly two, before any of them could return to Chicago. Then Paul Arcadio would reward them.

Now two of them would never embark on their circuitous escape routes because they were dead.

When the cop shot off the lock and kicked the door open, the two dead Mafiosi had been standing on the east side of Ryan's living room near the kitchen entrance. They were exposed when Larry Cole returned Sal Marino's fire with a volley of four bullets from the .45 and three from the .38. The henchmen were each hit twice by Cole's .45 and once each with the .38. The remaining .38 caliber round singed the hair on top of Marino's pomaded head, before becoming embedded in the wall. Now there was just Marino and a single Mob soldier against the lone cop.

*   *   *

The accountant the mobsters had kidnapped dropped to the floor when the shooting started. He scrambled behind a couch and curled himself into a fetal ball. He was out of the line of fire and would remain there until this was over.

Prior to December 2, 1977, Officer Larry Cole had fired his gun only once before in the line of duty. That incident had occurred exactly a year and a day ago, almost to the minute. Now, in a span of less than twenty-four hours, Cole had become engaged in two separate gunfights.

Armed combat can be simultaneously terrifying and breathtakingly thrilling. As he blasted away at the gunmen attempting to kill him, Cole felt an adrenaline rush that made him light-headed, but which also enhanced his powers of perception remarkably. His vision was so acute that each time he looked around the edge of the doorjamb, he could see everything inside the apartment with a crystal clarity. The images of the chessboard, the books on their shelves, the dead bodies and, of course, the men who were trying to kill him, became etched in his mind.

When Cole shot the first two men, he could have sworn he saw the bullets leave the barrels of his guns, zip across the space separating him and the killers, and strike their bodies. With two of the four out of the way, the cop's sense of dangerous excitement increased, and he pressed the attack.

Cole squeezed off the last rounds from the .45 into the apartment and quickly reloaded both the automatic and the snub-nosed .38. He braced himself against the outside wall. He fixed in his mind the last place that he'd seen the surviving shooters. He recalled the position of each piece of furniture and came to a decision. There was a leather armchair just inside the door on the left. It looked fairly sturdy, but he doubted if it would provide much protection against bullets. However, it would place him in a better strategic position to continue the attack.

The word "attack" made Cole hesitate a moment in the midst

of the violent excitement raging through him. As a police officer, he was not supposed to be attacking the men who were shooting at him from inside apartment 12A, but was to first summon assistance, and then order them to surrender. However, his radio was dead, and the deadly force, that soon-to-be Sergeant Larry Cole was throwing around the inside of Chief John T. Ryan's apartment, was supposed to be used only as a last resort. But they had fired first. What Cole was doing was meeting the force utilized to resist a lawful arrest with superior force.

Clutching the two fully loaded handguns tightly in his fists, and firing a round from each pistol to provide a diversion, Cole charged through the open door into the apartment.

Sal Marino was not a cowardly man. In fact, he had gotten a reputation within the ranks of the Chicago mob for being not only tough, but fearless. He had carried out hits before. Thirty-seven of them. He had whacked guys and a few gals using guns, knives, baseball bats and, on one occasion, an ice pick. He had also exchanged gunfire with cops.

When he was twenty-two, he had robbed a Cicero bank single-handedly. A silent alarm resulted in three police cars racing to the scene to intercept the robber, as he exited with a stocking mask over his face and a .357 magnum in his hand.

The cops had made the mistake of demanding that he surrender. Marino opened fire immediately and succeeded in hitting and disabling two of the officers before the third put three rounds into him. The stickup man managed to wound the third cop and make good his escape. That incident had also added to Sal's reputation.

Now the Mob underboss was facing a lone cop, who had killed two of his soldiers, and had him and the third pinned down.

Marino realized that with each second he remained in the apartment, the odds of his escaping were becoming extremely slim. There were more cops on the way, and they wouldn't be as stupid as the Cicero cops had been thirty years ago. So he had to get out of this apartment as soon as possible.

The underboss was partially concealed behind a bookcase that provided very poor cover. One of the cop's bullets had come within a millimeter of taking off his nose. If the cop got any closer, then it would all be over.

Sal had two bullets left in his gun and could see his dead henchman's Uzi on the living-room floor, where he had fallen. If he could get to it, he might have a chance.

Then the cop outside made his move.

Cole charged through the door, firing as he did so, and took cover behind the leather armchair. Only one shot came his way to embed itself in the wall above the policeman's head. Cole rose to place his head above the edge of the chair and caught a glimpse of a figure standing partially concealed behind a bookcase near the entrance to the kitchen. Cole ducked back quickly behind the chair. He had sufficiently established his position of strength. Now was the time to employ basic procedure.

"Okay, you people! I'm giving you one more chance! You are under arrest! Toss your guns in the center of the floor, raise your hands, and come out where I can see you!"

Marino decided that this was it. He motioned to the remaining soldier, who was crouched behind an end table. Marino whispered urgently, "Pick up the Uzi and cover me!"

The henchman was obviously terrified, but fear came in degrees. He was infinitely more afraid of the mobster standing a few feet away from him than he was of any cop. So he reached out obediently and picked up the machine pistol. Getting to his feet, he pointed the weapon, which was set on semiautomatic fire, at the armchair across the room. His hand was shaking badly, but he presented enough of a presence to stop the cop long enough for Marino to make it out the back door. Then he would attempt to follow the underboss.

The cop's head came up from behind the leather chair, and the Mob soldier opened fire. Marino didn't wait to see the result of his covering fire and ran as fast as his rotund, out-of-shape body would carry him into the kitchen. He bolted out the back door and ran for the stairs leading down to the parking garage.

The Mafia soldier's bullets punched holes through the leather chair Cole was using for cover. The cop came so close to being hit that he was forced to stand up immediately and return fire. Cole and the henchman stood toe-to-toe in the living room of apartment 12A of Marina Towers and blasted away at each other. Sal Marino's henchman missed Cole; the cop hit him four times. The Mafioso was dead before he hit the floor.

The tactical cop searched the apartment for any signs of additional danger before he advanced. He stepped over the bodies of the men he had killed until he reached the man dressed in a silk smoking jacket. Most of his face had been blown away by a bullet fired at close range. There was enough left for Cole to recognize the dead man as the chief of detectives, to whom the young cop had been delivering reports when the shooting started.

Cole caught movement out of the corner of his eye and, with both guns raised, spun toward it. The terrified accountant cringed behind the sofa in terror.

After Cole verified his identity, the accountant said in a trembling voice, "One of them got away."

Cole headed for the back door and said over his shoulder, "No, he didn't."

Sal Marino fell hard twice as he scrambled down the stairs. Either the shooting in 12A had stopped, or he was too far away to hear it now. He made it as far as the sixth floor when he heard the pounding of someone coming fast down the stairs from above. The image of the black cop leaped into his mind, making the underboss's blood run cold. He forced himself to run faster, but knew that the cop was gaining on him.

He reached the sublevel garage and rushed out of the stairwell into the glare of headlights and revolving Mars lights from a squadron of police cars.

"Hold it right there, mister!" a voice boomed over a loudspeaker. *"Drop the gun now!"*

Marino tossed the revolver on the cement floor and raised his hands.

From inside the stairwell, Cole heard the loudspeaker. A few seconds later, he stepped out into the glare of the spotlights with his badge held high over his head.

17

DECEMBER 2, 1977
8:04 P.M.

Alain Marcus Casimir von Rianocek finished his preparations and left the room in the Hyatt Regency Hotel on Wacker Drive in downtown Chicago. He was dressed in dark clothing from head to toe. The snap-brim cap covering his brown hair was charcoal gray, his three-quarter-length cloth coat was navy blue, his thick turtleneck sweater was black, his trousers were dark blue, and the soft-soled boots were black suede.

As he waited for the elevator, he pulled on a pair of thin black leather gloves. In the right pocket of his coat was a device consisting of a metal wire attached to two oblong pieces of wood. It was called a garrote and the Bavarian baron was a master with it. He also had a razor-sharp stiletto strapped to his left calf.

Rianocek crossed the lobby and exited the hotel into the cold December night. He walked west on Wacker Drive. Approaching the bright lights of Michigan Avenue, he noticed that the downtown area was already decorated for the upcoming holiday season. The Christmas trees, Santa Claus figures, and ornamental lights reminded him of another time and place, which he really didn't have the time to dwell on right now. He crossed the street and was about to enter a public parking garage when the sound of numerous sirens echoed off the skyscrapers surrounding him. He stopped.

Three marked police cars, their twin blue Mars lights spinning and their sirens alternately blaring the "wail" and "high-low" frequencies, crossed the intersection of Wabash and Wacker Drive 150 feet away from where Rianocek stood. Although he was fairly certain that the cops knew nothing about him, the assassin wasn't about to do anything that would call attention to himself, even if the cops in the squad cars appeared somewhat preoccupied. He waited until the trio of vehicles raced away before he proceeded into the garage.

An envelope was in his hotel room when he arrived. The envelope contained a claim check for a car which was parked in the Wacker Drive garage. Rianocek gave the ticket to the cashier in the glass-enclosed booth, paid the five-dollar charge, and waited for an attendant to deliver the car to the garage exit.

The assassin got behind the wheel of a black Lincoln Continental Mark IV and drove from the garage. He traveled slowly from the Loop area onto West Madison Street. Driving carefully, he noticed four more police cars flying down Wacker.

A block from the entrance to the expressway, he pulled to the curb and opened the glove compartment. There was another envelope inside, along with a Walther PPK semiautomatic pistol equipped with a silencer. Checking to make sure that it was fully loaded, he chambered a round and slipped the weapon into his coat pocket. Ripping open the envelope, he found a map, the diagram of a house, instructions for entering the house, and a name: Paul Arcadio.

Putting the car in gear, he drove to the expressway and turned north.

18

DECEMBER 2, 1977
8:15 P.M.

Deputy Chief of Detectives William Riseman and Area Six Detective Commander Jack Govich arrived at Marina Towers in a black unmarked Chevy equipped with a buggy-whip antenna. A uniformed sergeant was waiting at the entrance to the tower in which Ryan had lived. The two high-ranking cops brushed past him and raced across the lobby to the elevators. They rode up in a car alone to the twelfth floor. They had been here many times before; however, on those prior occasions, their faces had never held such grim expressions.

Riseman was a tall man, who gave more of the impression of being a scholar than a cop. He was dressed in blue jeans, a windbreaker, and white tennis shoes. Govich was wearing a blue suit, white shirt and red-and-white-striped tie beneath a beige trench coat. His black hair was graying at the temples. It looked as if it had been styled recently. Govich could have just stepped off the pages of a male fashion magazine, but he was all cop and had the reputation as being one of the best detectives on the force. Govich had modeled himself after John T. Ryan.

In fact, both of the men riding in the elevator had been profoundly affected by the man whose death they were here to investigate. Riseman had been Ryan's administrative deputy, or second in command, for five years. Riseman was the detail man and kept the paperwork up to date in the detective division of the second largest police department in the nation. The deputy chief had not always agreed with Ryan's tactics, but one thing was certain, Riseman definitely respected him, which bordered on profound admiration.

It was different with Govich. The commander had been a detective for all but two of his sixteen years on the force. During that time, he had worked almost exclusively for John T. Ryan. Govich had patterned himself in the image and likeness of the chief of detectives. At times he referred to himself as "The First Disciple of the Dogma of Policing According to Ryan." The loss of the chief of detectives was going to affect Govich as deeply as the loss of his own father.

The two men exited into the twelfth-floor corridor, which was packed with cops. A uniformed captain shoved his way through the throng and approached Riseman and Govich. They conversed in whispers before the captain turned and led the deputy chief and the commander solemnly to the door to apartment 12A.

There was a frightened female officer stationed at the door. As the captain led the two men in plainclothes past her, she recalled the precept she'd been taught in the police academy about protecting the crime scene. She opened her mouth to mention this to her watch commander, but the captain gave her a stern look, tinged with anger. This succeeded in forcing her back into the inanimate mannequin in uniform she had been since she'd been assigned to this task.

However, what the deputy chief of detectives, the detective commander, and the uniformed captain were doing was, in fact, violating the crime scene. Despite their high ranks, they were unauthorized personnel who should not have been permitted into apartment 12A until the mobile crime-lab-unit technicians, who were speeding to the homicide scene at this very moment, had finished processing the area. When photos had been taken, a schematic drawing called a "plat" completed, and as much physical evidence as possible collected, then the scene would be turned over to the assigned detectives. The detectives would then make a determination as to exactly who would be considered "authorized" personnel. As yet, no detectives had put in an appearance at the scene, but they, like the crime-lab techs, were on the way.

Riseman and Govich knew the rules of evidence as well as any other cop. What they were doing by entering the crime scene of apartment 12A was unprofessional. But this wasn't about the profession of being a law-enforcement officer. It was personal. Very personal.

Ryan's body had been draped with a beige blanket that one of the cops had found in a linen closet at the rear of the apartment. This was another violation of the rules of evidence on protecting the crime scene. The bodies of the other dead men remained uncovered and blood from the four exsanguinating bodies had formed a mini-lake on the varnished hardwood floor.

The three cops walked through the blood to reach the blanket-covered corpse of John T. Ryan. The captain stopped. Riseman and Govich did the same. The eyes of each of the men rested on the blanket-shrouded body. Then, unable to contain himself any longer, Govich squatted, making sure not to get any blood on his trousers, and pulled back the edge of the blanket. The commander stared at the corpse with wide-eyed horror. Riseman took one glance at the dead man before turning to the captain.

"Where is the tactical cop?"

"Down in the garage, Boss."

"We need to talk to him."

"I'll get him, sir."

"No. We'll go downstairs."

Riseman turned back to where Govich was still squatting beside the body. "Jack," he said softly.

It took the detective commander a moment to pull himself away. Then Govich covered the dead man once more, stood up slowly, and turned around. His face was rigid and his jaw muscles rippled as he fought to control his emotions.

Riseman reached out and touched Govich's arm. "C'mon. We've got work to do."

The parking garage had been turned into a makeshift Chicago Police Department command post, much to the consternation of Marina Towers management. A handcuffed, impassive Sal Marino was being held in the backseat of a marked police car. Two uniformed officers stood a very close watch over him.

Larry Cole had driven his unmarked Dodge into the garage and parked a short distance from the car where *his* prisoner was being held. The young tactical cop was numb from all the violence he had been through that day and, despite his being surrounded by fellow cops, he felt very much alone.

Now he would be forced to endure the same type of inquisition he had this morning. Commander O'Casey, the IAD, and Office of Professional Standards investigators were on the way.

The prospect of what the remainder of the night held for him made Cole's shoulders sag. He spied a public telephone mounted on the garage wall a short distance from where he was parked. Getting out of the car, Cole crossed to the phone and dialed the number of St. Joseph's Hospital.

He was forced to threaten, cajole, plead, and even tell a small lie before the nurse would put him through to Blackie's room.

"Yeah." It was obvious that Blackie was talking around a cigar.

"How are you feeling?" Cole said, attempting to keep his tone light.

It didn't fool Blackie for a second. *"What's wrong, kid?"*

Cole heard Maria Silvestri's concerned voice in the background. Blackie shushed her, saying, *"He hasn't told me yet, babe."*

So Cole told him.

When he was finished, Blackie said, *"You did real good, Larry, but you were lucky. A lone cop against four Mafia guns, with one of them being that scumbag Sal Marino, stacked the odds against you."*

"I guess so," Cole said, "but I had a good teacher."

"Just promise me one thing. That you won't go pulling anything like this again unless I'm with you."

"I promise."

"So what now?"

At that moment Deputy Chief Riseman and Commander Govich entered the garage. The watch commander accompanying them pointed to Cole.

"There are a couple of bosses who want to talk to me," Cole said.

"Who are they?"

"One of them is Deputy Chief Riseman. I think the other is Commander Govich."

"Okay, kid, this is how you play it. Just tell them how, in one day, you whacked out four members of the Arcadio Mob and busted Sal Marino, after being tutored by none other than the best street cop in Chicago, who incidentally happens to be of Italian descent, and they'll make you a detective before dawn."

"But I don't want to be a detective," Cole protested.

"How do you know, kid? You ever been one?"

19

DECEMBER 2, 1977
8:17 P.M.

Despite his great size and energy, Cleveland Emmett "Clevey" Barksdale III was very sensitive. So he had been able to detect that there was something not quite right with his grandfather when they had talked earlier in the dining room. Clevey had done his homework and gone down to dinner. He was forced to eat alone because his grandfather had not returned.

After dinner, Clevey watched a little TV, but was unable to concentrate on the mindless chatter on the idiot box. Switching off the set in the living room, the muscular young man went into his grandfather's study.

The walls were lined from floor-to-ceiling with books. Most of them were volumes on the law. Often, Clevey would take one of them off the shelf and read a case at random. He loved the law or, more appropriately, the power that a master practitioner of the law could wield. He sat down behind his grandfather's desk and opened the law book he'd selected to the *State of Illinois* v. *Thomas Ward*. This was a murder case tried in the Circuit Court of Cook County in August 1962. Cleveland Emmett Barksdale Sr. of the law firm of Barksdale and DeVito, P.C., was the attorney of record for the defense.

The young man reading a law book in the study of his grandfather's mansion in the Beverly Hills neighborhood of Chicago was an orphan. Clevey understood from the little his grandfather had said about him, that his father was the total opposite of both grandfather and grandson.

While in high school, Cleve Jr. had become a drug user. After failing to earn a college degree, he had left home to take a job as a blackjack dealer in a Las Vegas casino operated by the Arcadio Crime Family. Cleve Sr. had kept tabs on his son and, when he got into trouble with casino management for failing to show up for work or being too drunk to deal the cards, the Chicago attorney had intervened on his behalf. Then Cleve Jr. met a showgirl, whom he impregnated with Clevey.

The young man sitting in the study reading a law book on this winter night had no recollection at all of his father or his mother. He had never seen a photograph of either of them and had promised his grandfather a long time ago that he would never ask any questions about them. Periodically, Clevey had brief bouts of curiosity about his natural parents, who were dead. However, other than that, he respected his grandfather's wishes.

Clevey finished reading the 1962 case and closed the law book. Returning it to the shelf, he walked around the study. His grandfather was Clevey's only living relative. They lived together here in this mansion, attended by a staff of servants. Cleve Sr. took care of his grandson, and Clevey reciprocated by excelling in academics and sports. Someday Clevey would also become a lawyer. They had already discussed it. On the day that Clevey passed the Illinois bar exam, the firm name would be changed to Barksdale, Barksdale, and DeVito, P.C.

Clevey walked over to the window and looked out at the side of the house where the driveway, leading from the street to the garage, was located. It was 8:30, and his grandfather should have been home by now.

The fifteen-year-old knew that Barksdale and DeVito had a very select client list. When Clevey was a freshman in high school, he had broken a big-mouth senior's jaw for calling his grandfather a "Mob lawyer." But if Cleve Sr. did have contacts with organized crime, they were merely in line with his successful legal practice. After all, everyone was innocent until proven guilty.

The lights of a car illuminated the driveway. Clevey waited, expecting his grandfather's chauffeur-driven Cadillac to pull into view. But, although the lights remained on, no car appeared. From where he was standing, Clevey could not see the end of the driveway where the illumination originated. Then the lights were extinguished.

This alarmed the young man and made him curious. Turning from the window, he went downstairs to investigate.

20

Commander Jack Govich stood outside the police car inside of which Sal Marino sat handcuffed in the backseat. The policeman stared through the window at the mobster who, although aware of Govich's presence, refused to return his gaze. Instead, Marino kept his eyes cast forward stonily.

After five minutes of this intense scrutiny, Govich turned and walked across the garage to Larry Cole, who was standing next to the unmarked Dodge. Cole stiffened to attention when he saw the commander approaching.

"Relax, kid." Govich removed a package of Marlboros from his pocket and offered one to Cole.

"No, thank you, sir. I don't smoke."

"Good for you." The commander lit a cigarette and leaned against the front bumper of Cole's police car. "You did one helluva job today, Larry. I don't ever recall a cop getting involved in two shoot-outs on the same day and walking away without a scratch."

Cole shrugged and looked down at the garage floor. "I was lucky, sir. My partner was wounded."

"I heard about that. I'm sorry, but I heard he's going to be okay."

"I talked to him a little while ago. Blackie sounded like he could get up and come back to work right now."

Govich drew on his cigarette and exhaled a thick cloud of smoke. "You ever meet Chief Ryan?"

"No, sir. I never had the pleasure."

The commander's face went slack and his eyes blurred. Finally he cleared his throat and said, "He was a terrific cop and a good man. The department won't be the same without him."

Deputy Chief Riseman exited the stairwell and walked quickly over to Govich and Cole. He was slightly out of breath as he said, "I just talked to the state's attorney. He was able to obtain an arrest warrant for Paul Arcadio, charging him with conspiracy to commit murder. A deputy sheriff is going to meet us at the Rabbit's North Shore home with the warrant, so we can serve it on him tonight."

"Okay, let's go," Govich said, stomping his cigarette out on the garage floor.

"Excuse me, sir," Cole said.

Riseman and Govich stopped and turned around.

"May I go along?"

Riseman frowned and began shaking his head when Govich replied, "I guess this is your case, Cole. You've been on it since the start. It's only fitting that you be in on the finish." The commander looked at the deputy chief. "Don't you think so, Boss?"

Riseman thought for a long minute before saying, "Okay, Cole. You can come along. Just don't get in the way."

"Yes, sir."

21

DECEMBER 2, 1977
8:22 P.M.

Antonio "Tuxedo Tony" DeLisa entered the study of his Oak Park home. His wife, Helen, and his four-year-old daughter, Rachel, were confined to the second floor for the rest of the night. One of DeLisa's soldiers, armed with a .44 magnum revolver concealed in a shoulder holster beneath his jacket, was stationed outside the bedroom where the two most important women in the mobster's life were watching television. There were two armed wise guys stationed in the front alcove and four more down at the entrance to the driveway. The iron gates at the entrance were closed and padlocked. A steel-reinforced, four-door sedan was parked across the driveway.

DeLisa had turned his home into a fortress in which he would remain while a gang war raged around him. When the smoke cleared, he would be ready to take over the Chicago mob.

Cleve Barksdale's chauffeur pulled the Cadillac limousine into the driveway of his Beverly Hills home. He stopped at the walkway leading from the garage to the house. The attorney got out of the rear seat, leaving the chauffeur to park the car in the four-car garage.

The front of the house was equipped with a pair of strategically placed spotlights, which illuminated the corner lot on which the Barksdale residence was located. But to add to the grounds' ambience, rows of evergreens had been planted, which cast some areas in shadow. Now, as Cleve Barksdale approached the front door of his home, Tony Lima, brandishing a nine-millimeter semiautomatic handgun, stepped from behind a bush. When the attorney saw the weasel-faced little man, he froze.

Lima smiled. "It's time, Counselor. The Rabbit told me to tell you that this is for Frankie. He also wanted me to let you know that it's personal. Very personal."

Lima was about to pull the trigger when the hulking figure of Clevey Barksdale loomed up behind the Mafia killer. The high-school football player was wielding a snow shovel, which he swung at Lima's head with all of his might. The sound the metal made on impact with the little man's skull was as loud as a pistol shot.

Lima dropped the gun and collapsed. Clevey stepped over the prone man and swung the shovel down to strike him again, and again, and again until his grandfather shouted, "Clevey, stop!"

He halted the shovel in mid-swing and looked from the carnage lying at his feet to his grandfather. There was a mixture of fury and terror on his face.

The older man stepped forward and, with some difficulty, took the shovel from his grandson's hands. Then the lawyer checked Lima's body. The head had been bashed in. It was probable that the first blow had killed him instantly. But the Mob lawyer left nothing to chance.

Standing up, Barksdale said, "Clevey, go into the house."

At first the young man didn't acknowledge his grandfather's order. Then he shook himself, as if attempting to escape from a bad dream, and went inside.

Barksdale took one last look at the man who had come here to kill him, picked up the pistol and, carrying the shovel, went to get his chauffeur to assist him in disposing of the dead body.

Four Chicago Police cars—two marked and two unmarked—raced north on Lake Shore Drive with all emergency equipment activated. Before the convoy crossed the northern city-limit line at Howard Street and Sheridan Road, Govich had radioed ahead to the Evanston Police Department to announce that the four CPD units would be passing through their jurisdiction en route to the unincoporated North Shore area where Paul "the Rabbit" Arcadio lived.

At the Chicago city limits, two marked Evanston PD cars joined the caravan to provide an escort through the northern suburb, where the Northwestern University campus was located.

Riding in the unmarked yellow Dodge police car, which Larry Cole was driving, Govich mumbled, "So much for stealth and subtlety."

Cole heard him and couldn't help laughing.

All the cars shut off their emergency equipment when they were half a mile from the Arcadio mansion, which sat on a bluff overlooking a private beach. The Mafia boss's estate occupied ten tree-lined, manicured acres. There was no fence surrounding the property. Prior to this December night, security had never been an issue. A curving driveway led up to the front door. The six police cars pulled into the driveway and the cops got out.

Although he was the ranking officer, Deputy Chief Riseman deferred to Commander Govich, who was a field officer and a good one. The Evanston cops had horned in on the CPD operation, but Govich wasn't about to turn down the additional help.

"Cole, take two of the Evanston guys and cover the back," Govich ordered. "I don't think the Rabbit is going to do anything stupid, but we're not taking any chances."

"Yes, sir," Cole said, nodding to two of the Evanston cops.

As they followed the tactical cop around the side of the house toward the beach, Govich led the other cops to the front door.

Alain Rianocek had arrived in the unincorporated area, where Rabbit Arcadio lived, fifteen minutes before the cops. Ordinarily, he would not have moved against a target on such short notice, but the price was not only right, it was the highest fee he had ever received for a "sanction." He refused to call the murders he committed "hits," as his American counterparts did.

He left the Lincoln on a side road running parallel to the beach a quarter mile away and proceeded on foot. The night was cold and the sharp wind blowing off the lake stung his face and made his eyes tear. He kept to the shadows lining the stretch of beach on which were displayed prominently posted signs proclaiming. "Private Property—Keep Out—Violators will be prosecuted."

Rianocek was aware that a private security firm patrolled the area. There were also the Arcadio Family soldiers. But the assassin had been told that there would be no guards or wise guys prowling the area tonight. Then there was his contact inside the house.

The assassin made it to the edge of the mansion grounds and stopped. He was in a small grove of tall cedars. He studied the south portico of the mansion. It was connected to a balcony surrounded by a short ornamental stone railing six feet above the ground. Giving his eyes a moment to adjust to the darkness of this moonless night, he studied the area.

Then he saw it. A dim light flashed in one of the ground-floor windows. It could have come from the open flame from a cigarette lighter or a pencil flashlight. Rianocek waited until it flashed twice more. Then he moved toward the window.

The assassin reached the south portico and climbed onto the balcony. He crossed to the window. It was open. He climbed inside just as the six police vehicles pulled up in front of the mansion. He was unaware of their presence.

The room he entered was dark. The assassin backed against a wall and willed himself to become one with his surroundings. Then he became aware that he was not alone.

"The man you are here for is in the study on the other side of the entrance alcove," a voice said from the shadows.

The assassin was unable to see who had spoken to him. He didn't like this. The front doorbell rang.

"Wait here," the man in the shadows said.

The assassin sensed—rather than saw—movement on the other side of the room. Then there was a brief flash of light as the door opened, momentarily illuminating the silhouette of a tall, thin man. Then the door closed plunging the room into darkness once more.

The assassin reached into his pocket and removed the garrote. He was ready to kill.

Arthur Maggio looked through the peephole into the scowling face of Commander Jack Govich. Without opening the door, he demanded, "What do you want?"

"Your boss, Maggio. We've got a warrant for his arrest."

The cop held up the warrant, which Maggio recognized from prior experience. He glanced back at the door off the alcove behind which the assassin, who had come here to kill Paul Arcadio, waited. If the cops searched the house, his presence would be discovered. That would be a disaster.

Govich leaned on the doorbell. The study door opened and Paul
Arcadio stepped into the alcove. Maggio jumped when he heard the
Don's voice.

"What is it, Art?"

"The police are outside," his assistant said, glancing frantically
from Arcadio to the assassin's hiding place. "They've got a warrant
for your arrest."

Arcadio smiled. "Let them in."

With a final glance across the alcove, Maggio opened the front
door.

Larry Cole stood in the sand at the foot of a staircase leading up
to a sundeck behind the Arcadio mansion. The two Evanston cops
were spaced at twenty-yard intervals on each side of the Chicago
tactical cop. Cole had the .45 in his hand, his fur-lined jacket but-
toned, and his coat collar up, but he still felt chilled to the bone.
He thought that his shivering was due to the cold, but it was actually
his nerves beginning to overload. Cole was on the verge of emotional exhaustion, but he called up what little strength he had left
so that he could complete this final duty of the most hectic day so
far of his career.

Before they started for the North Shore, Cole had been given a
charged battery for his radio. The walkie-talkie was set to the frequency all of the units engaged in the arrest of Rabbit Arcadio were
on. Now Commander Govich's voice came over the air.

"We've got him, Cole. Meet us back out front."

"Okay, guys," Cole called to the Evanston uniforms, "let's go."

They were passing the south side of the house when Cole happened to glance up and see the open window. He stopped. The
frozen Evanston cops kept going.

The assassin's sanction had to be aborted. The police were inside
the house, placing the killer in danger of being discovered. He had
to get out of here as quickly and silently as possible. Going to the

window, he looked out and saw the black man standing outside. It was obvious that he was a cop. The assassin tensed, but was aware that he could not be seen.

Cole thought he detected movement inside the house. The incongruity of a window being open on a night like this haunted him. However, he was exhausted and didn't think he possessed the strength to climb up there and check it out. His cop instincts began acting up. He remembered the talks he'd had with Blackie, as they patrolled the streets on quiet nights. Conversations about going the extra yard to make the arrest. About giving just a little bit more to ensure that the bad guys didn't get away. Now Cole rationalized that he had done his bit on this day for God, country, and the Windy City. Slowly, he turned and walked back to the front of the mansion. The handcuffed Mafia boss was being placed into the back of a marked Chicago Police car when Cole joined the other officers.

For a brief moment, the assassin was certain that the cop was going to enter the house. He had returned the garrote to his pocket and had the silenced automatic in his hand. Now he waited. When the cop finally walked away, the assassin's tension eased. Only then did he realize that he had bitten his bottom lip so hard he'd come close to drawing blood.

Waiting a moment longer, he slipped out the window, dropped to the ground, and ran off into the dark. His thirteenth assassination had failed.

22

L arry Cole had slept soundly for nine hours. He hadn't set the clock on his nightstand when he went to bed at about 1:00 A.M. because he'd been given the day off by Deputy Chief Riseman with the acquiescence of Commander O'Casey. Swinging his feet to the floor, Cole cradled his head in his hands for a moment waiting for the cobwebs, left by the long hours of slumber, to recede. He was not used to more than four to six hours of sleep a night. He thrived on a schedule that usually had him on the go from dawn until midnight. However, yesterday had not been a normal day in the life of Nineteenth District Tactical Officer Larry Cole.

Finally, Cole pushed himself off the bed and went into the bathroom. After a shower, shave, and a fried bacon-and-egg sandwich, the young cop called St. Joseph's Hospital. Blackie was fine and demanded to be filled in on every detail of what had occurred the previous night. After telling his partner that he would be by to see him later, Cole hung up and was preparing to go out for his daily run when the telephone rang.

"Officer Cole?" a female voice inquired.

"Yes."

"This is Detective Blackledge from Detective Division Headquarters. Would you please hold for Deputy Chief Riseman?"

A moment later, Riseman was on the line. *"How are you feeling this morning, Larry?"*

"A little groggy after the long hours yesterday, sir, but I plan to clear that up with a nice long run."

"Excellent. Listen, I wonder if you could drop by my office at police headquarters in the next day or so? I understand you're high up on the sergeant's promotion list."

"Yes, sir."

"Perhaps, after you finish preservice sergeant's school, you would consider an assignment in the detective division."

After his talk with Blackie last night, Cole had given this some thought, so he said, "That would be great, sir."

"Good, but stop by and see me anyway when you get a chance and we can explore some ideas I have about your career. But that's not the real reason why I called. Our Mob plot continues to thicken.

"Somebody caved in Tony Lima's head last night and dumped his body in a vacant lot out in Oak Lawn. Rabbit Arcadio made bond in court this morning and is scheduled for trial in January; but without a corroborating witness to the conspiracy charge, we're whistling in the wind. But, thanks to you, we've got Sal Marino dead bang behind the eight ball."

"What do we do next?" Cole asked.

"Right now nothing, until a grand jury convenes. There's not a judge in the state who will dare grant bail to the alleged killer of Chief John T. Ryan." Riseman paused for a moment. *"I would say that the Arcadio Family is dealing with some very serious damage control right about now."*

23

Monsignor Maurice O'Keefe concluded the 12:00 mass at St. Peter's Cathedral on West Madison Street in the Chicago Loop. After blessing the congregation, the 6'5" priest left the altar.

Inside the sacristy, he removed his vestments and washed the chalice. Putting everything away, he went back onto the altar. The cathedral was open twelve hours a day to service transient worshipers in the downtown area. Even though the next mass would not be celebrated until 5:00 that evening, there were still a number of people inside the church. The monsignor genuflected in front of the altar and made the sign of the cross before proceeding to the rear of the building.

In the vestibule, he nodded to the usher on duty and proceeded down the steps to the lower level of the cathedral. St. Peter's was one of the most beautiful Catholic churches in the country. It was constructed of marble and was designed in a modernistic architectural style. The cathedral was not really considered a parish, as was the case with the numerous "neighborhood" churches in the Chicago archdiocese, but designated for the commercial worshiper. It was there for those Catholics who dropped in to say a quick prayer between business deals or were visiting Chicago and staying at a Loop hotel and wanted to attend a conveniently brief Sunday mass, or those who simply wished to drop in during the hours the cathedral was open to experience the quiet reverence and stately ambience of the magnificent structure.

The lower level stretched the entire length of the block-long building and was lined with doors leading into a library lined with shelves containing texts on theology, the offices of cathedral administrative personnel, and two spacious conference rooms.

Monsignor O'Keefe went to one of the conference rooms. Three people were waiting for him. The monsignor went to the head of the conference table and remained standing. After surveying those present, he said, "Before we begin our deliberations, let us join hands and pray."

The three men rose from their seats and did as the prelate instructed. Monsignor O'Keefe took the left hand of Paul "the Rabbit" Arcadio, who took the hand of Antonio "Tuxedo Tony" DeLisa, who, in turn, joined hands with Cleveland Emmett Barksdale, Esq.

Monsignor Maurice O'Keefe had been born Alphonse Soristino in Casca, Sicily, in 1917. At the age of seven, Alphonse's father, Giuseppe Soristino, who had Mafia connections, moved his family to the United States. They settled originally in New York City, where "Joe" Soristino went to work for the Maranzano Crime Family. Soristino became an underboss and chose to follow Lucky Luciano, who murdered his way to the top of the organized-crime underworld in 1931.

Soristino had six children, four boys and two girls. Alphonse was the fifth child and youngest boy. At an early age, he was seen to be "different." He was quiet and studious, didn't show much interest in playing with other children, and spent most of his time alone reading or daydreaming.

The other Soristino boys—Joe, Jr., Pete, and Ray—followed in their father's footsteps. Each of them accumulated lengthy arrest records for everything from murder to petty theft, before their twenty-first birthdays. Big Joe Sr. was a giant of a man who stood over 6'6" inches tall, and envisioned one of his sons becoming the head of a Mob family some day. But in a 1934 gang war between

Luciano and Dutch Schultz, the three young mobsters were gunned down. This was the same year that young Alphonse graduated from high school.

Unable to bear the burden of losing his only surviving son, Joe Soristino sent Alphonse to Chicago, where he came under the protection of Frank Nitti. In Chicago, two things of great importance happened in the life of Alphonse Soristino. To protect himself from his father's enemies, he changed his name to Maurice O'Keefe, and he decided to become a priest.

Father O'Keefe was a good priest. He was also smart and earned a master's degree in business administration from Notre Dame University. After serving in local parishes for ten years, he was assigned as an aide to the archbishop of Chicago. This placed him on a fast track for an appointment to monsignor. He built a reputation for being something of a diplomat and a skilled arbitrator of disputes. It was said that he could mediate even the most bitter disagreement. Monsignor O'Keefe's ability in this regard was utilized not only by the Catholic Church.

With the prayer concluded, the four men took seats around the conference table. Before beginning the negotiations, Monsignor O'Keefe studied his "guests." They were a group of very dangerous men. He could employ all of his arbitration skills, and they still could opt to disregard his decision. But he realized that he had a power over them which they not only recognized, but respected and feared.

Monsignor O'Keefe's power existed on two levels. One level was purely physical; however, it was not due to his impressive size, but rather by way of his unique position in the Mafia hierarchy. The title of "Intercessore" or "mediator" had been bestowed upon him by the joint commission that oversaw all Mob activities within and having any connection to the United States. Because of his Sicilian background, and despite his involvement with the Catholic Church, the monsignor was considered a member of the Family.

O'Keefe did not benefit directly from his unique position with the Mafia, but he would ensure that the appropriate fees for his services were donated in his name to the proper charities.

The Intercessore's word was law. If anyone seeking his services failed to obey his dictates to the letter, the wrath of the entire Mafia apparatus would be brought to bear on the recalcitrant. Only two men had ever gone against the Intercessore's dictates. The two Las Vegas gamblers were supposedly buried somewhere in the Mojave Desert.

The other level Monsignor O'Keefe operated on was spiritual, which to him was paramount. He had never considered the morality of the mediations he conducted for the Mafia. Who they were didn't matter to him; the fact that they needed his guidance to keep from killing themselves and others, did. Long ago he had come to the decision to let God judge him and them in the hereafter.

To effectively do his job as Intercessore, it was necessary for Monsignor Maurice O'Keefe to first listen and listen patiently. Now he nodded to Paul Arcadio. The Mafia don began.

The hearing took over an hour. Arcadio did most of the talking. Barksdale spoke briefly, but was extremely guarded. DeLisa said nothing. Monsignor O'Keefe understood their respective positions.

Arcadio was playing the aggrieved, betrayed Mafia boss. He couldn't believe that his organization had been decimated by a lone tactical cop, who had less than three years on the job. He saw himself as the target of a plot which had been hatched by Cleve Barksdale.

For his part, the attorney did little more than deny Arcadio's charges. Barksdale did manage to skillfully—but surreptitiously, point out what a complete mess Arcadio had made of things. Particularly the assassination of Chief of Detectives John T. Ryan, which had resulted in the deaths of three of Arcadio's soldiers and the arrest of underboss Sal Marino with a smoking gun in his hand. Barksdale saved Marino's arrest until the end of his short remarks because it had the most devastating implications.

The Arcadio underboss was facing the death penalty. Despite Marino having sworn a blood oath of silence—*"Omertà"*—he was in the perfect position for the government to apply pressure to make him turn state's evidence in exchange for his life. This could be disastrous for organized crime families nationally, because Sal Marino knew—literally—where a lot of bodies were buried.

When the attorney finished his remarks, Monsignor O'Keefe looked down the table at DeLisa. Despite his high calling, the cleric could not help feeling a deep dislike for this man.

Tuxedo Tony sat at the end of the table opposite O'Keefe. The underboss kept his gaze cast down at the table surface and his face expressionless. If there would be a winner coming out of the deliberations of the Arcadio Crime Family with the Intercessore, it would be DeLisa. Due to Rabbit Arcadio's mismanagement and errors, within a span of little more than twenty-four hours, DeLisa had gone from being an "also ran" to next-in-line to be the Chicago mob boss. If and when that day did come, Monsignor O'Keefe was certain that none of them would be safe.

Now, all of the statements had been made. The evidence was in and it was time for the Intercessore to make a decision. Sitting forward he addressed his guests.

"It is unfortunate that this situation has deteriorated to this stage. It is my understanding that prior to yesterday's events, the Arcadio Family shunned violence." The monsignor sighed. "Hopefully, that pattern will reassert itself in the future. Now to the matter of hand."

"Don Paolo Arcadio"—the Mafia boss sat up a bit straighter when the Intercessore addressed him—"your actions have not only jeopardized your own business, but imperiled the activities of your colleagues from coast to coast. For that you will be penalized the sum of five million dollars, which will be collected within twenty-four hours."

Arcadio looked away from the monsignor at the far wall. The Mafia don's jaw muscles rippled furiously, but he held his tongue.

To do otherwise could be dangerous, even to a man as powerful as Rabbit Arcadio. However, the Intercessore was not finished.

"In addition to the fine, Don Paolo, you will relinquish your interest in the Satin Slipper Hotel and Casino in Las Vegas. That interest will be transferred to the heirs of Salvatore Marino as a guarantee that during his time in prison they will be taken care of and he will remain faithful to his oath of *Omertà.*"

Arcadio had become so rigidly still that he appeared to have turned to stone.

"Do you understand and accept these terms?" Monsignor O'Keefe asked.

In a hoarse voice, the Rabbit said haltingly, "I understand and . . . I accept the . . . terms."

The Intercessore turned his attention to Cleve Barksdale. "To a certain extent, Attorney Barksdale, I see you as something of a victim in this interfamily conflict. At the outset, you were attempting to serve your Don as best you could; however, somewhere along the way, you lost sight not only of your function, but also where your ultimate loyalty should be."

Barksdale was more relaxed than Arcadio, but his tension was quite obvious.

"You conspired against your Don and plotted his death. The fact that Don Paolo attempted to kill you without justification is the only factor mitigating my decision as it applies to you."

Barksdale waited.

"You will be assessed a monetary penalty of one million dollars, which will be collected in twenty-four hours. Your law firm will provide Salvatore Marino pro bono assistance with his legal difficulties. You will do everything that you can to obtain his acquittal. In the event of a guilty verdict, you will file the appropriate appeals until all legal options have been exhausted."

The monsignor paused for a moment before concluding, "And finally, Attorney Barksdale, you will sever all contacts with the Arcadio Family, and any organization or individual associated with the Arcadio Family. Neither you, nor your law firm, will represent, handle any legal business for, or advise any such organization or individual in any way. Do you understand and accept these terms?"

Solemnly, Barksdale nodded.

The Intercessore looked at Antonio DeLisa. "As of right now, Mr. DeLisa, you are in the clear; however, I suggest that you proceed cautiously in your dealings in the future. A number of people are aware of not only your sentiments, but also your ambition."

The look Tuxedo Tony gave Monsignor O'Keefe was of such menace that it conveyed a threat quite clearly. But in keeping with the decorum of the other participants attending these proceedings, DeLisa remained silent.

Monsignor O'Keefe smiled and got to his feet. "Let us now join hands once more and pray for the Lord to guide us in the future conduct of our lives in his service."

24

DECEMBER 3, 1977
4:00 P.M.

Cleve Barksdale was in a solemn mood when he returned to his LaSalle Street office. He went to his desk, slumped down in his chair, and stared out the window. He felt very tired, but realized that this was not the end of the world. The attorney craved a cigarette, but didn't feel that he had the strength to remove the pack of Marlboros and the gold lighter from his coat pocket. He could take some consolation in the fact that he was still alive. Arcadio would not go against the Intercessore's decision.

The law firm of Barksdale and Devito, P.C., would survive. There would be a few lean years until they built up their client list by accepting cases "off the street." Barksdale and Devito, P.C. would never again be the elite, very private firm that it had been in the past. But things would work out eventually. There was still tomorrow.

Barksdale's intercom buzzed.

"Yes."

"A telegram just arrived for you, sir," his secretary said.

"Bring it in."

Barksdale managed to drag himself out of the depression by the time she walked through the door to place the yellow envelope on his desk blotter. When she was gone, he opened it.

```
Was unable to carry out the assignment.
Your fee will be returned. I owe you one.
                                      A.
```

PART 2

"Commander Cole and I are far from through,
Mr. Shade. Far from through."
—A. Rianocek

25

B aron Alain Marcus Casimir von Rianocek entered Caruso's Restaurant on East 57th Street in Manhattan. The maître'd' recognized the guest and graced him with a cordial smile. "Good evening, Baron von Rianocek. Right this way."

The tall, aristocratic European followed the maître'd' across the exclusive restaurant to a private room, where a dinner party for six was being held. As they passed other diners, a number of admiring stares, from both male and female patrons, were cast Rianocek's way. The aura of charisma he generated was quite evident and he transmitted to everyone he encountered that he was "someone."

The maître'd' opened the door to the private dining area and held it for Rianocek. "Madame Sharp and her party are waiting for you, sir."

"Thank you," the baron said imperiously.

"Baron von Rianocek!" the high-pitched scream of Madame Christina Sharp echoed through the private room.

Etching a tolerant, slightly bored expression on his face, Rianocek took in the assemblage.

There were six people present including his hostess. Madame Christina Sharp was an aging, spectacularly ugly New York society fixture, who could trace her family tree and fortune back to the *Mayflower*. The attendees were a mixed bag of academics, politicians, and social hangers-on. There was a current New York City councilman, a black Harlem activist preacher, a novelist who hadn't published a book in ten years, a Broadway actress who hadn't been in a hit play since the sixties, and a former New York City mayor. The guest of honor at Madame Sharp's little soiree was Baron Alain von Rianocek.

Madame Sharp approached her guest with her hand extended. Rianocek took it and rendered a perfunctory shake, noticing with an inner delight that the horrid woman was disappointed that he didn't kiss the hand. Then she led him to the place of honor at the table, at her right.

For the next hour and a half, the Bavarian national endured the inane dinner table talk of his hostess, who had the irritating habit of talking with food in her mouth, and the other bores in attendance. He performed the role of the arrogant, rich international playboy to perfection. However, he was in New York City for something far more important to him than being the guest of honor at this stupid dinner party.

In the twelve years that had passed since the aborted assassination of Rabbit Arcadio in Chicago, Alain Rianocek had been responsible for the deaths of over eighty people. He had taken the assassin's profession to the level of fine art. His repertoire of methods and range of weapons was vast. To get to a target he would use whatever means necessary.

To carry out the assassination of an Eastern European dictator who never went anywhere without being surrounded by six bodyguards, the assassin had stood in a crowd while the target gave a speech from the balcony of a palace. Carefully disguised as one of the natives of the impoverished capital city of the dictatorship, Rianocek had fired a curare-tipped dart from a spring-operated compressed-air tube, which was concealed in the palm of his hand. The dart pierced the dictator's neck, appearing to cause little more damage than a mosquito bite. He collapsed within minutes and died before they could get him to a hospital. After firing the dart, the assassin had simply dropped the metal tube and walked away.

To dispose of a British industrialist, the assassin had rigged a stick of dynamite inside a cigar box. The booby trap had been slipped into the closet of the industrialist's office where he kept his private tobacco stock. When the target opened the rigged box, he was quite effectively blown to bits.

The elimination of a gambler in Los Angeles, who had defaulted on a Mob loan, had entailed the assassin getting close to the target on a crowded downtown L.A. street. Rianocek had stepped up beside him and plunged a razor-sharp six-inch-blade stiletto into his heart. The assassin was a quarter of a block away before the gambler fell to the sidewalk.

Alain Rianocek studied each job as thoroughly as was humanly possible and employed a research staff, as well as an on-site backup crew. He did not want a repeat of what had occurred with the aborted assassination attempt in Chicago back in December 1977. His anonymity and safety were of paramount importance. Rianocek had gone to great lengths to maintain this status.

When the assassin began his career, each job had been deeply personal. Rianocek attempted to get as close to his victims as possible. Close enough to look into their eyes at the instant that they died by his hand. However, being so close finally proved to be dangerous for the killer.

In April 1978, on the third assignment after the failure in Chicago, the assassin had been hired to kill the heiress to a Greek shipping empire. The seventy-six-year-old woman lived in a villa in Monte Carlo and was attended by a small, aging domestic staff which included a nurse. Research revealed that the household turned in for the night at 10:00 and that security was minimal. Rianocek figured that this assignment would be not only simple, but easy.

Entering the villa at midnight on a moonless night, the assassin had proceeded to the woman's bedroom. With a garrote stretched between clenched fists, he approached the bed. It would have all been over in a matter of seconds, but his target was not a sound sleeper. She awoke before he was in position, spied him, and started screaming.

The staff became alerted and the nurse rushed to her charge's aid. The quiet kill he had anticipated became a brawl, with the skilled assassin battling two terrified, hysterical women. He managed to prevail with some difficulty, but it had forced him to change his tactics. He depersonalized his kills, which resulted in the body count from his operations rising significantly.

"Baron von Rianocek," Madame Christina Sharp's shrill voice broke into his postprandial dinner reverie.

The assassin said wearily, "Yes, dear lady."

"You've been so quiet. Didn't you enjoy the meal?"

"Actually, no."

This was not really true. The food at Caruso's was good, if not exceptional, and Rianocek had eaten here many times in the past when he was in New York. But to be too effusive in his praise would be out of character for the snobbish aristocrat Christina Sharp thought him to be.

Stifling a yawn, Rianocek murmured, "The food was bland and terribly overcooked. I've consumed tastier hot dogs from curbside vendors out on the street."

"Oh, dear!" his hostess said in obvious distress.

The assassin checked the time on his gold Patek Philippe wristwatch. This dinner was not an idle waste of time for him. He was in the city to do a job, and his dinner companions were part of the scenario he had planned to set up his access and egress from his target's location. He had five minutes to go before the operation was scheduled to commence, but he'd had enough of Madame Sharp and her guests.

Tossing his napkin on the table, Rianocek rose. "I have an important phone call to make. Please carry on without me. I'll return shortly."

"Of course, Baron," the flustered hostess said. Then, as he walked rapidly from the private dining room, she turned to the former New York City mayor and whispered a horrified, "He didn't like the food. Do you think I should speak to the maître'd?"

26

OCTOBER 15, 1989
8:00 P.M.

Caruso's Restaurant was located on the ground floor of the M. D. Hines office building. The Hines Building, as it was called, leased office space primarily to businesses specializing in legal work, accounting and insurance. After 6:00 P.M., the twenty-eight-floor structure was closed to the public. A uniformed security guard, who was an ex–NYPD detective, manned the desk at the center of the lobby and was responsible for checking the identification and making authorized visitors sign in on a log.

The sixty-five-year-old ex-cop was not supremely dedicated to his second career. There was really nothing in the building worth stealing. No jewelers, banks, or watch-repair shops leased space in the Hines Building. So he went through the motions without being unduly concerned with the comings and goings through the ornate lobby.

There were two entrances from 57th Street. One was through a revolving door directly off the street; the other was from Caruso's Restaurant. To make the long hours of the night watch more tolerable, the guard took an occasional swig from a metal hip flask containing vodka. He had started his shift at 6:00 P.M. and would go off duty at 2:00 A.M. By that time the flask would be empty and he would be drunk. Now, after two hours on the job, he had taken only two shots of the liquor, which left him more-or-less sober. He had just returned the flask to his pocket when the man with severe breathing problems entered through the revolving doors.

As the newcomer approached the security station, the guard studied him. He was a rotund man of medium height wearing thick glasses with black plastic frames and sporting a bushy mustache. He was dressed in a drab brown suit under a wrinkled beige raincoat and wore a battered gray-plaid hat. He was carrying a worn leather satchel. To the ex-cop he looked like the ambulance-chasing shysters and bail bondsmen who infested the halls of the New York Criminal Courts buildings looking to score clients. Then there was his ragged breathing.

When he came in from 57th Street, the man was fifty feet away from the guard; however, the wheezing noise he made with each inhalation was audible even at this distance. His breathing sounded like an old locomotive chugging up a hill.

He came up to the desk, leaned against it, and took a couple of deep breaths before saying, "Good evening, my good man. I am Cornelius Shade."

The guard stared back at him with a deadpan expression.

"You *were* expecting me?" he said between gasps.

"No. I wasn't," the guard replied. "I never heard of you before."

With some effort, Cornelius Shade lifted his tattered briefcase and placed it on the security desk. The guard didn't notice that the newcomer had blocked his line of sight to the door leading from Caruso's Restaurant and the stairwell door.

Then the woman arrived.

She came in from 57th Street and walked across the lobby with long-legged strides. She was blond, beautiful, and had a figure stuffed into a red two-piece suit that made the guard's eyes widen.

Cornelius Shade merely glanced in her direction before saying, "Now, see here, my good man, I have an appointment here at 8:00 P.M., and I've come a long way to keep it."

The woman ignored the guard and headed for the elevator, passing the security station on the side of the lobby opposite Caruso's Restaurant and the stairwell door.

The guard shook himself out of his sensual daze and said, "Excuse me, ma'am, but the building is closed."

She stopped and, exuding indignation, turned to glare at him. "Don't you know who I am?"

The guard was so completely occupied that he didn't see the tall man exit the restaurant and enter the stairwell.

27

OCTOBER 15, 1989
8:07 P.M.

The assassin was on a tight schedule. He had a maximum time of fifteen minutes to carry out the assignment in the M. D. Hines Building and return to Christina Sharp's dinner party in Caruso's Restaurant. And this sanction had to look like an accident.

He raced to the seventh floor with ease. In his profession, it was a strict requirement that he keep himself in top physical shape. He opened the stairwell door and carefully examined the corridor. He didn't want to encounter any late-working employees or building maintenance personnel, who could later give his description to the police. He was still as much of an anonymous figure now as he had been in 1977. Only one law-enforcement official in the world suspected him of being an assassin. That was Scotland Yard Chief Inspector Gordon Edwards. However, Edwards had no proof, and Rianocek planned never to work in England again.

Satisfied that there was no one present to observe him, he left the stairwell and walked rapidly down the corridor. At the door to suite 732, he stopped and slipped on a pair of thin black leather gloves. The gold stencil on the door read. "Gross and Sheppard, Certified Public Accountants."

The door was unlocked, as his researchers had told him it would be. After all, management had the ex-NYPD detective handling security in the lobby, and there wasn't anything of any great value in the building worth stealing. However, Alain Rianocek had not come here to steal.

The interior of the outer office of Gross and Sheppard was dark, but there was light coming from one of the offices in a corridor adjacent to the entrance. Moving silently, Rianocek approached the door to this office.

He was inside before the lone woman seated at the desk looked up from the papers she was working on. Initially, she was surprised by this handsome man's presence. But her surprise turned quickly to fear as he advanced toward her.

28

OCTOBER 15, 1989
8:10 P.M.

L ook, nobody told me nothing about meeting a Cornelius Shade, and I don't know who you are, lady!" the lobby security guard argued with the two people who had turned his postretirement job into a confusing nightmare.

They were both badgering the guard in such a shrill, incomprehensible manner that he couldn't understand a word that they were saying.

"This isn't getting us anywhere," the outraged ex-cop finally bellowed. "Neither one of you is getting into this building without authorization, which has to come from the building manager, who ain't here. Now, both of you have got to vacate the premises right now, or I'm calling the cops."

The guard still had his back turned to the stairwell door. At the instant he concluded his angry speech, Rianocek slipped silently into the lobby and reentered the restaurant.

Cornelius Shade removed his briefcase from the desk and said breathlessly, "Since you put it that way, my good man, I won't trouble you any longer. Good night."

Spinning on her heels, the woman snapped, "You haven't heard the last of this!"

Then, to the ex-NYPD detective's amazement, the troublesome pair walked out.

To celebrate his expert handling of the situation, the guard pulled out his hip flask and took a long pull. The vodka burned its way down into his gut, giving him a warm glow. He'd dealt with this problem just as effectively as he'd done all the years he worked as a cop in some of the busiest hellholes in the Big Apple. As a salute to his law-enforcement prowess, he took another swig of booze.

At that moment, the fire alarm sounded. He almost dropped his flask. The seventh-floor fire-indicator light was blinking, and the alarm echoed around him. Shutting off the alarm, it took him a moment to remember the proper procedure. He was supposed to make a backup call to the fire department in case the automated alarm signal didn't go through to 911. However, before he did that and got a squadron of firemen tramping in here, he would check out the seventh floor himself. A female accountant had signed in to work late in an office up there.

Leaving the security desk, he took a lobby elevator to the seventh floor. The instant the doors opened, he smelled smoke. He started to return to the lobby and make the call, but his vodka-soaked brain again flashed back to his NYPD career. He had once received a medal for valor after rescuing a family from a burning tenement in the Bronx. The fact that he had performed this heroic feat twenty-eight years ago and that the rescued fire victims lived in a first-floor apartment didn't register with the guard as he went in search of the accountant.

He came up to the door of suite 732 and entered to find that the smoke here was more dense than out in the hall. He switched on the overhead lights, which flickered on momentarily before blinking off again. Locating the office, from which thick smoke billowed from beneath the door, he checked the outer surface for heat. He had seen this done in a movie once. He was forced to jerk his hands back because the wood was as hot as the top of a burning stove.

Squatting down, he took out his handkerchief and grasped the door handle. With one motion, he twisted and shoved.

The security guard on the night shift in the M. D. Hines Building in midtown Manhattan lived long enough to witness a bizarre sight inside the burning office.

The accountant was tied to a chair at the center of the room. She was either dead or unconscious. The source of the fire was an outlet beside her desk, which was spewing sparks onto the carpet. Every combustible surface in the room was burning and there was a strong chemical odor present. Then one of the windowpanes, providing a view of 57th Street seventy feet below, exploded. Fresh air blowing into the office caused the flames to flare with an explosive force, consuming the entire suite of offices on the seventh floor of the M. D. Hines Building and incinerating both the accountant and the security guard.

29

Larry Cole was riding in the backseat of a 23rd Precinct Detective Squad car. The Chicago Police officer, who had been promoted to the rank of commander a year ago, was not a prisoner, he was a guest of the NYPD. After attending a seminar on urban terrorism given by the FBI in Washington, D.C., Cole had flown to New York to spend a couple of days with his old friend, Assistant Deputy Commissioner Joseph E. Leak. The two cops had become fast friends while attending a management class at the Northwestern Traffic Institute in Evanston, Illinois. Cole, like his counterpart in the Big Apple, signed up for every law-enforcement and criminal-investigation class that was offered. Since entering the CPD Detective Division twelve years ago, the commander's rise through the ranks had been swift, but he had never been one to rest on his laurels.

"This Caruso's Restaurant you're meeting Deputy Leak at," Detective First Grade Frank Azzoli said from the shotgun position in the front seat, "is one of the best eating spots in Manhattan. The food is excellent, and they've got a wine cellar that'll rival anything you'll find in Europe."

"Yeah, Commander," Azzoli's partner, Detective Ted Willis, added, "Caruso's is dining at its finest in the Big Apple."

Larry Cole smiled. Azzoli was a short, dark-haired Italian from Brooklyn; Willis was a tall, thin African-American from Harlem. However, they both spoke with distinctive New York accents and sounded so much alike that Cole didn't think he could tell them apart in the dark.

"I'm sure that the assistant deputy commissioner's tastes are up to their usual high standards," Cole said.

"You can count on it," Azzoli added as his partner turned the police car onto 57th Street to find it clogged with emergency equipment.

Detective Willis pulled up to a wooden barricade manned by a uniformed cop. The detective rolled his window down, flashed his badge at the cop and asked, "What's going on?"

With a characteristic New York accent, the cop leaned down to look inside the car and responded, "We got a high-rise building fire with a couple of people dead."

"We're from the Twenty-third Precinct," Azzoli said. "We're transporting a commander from Chicago to meet Assistant Deputy Commissioner Joseph E. Leak at Caruso's Restaurant."

"The deputy commissioner is already here, Detective," the cop said. "He's taken command of the investigation. The fire occurred in the M. D. Hines Building. Caruso's is on the ground floor."

"Where can we park this thing?" Willis asked the cop.

He looked around and spied a space behind a fire engine and pointed. "Put it over there, but you're gonna have to leave the keys with me in case the smoke eaters need it moved."

"No problem," Willis said.

"Yeah, we're all cops here. Right, Commander Cole?" Azzoli added.

"Whatever you say, Detective Azzoli. At least I'll get a chance to see you Big Apple cops in action."

Assistant Deputy Commissioner Joseph Eduardo Leak had been a New York City cop for twenty-two years. The barrel-chested, 5'10", forty-five-year-old of African-American and Hispanic descent, was a dead ringer for the 1960s French actor Jean-Paul Belmondo and had a great deal in common with Larry Cole, his Chicago counterpart. Besides being a dedicated career cop, Leak had become a legend on the NYPD by breaking more tough, headline cases than any other cop in the city's history.

Right out of the police academy, he was assigned to Midtown Manhattan traffic duty when he responded to a bank alarm. Entering the bank, he came face-to-face with a stocking-masked stickup man wielding a sawed-off shotgun. The robber opened fire, wounding Joe in the shoulder. Leak put six bullets from a .38 Colt Police Special into the stickup man's head. A gold detective's shield was waiting for Leak when he returned to duty.

Joe Leak's career from that point on became storied to the point of approaching fantasy. By his fifth year in the detective bureau he was being referred to openly as "the Spanish Kojak," "Zorro," and "El Detective Magnifico." The chief of detectives, headquartered at One Police Plaza, began calling on Joe Leak whenever there was a tough case breaking, and Leak never let his boss down.

In twenty-two years, he had solved numerous murders, robberies, and burglaries, and had caught every serial criminal he had gone after. A number of his fellow cops had attempted to discover the secret of Leak's success. If they had simply asked, Joe would have told them. There was no secret. He simply utilized hard work, experience, common sense, and the occasional hunch that all good cops employ to catch bad guys.

Now, as he stood in the smoky, fire-blackened corridor on the seventh floor of the M. D. Hines Building, he was once more facing a complicated case.

A uniformed lieutenant approached the assistant deputy commissioner. "Begging your pardon, but there are a couple of Twenty-third Precinct detectives down in the lobby. They've got a Chicago cop with them and are telling my people that they're supposed to be meeting you here."

"Actually, they're supposed to meet me in the restaurant on the ground floor," Leak said, rubbing his eyes to ease the smoke irritation.

"Should I have them wait down there?"

"No. Send them up. I want to get the Chicago cop's take on this."

The lieutenant laughed. "No cop from the Second City has anything on you, Deputy."

"Don't bet on it, Lieutenant. Don't bet on it."

Flanked by Azzoli and Willis, Larry Cole stepped off into the seventh floor corridor of the M. D. Hines Building. The NYPD detectives had pinned their shields to the lapels of their trench coats, and the CPD commander walked between them. The uniformed lieutenant was waiting.

"Assistant Deputy Commissioner Leak is right this way, sir," the lieutenant said to Cole.

They entered the burned-out shell of suite 732. There were a number of cops and firefighters stomping through the area, causing Cole to raise a skeptical eyebrow. So much for protecting the crime scene.

Leak was standing outside the office a few feet away from the rubber sheet–covered body of the building security guard. Like that of the female accountant found inside the office, it was burned beyond recognition. When the New York Police Department assistant deputy commissioner turned and saw the Chicago police commander, his somber expression dissolved and he broke into a broad grin. "My main man!"

Cole smiled and said, "What's happening, Joe?"

They shook hands and the effusiveness of their greeting caused a couple of the cops who knew the deputy to exchange amused glances.

"So you need my expertise to help you crack this case?" Cole said.

"That'll be the day," Leak responded. "You guys out in the Windy City wouldn't know where to begin with a complicated investigation like this." Then the assistant deputy commissioner became all business. "If a crime was indeed committed."

Cole looked into the burned-out office. "You suspect arson?"

Leak shrugged. "I suspect everything, I suspect nothing."

Cole laughed. "Sounds like something from one of Colonel Lohrman's criminology classes at Quantico."

"Yeah. And it made as little sense then as it does now. Why don't we take a look? With all the damage the smoke eaters had to do to put the fire out, I doubt if we'll find a lot of collectible evidence." Motioning to the uniformed lieutenant, Deputy Leak said, "Have everyone clear out of there so that me and the commander can examine the scene."

"Yes, sir."

The two cops stood in the center of the room and looked around. Portable lights had been set up to provide illumination. The only other light source was from the street below. They stood like that for a long time, taking it all in and saying nothing. The body of the horribly burned woman was also there, and they examined it with the detached, but carefully scrutinizing eye of the professional investigator. Then they proceeded to canvass every square inch of the room, but they were careful not to touch anything. Despite what Leak had said about the fire department's contamination of available evidence, there was still a chance that something of relevance could be collected.

After fifteen minutes of engaging in this examination, Cole and Leak returned to the hall. The other cops and firefighters stood in groups a short distance away and watched them with curious stares.

"That was a pretty smooth operation, Joe," Cole said. "Whoever did that came very close to thoroughly covering their tracks behind them."

"Very close indeed," Leak agreed. "But one thing is certain. The two people who died here were definitely murder victims."

30

Alain Rianocek had returned to Madame Christina Sharp's dinner party. He was experiencing the pleasurable rush that always followed a kill; however, he concealed his excitement behind his bored, arrogant, aristocratic mask.

"Were you able to make contact with your party?" Madame Sharp asked her guest of honor.

A slight smile curled the corners of his mouth. "As a matter of fact the conversation was brief, but quite enlightening."

"How very nice."

"Well," the baron said, getting to his feet, "it's getting late and I'm off to Miami in the morning."

Actually, Rianocek had wanted to leave New York that night, but he couldn't book a connecting flight to Buenos Aires out of Miami until the next day. This required the overnight stay in the Big Apple. Following a sanction, he seldom stayed overnight in the city where the operation had been carried out. This had kept him from having any dangerous contacts with the law. At the moment he had that thought, Rianocek recalled the black cop on the beach in Chicago twelve years ago. But that cop hadn't even seen him.

Finally, in response to the socialite's question, Rianocek responded, "I'll only be there long enough to transfer to a Pan-Am flight home."

Madame Sharp got to her feet. "Could I have everyone's attention please?" Her shrill voice made the assassin wince. "Our guest of honor must leave, so why don't we give him a round of applause?"

Those present gave Rianocek a brief, halfhearted clap and then went back to their after-dinner cocktails.

"I'll walk you out," Madame Sharp said.

"That won't be necessary," Rianocek said, walking rapidly toward the exit. "I can find my own way." This stuffy dowager and her boring guests had served their purpose.

He left the private dining room. Cornelius Shade and Hannah Spencer, who had set up the diversion enabling him to slip past the lobby guard, would be waiting for him in a car at 57th Street and Eighth Avenue. Rianocek always made sure that his escape route was covered even though this assignment had gone off without a hitch.

Rianocek entered the restaurant proper and was crossing to the door leading out to 57th Street when four men entered through the side entrance from the M. D. Hines Building lobby. Three of these men the assassin had never seen before; however, the fourth one he had. In fact, Rianocek had been thinking of this same man only a few moments ago. It was the black cop from Chicago. The assassin's surprise at the cop being here now registered on Rianocek's face. The Chicago Police Commander's eyes locked with those of the international assassin.

Due to Assistant Deputy Commissioner Joe E. Leak and Commander Larry Cole's investigation, the fire deaths on the seventh floor of the M. D. Hines Building had been classified as homicides. A joint homicide/arson investigation squad was at that moment examining the crime scene, which had been almost completely destroyed by fire. Part of the investigation would encompass finding out why the sprinkler system had not gone off. It would later be discovered that the system was defective.

Now, with the investigation progressing, Cole and Leak were on their way to dinner. They had just entered Caruso's when Cole stopped. Leak, Azzoli, and Willis turned to see why. The Chicago cop was staring off across the restaurant.

"What's the matter, Larry?" Leak asked.

"That guy over there just gave me the look," Cole said.

Leak turned to see who Cole was talking about, but Rianocek had already turned away and was striding toward the exit. "What guy?"

"The tall one with the light brown hair," Cole said. "He just went out the door."

"You want him checked out?"

"There was a double homicide upstairs and I've been given that look before," Cole said. "I'd be willing to bet my pension that the guy who just left is dirty, but I can't tell you how."

"You did say that he only eyeballed you, Commander," Detective Willis interjected. "But he didn't pay any attention to us, so it wasn't just a bad guy recognizing a cop. He only recognized you, so it was something more personal. Maybe he's seen you someplace before or he's a perp you once collared."

Before Cole could respond, Leak said, "We could debate this all night, while our man gets away. Now my friend here has got a hunch, which I respect. We can sort out the probable cause later. Let's go talk to him."

The four cops exited Caruso's Restaurant onto 57th Street in pursuit of the assassin.

Rianocek walked quickly west from the restaurant and didn't look back. He attempted to blend in on the crowded Manhattan street, but for once in his life he cursed his 6'4" height. Everyone around him didn't appear to be an inch over 5'2". He willed himself to relax. Shade and Hannah Spencer were less than a block and a half away. In a few minutes Rianocek would launch himself onto an escape route that would transport him from New York City back to the security of his villa in Argentina. If he could just make it. . . .

"Hey, mister!" Detective Assoli called. "We're with the NYPD! Hold it! We want to talk to you!"

Rianocek looked back over his shoulder to see two of the men who had been with the black cop back in the restaurant coming down the street after him. They were about twenty feet away and closing the distance rapidly. The Chicago cop and another man were a short distance behind the policemen rushing after the assassin.

Panic seized him and he ran.

The chase was on.

The asthmatic Cornelius Shade and the shapely Hannah Spencer were seated in a silver Lincoln Continental parked near the corner of Eighth Avenue and 57th Street. They were waiting for Rianocek. They expected him to arrive at any minute.

The engine idled softly and the radio was turned to a classical music station, which Shade had selected. The music grated on his young female companion's nerves.

"Do you think we could listen to something a bit more twentieth-century?" she asked with irritation in her voice.

"What do you want to hear," he asked, "rock and roll?"

"For your information there is a great deal more to contemporary music than rock and roll. There's jazz, pop rock . . ."

"Something is wrong," Shade said, hunching over the wheel and staring through the windshield at the street. The woman also stared and saw Alain Rianocek sprinting in their direction. It was obvious that the four men pursuing the assassin were cops.

Shade put the car in gear and pulled from the curb, cutting off a taxicab that was speeding up the avenue. The cab sideswiped the Lincoln, doing extreme damage to the front quarter-panel. But the assassin's escape vehicle was still drivable. Ignoring the accident, Shade drove to a spot where he could intercept Rianocek.

The Lincoln was still rolling when the assassin yanked open the back door and leaped inside. The cops were close, but not close enough to reach the car before Shade pulled away and crossed 57th Street, barely managing to avoid another collision.

Leak, Cole, Azzoli, and Willis reached the intersection just as the Lincoln disappeared up Eighth Avenue.

"I got the license plate number," Azzoli said, breathlessly, as he pulled a notebook from his pocket and jotted the number down.

"One thing is certain," Leak said to Cole. "You were right about our boy there being dirty."

"Yeah," Cole said, staring off down the street at the escaping getaway car. "Now we've got to find out what he's done that made him nervous enough to run."

31

OCTOBER 15, 1989
10:03 P.M.

His name is Baron Alain Marcus Casimir von Rianocek," the maître'd said in nasal-sounding imperious tones, "and I assure you that he is, in every sense of the word, a gentleman of class and noble lineage."

"Oh, dear," Madame Christina Sharp said with obvious distress, "what did poor Alain do to get himself into difficulties with the police?"

"The guy's a fraud," the inebriated ex–mayor of New York City said in a voice so badly slurred that they could barely understand him. "Putting on airs like, because he was born into it, he was better than everybody else. Well that don't play in the good old U. S. of A., brother. Over here you earn your way. Am I right or what?!"

*   *   *

Detectives Willis and Azzoli conducted each of the interviews, while Cole and Leak remained in the background observing the investigative process taking place. They were looking for any undercurrents of deception or some guilty nuisance from any of the people who had either eaten dinner with Rianocek or seen him in the restaurant during the evening. So far, they had come up with nothing. It was at that point Cole and the NYPD assistant deputy commissioner left Caruso's Restaurant and entered the relative security of the M. D. Hines Building lobby.

"This isn't looking too good, Larry," Leak said, plunging his hands into his trench coat pockets. "We don't have anything on this guy except that he ran from us."

"I know," Cole said with a sigh. "But this Rianocek was absent from the private dining room at about the same time that the homicide occurred upstairs. No one actually saw him go to make the telephone call that he claimed. He could have slipped into the lobby and managed to get upstairs. Then he started the fire and returned to the restaurant."

"That's a valid scenario, but we haven't got one single, solitary piece of evidence to support it."

"Then why did he run?" Cole asked.

"Because he got spooked when he saw you, but without having him to ask in person, all we can do at this point is guess," Leak said. "But one thing's for certain, kiddo: He recognized you as a cop because he's seen you before—and that was obviously back in Chicago and not in New York."

"Joe, I never set eyes on that guy before tonight. I'm certain of it."

Detective Azzoli entered the lobby. "Excuse me, Deputy, we've got a new development."

"Don't just stand there, Azzoli, tell us what it is," Leak bellowed.

"Alain Rianocek, accompanied by his attorney and a representative from the French consulate, just walked into the Midtown

North station over on 54th Street. They want to make a complaint against the NYPD. Now get this, boss. His lawyer is none other than Mob attorney Ben Crenshaw, who is claiming that four plainclothes cops assaulted his client on 57th Street and Eighth Avenue about a half hour ago."

Leak and Cole exchanged looks.

"So what do you think of that, Larry?"

"I'm totally speechless, Joe. Totally speechless."

32

OCTOBER 15, 1989
10:47 P.M.

The Manhattan North police precinct station was on 54th Street between Eighth and Ninth Avenues. The desk sergeant on duty had just remarked to one of the officers, who was leaving the precinct after making a routine arrest, that it had been a relatively quiet night. Then the shaved-head, nattily dressed Ben Crenshaw stormed into the building.

The high-profile mouthpiece for New York's crime families were instantly identifiable anywhere in the country. He was known for his courtroom dramatics, his representation of famous clients, and his flamboyant lifestyle. Crenshaw didn't walk, he sauntered. He didn't talk, he orated. He lived his life as the star in the spotlight on the stage of life, and he was not going to let anyone upstage him.

Now he had a case that he could sink his teeth into. A foreign national had been "roughed up" by the NYPD, and there would be hell to pay. Of course, Alain Rianocek did not actually say that he'd been "roughed up." The Bavarian baron, as he wished to be called, had used the word "accosted." Crenshaw preferred his own terminology. It would look better on a multimillion-dollar lawsuit, which the City of New York would settle after Crenshaw threatened to try the case in the court of international public opinion. That would further smear a police department which already had a poor public image. This case was a moneymaker, and Ben Crenshaw knew how to make money.

Rianocek had located Crenshaw at the lawyer's private club, which was only a few blocks from Caruso's Restaurant. He was in the bar with the French consul when he received the call. The attorney had never heard of him and was about to tell Rianocek to get another lawyer when the European mentioned some very influential people as references. Obviously, this so-called "Bavarian baron" was much more than he seemed to be.

Now Crenshaw, the French consul, who was along merely for show, and Rianocek had been shown to a filthy interview room on the second floor of the Manhattan North station.

The sergeant downstairs had told the flamboyant attorney that Assistant Deputy Commissioner Joe E. Leak was on the way to the station to handle the complaint against the NYPD personally. Crenshaw was too smart not to realize that something was up. Assistant deputy commissioners did not come out to take complaints from citizens, even if they were represented by Ben Crenshaw.

Rianocek sat beside Crenshaw in one of the scarred wooden chairs next to a table onto the surface of which several generations of suspects had carved and scratched a history of graffiti. The assassin stared across the room at a mirror set in the wall. He was aware that this reflecting surface was not placed there to enhance the grooming of those who spent time in this place. The killer was 100 percent correct.

On the other side of the glass, Assistant Deputy Commissioner Joe Leak and CPD Commander Larry Cole stood side by side, examining the trio of men seated inside the interview room. Ben Creshaw had an expression on his face that reminded the cops of a salivating predator preparing to devour defenseless prey. The French consul, a thin, nervous little man, who sported a cheap toupee, looked confused at finding himself in this place. Alain Rianocek was staring at the mirror with such intensity, it seemed that he could see the policemen concealed behind the glass.

"I'm certain that I've never set eyes on this guy before, Joe, but I know he recognized me back in the restaurant."

"So let's find out what he's got to say," Leak said. With that he headed for the interview room.

When Leak walked in, Ben Crenshaw leaped to his feet and went into his act. "This is an outrage, Deputy Commissioner Leak! An outrage! My client is a foreign national and a guest of the United States government, who was . . . !"

"He was one of them," Rianocek said, causing the attorney to halt in mid-sentence. Despite Crenshaw's esteemed reputation, he had heard of Joe Leak and didn't relish the idea of crossing this particular cop.

Crenshaw quickly changed his tactics with the same expertise he would have employed had he been faced with an unexpected development in a courtroom. "Do you want to explain to me why you and three of your cop goons attacked my client on a Manhattan street?"

Leak smiled. "Why don't we sit down and discuss this thing like reasonable men, Counselor?"

Crenshaw glared at the cop for a moment before finally resuming his seat. Rianocek looked from Leak back at the mirror.

When they were all seated, the assistant deputy commissioner began by saying, "A short time ago there was an arson at the M. D. Hines Building on 57th Street in which two people were killed. Me and my 'goons,' as you called them, Mr. Crenshaw, were investigating that crime when we attempted to interview your client and he ran."

"So you're saying that my client was a suspect in this arson?" Crenshaw demanded.

"Not necessarily."

"What in the hell is that supposed to mean?"

Leak's relaxed demeanor didn't alter one bit. "Just what I said, Counselor. We were in the process of conducting our investigation and your client fled the scene under rather mysterious circumstances. We would like to ascertain why?" Now the assistant deputy commissioner looked at Rianocek.

Crenshaw jumped in before the assassin could say anything. "I would advise against making any statements at this time, Baron von Rianocek."

"Baron?" Leak questioned. "Are you nobility, sir?"

"Yes," Rianocek said, much to Ben Crenshaw's consternation. "My Bavarian lineage dates back to Duke Maximillian and the Thirty Years' War in the seventeenth century."

"I thought Bavaria was a German state?" Leak said.

"To those who recognize it on those terms," Rianocek replied, imperiously.

"So that's where you live? In Germany?"

"No. I am now a resident of Buenos Aires, Argentina, but I travel abroad quite frequently."

"Could I see your passport?"

"Now wait a minute!" Crenshaw said, his face reddening with outrage.

"I don't have a problem with that, Mr. Crenshaw," Rianocek said, removing the document from his inside jacket pocket and handing it to Leak.

The document had been issued in Argentina. After a brief examination, Leak gave it back.

"How long will you be staying in the United States?" Leak asked.

"I'm leaving in the morning."

"The only question I have left is, why did you run from us?"

Crenshaw again spoke up. "Before you answer that I must warn you that you are doing so against the advice of counsel."

"I understand, Mr. Crenshaw," Rianocek said, "but perhaps all of this can be cleared up if I provide an honest response to this officer's question."

Leak waited.

"I was a foreign national walking alone on a street in one of the most crime-ridden cities in the world when I chanced to glance back and see three black men running down the street after me. Naturally, I ran."

Leak displayed no reaction to Rianocek's statement. "Didn't you hear the white man with us shout that we were the police?"

The assassin smiled. "Alas, no. I was so frightened that I didn't hear anything."

"The car you jumped into was involved in an accident. It was also stolen from a police impound garage."

"I really can't tell you anything about the driver or that vehicle, officer," Rianocek said. "He was apparently a Good Samaritan I had never laid eyes on before, who saw me in distress and came to my aid. He let me out a couple of blocks away. That's when I contacted Mr. Crenshaw."

"And told him that you were attacked by four police officers. I thought you said that you didn't know that we were cops."

Rianocek graced Leak with a cold stare. "My Good Samaritan driver informed me that he believed you were with the authorities."

"Can you describe this informative 'Good Samaritan'?"

The assassin's stare never altered. "I'm sorry, but I glimpsed him only briefly."

"Were you hurt?" Leak asked.

"I beg your pardon?" Rianocek said with confusion.

"In the collision the Lincoln had with the taxi," Leak explained. "Were you injured?"

"No. I wasn't."

"Well, I guess that's it," Leak said.

"No, it's not, Deputy," Crenshaw said. "My client still wishes to lodge an official complaint. . . ."

Rianocek raised his hand, silencing the high-priced attorney. "I think that, under the circumstances, we can drop the complaint against the officers."

Leak returned Rianocek's chilly smile. "That's very noble of you, Baron von Rianocek."

They all stood up. The French consul looked visibly relieved to be escaping the confines of this menacing place.

Leak escorted them to the door and shook hands first with Crenshaw, then the French consul and finally Rianocek. "It was a pleasure meeting you, Baron." Still grasping the hand, he added, "Oh, by the way, have you ever visited Chicago?"

Rianocek's eyes narrowed and he glanced back into the room at the two-way mirror before responding, "No, I've never had the pleasure, but I've heard that it's a beautiful city."

"Next time you're in the States, you should check it out. You folks have a good night, and I'm sorry for any inconvenience we caused you."

33

OCTOBER 15, 1989
11:55 P.M.

Rianocek, Crenshaw, and the French consul exited the Manhattan North police station onto 54th Street. The attorney exuded pronounced self-satisfaction.

"I think that went very well, Baron."

Rianocek gave Crenshaw a glare that frightened the usually unflappable attorney to the very core of his being.

"If you ever do any legal work for me again, I suggest that you give my interests priority over your own."

Before Crenshaw could respond, the assassin charged off down the street in the direction of Ninth Avenue. He called over his shoulder, "My personal solicitor in Buenos Aires will contact you to settle your fee."

Crenshaw stood watching Rianocek's receding back for a long time. Then he said to a totally bewildered French consul, "That arrogant bastard will never get me to represent him again."

The assassin strode to 56th Street and Ninth Avenue, where a black commercial van was parked. The side panels of the van displayed the sign "Holiday Gift Delivery" in stenciled silver script and had been stolen from a garage at 24th Street and Fifth Avenue. Its absence wouldn't be noticed for four days.

After carefully checking the street to make sure that there was no one present to observe him and make this night any more of a disaster, he knocked on the back door. Hannah Spencer opened it and the assassin climbed inside.

Cornelius Shade, breathing heavily, was driving the van. He leaned around the partition which partially separated the driver's pod from the cargo area and inquired, "Did everything work out to your satisfaction, sir?"

Rianocek gave Shade the same fierce glare he had given Ben Crenshaw back in front of the police station. Slowly, Shade turned in his seat to face front once more.

The assassin was seated on a wooden crate. Hannah Spencer, still clad in her red suit, sat on another crate across from him. She watched Rianocek closely, as she had never witnessed him in such a state before. To her it was at once fascinating and at the same time quite terrifying. Cornelius Shade and Hannah Spencer were aware that Baron Alain Marcus Casimir von Rianocek was an extremely dangerous man. Perhaps the most dangerous man alive.

However, as a team, the man and woman in the stolen "Holiday Gift Delivery" van with him were equally as deadly.

Cornelius Shade was English. He had been born in London's East End out of wedlock and raised by a distant aunt. His upbringing was not only impoverished but further complicated by his developing severe asthma before he reached school age. Growing up in a cold, damp slum nearly killed him before he reached adolescence, but somehow he survived. The sickly youth thrived on adversity, and by the time he reached his early teens his feet were firmly planted on a criminal path.

At sixteen he adopted the street name of "the Wheeze" and became the leader of an East End gang of thugs, who engaged in everything from hijacking to extortion. At the age of nineteen he committed his first murder. The shotgun death of a rival gang member was a milestone in Cornelius Shade's life. He discovered he had no compunctions about killing and he was also very good at it. Before he was twenty-one the East End of London street gang leader had taken his place as an assassin on the international scene.

Hannah Spencer's story was a great deal different from Cornelius Shade's. She was born in San Diego, California, the only child of an electrical engineer father and dental hygienist mother. Hannah was an honor student and became a cheerleader at Oceanside High School. She was beautiful and talented and appeared to have a tremendous future unfolding for her. Then something went terribly wrong.

At the age of sixteen, the attractive young woman began getting unusual urges. She started viewing her fellow students and some of her teachers oddly. She experienced morbid fantasies in which she envisioned herself torturing and killing each of them. A short time later, people began disappearing from Oceanside under mysterious circumstances. Then the bodies of dead teenagers started popping up all over town.

It didn't take any great feat of law-enforcement investigative expertise to discover that each victim had a connection to Oceanside High School. In particular, a connection to a cheerleader named Hannah Spencer.

A pair of homicide detectives named Sonny Adams and Gene Gibson "invited" the young woman and her parents down to the police station to "discuss" the murders. Hannah Spencer had been the last person seen with each of the murder victims before their deaths.

After a half-hour interview, the detectives retreated to a glass-enclosed office. They were able to see Hannah and her parents in the adjoining room through the partition windows.

"They look like the all-American family you see portrayed in TV ads," Adams said.

"Yeah, and butter won't melt in Little Miss Muffet's mouth," Gibson added, referring to the glacially cool teenager.

"So what now?"

Gibson shrugged. "We keep digging until we get enough evidence to send our golden-haired cheerleader away for the rest of her life."

But Hannah's parents, despite being aware that their only child was extremely dangerous, were not about to let Adams and Gibson send her to prison. So they shipped her out of the country to live with relatives in South America. Relatives living in Buenos Aires, Argentina. There she met the German expatriate Baron Alain Marcus Casimir von Rianocek and discovered her true vocation.

Cornelius Shade and Hannah Spencer were the assassin's primary backup team. They had assisted him on sanctions all over the world and they were very good at what they did. Rianocek would not have accepted anything less.

Now, after some moments of protracted silence had ensued inside the "Holiday Gift Delivery" van, the assassin shook himself out of a furious trance and said, "I've got to deal with the policemen who came after me tonight. All of them must die before we return to Argentina or I'll never be able to work in the United States again."

Shade and Spencer didn't respond, because they didn't have to. They knew what their jobs were. They would have to find out as much as they could about their targets, then assist the assassin in killing them. There was no way that the four cops who had pursued the assassin would survive.

34

OCTOBER 16, 1989
1:07 A.M.

Caruso's Restaurant closed at midnight, so Larry Cole and Joe Leak ended up at Mike's Tavern on East 43rd Street. Mike's was, in the vernacular of the trade, a "cop bar" frequented by New York City, New York City Transit Authority, New York City Housing Authority, and New York/New Jersey Port Authority police officers. A smattering of firefighters, paramedics, and cop groupies rounded out the clientele. As the number of females in law-enforcement service had increased remarkably over the last decade, there were almost as many women present in the jam-packed saloon as there were men, when Cole and Leak arrived.

"What are they having, a party?" Cole was forced to shout to be heard over the loud music that was blasting from ceiling speakers.

Leak surveyed the dance floor and replied, "Shift change."

But despite the crowd, the deputy commissioner had enough

weight to requisition a booth, which provided him and his guest from Chicago a modicum of privacy in the midst of this cop social riot.

Once seated they ordered bottled beer. Leak insisted on an imported brand that Cole had never heard of before and Mike's special hamburgers with fries. When they were served by a heavyset woman, who had the disposition, vocabulary, and as many tattoos as a bo'sun's mate, Cole remarked to himself that the foreign beer tasted like cold cough syrup, but the burgers could compete with those served at the famous Billy Goat tavern back in the Windy City.

"How's Lisa?" Leak asked, after they were served.

"She's fine," Cole responded. "I wanted her to come along, but she didn't want to leave Butch. He just got over a bad cold and she's still keeping a close eye on him."

"How old is Butch now?"

"Four," Cole said. "But he can move faster than an Olympic sprinter. You can't take your eyes off him for a minute or he'll be into one thing or another."

"Yeah," Leak said, a sad expression dropping over his face. "Kids are always into something."

Cole knew that the assistant deputy commissioner was divorced and had three teenage children—two boys and a girl. Cole also knew that because of complications with his ex-wife, Leak didn't see as much of his children as he would have liked. The Chicago cop decided to let his friend raise the subject if he wanted to talk about it.

They sipped beer and chewed on their burgers for a time before Leak spoke again. "I'm running our friend Baron von Rianocek's name through some contacts I have with Interpol. I'm also having the detectives assigned to the Hines Building fire looking into any possible links between the accounting firm of Sheppard and Gross and our so-called Bavarian Baron."

Cole chanced another swallow of the horrible-tasting beer only to discover that it had not improved at all. A portion of his brain was attempting to come up with a way to dispose of the rest of this alien concoction without offending his host as he said, "I'm sorry I couldn't be more help in identifying him for you."

"Don't worry, Larry," the assistant deputy commissioner said. "We'll find out what Rianocek was up to in New York. You can bet on it. How about another beer?"

Cole was certain that he was going to be sick.

It was after 3:00 A.M. when Joe Leak dropped Larry Cole off at the New York Hilton. Cole had finally convinced his host to let him switch to a domestic beer, so they had spent an hour reminiscing about their time in school and discussing some of the cases they had handled since the last time they'd seen each other. When Cole entered the hotel lobby he was stone-cold sober, but feeling pretty good.

It wasn't until he went to his room, undressed, and was brushing his teeth that he again thought of Alain Rianocek. Cole recalled the look Rianocek had given him back in the restaurant. Cole had seen this look before.

The first time was the night before Thanksgiving, when he was a rookie. The young cop had been writing a parking ticket when he saw two men come off of a side street on Chicago's North Side. One of them, a rapist and murderer named Martin Zykus, had given Cole a surprised look tinged with guilt. Then Zykus ran, just like Alain Rianocek had done tonight in New York. The difference between that incident and this one was the fact that Cole was in uniform when Zykus first saw him. However, Rianocek had made the identification of Cole as a cop, despite the commander's being out of his jurisdiction and dressed as a civilian.

Cole stepped back from the mirror and examined his reflection. He didn't think that he gave off that much of an impression of being a cop. Blackie Silvestri, his former tactical partner and current case-management sergeant in the detective division back in Chicago, left no doubt in anyone's mind as to his occupation. Once Cole had seen one of Blackie's baby pictures. At the age of six months, he already possessed the menacing scowl of the veteran cop.

Now, examining himself in the mirror, Cole thought that he looked more . . . he searched for the appropriate word. The best he could come up with was "generic." He could have any number of occupations, which would not make him easily identifiable to the average person. Yet Baron Alain von Rianocek had made him with one glance.

But as the case was out of his hands, Cole got into bed, switched off the lights, and went to sleep. Rianocek was forgotten.

35

OCTOBER 16, 1989
6:20 A.M.

Rianocek's assassination team was set up in a six-room suite in the Rihga Royal Hotel on West 54th Street. They were unaware that Larry Cole was registered at the New York Hilton, which was right across the street.

The accommodations were in Cornelius Shade's name. This was not a problem for Shade, as he had never been arrested and had merely been mentioned as a suspect in a smattering of crimes in the United Kingdom. The asthmatic was as dedicated to anonymity as Rianocek; however, he did not employ secrecy to conceal his true identity. He simply hid in plain sight. He was overweight, stooped, nearsighted, and had a severe breathing problem. Not even the most suspicous law-enforcement official would suspect him of being an assassin. Nonetheless, he was extremely adept at dispensing violent death.

Now he was entering data into a computer console. Since arriving at the hotel last night, Shade had been accumulating information on the four cops Rianocek was after. To do so, he had tapped into the personnel files of the New York Police Department, which was not an easy task. Computer hacking was one of Shade's many talents.

So far, he had identified three of the four cops who had pursued Rianocek last night. Assistant Deputy Commissioner Joseph Eduardo Leak, who was assigned to the staff of the chief of detectives out of NYPD Headquarters at One Police Plaza, and Detectives Frank Azzoli and Theodore Willis of the 23rd Precinct Detective Squad. Shade had also obtained their shield numbers, home addresses, and the names of their next of kin. Leak's law-enforcement career was fascinating to Shade. In fact, for a criminal, having this particular assistant deputy commissioner on your trail could be disastrous.

The door to one of the bedrooms opened and Alain Rianocek came out. The assassin was dressed in a short black silk robe that barely covered his genitals. He had nothing on beneath the abbreviated garment. Shade could see Hannah Spencer lying nude on the bed inside the room. She and Rianocek had been engaged in nonstop passionate sex for hours. The assassin possessed a voracious sexual appetite, and Hannah Spencer was just as insatiable as he was.

Closing the door behind him, Rianocek crossed the room to stand behind Shade. "What have you found out?"

Shade pointed at the screen. "I have all the information on the New York cops. But we're going to have to cultivate a source within the NYPD to find out about the one from Chicago."

"Do what you have to, but I want that information before dawn. We've got work to do later today." With that Rianocek returned to the bedroom to awaken Hannah Spencer. A moment later, Shade heard her moan with pleasure through the closed bedroom door.

*   *   *

Police Officer B. J. McNamara worked a patrol car out of the 42nd Precinct in one of the worst sections of the Bronx. A thin, visibly unhappy man, McNamara wore his shabby, unclean uniform with the same disregard that he had for the people in the community he was supposed to serve, his fellow officers, and, in fact, all of the human beings inhabiting the planet Earth. He had compiled an unimpressive work record, tainted by numerous rule violations, during his nine years with the NYPD. He was also having credit problems and always short of cash. Most of this information was contained in B. J. McNamara's computerized personnel file, which Cornelius Shade had tapped into. But Shade was not only interested in McNamara because he was a lousy cop. There was also his graduating-class members from the New York Police Academy in the summer of 1980.

Now, as McNamara left the station after the day shift roll call, the man in a wrinkled trench coat and horn-rim glasses was waiting for him.

"Excuse me, Officer McNamara," Shade wheezed. "I wonder if I could have a moment of your time?"

The policeman stopped and turned around, thinking that this was one of his creditors. He grumbled, "What do you want?"

"To offer you a proposition, sir, and a lucrative one."

Detective Ted Willis was at his desk at the 23rd Precinct Detective Squad when a call came in for him. The detective and his partner, Frank Azzoli, were logging overtime authorized by Assistant Deputy Commissioner Leak to run down any possible leads on Alain Rianocek.

Answering the telephone, Willis was surprised to find that his academy classmate Benjamin James McNamara was calling.

"How's it going in the Two-three, Ted?"

A puzzled Willis responded, "Good, B. J. How are things with you?"

Azzoli was working at a computer terminal on the adjoining

desk. He noticed the quizzical look on his partner's face. When Willis hung up, Azzoli asked, "What's the mystery?"

It took him a moment to realize that his partner had spoken to him. "Huh?" Willis said.

"You've got this real puzzled look on your face. Like you need to put in a call to Hercule Poirot or Sherlock Holmes to give you a hand."

"That was a guy I went through the academy with. He's assigned to the Four-two in the Bronx. I haven't heard from him in nine years. Now he calls me out of the blue and asks if I know any cops from Chicago."

Azzoli stopped typing. Now he had a look that mirrored his partner's. "What did you tell him?"

Willis shrugged. "I mentioned Commander Cole, since I've never met . . ."

"Did you tell him that Cole is in New York?"

"No. He didn't ask."

"What's this classmate's name?"

36

Officer B. J. McNamara arranged to meet Cornelius Shade at a greasy-spoon diner two blocks from the 42nd Precinct station house. Driving the police car to the rendezvous point, the policeman decided to alter the agreement he had made with the rumpled little man with bad lungs. McNamara had been offered $500 to obtain information from Detective Willis of the Two-three. Five C-notes for a name. Larry Cole. A name that meant nothing to McNamara, but obviously meant a great deal to anyone willing to pay that much money. And if they would pay $500, they might pay $1,000 or maybe even double. Needless to say, B. J. McNamara planned to test the market.

He parked the police car in front of the diner and went inside. The place was like thousands of others in New York. The menu was listed in black plastic letters on a Royal Crown Cola sign. There was an aging, tired-looking waitress, who wore a stained uniform and had a run in one of the legs of her panty hose. The combination cook/cashier spent his time between a hot plate and a television set broadcasting game shows.

There were a couple of patrons in the place seated at a counter hunched over plates of food. They glanced up only when the uniformed policeman entered. White cops were not an unusual sight in the Bronx. Everyone present was black. That is, with the exception of the little man with bad lungs seated in a back booth.

McNamara ignored the others and sat down across from Shade.

"I wouldn't drink or eat anything they serve in this joint," McNamara said loud enough for the others to hear. "It ain't sanitary." He pointed at the cup of tea and plain doughnut on the table in front of Shade.

"Just a simple comestible, officer," he said with difficulty. He removed a handkerchief from his pocket and coughed into it noisily. "Do you have something for me?"

"You should do something about your condition, pal," McNamara said. "It'll eventually kill you."

"Thank you for your concern, sir, but I've lived with it all my life. Now I would like to conclude our business." He opened his worn briefcase and removed a white envelope from it. "I have the agreed-upon sum. Do you have the name?"

"I've got it, but there are one or two problems."

The waitress came over to inquire if the cop would like to order anything. He replied coarsely "You gotta be fucking kidding."

After she rolled her eyes and walked away, Shade said, with an edge in his voice, "What kind of problems?"

McNamara looked around to make sure that no one could hear what he was about to say. Then, "The name I obtained for you, my friend, belongs to a Chicago Police commander. Now I ask myself, why and to who is that information worth five hundred dollars?"

"Does the fact that this gentleman is a fellow law-enforcement official offend your sense of professional honor, Officer McNamara?"

"Not really, but the fact that he is a cop ups the price a bit."

"How much is 'a bit'?" Shade asked.

Again McNamara looked around. "Instead of five hundred dollars, shall we make it two thousand? That's a grand for the first name and a grand for the last name."

Cornelius Shade had gone completely still. He stared across the table at the corrupt cop, who returned his gaze without flinching.

Finally, Shade coughed into his handkerchief, laughed, and said, "My goodness, sir, you are quite the businessman. You are also quite astute; however, the people I represent have not authorized me to go higher than fifteen hundred dollars in this transaction."

McNamara looked away for a moment. Finally, he said, "Okay, give me the fifteen hundred."

Shade opened his briefcase and extracted another envelope. From it he removed ten $100 bills, which he counted out on the chipped, Formica-topped table. He placed the sealed envelope which he had initially offered McNamara next to them.

"Now, sir, may I have the name?"

McNamara grinned and responded, "It's Cole, Larry Cole."

As he reached for the money, Shade removed a Montblanc fountain pen from his pocket and began unscrewing the cap.

"I hope you're not expecting me to sign for this," McNamara said.

"I would never dream of such a thing, Officer."

Then the little man with the bad lungs plunged the sharp tip of the fountain pen into a vein in the back of the policeman's hand.

McNamara's initial reaction was surprise, which dissolved quickly into anger. He was attempting to come up with a plausible excuse for his lieutenant, to explain why he was forced to kill Shade, when the paralysis set in.

Shade picked up the money and the envelope from the table, and returned them to his briefcase. He replaced the cap on the fountain pen and put it back in his pocket. He left a five-dollar bill to cover the cost of the doughnut and tea he had not touched. Using his handkerchief, he wiped every surface that he could have left fingerprints on. Before getting to his feet, he examined Officer McNamara.

The corrupt cop was already dead. Cornelius Shade had injected McNamara with a potent poison which shut down the human nervous system in a matter of scant seconds. First it affected the limbs, then the internal organs, and finally made everything stop functioning. McNamara's body remained upright, with his eyes open in the stare of death.

Shade struggled out of the booth and headed for the door. The patrons kept their heads down as he passed, but the waitress and cook did look up.

The wheezing man said cheerfully, "You folks have a nice day."

Then he was gone.

As time passed, the cook and the waitress became increasingly nervous. This greasy spoon did not merely sell blue-plate specials and hamburgers, it was also the delivery point for a street-drug operation. The buyer would pay a dealer out on the street and then come to the restaurant to pick up the narcotics. Packets of heroin, cocaine, and crack were concealed in brown paper bags containing a fossilized donut or slice of stale pie. Now this operation was imperiled because of the cop remaining in the back booth.

A few customers, both legitimate and not, came and went, but the policeman didn't move. Finally, the cook decided to check out the man in blue.

The waitress watched as the cook walked to the back booth, stood over the cop, and said, "Something we can get for you, Officer?"

There was no response. The cook stood looking down at the policeman for a long time before crying out, "Damn, this man is dead!"

37

OCTOBER 16, 1989
10:32 A.M.

Assistant Deputy Commissioner Joe E. Leak was waiting for Larry Cole in the lobby of the New York Hilton when his beeper went off. Going to the concierge's desk, he flashed his shield and used a hotel phone to call his office.

Detective Bobby Melendez, Leak's secretary, answered, *"Detective Division Headquarters, Assistant Deputy Commissioner Leak's office."*

"What's up, Bobby?"

"It might be nothing, sir, but I thought I should let you know anyway."

"Shoot."

"I got a call from Detective Willis at the Two-three. He said he's working on an investigation for you."

"Yeah. Willis and his partner Azzoli are checking out a foreign national named Rianocek with Interpol."

"Well, they supposedly have some information about this Rianocek guy, which is coming through from Scotland Yard. Seems that he was the prime suspect in the murder of a banker that occurred in England a few years back. An explosive was concealed in a cigar box, which was rigged to blow when it was opened."

Leak smiled. The South American baron had just taken another step toward becoming the prime suspect in the M. D. Hines Building murders.

Detective Melendez continued, *"But that wasn't the reason why Willis called. He said he got a kind of funny call from an officer working the Four-two."*

"What kind of funny call?"

Melendez told him.

"But why would this B. J. McNamara be interested in Larry Cole?" Leak questioned, as more of an exercise in thinking out loud.

"You've got me there, sir, but it just came over the wire from the Four-two. Patrolman McNamara is dead."

Now the assistant deputy commissioner frowned. Something was indeed wrong.

A few minutes later, Larry Cole, carrying his suitcase, stepped off an elevator into the lobby. Spying Leak, he waved.

Once they were in the NYPD unmarked car, Leak filled Cole in on this morning's strange events.

"Are you sure McNamara was interested in me?" Cole asked.

"Apparently, and then he got very dead in a very exotic manner in a greasy-spoon restaurant in the Bronx," Leak responded. "From the report that I got, he was found sitting up in a booth, dead as a doornail and as rigid as a board. The only sign of injury was a small cut on the back of his hand. The C.O of the Four-two is on the scene supervising the investigation, and we're going to have McNamara autopsied as quickly as possible. The witnesses either don't know much or aren't talking. The cook told the detectives that the dead cop was in the back booth with a short white guy, who talked funny, like he was a foreigner or something, and had trouble breathing, like he had emphysema or asthma. Doesn't seem the usual stomping ground for a lad of that type. I've put out an alert for this guy, but all we can do now is sit back and wait for something to develop."

"You know," Cole said, "this is the second time in less than twenty-four hours that someone has exhibited an interest in my being in the Big Apple. Somehow I can't help getting the impression that the two incidents are related."

"I wouldn't sweat it, Larry," Leak said. "Your flight leaves for Chicago at three. There's just enough time for us to stop at a restaurant in Queens that serves a great shepherd's pie and an exotic beer. You'll never guess what country this brew is imported from."

"Okay," Cole said, without a great deal of enthusiasm, "where's it from?"

"Tasmania."

38

OCTOBER 16, 1989
10:55 A.M.

I'm hungry," Detective Azzoli said. "Let's go grab a sandwich."

Willis leaned back in his chair and rubbed his eyes to ease the strain after the long hours he had spent staring at a computer screen. "Where do you want to eat?"

"The Ninety-second Street Deli."

Willis stood up and began putting on his sports jacket. "Don't you ever get tired of cold cuts?"

"So what would you recommend?" he asked, following Willis out of the squad room.

"We could have a hot lunch for a change," he said as they started down the stairs. "An open-faced turkey sandwich with gravy, corned beef and cabbage, or maybe some soul food."

"No way, Willis," Azzoli said. "That stuff is too heavy for me. I eat a lunch like that, I'd have to take a nap afterward."

The "Holiday Gift Delivery" van was parked a block away from the 23rd Precinct station. Cornelius Shade, wearing a snap-brim plaid cap and sunglasses, was behind the wheel. Rianocek and Hannah Spencer were in the rear of the van, which had been transformed into a mobile spy center.

Every type of surveillance equipment available was crammed into the cargo space. Listening devices, video screens, computers, and homing-signal monitors. At that moment, the assassin and his equally deadly paramour were studying a pair of homing-device monitors.

The monitors were equipped with blue screens with detailed computerized maps of all the streets in New York's five boroughs. Rianocek was studying the display on which a lone signal flashed from Woodhaven Boulevard in Queens. The other monitor, which Hannah Spencer was watching, transmitted a signal in Manhattan only a short distance from where the assassin's van was parked.

The sources of these separate, unauthorized signals were a pair of magnetized devices. One was attached to the undercarriage of the official police vehicle assigned to Assistant Deputy Commissioner Joe E. Leak. The other was beneath the back bumper of the unmarked car which had been signed out of the 23rd Precinct by Detective Ted Willis. At this moment, both signals indicated that the vehicles were stationary.

"Excuse me, sir," Shade said from the front seat. "The detectives are approaching their police car."

"Good," Rianocek said. "Give them a head start, and then follow at a discreet distance." He turned to the woman. "When they reach their destination, Hannah, they will be all yours. Shade and I will go after Leak and Larry Cole."

"Thank you, Baron von Rianocek," she said.

The assassin noticed that her eyes glistened and there was color in her cheeks. She was looking forward to committing murder.

The 92nd Street Deli consisted of tables and chairs at one end of an oblong room across from a glass counter behind which three white-clad servers made sandwiches to the customers' specifications and placed them on plates with potato salad, chips, and a pickle. Azzoli ordered corned beef on rye with mustard; Willis, a ham-and-cheese sandwich on pumpernickel with mayo, lettuce, tomato, raw onion, and sliced hard-boiled egg. While Willis was ordering, Azzoli rolled his eyes.

"What?" the black cop asked.

"You ordering a sandwich or a salad?"

"Hey, Azzoli, you order what you want to eat and I'll order what I want."

"No problem."

They were carrying their trays to a table when a blonde, wearing a black leather pants suit, dashed into the restaurant, screaming, "Somebody help me! There's a man with a gun chasing me!"

The detectives put their trays down on a table as the woman ran up to the counter. The servers looked to Willis and Azzoli, who they knew were cops.

"Okay, lady," Willis said, "calm down and tell us what happened."

"Who are you?" she said, cringing against the counter.

They both flashed their detective shields at her.

"There's a man out there." She pointed through the glass windows of the deli out at the street. "He pulled a gun on me and tried to get me to go into an alley with him, but I ran."

"Where was this?" Azzoli asked.

"Right outside a minute ago—I'm sure he's still there!" she screamed.

"What does he look like?" Willis asked.

"While you two are standing here asking me stupid questions, he's getting away. Come with me and I'll point him out to you."

"Okay, let's go," they said together.

Out on the street, they looked up and down the crowded avenue. The woman appeared confused. "He's not here, but he couldn't have gone far."

"No problem, miss," Willis said. "Our car is right there. We'll take a ride around the area and look for him."

Azzoli opened the back door of the police car and helped the blonde inside. Willis started the car, put it in gear, and pulled away from the curb.

"Which way was he going the last time you saw him?" Azzoli asked.

"Down there." She pointed in the direction that they were traveling.

They had gone less than a quarter of a block when something began bothering Willis.

Back in the delicatessen, she had said that the man had been chasing her and that he was still outside. So how did she know which way he ran? The detective glanced into the rearview mirror at their "damsel in distress." She was looking down as she pulled something from her pocket. At that instant, the world slowed down considerably for the three people in the unmarked New York City Police Department detective car.

Ted Willis turned completely around to see what their alleged victim was doing in the backseat. Azzoli noticed his partner's reaction and also began to turn. In the millisecond before Hannah Spencer reached for the silencer-equipped, .25 caliber Colt semiautomatic pistol that was concealed in her jacket pocket, she figured that the two detectives would remain facing front until they came to a red light. Then, when the car had stopped, she planned to fire two bullets into the back of each head. Now they were slowing to a stop at a red light at 90th Street, and her targets were turning toward her. She began raising the gun.

Willis detected the danger first and, acting on pure reflex, raised his hand. Confused, but aware that something was wrong, Azzoli began reaching for the snub-nosed Smith & Wesson .38 revolver in his belt holster. The female assassin opened fire.

The first bullet entered Willis's forearm, passed through soft tissue without striking bone, exited above the elbow, and struck him in the forehead. The bullet glanced off his skull, fracturing the cranium before continuing to smash into the windshield. She immediately fired a second round at Willis, which missed the officer completely, shattered the rearview mirror, showering the interior of the car with glass, before splintering the windshield. Then she turned her attention to Azzoli.

In the instant that had passed since Frank Azzoli had begun his turn in the front seat, he had managed to do two things. His left arm was over the backseat, and he was able to grasp the gun before the woman could swing it to bear on him. He had also pulled his own gun and was attempting to point it at the female assassin.

Then the dynamics of this deadly confrontation were altered dramatically when the foot of the unconscious Ted Willis slipped off the brake pedal and floored the accelerator. The police car leaped across the intersection on a green light, sideswiped the signal pole, and rammed headfirst into a light pole.

Willis was thrown against the steering wheel. Azzoli and Hannah Spencer were tossed around the interior of the car, but they both maintained a firm hold on the silenced automatic. However, in the collision, Azzoli had dropped his gun on the floor. Hannah Spencer was unable to bring her weapon to bear on the cop, so she changed her tactics. With her free hand, she reached into her left boot and removed a razor-sharp, stainless-steel throwing knife and stabbed Azzoli in the back of the hand holding the barrel of her gun. Screaming, he released the weapon. She shot the defenseless policeman four times.

The car was coated with blood and a crowd was gathering on the street. Hannah Spencer attempted to shove the door open, but it was stuck. She kicked at it, and a sharp pain shot from her ankle to her knee. The door flew open. Carrying the silenced pistol in her hand, she confronted the group of pedestrians. They melted away. She started walking up 90th Street favoring her left leg, which had been damaged in the crash. She was also covered with Willis's and Azzoli's blood.

"Hold it, lady!" The shout came from behind her.

The female assassin turned to find a uniformed New York cop running toward her. He was about fifty and carrying a blue-steel, four-inch-barrel standard police service revolver in his hand. He raised the gun, but she was faster and, shooting from the hip, hit him in the forehead and throat. He was dead before he hit the ground.

She'd again turned to continue her escape when she heard a loud bang followed by the back of her right thigh going numb. She'd been shot. Ignoring the wound, she spun around with her weapon raised.

Frank Azzoli, lying half in and half out of the damaged police car, had managed to retrieve his gun from the floor, open the door, and take aim at the assassin. He had aimed for the small of her back, but he was weak from the bullet wound in his neck, the two in his chest, and the nick in his right arm. He was lucky that he hit her at all.

Then she returned fire.

Hannah Spencer's next bullet killed Detective Frank Azzoli. It zipped from the barrel of her silenced weapon across the seventy-five-foot space between them to penetrate the policeman's brain through the left eye. His lifeless body collapsed back into the car, and the female assassin turned to continue walking away. Blood streamed from the wound in her leg, and she was limping badly. She made it less than a block before she succumbed to the pain and collapsed to the sidewalk. Police units responding to the shooting found her unconscious body on the street. She was still clutching the silenced weapon in her hand.

39

OCTOBER 16, 1989
12:02 P.M.

Traffic on the approach to the Queensboro Bridge was backed up, trapping the "Holiday Gift Delivery" van, which contained Alain Rianocek and Cornelius Shade. The assassin remained in the back of the van studying the monitor screen displaying the location of Assistant Deputy Commissioner Leak's car. The van was making slow progress, and Rianocek was worried about running out of time. Leak and Cole would not remain where they were indefinitely, and the assassin did not relish the idea of chasing them all over New York City.

Rianocek glanced at the traffic ahead. It didn't look as though there would be any letup soon. He returned to his study of the monitor screen.

Baron Alain Marcus Casimir von Rianocek was a handsome, intelligent man of noble blood. He had been educated at the most prestigious universities in Europe. He was well read and kept himself abreast of all of the advancements taking place in technological fields related to his profession. He was also very strong and could be as deadly with his bare hands as he was with any weapon. However, the assassin was also very superstitious. He was aware that there were forces in the universe not easily explainable by science and knowledge.

So he was worried. This operation should not have been so complicated. He had come to New York to kill one woman and make her death look like an accident. And all had gone well from the initial setup—he had been so subtle in recommending Caruso's Restaurant to Madame Christina Sharp that she actually thought that it was her idea to have dinner there—right through the completion of the assignment and his escape.

Then that Chicago cop Larry Cole had shown up.

Twelve years ago, there had been the aborted assassination of the Mafia don back in Chicago; now it was Cole's presence drawing attention to the assassin here in New York. Rianocek believed in unusual signs and bad omens with the faith of a primitive witch doctor. Besides Cole, there were the other small things. The Bronx cop demanding more money, forcing Shade to kill him. Now they were trapped in one of the Big Apple's frequent traffic jams. He would have left New York right now had it not been for Hannah Spencer's already being engaged against the two detectives in Manhattan.

Rianocek sighed. Perhaps it would work out; but if one more obstacle arose, he would abandon the targets and return to Argentina.

The traffic began to move. As the van picked up speed, some of his gloom dissipated. Maybe it would all work out, he thought. Then the signal being transmitted from Queens moved very quickly across the computerized map.

The assassin studied the path Assistant Deputy Commissioner Leak's police car was taking as it sped across Queens headed back for Manhattan. If Rianocek was right, the cop car would pass them going in the opposite direction. If he could anticipate where they were going to be . . .

"Excuse me, sir," Shade said. "There's something on the scanner that I think you should hear."

Due to the amount of equipment packed into the rear of the van, the police scanner was located in the driver's pod. Now Rianocek moved forward so that he could hear the transmission. And what he heard made all of the color drain from his face.

Larry Cole would remember this day for the rest of his life. The weather was beautiful in Manhattan. The sun shone down on the endless row of skyscrapers from a cloudless blue sky. The temperature hovered around seventy degrees and it would have been a great day to take a walk, visit a zoo, or eat lunch on a park bench. A great day to be anything but a cop at the scene of another cop's death.

Back in the restaurant in Queens, Leak and Cole had just been served a round of cold "Tasmanian" brewed beer, which was supposed to be the restaurant's specialty, when the New York cop's beeper went off.

"Does it ever stop?" Leak got to his feet.

"Not as long as you're a command officer, Joe."

While his host was gone, Cole tested the beer and was surprised to find, unlike the beer last night at Mike's Tavern, that this one was very good. Then Leak returned.

They had raced back across the Queensboro Bridge and, with the aid of Leak's siren and magnetized Mars light affixed to the roof, made it to the 90th Street and Third Avenue police shooting scene in record time.

New York is the most densely populated city in America. Whenever the police gather in large numbers to handle emergencies on the street, all traffic, both foot and vehicular, grinds to a halt. Then there were the spectators.

In the wake of the shooting of Detectives Azzoli and Willis, thousands of people lined the curbs and streets, and leaned out of the windows of the high-rise buildings towering over the scene. Extra cops had been called in just to handle the throng and had their hands full, as the curious pressed as close as they could to see for themselves what had occurred.

Leak, followed closely by Cole, shoved his way to the blue wooden barricade emblazoned with the stenciled words in white: "Police Line—Do Not Cross." A pair of uniformed cops manning the barricade let Leak and Cole through after the assistant deputy commissioner identified himself.

Later, Cole would remark that they had been granted admittance to hell.

The ranking officer at the scene was a uniformed captain from the Two-three. A white-haired, grizzled old veteran named Walsh, he strode toward the assistant deputy commissioner with a bow-legged gait and a scowl which reminded Cole of Blackie Silvestri's. After Leak cleared Cole as being authorized to hear the details of what had occurred, the captain began.

"Detectives Azzoli and Willis from the Two-three were having lunch in a deli down the street when a woman rushed in claiming she'd been assaulted by a man with a gun. The dicks put her in their car and began a canvass of the area. She was in the backseat, which is according to procedure. They'd traveled about a block from the restaurant when she pulled a silenced piece and opened fire. She hit Willis at least once and Azzoli five times. Azzoli didn't make it."

The captain paused when Leak lowered his head. Cole's heart went out to his old friend. The Chicago cop also felt a deep sadness over the death of the friendly Italian detective, whom he had known for only a brief time before his death.

Carefully, Captain Walsh continued. "After the shooting, the squad car collided with a lamppost. The woman broke her leg in the collision. She kicked open the back door and was walking west on 90th Street when Officer Joe Jackson, who is assigned to a walking post on Third Avenue, attempted to apprehend her. She shot him dead. It was at this point that Detective Azzoli managed to get off a shot and hit her in the leg. She returned the fire and killed him before she collapsed on the street. Right now she's on her way to Bellevue. She didn't have any identification on her. The crime lab picked up her gun, and it's a doozy. A twenty-five-caliber silenced Colt automatic loaded with hollow-points. If I'm not missing my guess, Boss, that woman is a professional killer."

Leak had listened with patient absorption to the captain's narration. Now he asked, "What hospital did they take Willis to?"

"Doctor's Hospital. He's in surgery right now. The last I heard, he's got a fifty-fifty chance."

"Okay, Captain, this is what I want. Put an extra guard on the perp at Bellevue. I want her printed right away and those prints run through every ident system there is until we get a match. I want to be personally notified when the doctors authorize us to question her and she's to receive no visitors without my authorization. Who's notifying Azzoli's next of kin?"

"The Two-three CO and a chaplain."

"I'm going to the hospital to see how Willis is doing. Anything breaks, call my office right away, and they'll patch you through to me on the car phone."

"Yes, sir," Captain Walsh said.

Turning away, Leak noticed Larry Cole still standing there. In all the excitement, the New York cop had forgotten his old friend.

"I'll get someone to take you to the airport, Larry, so you won't miss your plane."

"If you don't mind, I'd like to stick around, Joe. I can always catch a later flight home."

Leak stared at Cole for a moment. "I appreciate that, Larry. We'll all be running pretty hot with three dead cops so far today. Maybe you'll catch on to something I might miss."

"Don't worry, Deputy. I'll keep my eyes open and my mouth

shut unless I come across something I think that you really need to know."

They headed back for Leak's police car.

Three blocks from the scene, the "Holiday Gift Delivery" van was parked in a loading zone. However, the vehicle's occupants were not worried about a cop hassling them. At least not today, because they were all occupied with the shooting.

When the NYPD assistant deputy commissioner's car began moving, the van pulled out into traffic and followed.

40

OCTOBER 16, 1989
12:30 P.M.

Hannah Spencer jerked herself back to consciousness and discovered that there was an IV in her left arm, an intense pain emanating from the back of her right leg, and a cast on her left leg. Her right arm and leg were shackled to the bed.

Looking around she found that she was in a curtained cubicle and the window over the bed was covered with iron bars. And she was not alone. A pair of uniformed female NYPD officers were seated in chairs on either side of the bed. They were both large, sturdy-looking women, who gazed at the attractive blond assassin with unemotional, unflinching stares.

Hannah looked up at the high ceiling, which was covered with acoustical tile. She wondered how long it would take Alain Rianocek to get her out of this place.

*   *   *

At that exact moment, several miles north outside of Doctors' Hospital, the assassin and his henchman, Cornelius Shade, were in the back of the stolen black van attempting to come up with a plan to carry out Hannah Spencer's rescue.

"How old are these blueprints?" Rianocek pointed at the computer screen, where a floor plan of the jail ward at Bellevue Hospital was displayed.

Shade was seated on the wooden crate that Hannah Spencer usually occupied. Before responding to the assassin, Shade removed an inhaler from his jacket pocket, took a healthy breath, and emitted a cough that sounded like ball bearings rattling around inside a kettledrum. Then he replied, "They are the most current ones on file. I would say they are no older than a year, possibly two. Not much could have changed in that time."

Rianocek manipulated the keyboard. "We've got to figure that our friend, Assistant Deputy Commissioner Leak, will have extra security assigned to Hannah, so this won't be easy."

"Easy, sir?" Shade wheezed. "Now, that is quite the understatement. I would say that extricating Ms. Spencer from her current difficulties approaches the realm of the impossible."

Without taking his eyes off the computer screen, Rianocek said, "Nothing is impossible, my asthmatic friend. Nothing is impossible."

Joe Leak and Larry Cole stood over the bed of Detective Ted Willis inside Doctors' Hospital. The detective's head was completely covered with a turban of white bandages. His right arm was also bandaged, and there were tubes leading from his body to bottles and monitors all around the small private room. Although Willis had not regained consciousness since the shooting, the doctors attending him had informed Leak and Cole that the detective's condition was being upgraded from critical to serious. His prognosis for survival was excellent.

A nurse entered the room to check the monitors and the levels in the IV bottles. Silently, Leak and Cole retreated out into the corridor, where Detective Bobby Melendez, Leak's aide, was waiting for them.

"Commander," he said, nodding to Cole before turning to Leak. "How's Willis doing, Boss?" the short, muscular Hispanic asked.

"They say he's going to make it," Leak replied solemnly.

Detective Melendez got down to business. "I went over to the Two-three detective squad room and collected everything I could find that Azzoli and Willis were working on regarding this guy Rianocek." He handed over a manila folder. "It's all in here."

Leak was about to open the folder when a group of cops got off an elevator at the other end of the hall and began marching resolutely toward the wounded cop's room. Cole recognized the commissioner of the New York City Police Department, who was accompanied by Chief of Detectives Timothy Belcastle—Joe Leak's boss—and four high-ranking uniformed members of the NYPD.

"I've got to brief the commissioner, Larry," Leak said. "Wait for me in the visitors' lounge."

"Joe," Cole said, before his friend could turn away, "you mind if I take a look at the information on Rianocek?"

Without hesitation, Leak handed over the folder.

Cole waited until the commissioner, accompanied by Leak and Chief Belcastle, entered Willis's room before he retreated to the visitors' lounge.

A complimentary coffee service was available and, as Cole had not eaten lunch, he poured a cup and sat down with the information Willis and Azzoli had obtained from Europe prior to the shooting.

There were six pages of single-spaced computer print. Unbeknownst to Commander Larry Cole, Baron Alain Marcus Casimir von Rianocek would have been shocked to learn that he was not as anonymous a figure on the international crime scene as he believed himself to be.

The first page was headed:

CONFIDENTIAL   CONFIDENTIAL   CONFIDENTIAL

followed by:

Response to Inquiry #89-43291—

TO: New York City Police Department

FROM: Interpol

SUBJECT: Baron Alain Marcus Casimir von Rianocek

Baron Alain Marcus Casimir von Rianocek—born August 4, 1946 Buenos Aires, Argentina. Alleged claimant to the Bavarian royal noble line of succession Rianocek Baronet traceable to the Medieval Babenburgs.

Baron Otto Wilhelm von Rianocek (1866–1919) was a staunch supporter of the Bavarian monarchy overthrown by Kurt Eisner, who installed a socialist republic in 1919. Otto Wilhelm von Rianocek was believed assassinated by pro-socialist fanatics. Although the title Baron was not recognized by the socialist government, Otto Wilhelm's son, Hubert Walter Oscar von Rianocek, managed to maintain the family fortune and lands with a sizeable estate and castle located outside of Munich.

Hubert Walter Oscar von Rianocek (1896–1963) became actively involved in the volatile politics of the post–World War I period and was one of the earliest known members of the National Socialist German Workers Party (NSDAP). Hubert Walter Oscar von Rianocek became an avid follower of Adolf Hitler and was a high-ranking Nazi official, holding the rank of Oberst or full colonel in the SS. After the war, Hubert von Rianocek was placed on a list of war criminals and was believed to have escaped with other Nazis to South America. A 1956 intelligence report released by the United States Justice Department stated that Hubert Walter von Rianocek was no longer wanted by Allied authorities. This report further confirmed that he was currently believed to be living in Buenos Aires, Argentina. The Israeli government expressed an interest in learning the exact location of von Rianocek, but whether any action was taken against him by the Mossad is unknown. Rianocek built a large estate outside of Buenos Aires with what is believed to be contraband funds stolen from Nazi victims. He died in September 1963.

Alain Marcus Casimir von Rianocek was born in Argentina in August 1946. His mother was Anastasia Regina Maria Rothschild von Rianocek, who received a substantial inheritance from her French family at the time of her marriage to Hubert Walter von Rianocek in 1935. This inheritance was believed squandered by Hubert von Rianocek on his estate, high living, and women prior to his death. The von Rianoceks were believed bankrupt; however, as of this date, Alain Marcus Casimir von Rianocek has maintained the South American estate, as well as a number of other residences around the world, without any verifiable source of income. In 1973 Alain von Rianocek filed a claim in West German courts demanding that the family ancestral lands, confiscated after World War II, be restored to him as rightful heir. This claim was denied.

It is currently estimated that the alleged Baron Alain Marcus Casimir von Rianocek's net worth is in the vicinity of forty-four million dollars.

SPECULATIVE ANALYSIS

It is strongly suspected by Scotland Yard that Alain Rianocek was responsible for the death by explosive device of British financier William Cody, who was murdered on November 8, 1985, in London. An investigation into Cody's death revealed that the components of the bomb were obtained from a London East End street gang. A police informant inside the gang later revealed that a former street gang leader known as "the Wheeze," accompanied by a tall man with an aristocratic bearing that resembled Rianocek, picked up the dynamite. The former street gang leader is believed to be Cornelius Shade, who has no criminal record.

During the course of the investigation, which was supervised by Chief Inspector Gordon Edwards, Scotland Yard discovered that a rival banker named Ian Hamiltorn had bragged to his mistress that he had hired an assassin to kill William Cody. The fact that the mistress only came forward after Hamilton rejected her gave her account dubious reliability. When questioned, she was unable to remember the assassin's name, but she did say that Hamilton contacted him in South America and referred to him as "the Baron."

Due to the circumstantial nature of the evidence in the murder of William Cody, no arrests were made and the case remains open.

Criminal-intelligence agencies in Europe, the United States, and Canada have long suspected that an international assassin has been operating worldwide for many years while managing to avoid detection. It is further suspected that this international assassin usually employs a backup team consisting of a man and a woman.

Alain Marcus Casimir von Rianocek is known to travel extensively, and his presence has been documented in the vicinity of a number of murders and mysterious disasters leading to deaths around the world. However, there is no evidence directly connecting him with any crime at the present time. It is recommended that Alain Rianocek be kept under surveillance when he is reported away from his estate in Buenos Aires, Argentina.

The report ended. Cole looked out of the hospital windows across Manhattan. In America the police could not engage in random surveillances without establishing probable cause. To do so was a violation of First Amendment Rights, which not only protected American citizens, but also applied to foreign nationals within the United States, including Alain Rianocek. But the more the CPD commander thought about it, the more he was able to see a case for a probable-cause surveillance on Rianocek. In fact, there were grounds to go even further than that.

Joe Leak and Chief Belcastle entered the lounge. The commissioner's visit completed, he was on his way back to One Police

Plaza; however, he had left the chief of detectives and the assistant deputy commissioner with a strongly worded admonition to get to the bottom of the deaths of the three police officers who had been killed today.

They stopped at the entrance to the visitors' lounge, out of earshot of the few people who had been waiting there. Cole got up and went over to them.

"Fill me in, Joe," Belcastle demanded. When the Chicago cop walked up, the NYPD chief of detectives merely glanced in his direction. Belcastle knew who Cole was, but right now he wasn't very sociable.

Leak filled his boss in on everything that had occurred so far, including the double guard he had placed on the female killer in Bellevue. As he concluded, Belcastle frowned and said, "Why do you think that the shooter of Willis, Azzoli, and Jackson has any connection to this Baron Whatshisname?"

Leak sighed wearily. "Right now I can't prove it, but it fits. Willis and Azzoli were looking into Rianocek's background, and I bet, if we dig deep enough and long enough, we'll find a connection with this so-called Bavarian baron and last night's M. D. Hines Building fire."

"I think there's a connection in here," Cole interjected, holding up the folder.

"What's that?" Chief Belcastle's frown deepened.

"It's the information Willis and Azzoli compiled on Rianocek from Interpol," Leak said. "I let Larry read it, while we were—"

"I need to talk to you right now, Leak," Belcastle interrupted. "Alone."

"I'll step out into the hall," Cole said softly.

"Oh, and Commander," the chief of detectives added, "I'll take that file."

Cole handed it over and left the room.

*   *   *

A few minutes later, a red-faced Chief Belcastle walked out of the hospital visitors' lounge and glared at Larry Cole before stomping off toward the elevator. Joe Leak also left the lounge; however, there was a smile on the assistant deputy commissioner's face.

"What happened?" Cole asked his old friend.

"Tim, there, is bent out of shape about me having you give us a hand on this case. It's against unofficial NYPD policy to have outside law-enforcement officials working with us on a sensitive investigation. They're worried that something negative will get out and give us a bad name."

"So I guess I'm off the case," Cole said dejectedly.

"No, you're not, kiddo," Leak said, flashing a toothy grin. "I let Belcastle have his say. Then I reminded him of all the times I saved his ass by working around the clock to break a hot, controversial case. To say the least, he owes me, Larry, and today I called in my markers. Oh, it ticked him off, but he went along with me. In fact, he's calling your Chief Riseman in Chicago and requesting that you be assigned to us in an official capacity."

Cole smiled. "You *do* have a talent for getting what you want, Joe."

"Genius by any other name is still genius. Now, what did you find out from reading that file?"

Outside of Doctors' Hospital, the stolen "Holiday Gift Delivery" van was parked in a lot, which afforded the vehicle's occupants a view of the emergency-room entrance. Seated in the front of the van, Cornelius Shade watched the official cars come and go. Within a matter of minutes, the police commissioner had arrived, gone inside for a short time, and then left with his entourage. Next had come the mayor, who also went inside briefly before exiting to hold a press conference on a street behind the hospital. After the mayor left, Chief Timothy Belcastle, his florid face twisted into a furious scowl, stomped to his chauffeur-driven black sedan and was soon gone. Finally, the men whom Shade and Rianocek had tracked to this place, Larry Cole and Joe E. Leak, came out.

"Baron von Rianocek." Shade alerted his boss. "They're heading for the car."

The assassin was seated on one of the crates in the back of the van. He had placed himself into a hypnotic trance, which assisted in clearing his mind to deal with a serious problem. This problem was how to effect Hannah Spencer's escape from police custody. Because of the complexity of what the assassin would have to accomplish, he had to face the possibility that it would be necessary for him to abandon his mission against Cole and Leak. At least temporarily.

Remaining motionless, with his eyes closed, Rianocek said to Shade, "Continue to monitor their movements. If the opportunity presents itself, we will move against them."

Shade watched the cops get into the car, but they didn't move. He was close enough to see Cole reading aloud from a manila folder, while Leak listened.

"Excuse me, sir," Shade called to Rianocek. "Perhaps we should activate the eavesdropping equipment. Our police friends are having a rather involved conversation."

Coming out of his trance, Rianocek's hand snaked out to push the "power" button on a device which resembled a stereo set. There was an external antenna attached to the top of the van leading from this device. Rianocek manipulated controls inside the van, making the antenna move until it was pointing directly at Leak's police vehicle. The assassin donned a headset, adjusted the volume, and settled in to spy on the cops.

It took a moment for him to tune the device so that the voices came through as clearly as if Rianocek were actually sitting in the car with them. Then a deep voice, which Rianocek had never heard before, came over his headset. So this was what Larry Cole of the Chicago Police Department sounded like. Now the assassin had a voice to put with the face.

". . . but it fits, Joe. The Bronx cop, B. J. McNamara, calls Willis, asks about me, and ends up dead at the hands of a man who speaks with a foreign accent and has trouble breathing. Then this woman attacks Willis and Azzoli, which was obviously a setup from the start. Now, according to Interpol, Rianocek is suspected of being a professional assassin who has made a fortune killing people. But most of the information in this report is pure speculation. What happened last night on 57th Street brought him out into the open. The man who killed McNamara and the woman in Bellevue's jail ward are obviously his backup team. If we can make her talk, she'll blow the entire thing wide open and expose our so-called Bavarian baron for exactly what he is."

Now Leak spoke. "What we need to do now is bring Rianocek in. I'll put out an APB for him and also have anyone who is in his company detained as well. I think we'll have some answers on this thing before nightfall, Larry."

Cornelius Shade heard a strange noise coming from the rear of the van. As he had never heard anything like it before, he turned around. The source of the noise was instantly identifiable. Rianocek had his jaws clamped shut and was grinding his teeth violently to keep himself from screaming.

41

The special telephone rang in the offices of Zeefeldt and Gruen-wald, Solicitors, in Zurich, Switzerland. A thin young woman with an elaborately styled hairdo answered by saying simply, "Law office." The line was secured from eavesdroppers. Anyone attempting to listen in would hear nothing but continuous static.

"This is Black Rook. Repeat, this is Black Rook. I have need of the Mastermind's services in New York City as soon as possible. Black Pawn Two is in the custody of the New York City Police Department and is currently being held in the prison ward of Belle-vue Hospital in Manhattan. The Mastermind must effect Black Pawn Two's escape prior to her recovering sufficiently from injuries received during her arrest, which will enable the authorities to move her to a more secure facility. The Mastermind's fee will be paid along with all expenses incurred. Black Rook will call back for confirmation in exactly one hour."

The woman in Zurich replied, "The message will be relayed and a response obtained in one hour, as you instructed. Have a good day."

The connection was broken.

New York City
1:12 P.M.

The radios in all of the patrol cars in the New York metropolitan area crackled to life. *"All Points Bulletin #89-46327. Wanted for questioning in the murders of three New York City police officers and the investigation of murder by arson. Subject #One, Alain Marcus Casimir von Rianocek, male, white, forty-three years of age, six feet, four inches tall, approximately 190 to 200 pounds, medium build, light brown hair worn shoulder-length, blue eyes, fair complexion, no visible marks or scars. Subject #One is a foreign national, who is traveling on an Argentina passport. He is to be considered armed and dangerous. Subject #Two, who is possibly in the company of Subject #One, may answer to the name Cornelius Shade, is a white male, approximately forty to fifty years of age, five feet, eight inches tall, 245 pounds, stout build. This subject is a British national; however, there is no record of his authorized entry into the United States. Subject #Two has difficulty breathing and could be suffering from severe asthma or emphysema. Subject #Two should also be considered armed and dangerous. If contact made, apprehend immediately and notify the Office of Assistant Deputy Commissioner Joseph E. Leak, Detective Division H.Q."*

The broadcast was monitored on the scanner in the "Holiday Gift Delivery" van, which was in a vacant rest stop on the New Jersey Turnpike approximately fifty miles from New York City. Alain Rianocek, wearing dark glasses and a black knit cap, which concealed his long brown hair, used a can of black spray paint to cover the gold script of the "Holiday Gift Delivery" van logo. Cornelius Shade was removing the New York license plates and replacing them with Florida tags they had stolen from a recreational vehicle parked outside a McDonald's restaurant in Jersey City, New Jersey.

Soon they would be traveling south, away from the usual points of egress the police would expect the fugitives to use to return to South America. Instead their escape route was taking them to Washington, D.C. Leak and Cole would be shocked if they knew how Rianocek and Shade planned to leave the United States. Hannah Spencer was not forgotten. At 2:00 P.M. (EST) Rianocek would make another call to Zeefeldt and Gruenwald, Solicitors, in Zurich to confirm that the Mastermind would take the job of rescuing her.

The Mastermind was not primarily an assassin like Rianocek but was considered more of a meticulous planner, who viewed his assignments with the eye of a military tactician. One of the few people in the world who was aware of the Mastermind's existence, the assassin also knew his name. Karl Steiger was very good at what he did. His services would not come cheaply, but Hannah Spencer was very valuable to Alain Rianocek.

Their labors completed, Rianocek and Shade got back into the van. They planned to reach their destination in less than four hours.

Rianocek was driving. He possessed a forged New York State driver's license in the name of Edmund Collins and enough backup documentation to pass a routine examination of his identity by a highway patrol cop. If any attempt was made to take him in, the assassin and Shade were prepared to kill. However, Rianocek planned to drive as safely and carefully as possible to prevent the van from being stopped.

As he drove along in the right-hand lane of the turnpike, the wanted message came over the scanner again. Nothing in the text had changed. When it concluded, Shade said, "Begging your pardon, sir, but this cop from Chicago has become a real jinx to us. I'm glad that we're rid of him."

Rianocek stared through the windshield at the road ahead. "Commander Cole and I are far from quits, Mr. Shade. We are far from quits."

Joe Leak and Larry Cole exited the jail ward of Bellevue Hospital. They had attempted to interview the female prisoner, but she had refused to say one single word to them. In fact, she had behaved in such a cool, detached manner that it had infuriated the assistant deputy commissioner. She had displayed a definite, but silent, interest in Cole, which was evidenced by her stare intensifying whenever she looked at him.

In the corridor outside the jail ward, Joe Leak sighed exhaustedly. "Have you ever seen anyone like her before?"

Cole shook his head. "No one even close, Joe. That woman is a cold-blooded killer. There's not one ounce of emotion or regret in that pretty head of hers. As a matter of fact, when she looked at me, I got the impression that she was measuring me for a coffin."

Leak removed a folded telex from his coat pocket. "At least now we know who she is. Her prints identify her as Hannah Spencer. She was the primary suspect in a series of homicides in Oceanside, California, a few years back. A Sergeant Sonny Adams from the Oceanside P.D. is faxing us all the files from those murders. With them, the gun she used in the shootings, and that custom-made knife she stabbed Azzoli with, it won't be difficult to prove that she's a professional assassin. What we need to do is form a connection between her, Rianocek, you, and what happened at the M. D. Hines Building last night."

"But she's not talking, Joe," Cole said.

Leak's face turned hard and his eyes glistened with determination. "Oh, she's going to eventually talk to me, Larry. One way or another, I guarantee you she's going to talk to me."

Zurich, Switzerland
OCTOBER 16, 1989
8:00 P.M.

The secured telephone line in the offices of Zeefeldt and Gruenwald, Solicitors, rang exactly one hour after the assassin's initial call. The same receptionist answered it.

"This is Black Rook. Do you have a response from the Mastermind for me?"

"The Mastermind has agreed to accept the assignment and is en route to New York. You will immediately deposit the sum of $750,000 United States currency in his name in the Bank of Zurich. He will not take any steps to accomplish the assignment until confirmation of the deposit is received."

"Done."

"It will also be necessary for you to brief him on the details of the assignment."

"That will have to be done telephonically."

"Do you have a number where the Mastermind can reach you?"

"No. I will have to contact him. I am on the run. Obtain the information for me and I will call you back at midnight Zurich time."

"As you wish, Black Rook."

42

New York City
OCTOBER 16, 1989
3:02 P.M.

Finally, Leak and Cole found a connection, however tenuous, between the M. D. Hines Building fire in the offices of the accounting firm of Gross and Sheppard, and Larry Cole. The accounting firm handled a number of clients, which were located in the New York/New Jersey area. But as far as the geographic locations of the clients went, there was one major exception.

"Bingo!" Cole exclaimed, scanning a computerized printout of the Gross and Sheppard client list.

"What have you got?" Leak said.

They were in the assistant deputy commissioner's private office at police headquarters. The room was spartan in appearance with the furnishings being for the most part selected for function rather than style. Leak did have a private washroom, but other than a coffeemaker and photos of his children on his desk, there was little of the NYPD cop's personality in this place. Cole understood this because a cop's job, especially a detective's, was done out on the street and not in an office.

Cole pointed to an entry on the printout. "Barksdale, Barksdale, and DeVito, P.C., is a law firm in Chicago. The first big case I ever handled was connected with that law firm. It started out as a mob execution of an informant, which turned into a gang war." Then Cole sat up ramrod straight. "Wait a minute. Just wait one darn minute."

"Larry, you're killing me with the suspense," Leak complained.

Cole thought in furious silence for another moment before he turned to Leak and explained, "This Barksdale, Barksdale, and DeVito, P.C., was a mob law firm in Chicago. Back in December 1977, the law firm found out that Big Numbers Albanese, the outfit's bookkeeper was about to testify before a Cook County grand jury about the inner workings of the Arcadio Crime Family. The mob did manage to whack Albanese, but Blackie and I showed up before the hit men could get away. We were forced to kill Frankie Arcadio, the Chicago mob boss's nephew, and arrest his accomplice, Tony Lima. Lima ended up dead that same day.

"Now, my understanding is that Paul Arcadio blamed the senior partner at this Barksdale law firm for the death of his nephew, which touched off a short gang war, which also resulted in the murder of Chief of Detectives John T. Ryan. We were never certain, but it was rumored that Paul Arcadio put out a contract on Barksdale, and the attorney returned the favor. There was also some talk that Barksdale hired a professional assassin, but we pinched Rabbit Arcadio on a conspiracy charge before he could be assassinated."

Now it dawned on Joe Leak. "Do you think Rianocek could have been involved?"

Cole frowned. "I didn't see him the night we served the warrant on Paul Arcadio, but he could have seen me, which caused his reaction last night inside the restaurant."

"So we need to take a closer look at the operation of this Barksdale, Barksdale, and DeVito, P.C., and its connection to the Gross and Sheppard accounting firm."

43

OCTOBER 16, 1989
5:30 P.M.

The man stood outside the front entrance of Bellevue Hospital and studied the building facade. He entered the lobby and strolled around casually while glancing occasionally at his watch, as if he were waiting for someone. He took an elevator from the lobby up to the seventh floor, where the jail ward was located. Stepping off into the corridor, he saw a sign on a white cardboard background with red block letters, "This is a restricted area. Authorized personnel only."

The man got back on the elevator and rode up to the top floor before returning to the lobby. Exiting the front door of the hospital, he walked around to the emergency-room entrance. He examined the frenetic activity taking place there with the arrival of ambulances and police cars containing bleeding victims caused by the mayhem on the streets of New York City. He remained until he had seen everything that he had come to see.

Karl Steiger had been observed by any number of police officers and hospital personnel. His image had also been captured on closed-circuit TV cameras at various locations outside and inside of Bellevue. He was aware of this visual and electronic security, but was not concerned. He did not plan to ever return here.

Karl Steiger was a broad-shouldered, powerfully built man of about the same age as Alain Rianocek. He had blond hair worn in a close-cropped crew cut and cold blue-gray eyes that stared out at the world with an unemotional, calculating gaze. He was dressed in a brown tweed suit with a matching cap on his head. He possessed a pronounced European appearance, which couldn't be helped. He had arrived in New York only a short time ago, on the Concorde from Paris, and he was on a very tight schedule. Now Steiger had come up with a plan to extricate the lovely but lethal Hannah Spencer from the Bellevue Hospital jail ward.

A smile cracked the Mastermind's usually stony visage. His plan would require the talents of his son, Ernst Steiger. However, Ernst would be in disguise. A very different disguise.

And the information kept coming in, forming a connection between the accounting firm of Gross and Sheppard in New York City and the law firm of Barksdale, Barksdale, and DeVito, P.C., in Chicago.

"The dead woman found in the M. D. Hines Building was named Joan Rains," Joe Leak said, leaning back in his chair and reading the most recent computer printout they had received. "She handled a number of accounts for Gross and Sheppard, primarily specializing in tax returns and the investment accounts of some of the firm's major clients. She only recently took over the Chicago law firm's accounts, which had previously been handled by none other than Clarence Gross himself, who was one of the accounting firm's founding partners."

"Why did he give up the Barksdale account?" Cole asked, from the other side of the desk.

Leak looked up from the paper. "He died in late September."

Cole nodded. "That's a good enough reason."

Leak continued. "Now according to Michael Sheppard, the surviving senior partner, who was also Joan Rains's supervisor, she had discovered some discrepancies in the audit of the Chicago law firm account. Now get this, Larry. She discovered that Barksdale, Barksdale, and DeVito, P.C., had too much money."

"I don't get it," Cole said.

"Apparently, she found evidence that they had millions of dollars more than they were supposed to have, and she hinted to some other firm employees that she believed there could be some illegalities involved in the law firm's operation. She even threatened to contact the Internal Revenue Service if Barksdale, Barksdale, and DeVito couldn't come up with a plausible explanation for the discrepancies." The assistant deputy commissioner again looked up at Cole. "In the fire, all the records, both print and computerized, were very conveniently destroyed."

"This thing keeps getting deeper and deeper," Cole said. "Blackie is sending us as much information as he can come up with on the former Mob law firm. That will help us fill in the picture a bit better."

Leak glanced at his watch. "I'll have a messenger bring it out to the house when it comes in. Let's vacate this joint. If I spend too much time in the office I get jumpy. You can stay at my place tonight. I've got lots of room now. And I also have a treat in store for you."

Cole managed a smile. "Where's the beer from this time?"

"It's not beer, Larry," Leak said, pulling on his sports jacket. "I've got a box full of Corona Light ale. What we're going to do is pick up a Chicago-style pizza from an Italian restaurant near my house."

"Chicago-style?" Cole questioned with dismay.

"Yeah, that's what they call it."

As Cole followed the NYPD assistant deputy commissioner out the door, he mumbled, "I wonder why?"

The two female police officers assigned to guard Hannah Spencer were relieved by another pair of lady cops at four o'clock that afternoon. The sergeant who assigned them to this duty did not have to emphasize the importance of the assignment, as the Bellevue jail-ward inmate was a suspect in the murders of three NYPD cops.

In appearance, the officers looked a great deal like the ones they had relieved; sturdy-looking, no-nonsense veterans of the war on crime in the Big Apple. They did not say much to each other, and neither of them spoke at all to the shackled prisoner.

In turn, Hannah Spencer spent her time lying on her back staring up at the ceiling and dozing occasionally. The officers did not notice that she appeared relaxed to the point of being almost serene. It was as if she was waiting patiently for something to happen.

The female assassin's guards were going to devote this tour of duty to making sure that nothing—other than the strictly official—did happen.

A male orderly in a white uniform delivered a dinner tray to the wounded inmate at 6:45 P.M. The orderly was a young man with a baby face, who looked to be barely out of high school. One of the officers checked the tray before allowing him to place it on the movable table beside the bed. Using the control buttons, the prisoner raised herself into a sitting position and pulled the table toward her. There was a dry Swiss steak, a dab of lumpy mashed potatoes, some green beans, white bread with butter, applesauce, and a carton of skim milk. As the guards watched, the assassin ate it all.

A half hour later, the same orderly returned to retrieve the tray. Then he was gone.

The cops were scheduled for staggered meal periods at 8:00 and 8:30 P.M., respectively. At that time, an additional female officer would be dispatched to the jail ward to allow first one and then the other to go to the hospital cafeteria. At midnight they would be relieved. In the interim, they passed the time reading the newspapers and magazines they had brought with them.

By 9:00 they were bored silly and were doing their best to stay alert. Then, within less than thirty minutes, three things occurred to break the monotony.

A Bellevue Hospital doctor came in to check the prisoner. He was an elderly man with disheveled gray hair and tired eyes. He wore a wrinkled lab coat and had the obligatory stethoscope dangling from his neck. He woke Hannah Spencer up before poking and prodding her for a few moments with the sensitivity of a housewife examining a roast in a supermarket. Then, after a glance at the chart hanging from the railing at the foot of the bed and a noncommittal grunt, he was gone.

The female cops exchanged quizzical glances and returned to their boredom.

Then a blond female nurse walked in carrying a portable TV set.

"Good evening," she said, breezing past the officers and placing the set on top of the tray table. She began searching for an outlet to plug it in, saying over her shoulder, "The doctor told me to bring this in for you. He said it would help pass the time."

Although glad for the diversion, the guards were still aware of the sensitivity of this assignment.

"Where's your security badge?" the senior officer demanded.

The nurse, who was tall and slender and possessed large but attractive features, stood up and turned to face them. She smiled, displaying very white teeth. "You know, I'm always getting into trouble for not wearing it." Reaching into her pocket, she removed a laminated photo identification card attached to a metal chain. She slipped the chain over her head so that the ID card hung across her flat chest.

The cops remarked to themselves that, like most official photographs, this one bore an unflattering resemblance to the nurse. The name, in large block print, was "Angela Dizido."

Nurse Dizido turned the TV on. "Enjoy, ladies. I'll be back later." With that she left the cubicle.

"I thought television sets, radios, and other electronic devices weren't allowed in the jail ward," the less senior of the pair said.

The other cop shrugged. "The nurse said that the doctor ordered it. Who are we to argue with him?"

They turned their attention to the small screen, which was broadcasting a rerun of one of the *Star Wars* movies. Hannah Spencer abandoned her ceiling stare to also watch.

The nurse, pushing a stretcher on wheels, returned twenty minutes later.

"What is this?" the senior officer demanded, getting to her feet.

The nurse opened her heavily mascaraed eyes as wide as a Kewpie doll's. "Doctor's orders. The patient is supposed to have an X ray of her right leg."

"It's the left one that's broken," the other officer said, also standing up.

"I can see that," the nurse said, placing her hands on her hips in a defiant gesture. "The doctor wants the other leg X-rayed now. After all, he is the doctor."

"We've got to get authorization," the senior cop said.

"I already *have* authorization," the nurse said, snatching the patient's chart from the railing at the foot of Hannah Spencer's bed. "Right here."

"Just hold on!" the senior officer snapped. "Before this patient moves an inch, we've got to get an okay from Assistant Deputy Commissioner Joseph E. Leak."

"Fine!" The nurse raised her arms in a gesture of frustration. "This is only going to waste a lot of time, and I go off duty at ten o'clock."

"This won't take long," the other cop said.

The nurse went to stand against the wall beside the windows and the senior officer picked up the telephone. Opening her notebook, she dialed the home number of the NYPD assistant deputy commissioner, which had been given to her by the sergeant when she came on duty. As the phone began ringing on the other end, Hannah Spencer watched her escape begin to unfold.

Joe Leak's house was big—perhaps too big. It was located on a two-acre lot out on Long Island and, in Cole's estimation, could

easily rival any of the mansions in the wealthiest areas of Chicago.

"How many rooms have you got here, Joe?" Cole asked as they
stepped across the threshold.

"Fifteen," Leak said, carrying the extra-large, Chicago-style
pizza like a waiter. "It was a bit run-down when we bought it, so
I got a good price. I put a few dollars into the renovation, and it
appreciated substantially in value." He looked around as if suddenly
finding himself in an alien environment. "Someday I'll be able to
sell it for somewhere in the high-six or maybe even seven-figure
range."

"You really take good care of it," Cole said. "The grounds and
interior of the house are immaculate."

"I have a fairly inexpensive maid and gardener service. They
come over once a week. I spend most of my time in the city. Let's
eat the pizza before it gets cold."

They were sitting down to eat at a dining-room table that could
seat twelve, under a crystal chandelier, which could easily light up
Times Square, when the phone rang. Leak went to the kitchen extension to answer it. He returned a couple of minutes later.

"Anything wrong?" Cole asked, biting into a slice of the
Chicago-style pizza. He had to admit that with onions, green peppers, pepperoni, sausage, mushrooms, and a few other ingredients
that only a lab analysis could uncover, it wasn't half bad. But Cole
hadn't eaten lunch either.

"That was the Bellevue detail on Hannah Spencer," Leak
said, taking a chair across the wide table from Cole and snatching
up a wedge of pizza. "One of the doctors ordered X rays for the
prisoner. The officers guarding her won't let them do it unless I
say it's okay. I had them check the credentials with Bellevue Security on the doctor who asked for the X rays and the nurse who
is going to take the Spencer woman to the lab. They both
checked out as bona fide. I'm also having the officers go with the

nurse, so everything should be okay. I told them to call me when they get back to the jail ward."

The officer at Bellevue failed to mention anything about the orderly who had brought Hannah Spencer's dinner. He would not have checked out with Bellevue security.

Nurse Angela Dizido, flanked by the two NYPD officers, pushed the wheeled stretcher bearing Hannah Spencer through the corridors of the Bellevue jail ward. They reached the elevator and the nurse pushed the "down" button. She had not said a lot since the confrontation back in the cubicle. She was scheduled to get off at 10:00 P.M. and it was now approaching 9:45. She knew that she would never make it, so she pouted.

The cops maintained their alertness, but at this time of night there were few people in the halls of the hospital. They rode down to the lab floor and exited into a corridor that reeked with the odor of X-ray developing fluid. The nurse pushed the stretcher over to a desk and looked around quizzically. The cops noticed her frown.

The senior officer inquired, "What's wrong?"

"There should be someone here," the nurse responded.

"Maybe they stepped away," the other cop commented.

"No . . . ," she had started to say when the orderly who had delivered Hannah Spencer's dinner stepped from the corridor adjacent to the elevator. The three women saw him at the same time. The filter mask he was wearing over his nose and mouth didn't register immediately with them. Then he threw three golf ball–sized pellets to the floor. They exploded on impact, enveloping the area in a dense cloud of white smoke.

The officers didn't have time to react before the chloroform-based nerve gas entered their lungs. It took only seconds for the four women to be rendered unconscious.

The masked orderly stepped over the bodies of the nurse and police officers. He pushed the stretcher to the elevator and de-

scended to the main floor. He removed the mask and tossed it on
the floor of the car and covered the female assassin's head with the
sheet before the doors opened. If anyone stopped him, he would
say that he was on his way to the morgue with a recently deceased
patient. If anyone tried to examine the body, then Ernest Steiger
would react. And his reaction would be very deadly.

However, he made his way out of the emergency exit to the
hospital without incident. There a hearse was waiting. A solemn-
faced attendant, wearing a black suit, helped the fake orderly load
the unconscious woman's body into the rear of the vehicle.

As soon as the door was closed, Ernest Steiger snatched off the
white jacket he had worn and threw it behind a clump of bushes
outside the hospital. On this mission, he had wanted to impersonate
a doctor, but his father had demanded the lower profile menial's
guise. Ernest considered himself, in every sense of the word, a
Steiger in the long-standing, Prussian general staff military tradition
and a Steiger would never be anyone's orderly for any reason.

As the black hearse pulled away, Ernest Steiger walked from
the hospital. In less than a block, he flagged a taxi. As a reward for
having successfully carried out the escape of the female assassin
from Bellevue's jail ward, he planned to treat himself to a night on
the town.

44

The gray Buick sedan drove past the Smithsonian Institution Air and Space Museum and turned onto the Mall. The car traveled two blocks and pulled to the curb. There were three occupants inside, two men in the front and a lone man in the rear.

The pair in the front seat were stony-faced, broad-shouldered clones. Their job was to bodyguard the bald, nervous man seated behind them. They didn't know why they were here, but when they'd left Langley, Virginia, they'd been told to be ready for anything. To that end, they carried .45 caliber semiautomatic handguns in shoulder holsters beneath their size-fifty suit jackets and there were two .50 caliber machine pistols concealed inside secret compartments built into the door panels.

Their charge was a thin man who possessed the sharp features of a woodpecker. In fact, in high school back in Muncie, Indiana, he had been nicknamed "Woody," which was not intended to be complimentary. However, he had come a long way in the ensuing thirty years.

His name was Richard "Dickie" Fagan, and he was a Central Intelligence Agency deputy director. His current area of responsibility was Third World intelligence. He had made a reputation for himself for being ruthlessly efficient during a three-year stint he had done for the agency in Vietnam during the early seventies. Dickie Fagan was quite adept at interrogating captured Vietcong guerrillas to the point of mutilation and eventual death. He had also trained and dispatched assassination squads into North Vietnam.

When the war ended, Dickie was seen as a definite asset in the United States intelligence community and he rose rapidly in the Agency. He began operating in South America and was given the responsibility for keeping in place certain dictators who were sympathetic to the United States and opposed to communism. It didn't matter to Fagan's minders at Langley whether or not such despots were corrupt or engaged in horrendous human-rights violations. Dickie Fagan was charged with playing the intelligence game on a global scale and couldn't be concerned with the internal politics of backwater nations.

At times the men in charge of such dictatorships needed to be changed and Dickie took care of the necessary election procedures. However, only one vote was ever cast and that was Fagan's. Of course, he didn't do the actual "wet work" himself. After all he was a deputy director, so he farmed out the tasks to freelancers. One such freelancer was Alain Rianocek.

Dickie Fagan had gone to the assassin when it became necessary to eliminate a certain South American dictator who had forgotten where his true allegiances were. After the assassin had successfully carried out the assignment, Fagan had maintained contact with him and had used him three more times on jobs in Europe and South Africa. Each time, the assassin did an excellent job, with no lingering complications. So Dickie had decided to use the Bavarian baron on a sensitive mission a little closer to home, so to speak.

The Iran-Contra scandal disclosures of Lieutenant Colonel Oliver North before a congressional subcommittee shocked the nation. However, Dickie Fagan was a great deal more cunning and careful in his nefarious operations in Third World nations. But he was just as illegal as anything ever attempted in the Iran-Contra affair. In fact, the operations that Dickie Fagan was responsible for were more closely related to the Mob's than to any intelligence operation.

To keep some of the South American dictators happy, such as was the case with the criminally minded regime of Manuel Noriega in Panama, certain considerations were provided and courtesies extended. In impoverished Third World nations, no matter how oppressive the regime was, dictators were always short of cash. So they had to utilize the meager resources at their disposal to make money. Invariably, they turned to producing a product that yielded a big return for a small initial investment. That product was narcotics.

To prevent himself from having the same type of problems that Oliver North had experienced in connection with Iran-Contra, Fagan set up an elaborate network to transport the raw, unprocessed drugs from South America into the United States via secure military aircraft. The opiates, coca leaves, and marijuana plants were then processed in a factory inside the United States before the product was distributed throughout the northern hemisphere.

To prevent interference from organized crime and other narcotics purveyors, Fagan arranged from inside CIA headquarters in Langley, Virginia, to begin a massive takeover of street gangs and minor street-criminal enterprises. Despite the rivalries constantly raging within such groups, Dickie Fagan's experience in Vietnam and Central America served him well. Those he couldn't bribe, he threatened; those on whom threats didn't work, violence did. The gangs became the CIA's street merchants of death.

Then Fagan moved on to the next steps: taking the profits received from the streets and channeling them back to the dictatorships in Central America. Thus a massive, continuous enterprise began operating to bring the product in, process it, distribute it, sell it, and secure the profits. And everything worked very well. In fact, so well that there was more money available than Deputy Director Fagan ever dreamed of. Too much money to line the pockets of greedy, ignorant political figureheads in South America.

So Fagan made a select few of his trusted colleagues within the agency aware of the illegal fund he had established to finance secret operations. A fund which would not be reported to any congressional intelligence oversight committee. And at a time when the need was waning for a strong international supersecret spy organization in America, the CIA, funded by drug money, became more powerful and diabolical than ever before in its history. The banker of this new intelligence behemoth was Richard "Dickie" Fagan.

Any large, immensely powerful organization develops enemies, and the shadowy section of the CIA, that dealt drugs to an unknowing world, was no exception. But they disposed of these enemies with ruthless, cold-blooded efficiency. In fact, the operation Deputy Director Fagan was carrying out on American soil was illegal from so many different perspectives that if it was ever discovered, the televised tribulations of Oliver North would pale by comparison.

But the operation continued to flourish and made billions for the South American drug lords and the Agency. Dickie Fagan was too cunning a covert operative to remain closely associated with this operation for long, so he began disengaging himself from day-to-day activities during the third year of its existence. The few CIA executives aware of this illegal enterprise also demanded that Agency involvement be severely limited and Fagan managed to do just that. Now that decision was coming back to haunt him.

A black van bearing Florida license plates drove slowly onto the Mall and cruised past the Buick sedan before pulling to the curb a short distance away. The three men in the car studied the new arrival closely. Then the van's lights were extinguished and the driver got out. Even in the shadowy light of the streetlamps, Dickie Fagan recognized Alain Rianocek.

With a frown creasing his sharp features, the CIA deputy director snapped at the broad-shouldered men in the front seat, "Remain here, but stay alert and don't let me out of your sight."

"Yes, sir," they responded.

"You know," Rianocek said as Fagan approached, "I always loved this city. Despite the trite horror of your political system, the aesthetics of Washington are quite spectacular."

Standing six inches shorter than the assassin, the deputy director bristled with indignation. "I haven't got time for any bullshit, Rianocek. You know you're not—"

The assassin took a step toward Fagan, which startled the sharp-faced spy and caused the two bodyguards in the Buick to reach for their holstered weapons.

"I prefer to be called *Baron* von Rianocek, Dickie, and you'd better smile before those two muscle-bound idiots get themselves killed. My man in the van has them covered with a Britton Mauser sniper rifle. If they get out of the car, they'll both be dead within five seconds. Now, smile!"

Slowly, Fagan forced himself to relax and even managed a slight curling of his lips, which was enough to make the agents in the Buick remain where they were.

Rianocek continued, "I bypassed normal channels and came directly to you because I've developed some serious problems in connection with the job I did for your network in New York last night."

"So I've heard," Fagan said. "The police have got APBs out for you all over the East Coast. I'm surprised you made it this far without being apprehended."

Rianocek's stare was so intense, it was all that Fagan could do to keep himself from turning around and attempting to run back to the Buick, although he knew he'd never make it.

"You wouldn't want me in police custody, Dickie," Rianocek said in a voice dripping with menace. "I might decide to tell them all that I know about the actual inner workings of the American intelligence community. Especially the interesting connections between Langley, Colombia, and Panama."

Despite standing in such close proximity to one of the most dangerous men alive, Fagan managed an indignant "Is that why you wanted this meeting? To threaten *me,* Baron von Rianocek?"

The assassin looked from Fagan over at the Buick and then off into the distance at the floodlit Washington Monument. "It is un-becoming for men of our caliber and station to argue, Richard. Es-pecially with all of the confidences we share."

"So what can I do for you?"

"I need safe passage out of the country for myself and two others."

"Done."

"I also need you to take care of my recent problems with the New York City Police Department."

Although Fagan's stare was nowhere near as intense as the as-sassin's, it came close. "There are three dead cops back in New York, Baron von Rianocek, which had nothing to do with the reason we sent you there. The only thing I want to know is, why?"

Again Rianocek looked at the Washington Monument. He did not look back at Fagan as he replied, "Because I felt it was nec-essary. We all have our priorities in life." Now he *did* look at the CIA deputy director. "Don't we, Richard?"

Fagan didn't reply.

After a moment of protracted silence, the assassin said, "Are you going to do what I ask?"

"Consider it done. Check in at the Holiday Inn Capitol Mall using your Edmund Collins alias, and I'll take care of the rest. I assume you've made arrangements to obtain your lady friend's re-lease from NYPD custody?"

"I have. It should have been carried out by now."

"So we have no further business to discuss," Fagan said, turning away to return to the Buick. Before opening the car door, he stopped and once more faced the assassin. "Oh, and Baron, I think you should retire. I would also appreciate it if you stay away from me and any operations I'm engaged in."

Then CIA Deputy Director Richard "Dickie" Fagan got into the car and soon was gone.

45

There was a small group of commuters waiting at the gate for American Airlines Flight 1284 for Chicago when Larry Cole and Joe E. Leak arrived at LaGuardia Airport. Cole checked in with the attendant and joined Leak, who was standing by the windows overlooking the field. Anyone observing the two men would notice that there was a definite weariness surrounding them. A depth of fatigue that went beyond the physical and affected the spirit.

It had been a long night for Cole and Leak. They hadn't gotten any sleep and had seen the Rianocek investigation not only hit a dead end, but come crashing down around them.

They had just finished the Chicago-style pizza when Leak's phone rang again. When the assistant deputy commissioner returned to the dining room, Cole had taken one look at his friend's face and known that something was very wrong.

When they reached Bellevue Hospital, the two female officers who had been guarding Hannah Spencer had regained consciousness, but were very groggy. They had been treated in the emergency room and were being admitted to the hospital. At this stage of the investigation, the score was Rianocek and Company 6, NYPD 0.

Then the small brushfire turned into a raging inferno.

Major police departments in America have many similarities as far as their ranks, procedures, choice of weapons and, to some extent, even their uniforms. They also have something in common that is indicative of most Western bureaucracies when faced with a crisis. That something is called "fixing the blame," or "finger-pointing."

As Larry Cole looked on as a silent spectator, the "finger-pointing" by the NYPD brass began. And all of those fingers were pointed at his friend, Joe E. Leak.

A Bellevue conference room had been commandeered for the investigation. Leak had briefed Chief of Detectives Timothy Belcastle first. Belcastle looked as if he had been yanked from a deep slumber and had arrived at the hospital in a particularly foul mood. When he saw that Cole was still tagging along with Leak, Belcastle's mood deteriorated to the meltdown point.

"If you spent less time looking for help outside the NYPD and paid more attention to your job," the chief bellowed, "then we wouldn't be in this mess now, Leak!"

Barely able to control his own temper, Leak defended Cole. "Commander Cole was a definite asset to this investigation, Chief. Now we've not only got a motive for the M. D. Hines Building arson, but have also discovered some very interesting facts about this Alain Rianocek."

But Belcastle was not about to listen to reason. "All of this nonsense about an international assassin doesn't alter the fact that four New York police officers were killed and three more seriously injured today. And you don't have one single, solitary thing to show for it."

Cole could tell that Joe was close to exploding as he said, "What happened here with Hannah Spencer's escape was not my fault, sir. Obviously, there was no negligence. Our people were proceeding properly when they were overwhelmed by someone using chloroform. They had no defense against such an attack. In my estimation, they did all that they could."

It was at this point that Belcastle glared at Leak and said acidly, "Are you willing to stake your career on that 'estimation'?"

Then the police commissioner, the mayor and the media arrived. In the early hours of the morning on October 17, 1989, Bellevue

Hospital became the scene of a police/media circus. And in the center ring of this circus, the main attraction was pointing the finger of guilt at Assistant Deputy Commissioner Joseph E. Leak.

Now at the LaGuardia Airport gate, waiting for Flight 1284 bound for Chicago to board, Cole asked his friend, "Joe, are you going to be okay?"

Leak looked at Cole through tired, bloodshot eyes. "Things will work out, Larry. The commissioner and Belcastle will be hot under the collar for a while, but when they cool down and assess the situation logically, they'll be able to see that we are right about Rianocek. Then what happened at the hospital this morning will be forgotten, and we can bring in the Bavarian baron and his murderous crew and charge them all with multiple counts of murder."

"I hope so," Cole said. "But I still feel bad leaving you at a time like this."

Leak managed a smile. "Don't sweat it. Like you said, it goes with the territory."

A few minutes later, Cole boarded the plane for the flight home. En route, he thought about the case he was leaving behind in New York. Little did he know at the time, but Joe Leak was right about one thing and wrong about another.

The police commissioner and Chief Timothy Belcastle would indeed calm down and realize that Leak was not to blame for Hannah Spencer's escape. They were also not about to sack their best detective commander. But Joe Leak was wrong about being able to go after Rianocek. In fact, when the heat was off and Leak raised the issue with Belcastle, the assistant deputy commissioner would be strictly prohibited from looking into the matter any further. When Leak inquired politely as to the reason why, he was given the catch-all admonition, "Because it is in the interests of national security."

PART

"That drug plant is like something out of a
bizarre nightmare."
—Eurydice Vaughn, posing as Edna Gray

46

In the decade that passed following the aborted pursuit of assassin Alain Rianocek in New York City, the careers of Larry Cole and Joe E. Leak continued to skyrocket. Both men had risen to the ranks of chief of detectives of their respective agencies. They had solved their share of headline cases in the interim and were legends within law-enforcement circles.

Periodically, Cole and Leak talked on the telephone; however, they had not seen each other since the fall of 1989. Neither cop had forgotten Baron Alain Marcus Casimir von Rianocek. On the day that Leak was appointed NYPD chief of detectives, he called for the file on the three unsolved homicides of Detective Frank Azzoli and Police Officers Joe Johnson and Benjamin James McNamara. To his amazement, the investigations of their murders had stopped on the night of Hannah Spencer's escape. Joe Leak put the then-five-year-old files aside and promised himself that he would personally go back and resume the investigation himself. But the duties of his new office were too demanding. He never got the chance.

Back in Chicago, for Larry Cole, the memory of Alain Rianocek dimmed. Blackie Silvestri had compiled a folder containing information on the law firm of Barksdale, Barksdale, and DeVito, P.C., which was on Cole's desk when he returned to work. From all indications, the law firm was legitimate and had severed all connections to organized crime. But as the investigation in New York had stalled, the information on Barksdale, Barksdale, and DeVito, P.C., was worthless.

However, the events of the past were not isolated and would have great significance in the future. Larry Cole and Baron Alain Marcus Casimir von Rainoicek would confront each other again. Now Cole had an imminently pending collision with the affairs of Barksdale, Barksdale, and DeVito, P.C.

Cleveland Emmett Barksdale, Sr., had aged well, but not naturally. Twice a year, he received illegal injections containing extracts from the hearts and livers of human fetuses imported from China. Now he looked barely older than he had in 1977, as opposed to his current actual chronological age of eighty-two. He was almost completely bald and suffered from arthritis, making it necessary for him to walk with a cane; but other than that, he looked and felt exceptionally good.

Barksdale was seated in an easy chair in the lobby of the Barristers' Club on Plymouth Court in the Loop. The early crowd streamed past him on their way to meetings over breakfast in the many private dining rooms on the upper floors. A number of powerful, influential lawyers stopped to pay homage to Barksdale, who was the senior living Barristers' Club member. And the old man enjoyed every moment of the attention he received.

"Hello, Sam," he said to a well-dressed man who was a federal judge over at the Kluzynski Federal Building. "How's the family?"

"Bill," he called to another, "how's the wife? Give her my regards."

A young woman in a smart blue business suit strode up to him. "Penelope," Barksdale said with a smile, as she leaned down to kiss his cheek, "you get prettier every day. If you were a few years younger, I'd ask you to go dancing with me."

She laughed and asked, "Are you waiting for your grandson?"

"Yes," Barksdale said with a smile. "We're having one of those stuffy business breakfasts together. Seems like we only get together to talk business."

Penelope Josephson was one of the best criminal lawyers in the state, who had once been engaged to Barksdale's grandson. However, Clevey Barksdale had yet to satiate his voracious sexual appetite and was running around so much, Penelope had called off the wedding. She still remained close to her once-future grandfather-in-law.

"I'm sure that Clevey's quite busy," Penelope said with just a tad more emotion in her voice than had been present before.

Barksdale knew she would have been a good wife to Clevey and undoubtedly they would have produced many fine children. But with each passing day, fetal injections from China or not, Cleve Sr. realized that the odds of his seeing any great-grandchildren at all were becoming more and more remote.

"Well, here Clevey is now," she said, looking toward the entrance.

Barksdale followed her gaze. His heart swelled with pride and affection, as it always did when he set eyes on his grandson.

Cleveland Emmett Barksdale III was thirty-seven years old and radiated a charismatic aura that was so intense it seemed to possess physical dimensions. He was 6'5" but had shed the weight he carried, which enabled him to become an all-state linebacker in high school and then an all-American at Ohio State.

Clevey Barksale was selected in the third round of the NFL draft by the Denver Broncos; but after his last game as a Buckeye, he hung up his cleats and headed for Harvard Law School. Clevey was carrying out his part of the contract he had made with his grandfather years ago. When he earned his law degree and passed the bar exam, he entered the law firm as a full partner and the name was changed to Barksdale, Barksdale, and DeVito, P.C.

The "family business," as Clevey was fond of calling the law firm, had once more become exclusive and secretive. No one outside the firm knew exactly what type of law Barksdale, Barksdale, and DeVito, P.C., actually practiced. Upon joining the firm, Clevey had not only brought youth and enthusiam to the operation, but also some unique ways that the "family business" could make more money.

At Harvard, he had made a number of contacts. One of those contacts was a covert CIA operative named Richard "Dickie" Fagan.

Clevey walked up to his grandfather and Penelope Josephson with a broad smile etched on his handsome face. "I can tell that this is going to be a great day. After all, it's starting out with me seeing my two favorite people in the whole world."

Stepping forward, he grabbed Penelope by the shoulders and planted a lingering kiss on her lips. When he released her, she blushed. Then he hugged his grandfather.

Although the old man enjoyed the attention from the human being he loved most in the world—past or present—he blustered and said, "You must want something from us, Clevey, or you wouldn't be carrying on like this."

Clevey's grin never dimmed. "I've gotten more than anyone could ever ask from you, Granddad, and Penny knows how I feel about her."

"I've really got to go," she said with a tremble in her voice. Then, with tears in her eyes, she ran out of the Barristers' Club.

When she was gone, the old man chuckled, "You're just like I was with women at your age, Clevey. Just like I was."

Clevey helped his grandfather to his feet and, as they crossed the lobby to the elevators, he took the older man's arm. The two of them complimented each other. They acknowledged colleagues' greetings and once stopped to inquire into the health of a club member's ailing business partner.

They reached the elevators and boarded a car alone for their ride to the fourth floor for their private breakfast. The elder Barksdale still lived in the Beverly Hills mansion where Clevey had grown up. Now Barksdale was attended by a staff of servants, including a full-time nurse. He had not retired officially, but he no longer possessed the energy to go into the office every day. Clevey lived alone in a Lake Shore Drive penthouse apartment and was the law firm's managing partner. The younger Barksdale always kept his grandfather apprised of business developments. Today he had come not only to fill his grandfather in on one of their enterprises, but also to seek the senior attorney's approval to take action on a sensitive matter.

The elevator doors opened on the fourth-floor corridor. A number of the dining rooms on this floor had been donated by the Barksdales. The names of people who had been associates of Cleve and Clevey were on the private rooms. One room was dedicated to Joseph DeVito, Cleve's long-dead founding partner. The cost for dedicating each private dining room in the very exclusive Barristers' Club was $100,000. This morning the Barksdales were breakfasting in the Joseph DeVito Room.

A black white-jacketed waiter stood patiently at attention outside the private room door when they approached. He said diffidently, "Good morning, Mr. Barksdale, sir, and a good morning to you also, Mr. Barksdale."

"Good morning, Jimmy," Cleve said. "How's the family?"

The waiter grinned. "Granddaughter just had another one. That makes my sixth great-grandchild."

"Lucky you," Cleve said. "Clevey, make sure we send Jimmy's granddaughter some flowers and something nice for the baby."

"Thank you very much, sir," the waiter said.

Jimmy held the door for the two men and was about to follow them inside when Clevey stopped him. "Thanks, Jimmy, but my grandfather and I have some private business affairs to discuss. I can serve us. We'll signal you when we're through."

"Very good, Mr. Barksdale," the waiter said. Then he bowed and was gone.

The Joseph DeVito Room could have accommodated breakfast

for fifty but now contained only a lone white cloth-covered table with place settings for two. A steam table containing breakfast food, a coffee urn, and a buffet table containing glasses, along with iced pitchers of orange juice, tomato juice, and water, were arranged along one wall. A selection of breakfast pastries and croissants was also available.

Clevey Barksdale watched his grandfather eat. The younger man took it as a good sign that the old man had such a hearty appetite; however, he knew that Cleve would fall asleep on the drive back to the South Side. Clevey didn't mind; his grandfather deserved a rest.

The Barksdale fortune was now close to being worth $1 billion dollars and was increasing every day, due to the enterprises of Barksdale, Barksdale, and DeVito, P.C. The sole beneficiaries of this fortune were Cleveland Emmett Barksdale III and his venerable grandfather.

Eventually, the inheritance would be Clevey's, but he dreaded the day when his grandfather would finally leave this world.

Cleve Barksdale cleaned the last bit of scrambled egg from his plate and shoved it into his mouth. Then the old man dabbed his lips with a linen napkin, took a sip of coffee, and looked across at his grandson. There was a contented expression on the old man's face.

"Did you have enough?" Clevey asked. The young man had completed his own, less substantial, breakfast a few moments earlier.

"I think I'll have a small slice of that pecan coffee cake and some orange juice."

Clevey got up and returned to the buffet. A moment later he set a large slice of the pastry and a water tumbler full of orange juice in front of his grandfather.

Cleve frowned. "How in the hell am I supposed to eat all of this, Clevey?!"

"Eat what you can, Grandfather," Clevey said patiently. "Just leave the rest."

"Wasting food is a sin," the elder Barksdale said, picking up his knife and fork and cutting into the coffee cake.

Clevey waited a moment before saying, "Are you ready to hear about our current difficulties?"

Cleve swallowed a bite of coffee cake and nodded.

"Sylvester Merrill has been causing our operation some dangerous problems."

"Such as?" Cleve Barksdale said, swallowing the coffee cake and chasing it with a generous gulp of orange juice. Some of the juice dripped down his chin.

Clevey came forward quickly to wipe the liquid off his grandfather's face before it could stain his immaculately pressed suit.

Then the younger man explained, "A shipment of our product, possessing a weak chemical consistency, was shipped to Los Angeles. This is the third time in the last month that a shipment has been wrong."

The Barksdales did not only endow rooms in the Barristers' Club to honor the memories of dead colleagues. This room was guaranteed to be soundproof and secure.

The handsome young lawyer continued. "Our regional brokers and a number of dealers on the West Coast have begun complaining. There is talk of a war, but our emissaries have given them assurances that things will be rectified, so the situation remains stable."

Clevey Barksdale finished his speech and watched his grandfather continue to consume coffee cake and orange juice. There was no indication that he had either understood or even heard what the managing partner of Barksdale, Barksdale, and DeVito, P.C., had said. But then, that wasn't necessary.

If his grandfather commented, then Clevey would do what he was told. If the senior partner of Barksdale, Barksdale, and DeVito, P.C., had nothing to say, then Clevey would do it his own way.

Cleve finished all of the coffee cake and the orange juice. Then he pushed himself back from the table and looked at his grandson. There was an expression of amusement tinged with surprise on the old man's face. Then he spoke. "Has Dr. Merrill begun using the product he has been manufacturing for us in such an excellent manner over the past few years?"

"It is almost a certainty, Grandfather."

The older Barksdale tossed his napkin on the table and sat back in his chair. He shook his head, sighed deeply, and said, "We gave Sly everything. A new life, prosperity, and money. Now this is how he repays us?"

"I'm sorry, Granddad," Clevey said. "It was my fault that this happened. I recommended Merrill personally. I accept his failure as my responsibility."

"How are you going to handle it?" Cleve asked.

"I was going to give the job to Shelton Booker of the Peace Stones."

"Good," Cleve said. "But make sure the security of the plant is maintained and Booker doesn't make a mess of things."

"I'll take care of everything, sir," Clevey assured the older man. "Would you like another cup of coffee before we go?"

Cleve shrugged. "Why not?"

47

D r. Sylvester "Sly" Merrill was a short, plump man with a bald head and froglike features set in an ebony face. He kept irregular working hours, as it was best for the business he managed not to be operated on a predictable schedule. He pulled his black Mercedes up to the gate set in a cyclone fence, which surrounded the white-painted Barksdale Manufacturing Company building located in the 7300 block of South Chicago Avenue. The fence was electrically charged, and the gate could be opened only by the application of a remote-control device. After shutting off the juice to the fence and activating the remote mechanism from inside his car, Merrill drove onto the blacktop yard surrounding the building. The gate shut automatically behind him.

Merrill pulled up to a loading dock, shuttered securely by an impregnable metal door. His remote-control device opened this door as well. He got out of the Mercedes, walked to the loading dock, and entered the building. He activated the "close door" function on the remote device, which also turned on the lights throughout the 30,000-foot interior.

Merrill entered the main section of the plant. The area was devoid of any equipment, furnishings, or material. The heels of his shoes echoed throughout the empty structure. He was alone.

At the far end of the vacant area was an elevator door. It took a key to access, and he boarded the car to face a control panel with buttons mounted in descending order with the number "1" at the top, followed by "2" in the middle and "3" at the bottom. From the main floor, the car traveled in only one direction: down. The door sighed shut and, with nearly imperceptible motion and sound, the car descended twenty feet below street level.

When the doors opened again, Merrill stepped off the car and flicked a wall switch. Rows of fluorescent lights illuminated two long metal tables on a black tile floor. These tables contained computer terminals, pressure dials, thermal monitors, switches, and control levers. This was where Dr. Sylvester Merrill did his work as a chemist for the Barksdale Manufacturing Company.

This room, in the secret, secure subterranean structure, was the command center of the complex. Here, using computers and the most sophisticated robotic technology in existence, Dr. Sly Merrill assembled the product, which was located in its raw form in storage tanks on level 2 above the command center. Once everything was mixed mechanically and packaged properly, it was transported to the loading dock, where it would be picked up for shipment by members of the Peace Stones street gang. It was the Peace Stones who ensured that the product was delivered to wholesalers for distribution not only in Chicago, but all over the western hemisphere. To say the least, the Barksdale Manufacturing Company produced a very salable product.

Merrill entered instructions into a computer terminal, which caused the machinery on level 2 to begin humming. Although he still considered himself a high-tech chemist, Sly Merrill felt more like a mechanic or laborer. However, no laborer had ever been paid as much as the Barksdales paid him. The keyboard function and monitoring of the equipment dials was nearly automatic. Perhaps that was what had begun to bore Merrill and caused him to make a very critical error. He had started with small amounts before increasing to greater quantities of the cocaine he manufactured. Now he was an addict with a habit that was affecting his efficiency and threatening his job, as well as his life.

A graduate of the doctoral program in chemistry from M.I.T., Sylvester Merrill never considered the morality of what he was doing. He was paid to operate the largest drug-processing plant in the world. From behind its secure walls, the Barksdale Manufacturing Company produced a daily illegal-drug output greater than all of the South American nations exporting narcotics combined. It was also the largest purveyor of controlled substances in the world. As part of their very lucrative corporate legal practice and with the tacit protection of the U.S. government, through the nefarious, illicit operations of the Central Intelligence Agency, the Barksdales had upgraded the purveying of illegal substances from back-alley street dealing to a sophisticated corporate level.

Their operation was about to develop some very serious problems.

48

MARCH 22, 1999
12:16 P.M.

Joanna Bratton was a 90-pound, twenty-two-year-old junkie, alcoholic prostitute. Despite the problems of her existence, she considered herself lucky because she'd never contracted a venereal disease, didn't have AIDS, and had no children. She also thought of herself as smarter than the average street person. This caused her to play a very dangerous game of survival.

Joanna was a snitch for the cops, as well as the eyes on those same cops for Shelton "Bad Man" Booker, the leader of the notorious Peace Stones street gang. The Peace Stones were one of the most vicious and violent criminal organizations in Chicago.

On this chilly, overcast afternoon, Joanna, wearing the ragged waist-length leather jacket she'd worn all winter, walked with a rapid stride under the refurbished elevated train tracks on East 63rd

Street. Beneath the jacket she had on a skimpy halter top and child-size jeans that clung to her emaciated legs as if they'd been painted on, leaving no doubt in anyone's mind as to what she was advertising. Her high-heeled black shoes made her skinny figure appear as if it were on stilts; however, she managed to make steady progress. Her haggard face revealed that she'd had a hit of something potent enough to dim her eyes to half-mast before she began this journey.

At the corner of 63rd Street and Dorchester Avenue, she turned south. The entire area was being renovated from the rat-infested slums the Woodlawn area of Chicago had been for the last fifty years into an upscale neighborhood dotted with new luxury housing aimed at attracting young professionals back from the suburbs.

At 64th Street, Joanna turned east to pass under the elevated Illinois Central tracks. At the midpoint of the viaduct, a dark brown, official-looking Chevrolet was parked. Joanna walked up to the police car, opened the back door, and got in.

Tommy Becker and Mike Castigliano were sitting in the front seat. They were Gang Crimes cops assigned to the South Side, fairly new to this plainclothes assignment, and eager to make their mark on the squad. They had cultivated Joanna Bratton as their personal, confidential informant (CI) when they learned that she was one of Shelton Booker's on-again, off-again girlfriends.

Becker and Castigliano were white and had survived strenuous, very thorough prehire psychological testing, as well as intensive training at the Chicago Police Academy in the intricacies of cultural diversity across the multiracial, multinational population of Chicago. This should have imbued them with a greater respect, or at least wariness, for the 90-pound junkie. They didn't suspect that she was a great deal more cunning than either of them gave her credit for being. It wasn't that Tommy and Mike were racists, they were simply new to the job and naïve. But they were learning fast.

"So tell us what's happening, Mama?" Castigliano thought that he was a dead ringer for Emilio Estevez.

Joanna sniffled noisily. "Bad Man's got a hit going down to-day."

"Where and when?" Becker said, turning around in his seat to stare at her. He was the all-American-boy type, who would have looked more natural in a high-school senior-class photograph than on a Windy City Gang Crimes squad.

"Up north of Forty-seventh Street," she responded. "He's going to do some Vice Lords for messing with one of his shipments. I hear the house the Peace Stones are going to hit is at Forty-third and Lake Park. The deal is supposed to go down at one o'clock."

Castigliano frowned, but made no comment.

"Where did you get your information, Joanna?" Becker asked.

She waved her hand through the air in a cross gesture. "It's all over the streets out here, white boy. If you all would get out of the car sometimes and listen to what folks got to say, you'd know what was going down."

Becker turned red and was about to respond angrily when Castigliano held up his hand. "Pay the lady, partner."

Becker looked skeptical for a moment before finally reaching into his shirt pocket and removing a $10 bill. The CI's payment came out of the cops' own pockets. If something came of the information, they would request a reimbursement from the Gang Crimes Unit's contingency fund. The cop tossed the bill unceremoniously in the prostitute's lap.

"Okay, Joanna," Castigliano said. "Thanks for the tip."

The fleeting sneer of contempt crossed her face too quickly for the cops to detect. Then she balled up the $10 bill in her hand and got out of the car.

After she was gone, a few minutes passed before Tommy Becker said, "So what do you think?"

Castigliano stared sightlessly out the windshield for a time before finally saying, "I think our girl's selling us a bill of goods, partner."

"Why?"

"That's b.s. about Bad Man going after the Vice Lords. The gang truce between the Peace Stones and the Lords has been in effect now for over eight months. On top of that, if someone *did* mess with one of the Stones' dope shipments, it wouldn't be talked about out on the streets. We'd have dead bodies all over the South Side."

"Why do you think she lied to us?"

"Remember the last time she gave us a bum steer?"

"Yeah, she told us there was a hit going down on Seventy-fifth Street, and the Peace Stones took out the leader of the Disciples over on West Fifty-ninth."

"Exactly," Castigliano said with a grin. "So, there's a possibility girlfriend's sending us in the opposite direction from where the action's really going down again."

"How do you want to play it?"

Castigliano's face took on a look that made him appear instantly older and wiser. "We keep an eye on Mr. Bad Man Booker's van. When it moves, we follow."

"Got you," Officer Tommy Becker said with a grin.

49

MARCH 22, 1999
12:32 P.M.

Shelton Booker was 6'4" and weighed 320 pounds. He was a light-complexioned black man with freckles and red hair "permed" back into a pompadour off his forehead. A rival once commented that "Bad Man," which was Booker's street name, looked like either a pimp or a fifties rock star. He aspired to be neither. In fact, he wanted nothing more from life than to die rich.

If pimping or singing could have gotten him the cash, Booker would have gone into those fields; however, the only road to riches he'd ever discovered was by way of the violence of the Chicago streets.

Booker was thirty-seven years old and had been the leader of the Peace Stones since his predecessor had gone to jail. Bad Man had personally killed the only serious rival for the position.

Booker's job was to oversee the activities of the gang, whose members were recruited from the streets of the city's ghettos.

He ran the gang with an iron fist and controlled all of his followers' activities, but his was not the last word when it came to the operations of the Peace Stones. Bad Man Booker had a boss. This "boss" actually dictated the flow of narcotics not only in Chicago but, if Bad Man's suspicions were correct, all over the country. The gang leader had never set eyes on this mystery man but was well aware that he was extremely powerful. Powerful enough to ensure the transportation of vast quantities of narcotics anywhere in the world without interference from the cops—local, state or federal. Powerful enough to arrange bond or legal representation for any arrested gang member on a moment's notice. Powerful enough to mastermind the escape of anyone he wished from federal correctional facilities, state prisons, or local jails. A man capable of keeping tabs on every move Booker or the Peace Stones made while keeping his identity secret.

To Booker, the "boss" existed as a voice on the telephone. A voice which could purr with pleasure or rumble with anger. A voice whose orders Bad Man Booker followed explicitly, because doing otherwise would result in certain death.

Now the head of the Peace Stones had received a telephone call from his "boss." Booker was the only one authorized to receive such calls, and the voice on the other end of the line had given him an order. He was to kill a man. The hit was to go down today. The target could be located at the factory on South Chicago Avenue, where his gang picked up the narcotics shipments. Booker had been there many times before but had never been inside. The shipments were in plain cardboard boxes stacked outside on the loading dock, along with specific delivery instructions.

Bad Man was given a name and description of the man he was ordered to kill. He was further instructed to keep everything simple. Just take the man somewhere and kill him. The body was to be left some distance from the South Chicago address. Booker was also told that he would need a remote-control device to deactivate the electrified fence that surrounded the factory. He had never been given such a device before. In the past, whenever there were shipments to be picked up, the gate was left open. As usual, the gang leader and his men were strictly forbidden from entering the factory building itself. The requisite device was delivered by a Loop messenger service to the gang leader's residence less than thirty minutes after the call from the "boss" was received.

Booker lived in a new town house on Sixty-fourth Street in the Woodlawn area. It was a three-bedroom unit consisting of a living room, dining room, and two baths. The unit sold for over $500,000, and Bad Man had paid cash for it. The neighbors on either side of the gang leader were a gynecologist, who was on staff at the University of Chicago Hospital, and a real estate broker, who was seldom at home. Booker's unit was encirled by a six-foot-tall wooden fence, which concealed his property from prying eyes. There was a two-car garage at the rear of the town house, which exited onto a paved alley. Booker's silver GMC van, with the painting of a cowboy riding a galloping horse across a desert mesa stenciled on the side, was parked in the garage next to a custom-made canary yellow two-seater Cadillac Seville.

As it approached 1:00 P.M., the leader of the Peace Stones and two of his most-trusted lieutenants prepared for action. The henchmen were dressed in dark business suits with white shirts and dark ties. They carried black leather attaché cases containing fully loaded, thirty-round-clip, automatic machine pistols with four extra magazines.

Booker was also dressed in a business suit, although he wore a mauve tie adorned with a pattern of rook and knight chess pieces. The gang leader always sought to stand out from the crowd, thus his desire to make a great deal of money by any means necessary. Also, unlike his two lieutenants, Bad Man was not armed with an automatic weapon. Instead he carried a .357 nickel-plated Colt Python six-inch barrel revolver with a custom-carved ivory handle. It was loaded with M-39 armor-piercing bullets, which were made especially for this weapon. Booker had owned the Python for fifteen years and had murdered fourteen people with it. To Shelton "Bad Man" Booker, killing was something extremely personal, therefore he had chosen his gun with the same care which an artist would use to select a paint brush, a musician an instrument, or a writer a pen.

The three gang members were about to enter the silver van when Booker stopped. Facing the lieutenants, he said, "This is the drill. We're to take this guy at the factory. Afterwards, we'll dump his body in a lot out in Hegewisch in the same area where we got rid of Mack Jackson."

Mack Jackson had been Booker's chief rival for leadership of the Peace Stones. His bloated, decomposing body had been found in a vacant field. The enormous hole in the dead man's head was caused by an M-39 armor-piercing round fired from a .357 magnum at close range.

"Any questions?" Booker asked his lieutenants.

There were none. One of the lieutenants drove. Booker sat in the front bucket seat beside him. They were headed for the 7300 block of South Chicago Avenue.

50

Gang Crimes Officers Tommy Becker and Mike Castigliano were parked a half block away when Bad Man Booker's van pulled out of the alley. They watched it proceed west to the nearest cross street and make a left.

"He's going south," Castigliano said. "Looks like our CI lied to us. Let's go, partner."

Maintaining a discreet distance, Becker put the police car in gear and followed.

51

The work was going well for the chemist. He was almost finished mixing the daily shipment. In actuality he had been a bit off in his calculations and the product was a bit more potent than what was desired. Had Sly known of the discrepancy he would figure that he could get by with it. He was wrong.

So he decided that it was time for a reward. Removing a cellephane envelope containing the white powder that now ruled his life and a small spoon from his attaché case, he prepared to snort himself into a euphoric oblivion.

Before he'd become a drug addict, Sly Merrill had possessed a genius IQ. He had been born in the Robert Taylor public-housing development, which was one of the most violent and poverty-stricken areas in the country. He'd never seen his father, and his mother had supported her brood of nine children by way of the Cook County public aid system. The chances of the young Sylvester escaping the cycle of societal oppression were not very good, but he had been fortunate.

The Chicago Public School system has often been vilified for undereducating its charges. But the grammar school that the child from the welfare household attended in the shadows of the monstrous sixteen-story project buildings worked hard to not only educate its students, but also identify the more gifted for special attention. Sly Merrill was such a student.

There were a great many things that the black chemist had forgotten during his forty-one years of life. Among them were his mother, brothers, and sisters, whose names he could no longer recall. The grammar school, where he had been identified as mentally gifted, was now only a vague memory. The classes that he had attended to earn the degrees that had brought him the wealth and position he currently enjoyed were like something that had been experienced by someone else. Everything that he was and had been was a blur. A white blur caused by the cocaine he injested in near-lethal proportions.

When he first went to work at the Barksdale Manufacturing Company, he had thought himself too smart to fall into the trap of drug addiction. After all, he had come out of a neighborhood where every other person encountered on the streets was an addict and overdose victim death rates were as high as those for gang violence.

However, being in such close proximity to large quantities of narcotics, along with some degree of suppressed guilt, drove Sly

Merrill to first sample and then become a frequent user of the de-spised product. This had led to a rapid deterioration in the chemist's ability to do his job competently. So the CEO of Barksdale Man-ufacturing was about to terminate Sylvester Merrill's employment and his life. A replacement for the chemist had already been se-lected.

Now, as Sly snorted the cocaine up his nose, he failed to notice activity on one of the security monitors scanning the exterior of the building. The chemist would have been alarmed to see the remote-controlled gate in the electrically charged fence swing open and a silver GMC van, with a cowboy riding across a desert mesa etched on its side, drive onto the property. As Sly Merrill snorted himself into a state of oblivion, his assassination began to unfold.

52

MARCH 22, 1999
1:00 P.M.

Ain't this the place where we pick up the shipments?" the Peace Stone lieutenant driving the van asked Shelton Booker.

The gang leader sneered. "Don't concern yourself with 'where' we are. Just do what I tell you."

At that moment Sly Merrill came out of the factory. In his drugged state he didn't see the GMC van. Slowly, the chemist began making his way across the loading dock.

Booker and the gang member who had ridden shotgun got out of the van and advanced rapidly toward the factory. Sly heard their footsteps and turned around. When he saw them, his eyes went wide with terror.

"Hold it a minute, buddy," Booker said in a non-threatening

tone, as he closed the distance separating him from his intended victim.

It took only a glance for Sly to notice that the intruders had weapons down at their sides. Turning, he ran back toward the factory.

"Shit!" Booker hissed, raising his nickel-plated magnum. Lining up the front and rear sights of his revolver on Sly's back, he pulled the trigger twice. The M-39 explosive rounds smashed into Sly and propelled him ten feet to slam into a brick wall. The discharged rounds sounded as if they had been fired from a howitzer. The gang lieutenant walking beside Booker was temporarily deafened, so he didn't hear Bad Man say, "Those shots must've been heard for blocks. Somebody's going to call the cops. We've got to move the body. C'mon, give me a hand."

The dark-suited gang member stood in dumbfounded silence and stared quizzically back at his boss. Then the brown unmarked police car containing Officers Becker and Castigliano skidded to a stop behind Booker's van in the factory parking lot. As the two Gang Crimes officers got out of the car, the gang member in the van, the one accompanying the trigger man, and Bad Man Booker all turned their weapons on the cops and opened fire.

53

MARCH 22, 1999
1:06 P.M.

Chicago Police Department Chief of Detectives Larry Cole had been the guest speaker at the "career day" conference at his high-school alma mater. Mount Carmel, where Cole had been an all-city defensive back in the mid-seventies, was located at 6410

South Dante Street. This was less than half a block from the spot under the Illinois Central Railroad viaduct where Gang Crimes Officers Becker and Castigliano had met with their CI, Joanna Bratton.

The speech was enthusiastically applauded by the attending students. Afterward, the school principal, Father David Dillon, walked with Cole as he left the student center. Lieutenant Blackie Silvestri, who had accompanied the chief to the school, was at the wheel of the black unmarked Chevrolet police car parked at the curb.

"Thank you for taking the time to come out and talk to our students, Chief Cole," the priest said. "You really had them fascinated with those stories about dangerous police work on the streets of the Windy City."

"I appreciate your invitation, Father." Cole shook the priest's hand. The policeman hesitated before getting into the car and looked at the front of the main school building a short distance away. Memories from his high-school days came back to him. He recalled the tall, thin kid with the skinny legs that he had been all those years ago running to football practice. Would he recognize that young man if he saw him now?

Finally he got into the car and said to Blackie, "C'mon, I'll buy you lunch."

The lieutenant stuck the stub of a cigar back into the corner of his mouth and replied, "This must be my lucky day, Boss."

They ate at the drive-thru White Castle restaurant at 79th Street and South Chicago Avenue. After displaying initial surprise at Cole taking him to lunch at this place, Blackie's face split into a broad grin. He ordered eight cheeseburgers with mustard and extra pickles, a large order of fries, and a liter container of orange soda.

Cole asked, "You weren't ordering for both of us, were you?"

"C'mon, Boss," Blackie protested, " 'sliders' are so small that I've got to eat at least four of them to equal one regular-sized burger."

Cole ordered four burgers and a cup of coffee for himself.

Blackie drove the car into a far corner of the White Castle parking lot, where they began consuming this high-calorie but tasty lunch.

"You know," Blackie said between burgers, "in all the time that we've been working together, I never knew that you liked White Castles."

"I haven't had one in years, but when we were back at Carmel, I remembered that Mack and I used to stop by here sometimes after football practice."

Clarence "Mack" McKinnis had been an all-state linebacker at Mount Carmel and went on to a sterling career at Notre Dame before playing a few years of pro ball. Then he had joined Larry Cole on the Chicago Police Department. In 1996, Sergeant McKinnis had been shot to death by serial killer Neil Dewitt.

Blackie was about to make a comment about the dead police officer when two loud reports echoed from off in the distance. There was a moment of silence before a virtual cacophony of shots echoed through the cool spring air.

Without a word, Cole and Blackie closed their drinks and put away what was left of their hamburgers. They didn't speak because they didn't have to. They also didn't have to speculate over whether what they'd heard were indeed gunshots or backfires from a truck. The two policemen had too much street experience for that. A backfire and a gunshot were both explosions of a sort; however, a backfire made more of a popping noise, whereas gunshots from heavy-powder-charge, high-velocity weapons possessed more of a crack.

Blackie pulled the black Chevy with the buggy-whip antenna from the parking lot and made a left onto South Chicago. He was traveling northwest in the direction from which gunshots still came. Now the loud reports were clear enough for the two cops to accurately home in on their location.

"Somebody has sure declared war," Blackie said, accelerating the police car.

Cole reached for the police radio concealed in the glove compartment. Keying the mike, he said, "Car Fifty, emergency."

"Go, Car Fifty," the dispatcher responded.

"We've got 'shots fired' in the vicinity of Seventy-fifth to approximately Seventy-third on South Chicago Avenue. This unit is operating 'ten-four' in civilian dress." The "ten-four" designation told the dispatcher that they were a two-man car.

"Acknowledged, Car Fifty," the dispatcher said. *"Be advised that Gang Crimes Beat 4244 has called a 'ten-one' at 7332 South Chicago Avenue. Forty-two forty-four is reportedly under fire, and a civilian has been shot. Use extreme caution, Car Fifty."*

Unkeying the mike, Cole said, "We always do."

54

MARCH 22, 1999
1:03P.M.

Gang Crimes Officers Becker and Castigliano were pinned down. They were fortunate that they had the time to get out of their police car and take cover behind it before the three Peace Stones opened fire on them. In the first spray of bullets from one of the machine pistols, Castigliano was hit in the left thigh and right arm. He screamed as he landed on the ground behind his partner. Becker was wildly and ineffectively returning fire with a .45 Smith & Wesson automatic.

Shelton Booker and his men took cover behind the van. They began concentrating their shots on the police car, which was rapidly becoming dotted with bullet holes. With each passing second the chances of more cops showing up increased dramatically. Booker was about to jump into the van, use it as a battering ram to back into the police car, shove it out of the way, and make a run for it. The gang leader reloaded the six-inch barrel Python from a speed loader containing M-39, armor-piercing rounds and was about to initiate his escape plan when a black Chevy skidded to a stop just inside the gate, flanking the gang members.

Frantically, Booker swung his gun to bear on the new arrival and opened fire.

55

MARCH 22, 1999
1:04 P.M.

Booker's first M-39 armor-piercing round destroyed the left front tire of Cole's car before tearing into the front quarter-panel and smashing the engine block. His second round missed the police vehicle completely and traveled half a mile to embed itself in the trunk of a ninety-seven-year-old tree. The point of entry left a six-inch-diameter hole in the wood. The third round blew out the car's windshield; however, by this time Cole and Blackie had taken cover behind the car and were returning fire.

Cole leveled his Beretta's sights on one of the Peace Stone lieutenants, who was still shooting at the Gang Crimes car. The chief's bullet smashed through the gang member's sternum and clipped his aorta. He fell to the ground with blood beginning to flood his chest cavity. In a matter of seconds he was dead.

Booker's next three rounds did massive damage to the black command vehicle. The explosive projectiles tore gaping holes in the car's body, pulverizing windows, gouging pieces out of the frame, and deflating the remaining tires. Other than being sprayed with flying glass, Cole and Blackie were unhurt.

Then Becker got Gang Crimes on the board when one of his bullets struck the other Peace Stone lieutenant in the shoulder. Dropping his gun, the gang member climbed inside Booker's van, curled into a fetal ball, and, clutching his wound, began whimpering softly.

Shelton Booker reloaded the Python with his final speed loader, which contained only two M-39 rounds. The other four bullets were standard .38s. The three cops concentrated their fire on the position that the gang leader had retreated to behind the dead Sly Merrill's Mercedes. To Booker it was as if he'd been caught in a hornets' nest. Hornets with lead skins. Then the sound of buzzing bullets was joined by another distinctive noise. This was one of police sirens rapidly approaching the South Chicago factory. As his escape opportunities evaporated, the gang leader decided on the more logical of the two alternatives facing him, surrender. The only other option was certain death.

With no regard for the nickel plating and ivory handle of his weapon, the gang leader tossed it over the hood of the Cadillac. It landed with a clatter on the paved surface of the factory lot. Booker screamed, "Hey, cops, stop shooting! I give up!"

Cole and Blackie stopped firing immediately. Becker let two more rounds go before halting as well. The exterior of the Barksdale Manufacturing Company became quiet. The only sound still evident in the wake of the gun battle was the continuing wail of approaching sirens.

56

The area around 7332 South Chicago Avenue had taken on the appearance of a war zone. Police cars and ambulances were parked and double-parked in every available space in the alley and on the streets surrounding the factory. Under the guidance of the chief of detectives and Lieutenant Blackie Silvestri, the area behind the factory had been cordoned off with barrier tape. Wounded Officer Mike Castigliano and the surviving Peace Stone were being stabilized inside ambulances before being transported from the scene to nearby hospitals. Shelton "Bad Man" Booker was handcuffed securely and seated in the rear of a marked police vehicle. A uniformed officer stood guard over the gang leader. Paramedics had examined the dead black man found on the loading dock and the dead Peace Stone; however, it was obvious that nothing could be done for them. A police wagon was called and waited for the crime lab to finish processing the scene before removing the bodies.

A crowd had gathered and was watching the cops with silent curiosity. The news media had yet to put in an appearance, but their arrival was expected imminently.

After giving their initial orders, Cole and Blackie stood back to watch the officers work. The responding cops knew their jobs, and they all worked quickly and efficiently. In half an hour, maybe less, everything would be wrapped up here. Then the follow-up would try to answer the question. Why had this happened?

Reading his boss's contemplative expression, Blackie said, "So what do you think?"

Cole responded, "This was a gang hit, just as Becker from Gang Crimes told us. Our man over there"—Cole nodded to the police car where the stony-faced gang leader was caged—"isn't about to tell us anything. In fact, I doubt if he knows much about why this went down anyway."

Cole paused a moment and then turned around to look at the facade of the Barkedale Manufacturing Company. "I'd say the answers to our questions are in there."

"And I'd say"—Blackie removed a crooked Parodi cigar from his pocket and shoved it into the corner of his mouth—"that you're absolutely right. Of course, that's why you're the boss, Boss."

With that, the two cops headed for the loading dock where the body of Sly Merrill still lay under a plastic sheet.

57

MARCH 22, 1999
2:00 P.M.

Cleve Barksdale finished eating lunch in the dining room of his Beverly Hills mansion on the South Side of Chicago. As the maid began clearing away the dishes, the old man got up from the table, went into his study, and locked the door behind him. Crossing the book-lined room, he sat down behind his desk. He unlocked the center desk drawer. Inside were an ashtray, a package of Carlton 100 menthol cigarettes, and a disposable lighter.

Cleve was not supposed to be smoking at all, and Clevey had given his grandfather's live-in nurse strict instructions to confiscate any tobacco products she found in his possession. Of course, the retired lawyer had led a devious life and easily managed to deceive not only the nurse, but also his grandson.

The elder Barksdale fired up a cigarette and took a deep drag, which made him cough. Removing a handkerchief from his pocket, he wiped his eyes, which had become irritated by the smoke. Despite this, Cleve had every intention of finishing his after-lunch smoke.

To keep himself company, while he engaged in his health-damaging pastime, Barksdale used a remote-control device to turn on the television set across the room. He wasn't really paying any attention to the program being broadcast, as the nicotine was starting to make him light-headed. Then a voice from the set managed to break through the tobacco haze surrounding him.

"Please stand by for a special news bulletin."

Cleve's eyes drifted to the TV. A "Special Bulletin" announcement filled the screen. Idly, Barksdale watched, wondering what type of disaster had occurred now.

As the subject of the "Special Bulletin" began to unfold, Cleve Barksdale forgot his cigarette. He became so engrossed in watching the events on the screen that he unconsciously dropped the still-smoldering butt to the floor, where it burned a large, irreparable hole in the priceless Persian carpet. Ignoring the odor of burning cloth, Barksdale picked up the telephone and pushed a "direct dial" button, which connected him automatically to his grandson's office. The old man's stare of horror never left the TV.

Clevey was sitting at his desk preparing to call Shelton Booker when the private line rang. Only a select few possessed the number, which was equipped with a scrambler. Deputy Director Dickie Fagan of the CIA was one such select person. His grandfather was another.

"What's up, Granddad?"

"Turn on Channel Nine."

"I beg your pardon?"

Although Cleve Barksdale's voice did not rise above a conversational level, there was a definite edge present as he repeated, *"Clevey, turn on the TV."*

"Yes, sir."

The old man had never called him before just to tell him to watch a television program. Something very serious must have happened.

Switching on the set in his office, Clevey turned to Channel Nine. Immediately, the face of John T. Govich, the Chicago Police Superintendent, appeared on the screen. There were microphones thrust in his face and he was standing outdoors. *". . . drug-processing plant, possibly the largest in the world."*

Behind Govich, Clevey could see the Barksdale Manufacturing Company, with cops running back and forth from inside the building, across the loading dock and into the parking area inside the fence. The gate stood open. Clevey was too stunned to think. Apparently, Shelton Booker had indeed made a terrible mess of things.

Off-screen reporters were questioning Govich.

"How did the police find out about this place, Superintendent?"

Govich responded, *"Larry Cole, my chief of detectives, Lieutenant Blackie Silvestri, who is assigned to Cole's staff, and Gang Crimes Officers Thomas Becker and Michael Castigliano responded to shots being fired at this location. Apparently, this place was the scene of a gang execution."*

"Who was killed?"

"Before releasing that information to the press I'm going to make sure that the relatives of that individual are notified," Govich said.

"Who are the alleged killers?"

"We have a suspect known as Shelton Booker in custody. Mr. Booker goes by the street name 'Bad Man' and he is reputedly the leader of the Peace Stones street gang."

In his LaSalle Street law office, Clevey Barksdale groaned.

"Was there anyone else injured?"

"A police officer suffered gunshot wounds to the leg and arm.

He's been admitted to the hospital in guarded condition. We're withholding his name pending notification of his next-of-kin. The other wounded individual is in police custody. He is a twenty-four-year-old black male, who suffered a gunshot wound to his left shoulder. We have not identified him yet."

Clevey knew that the dead man was Sly Merrill. Now not only was the factory compromised and millions of dollars of product gone, but the entire operation was imperiled. Also, Shelton Booker was alive and in police custody. Although the leader of the Peace Stones always carried himself like such a big, tough, stand-up guy, when the cops started laying life imprisonment with no chance of parole or the prospects of a lethal injection on him, the so-called "Bad Man's" backbone would turn to jelly.

A reporter asked a question that snapped Clevey back to the television screen. *"Superintendent Govich, was it necessary for the police to make a forced entry into the building?"*

"Not at all," Govich said confidently. *"When Chief Cole and the other officers arrived on the scene, that building was wide open, with the victim's body lying up there on the loading dock."* The camera switched to the chalk outline of a body on the cement surface of the loading dock. Govich continued, *"The officers conducted an investigation, which quite naturally took them inside to make sure that no one in there required assistance as a result of the violence which had occurred out here."*

"Who discovered that it was a drug-processing plant?" another reporter asked.

"Chief Larry Cole and Lieutenant Cosimo Silvestri."

Sergeants Manfred Wolfgang "Manny" Sherlock and Judy Daniels, also known as the Mistress of Disguise/High Priestess of Mayhem, were forced to park their police car in a bus stop at 73rd and South Chicago and proceed to the Barksdale Manufacturing Company on foot. Security had been put into place to keep the media and the curious from entering the property, where the investigation was still in progress. Flashing their badges to a pair of uniformed policemen stationed at the front gate, Manny and Judy crossed the blacktop to the factory entrance.

Judy drew a number of curious stares, as she wore a long ponytail hanging to the middle of her back and had on an enormous pair of horn-rimmed glasses. She was wearing a blue jumper over a white blouse, black flat shoes, and a waist-length black leather jacket. Carrying a black leather portfolio under her arm, she looked more like a high-school student than a police officer.

They were given directions to the descending elevator and a few minutes later joined Cole, Govich, and Blackie on sublevel 3.

"I've got the information you wanted, Boss," Judy said to Cole. Placing her portfolio on top of a computer console, she removed a stack of papers from it and handed them to the chief of detectives. As Cole scanned them, she explained, "The property is managed by Park City Realty, which has an office at 300 East 61st Street. Manny and I went over there and talked to the manager, Mrs. Jacqueline Moore. At first she started making noise about client confidentiality and demanded to see a warrant. But Manny took care of that."

"How?" Cole asked.

The baby-faced sergeant shrugged. "I told her in a nice way that we were investigating a homicide on the property and that there was also evidence of a wholesale drug operation being run from inside the factory." The sergeant paused for a moment. "I might have mentioned a thing or two about possible charges of conspiracy to commit murder and her being named in a grand-jury indictment as an accessory to the distribution of controlled substances."

"But you didn't threaten her?" Govich smiled.

Manny's expression of wide-eyed innocence made Blackie cover his mouth to keep from laughing, as the sergeant replied, "Oh, no, sir, I would never do such a thing."

Judy interjected quickly, "So she gave us copies of the file Park

City Realty was keeping on the property." She pointed at the papers Cole was holding.

Cole began reading and, as they watched, his eyes widened in surprise.

"What is it, Larry?" Govich asked.

"This place has been owned by a gentleman by the name of Cleveland Emmett Barksdale, Esquire, since May of 1969. He has listed the types of businesses operated here as a toy manufacturer, machine shop, and currently a storage facility."

"Haven't I heard of this Barksdale before?" Govich asked.

Cole responded, "He was Rabbitt Arcadio's attorney back in 1977, when me and Blackie blew away Frankie Arcadio."

"Barksdale and DeVito, P.C." Blackie exclaimed, snapping his fingers loudly as the memory came back to him. "You heard Frankie talking outside their offices about going after Big Numbers Albanese. You've got a good memory, Boss. That was over twenty years ago."

But Cole's face had turned hard as he continued to read the photocopied file from Park City Realty. "Now the law firm is called Barksdale, Barksdale, and DeVito, P.C. About ten years ago, I got involved in a case with Joe Leak in New York City. A professional assassin named Rianocek was involved, who could have had a connection to this Barksdale's law firm, but we were never able to prove it."

"What did your real-estate agent have to say about this Barksdale character, Judy?" Blackie asked.

"She never met him, but she did say that he's the co-owner of the factory with his grandson, Cleveland E. Barksdale III. Mrs. Moore talks to the grandson occasionally, and he is very insistent about the building's security. No one is supposed to enter this place without his specific authorization. And although the real-estate agent is listed as the property manager, she said that she's never set foot inside of it."

"How is the inventory coming?" Cole asked Blackie.

"It's almost finished. We're talking about tons of heroin and cocaine here. If I hadn't seen this for myself, I wouldn't have believed it."

"Okay," Govich said, "let's get a Cook County state's attorney down here so we can start the process of getting warrants for both of the Barksdales. Larry, I want you to personally handle the interrogation of Shelton Booker. If we can get him to flip, we'll have a case on the Barksdales that is going to make history."

Cole and his crew nodded. They were indeed going to make history.

58

MARCH 22, 1999
4:17 P.M.

Shelton Booker had been transported by police van to police headquarters. After being booked on charges of murder, aggravated battery, and armed violence, he was signed out of the central detention facility by Lieutenant Blackie Silvestri and Sergeant Manny Sherlock. Handcuffing Bad Man's wrists securely behind his back, they escorted him via the rear headquarter's elevator from the twelfth-floor jail down to detective division headquarters on five.

"Where are we going, Silvestri?" Booker demanded as they entered the office. The main office bay was crammed full of desks at which detectives sat in shirtsleeves working at computers or talking on telephones.

"To see someone who is interested in your welfare, Shelton."

"My welfare?" Booker sneered. "That's bullshit!"

At the chief of detective's office, Manny stepped forward to open the door. Blackie, maintaining a firm grip on the prisoner's upper arm, stopped. "I wouldn't say that, *'Bad Man.'* " he said sarcastically. "There's quite a difference between life imprisonment and a date with a lethal injection."

Then they entered the office to find Larry Cole seated behind the desk, waiting. Blackie handcuffed Shelton Booker to a chair across from Cole. The lieutenant and Manny took up positions flanking the hefty gang leader.

After a moment of protracted silence, Cole said, "Have you been advised of your rights, Mr. Booker?"

Bad Man sneered, "Is that why you brought me down here, Cole?"

Blackie laid a heavy hand on Booker's shoulder. "Answer the Chief's question, *Bad Man.*"

The prisoner shook the lieutenant off. Glaring at Cole, he responded, "Yeah, I've been read my rights three times since you cops picked me up."

Cole smiled. "Did they tell you about the right to remain silent?"

"They told me."

"Good," Cole said, beaming across the desk and fixing Booker with a soul-chilling stare. "Now I want you to exercise that right and listen. *I'll* do the talking."

And when Cole was finished, Shelton "Bad Man" Booker waived his rights to have an attorney present and gave the cops a full confession.

In Langley, Virginia, the news of the discovery of the drug factory in Chicago was carried on CNN, the cable station from which most of the world received up-to-the-minute news. The Central Intelligence Agency also found the twenty-four-hour news station an excellent source for obtaining domestic intelligence. Now Deputy Director Dickie Fagan was very glad that one of the senior agents assigned to his office, who was aware of the Colombia-Chicago-Langley connection, had been monitoring the broadcast.

Fagan watched a rerun of the interview Superintendent Jack Govich had given. Then Chief of Detectives Larry Cole was interviewed.
The cop's name was vaguely familiar to Fagan, but he had no time to
order a computer search to uncover specifics about him. The deputy
director's attention became riveted to the television set in his office
when the policeman said, *"So far our investigation has revealed no
money or financial records indicating who actually profited from the
operation, but we're going to keep looking until we find out."*

Fagan knew that this Larry Cole wouldn't find any money or
financial records at the factory because there were none. It was an
old intelligence precept called "asset isolation." The profits from the
drug business were handled through a financial institution thousands
of miles away from the location where the actual product was processed. There was no direct link between them.

Dickie Fagan freeze-framed the shot of Cole. All of the TV
broadcasts received in this office were videotaped. He looked at the
Chicago cop's image on the screen. The equipment was state-of-
the-art and Cole's image came across with such a high degree of
clarity that he could have been standing in the flesh on the other
side of the room.

Fagan mumbled into the emptiness of his spacious office on
the executive floor of CIA headquarters, "Mr. Cole, you are just the
type of meddlesome fool who will find a connection between the
product and the profits, if given enough time. We can't have that,
now can we?"

Only electronic broadcasts coming into Fagan's office were
taped. High-ranking American government officials had learned
their lessons from the disaster caused by Richard Nixon's Oval Office tapes during the Watergate scandal.

Fagan got up and crossed to a computer console in a corner of
the room. After entering a password, a program appeared on the
screen. The data was encrypted and required the deputy director to
enter another password to decode it.

Every item of the data connected to the CIA-sponsored domestic drug program was contained in this file. The names of each individual who had ever been involved, along with their dossiers; the locations where the raw drugs originated outside the country; the means by which these drugs came into the United States; the locations to which the processed drugs were shipped; and, finally, the profits and the individuals to whom those profits were disbursed, was contained in the program.

Deputy Director Dickie Fagan's face twisted into a cruel smile when he read some of the limitations that had been placed on the drug distributors at street level within the continental United States. Certain areas were "off limits" to the drug dealers. Other areas, based primarily on racial and social demographics, were targeted. Fagan knew that this information was pure dynamite and could erupt into a war that would make the racial strife of the sixties look like a picnic.

Dickie Fagan, who had learned to touch-type in high school back in Muncie, Indiana, began to alter the top-secret computerized file. Any connection between the CIA and Barksdale Manufacturing was erased. Then the deputy director began adding disinformation. When he finished, he made a single hard copy and erased the program.

Fagan held the stack of documents in his hand. Now he had to figure a way to get them into the hands of Chicago Police Chief of Detectives Larry Cole.

The CIA assistant deputy director was also faced with a more pressing problem. The Barksdale Manufacturing Company would have to be erased from the face of the Earth. Fagan couldn't afford to use his own people in case something went wrong and one of them was captured. Then it came to him. Picking up the telephone, he placed a long-distance call to Europe. Instantly he was connected to a castle in Bavaria. It was time for Baron Alain Marcus Casimir von Rianocek to come out of retirement.

59

Baron Alain Marcus Casimir von Rianocek had moved his residence from Buenos Aires back to the ancestral von Rianocek Castle outside of Munich, Germany. The estate in Argentina had been sold and now he operated from the structure that had belonged to his family for hundreds of years.

The castle was part fortress, part castle, and all palace. The basic structure had been built in the sixteenth century, when the objective was to provide a formidable defensive position for the Rianocek army. As the centuries went by, the severe lines of the castle softened a bit, but not much. The place was meant to be efficient at the cost of any aesthetic value.

From the late nineteenth century until the mid–twentieth century, the Bavarian castle fell into a state of abject neglect. After the defeat of Nazi Germany, the structure was abandoned. Then, in the early nineties, the current baronet was finally recognized and purchased the estate outright.

Now the castle had been restored to a state of such perfection that it was one of the most beautiful such structures in the world. Alain von Rianocek had personally designed the refurbishment and supervised the renovation over a period of sixteen years at a cost that continued to rise into the millions. Electric lights, central air-conditioning and heating, wall-to-wall carpeting, plastered walls, and luxurious furnishings went inside. Calls went out from Bavaria all over Europe for stained-glass windows that had survived the war intact. At great cost they were shipped in from France, Portugal, the Netherlands, and as far away as Brazil. The installation of these windows made von Rianocek Castle take on the appearance of a cathedral, although a very modern cathedral by current-day standards.

The final touch was the weathered stone walls being sandblasted white. Floodlights were installed around the exterior grounds, which made the castle stand out at night like a searchlight in the dark. A very beautiful searchlight.

The von Rianocek Castle was listed on the route for every tour bus in Germany; however, the castle grounds were off-limits to anyone but the invited. It was rumored that a couple of curious trespassers had invaded the castle grounds in 1994. They were never seen or heard from again.

A staff of fifteen servants attended the reigning baronet and his guests. There was always a guest or two visiting the castle. Generally, since 1992, Baron von Rianocek had spent a great deal of time at the castle, whereas in the years immediately following his assumption of the title, he had traveled extensively. Now he seldom left Germany, and had relinquished all ties to Argentina.

Invited visitors to the castle consisted of the world's jetsetters, including well-known movie stars, royalty, the fabulously wealthy, and the otherwise socially noteworthy. Rianocek gave frequent parties, which were known to go on all night and at times became quite raucous, but there had never been a problem between local authorities and any of the baron's guests.

There were two permanent castle occupants besides the baron. One was a beautiful young American woman, who walked with a limp, and the other was an Englishman with a severe breathing problem. Their identities were never disclosed to the outside world, as the internal affairs of the castle were kept secret.

On this night there was a relatively small gathering being held in the main hall of the castle. The room was large enough to have accommodated an NBA basketball game with room for five thousand spectators. The banners of ten generations of von Rianoceks hung from the rafters. There was a fireplace large enough to walk around in at one end of the room and, against the chill of the frigid night, a fire roared inside of it. This open flame could not keep the immense room sufficiently warm and was more for effect than function. Vents placed at floor level around the room kept the hall at a comfortable seventy-two degrees.

Twenty-seven people mingled around a buffet table, which was loaded with a sumptuous feast, including hams, beef roasts, turkeys, and a number of salads, breads, and delicacies. White-coated attendants ladled food onto expensive china plates, which the diners would then carry to white-cloth-covered tables arranged around the huge room. A four-piece string quartet provided softly played music, ranging in their selections from classical to jazz. There was a bar in operation along with two circulating waiters carrying trays containing glasses of champagne.

No occasion was being celebrated. It was no one's birthday or anniversary. Baron von Rianocek entertained in this fashion almost every night. It was expensive, but he could definitely afford it. In addition to his frequent parties, he engaged in a number of hobbies, including exotic weapon and rare book collecting. Many people envied Alain Rianocek, because he lived a life of idle ease in conspicuous opulence. But the descendant of Bavarian royalty was far from being a happy man, because he was terribly bored.

In attendance tonight were an English female movie star, who could boast that she had made love with half of the men present; a retired United States Army major general; an Italian poet of some renown; and a painter who specialized in pornographic art. Also present were Baron von Rianocek's constant companions, Hannah Spencer and Cornelius Shade. The former assassin was seated in a high-backed chair, which rested on a platform constructed six inches above the floor.

Rianocek had aged well. His brown hair had a few streaks of gray but was still thick and luxurious. His skin was unwrinkled and his eyes were still capable of producing a chilling stare. Perhaps the one betrayal that the years had inflicted on him was a twenty-pound

weight gain, which was the result of his lavish lifestyle. Periodically, he went on diets and exercised, but the rich food and alcohol
he consumed nightly had taken a toll.

Hannah and Shade were mixing with the guests. Rianocek spent a
moment watching them. In the years since they'd made their escape after that debacle in New York, he had been very good to them. This
could be evidenced by their displaying a degree of additional weight
similar to the baron's, especially the asthmatic Mr. Shade. They
were often amused by some of Rianocek's more bizarre guests, but
they mingled well. Hannah and Shade enjoyed a high standard of
living and wanted for nothing. But the assassin could tell that there
was something missing in their lives. In their lives and his.

Since leaving the United States in 1989, Rianocek had taken
Dickie Fagan's advice and retired. At least that was his intention as
far as his activities in the Western Hemisphere went. But upon his
relocation to Europe from Argentina and the recognition of his title
by the German courts, he realized that he would no longer be able
to operate like he had in the past. This was due to his coming under
almost constant surveillance by the police. Larry Cole and Joe
Leak's prying in New York had led to his exposure. For that Alain
Rianocek hated them.

The demand for his services diminished worldwide. The reason
for this was not the cops, but instead the Central Intelligence
Agency, which had put out the rumor over the intelligence wire that
the assassin had become unreliable. With no other options available
to him, Rianocek took up residence in his luxurious castle outside
of Munich to live the life of the idle rich. A meaningless, wretched
existence that was slowly killing him.

Rianocek's personal secretary, a bearded man of fifty, who was
a graduate of the Harvard Business School and took care of all
castle affairs, entered the hall. The secretary generally avoided the
parties and devoted his time strictly to business. For this Rianocek
was grateful, so the baron was surprised when the man made an
appearance at the party.

The secretary crossed to his employer's side and whispered, "There is an urgent call for you from America, sir. A Mister Fagan."

Rianocek's eyes widened in surprise and for a moment he was unable to move. The secretary was about to repeat the message when the master of Rianocek Castle got to his feet.

Across the hall at their respective locations among the dinner guests, Hannah Spencer and Cornelius Shade noticed the expression on the assassin's face. They didn't know it at this exact moment, but their lives had once more changed.

60

Chicago, Illinois
MARCH 22, 1999
3:53 P.M.

Assistant Cook County State's Attorney Gus Lindsay was assigned to be the Felony Review liaison with the Chicago Police Department. A twenty-year veteran of the county prosecutor's office, Lindsay was a powerfully built black man of average height. His head was shaven in a style made popular by Chicago Bulls basketball star Michael Jordan. Lindsay had been selected for this assignment, because he had one of the most astute criminal-law minds in the country. He had worked with Larry Cole and Blackie Silvestri before.

The prosecutor had been given a tour of the impounded narcotics-processing plant by Manny Sherlock and Judy Daniels, whose schoolgirl outfit had drawn a questioning glance from Lindsay. There were police officers from the Narcotics Unit and the crime laboratory on sublevel 2, inventorying the volume of raw opium, coca leaves, and marijuana plants in one area. The processed final product was packaged in plastic bags and robotically loaded into cardboard boxes, which were then sealed and stenciled with black lettering, "Contents Fragile—Handle With Care." There were no other markings on the box.

All of the officers working in the processing area wore filter masks to protect themselves from the narcotics dust in the air. The assistant state's attorney, Manny, and Judy also put on masks.

"This is monstrous," Lindsay said. "Have you estimated the street value of this poison?"

"By the standards we use to approximate such things," Manny replied, "this stuff is incalculable. One of the Narcotics Unit supervisors gave an estimate of 18.3 million wholesale, which translates to a street value of fifteen billion dollars."

Even with the mask over his face, the prosecutor's angry grimace was evident. "I'm going to make sure that whoever is responsible for this goes away for a long time."

Manny and the Mistress of Disguise/High Priestess of Mayhem were quite certain that the assistant state's attorney was in deadly earnest.

After the tour, Gus Lindsay met Cole at detective division headquarters.

"So what did you think of that place?" Cole asked.

The assistant state's attorney told him.

"So far," Cole said, "the only thing we've come up with is the dead chemist, whom Bad Man Booker confessed to killing. Booker also admitted that he and his gang have been making deliveries to and picking up shipments from the plant for the past eighteen months. Now get this," Cole said, adding emphasis to his next words, "everything has been going through a hangar on the military side of O'Hare Field."

"Are you saying that this stuff is being transported by government aircraft, Larry?"

"We can't prove it right now, Gus. Booker and his gang were kept pretty much in the dark about what they were doing. Bad Man was controlled by an anonymous male voice on the telephone. Until today, he never saw anyone either at the narcotics plant or at the airport hangar, where he made the pickups and deliveries. Blackie is out at O'Hare right now with a squad of detectives and some CID investigators, but I doubt if they will come up with much."

"This sounds like an organized-crime operation," Lindsay said.

"I thought the same thing at first," Cole said, "especially since one of the listed owners of the property used to be a Mob lawyer. But the more I think about it, the more I doubt that there is any Mafia connection at all."

"Why?"

Cole shrugged. "The Mafia would never trust a black street gang with an operation of this magnitude. They'd use wise guys. What we've got here is an international operation on a gigantic scale. There is no way of knowing how long that plant has been turning out those kilo-sized packages of death. If it wasn't for the botched hit on this chemist, Sylvester Merrill, they could have continued operating indefinitely."

The assistant state's attorney's beeper went off. Cole turned his desk phone around so that Lindsay could get to it. As he dialed, he said, "So where do we go from here?"

"We've got to bring in the Barksdales for questioning," Cole said. "That's where you come in. We'll need search warrants for their offices and homes. There's got to be a lot of money from this deal lying around."

"Let's talk about that when I get through calling my office."

A moment later, Gus Lindsay hung up the phone and smiled at the chief of detectives. "Guess what?"

"What?"

"Penelope Josephson called my office a little while ago."

"I know Ms. Josephson," Cole said. "She's hell on wheels in a courtroom."

"She's beaten me more than once on cases that I thought I had a lock on. Now she's got a couple of new clients, who believe that they are about to have some serious legal difficulties. Before we arrest these clients, Ms. Josephson wants to arrange a voluntary meeting between them and us."

Cole saw it coming. "Would her clients possibly be named Barksdale, Gus?"

"You must be psychic, Larry."

Munich, Germany

In Munich, the supersonic United States Air Force transport plane was waiting on the tarmac when the black Mercedes limousine raced onto the private section of the airfield and skidded to a stop by the aft section door of the plane. A flight of folding steps extended from the plane's opening to the ground. Two muscular men in black jumpsuits stood by waiting. When the Mercedes came to a stop, one of the men stepped forward and opened the rear door.

Hannah Spencer, clad in a full-length mink coat, came out first. A heavy-breathing Cornelius Shade, wearing the same wrinkled raincoat and battered snap-brim hat he had worn in New York ten years ago, came out next. Then Alain Rianocek, wearing a black cape over a dark suit and white turtleneck, came out last.

The muscular door opener didn't hesitate. "Right this way, Baron von Rianocek. We're cleared through to the military field at O'Hare Airport in Chicago. Deputy Director Fagan has instructed us to provide you with anything you need."

Rianocek didn't move or respond right away. Instead he looked up at the cloud-covered night sky. His lips moved and the two men dressed in black assumed that he was praying. However, Hannah Spencer and Cornelius Shade knew that Baron Alain Marcus Casimir von Rianocek had never prayed to any deity in his life. And although no sound came from the assassin's mouth, his assistants guessed what he was doing. He was proclaiming to an unknowing world that he was back and there would be hell to pay.

61

Larry Cole got home late. He lived in a ranch-style home on the South Side of Chicago. Like his New York counterpart, Joe Leak, the chief of detectives was divorced. His son Larry "Butch" Cole, Jr. lived in Detroit with Cole's ex-wife, Lisa. Most of the time Cole spent his nights alone in a solitary, sometimes lonely mode. Tonight would be an exception.

After parking the pool car, which he had been given to temporarily replace the black command vehicle that Bad Man Booker and his Peace Stones had destroyed during the gun battle at the South Chicago narcotics factory, Cole headed for the front door. It was a cool night with a stiff wind holding the promise of rain or, if it got cold enough, snow. As he stepped across the threshold, he was attempting to come up with some idea of what to concoct for dinner. He had frozen pot pies, frozen hamburger patties, and frozen steak, all of which could be thawed in the microwave before cooking. Vegetables and side dishes would either come out of a can or the freezer. He remarked to himself that the late supper he was planning might not be tasty, but at least it would be filling.

The instant he opened the front door, his concerns about dinner evaporated. The delicious aroma of cooking food drifting from inside the house revealed that someone had solved his meal problems for him. Cole knew that this someone was his very reclusive and often-strange girlfriend Edna Gray. At least on this early spring night in 1999, Cole thought that the woman who had fixed dinner for him was Edna Gray.

The house was in semidarkness, which was the way she always preferred it when she visited. At times this annoyed Cole, because the house was fairly large and, with the lights out, there were too many shadows lurking. However, he went along with it to humor her, as well as not wanting to admit that he became apprehensive in the dark.

She appeared at the entrance to the kitchen. The only light came from the stove fixture framing her stunning figure and casting her features in shadow. She was wearing a sheer nightgown, which indicated to Cole quite clearly what she had in mind for later in the evening.

"I saw you on television," she said. "That drug plant is like something out of a bizarre nightmare."

Cole crossed the dimly lighted living room to the bar, where he began mixing a drink. She had filled the ice bucket and there was an unopened fifth of Wild Turkey on the sideboard. "You should have seen the inside of the place," he said, dropping ice cubes into a glass and pouring a couple of fingers of liquor over them. Adding a dash of water, he turned around, glass in hand. "Mass-produced, assembly-line dope. They've got to have made millions, possibly billions of dollars from that place. Yet we haven't been able to find anything indicating where all the money went. We've got the owners of the factory coming in with their attorney tomorrow."

"Do you plan to arrest them?"

"Hopefully," Cole said, taking a pull of his bourbon. "Gus Lindsay from the state's attorney's office is working with us and together we'll come up with a strategy to deal with them. Is there something wrong with your voice?"

Her shadowy figure tensed. "I think I'm coming down with a cold." Then she turned and walked back into the kitchen.

He stood at the bar for a moment, staring at the spot she had just vacated. Each time she came here she was different, yet the same. Her strange manner made her quite unique, which was at times intriguing and at other times confusingly frustrating.

But he had other more pressing problems on his mind. Finishing his drink, he went in to dinner.

Later, they were lying in bed. Cole was staring up at the ceiling again pondering the paradox of the woman lying in his arms. To-night, right after they'd cleaned up the kitchen and put everything in the dishwasher, she had virtually flung herself at him. She had displayed such unbridled passion that he had come close to telling her to calm down and take it a bit easier. But he managed to match her passion, and that first time they had made love so vigorously that at the conclusion they were both drenched with sweat and breathing heavily. But she was far from satisfied. It hadn't taken him long for his own batteries to recharge and they made love again, only this time with less abandon. Now they were resting, and he anticipated her becoming sexually aroused once more before they finally went to sleep.

That was what was bothering him. This time she had been a demon in bed. On her last visit, she had been so standoffish that she flinched when he attempted to even hug her.

"A penny for your thoughts," she said, placing the front of her body flush against his side.

He turned to look at her, but in the dark it was difficult to see her features. It was almost as if she was using the darkness as a mask. "I was thinking about you."

"That's nice. Exactly what were you thinking?"

"I'm puzzled."

Her weight shifted as she moved away from him. "What puzzles you?"

He didn't feel like getting into an argument, so he said, "I guess nothing, really. It's been one of those days."

"But it was a good day, wasn't it?"

"More or less. I keep wondering if closing that drug plant will cause any lasting reduction in the amount of narcotics out there on our streets."

Cole could feel her relaxing. The tension had only been present for an instant. Now that they were talking about something else, she had thawed.

"What you and Blackie did today helped put that mass-production operation out of business."

"That's another thing I'm having trouble understanding." He turned on his side to face her and propped his head up on his open palm. "The efficiency of the operation is unheard of, and how could they possibly get that amount of unprocessed narcotics into the country without any law-enforcement agency at the federal, state, or local level getting even a whiff of what was going on?"

"Do you think that someone in the government could be involved?" she asked.

"I don't know, Edna. I don't know."

A Chicago Police detail of two officers from the Grand Crossing District was assigned to guard the drug plant on South Chicago. The fence gate remained open, and the cops were seated in a marked police car parked on the blacktop area surrounding the building. As the evening progressed, the officers passed the time reading newspapers and paperback books.

Chief Larry Cole had recommended that four officers be assigned to security inside the factory and an additional four outside in two strategically placed police cars. Superintendent Govich had turned over security of the drug plant to the Third Police District, headquartered two blocks away. The watch commander on the afternoon shift decided that one patrol car would be enough. However, he had not consulted with Cole or anyone else in the command hierarchy before he made this decision. After all, the Third District was understaffed; the watch commander would assign alert young officers, who wouldn't be caught sleeping on the job no matter how boring things might get; and, last but not least, he was the frigging watch commander and he would damned well do as he pleased without interference from any brass-hat paper pusher from downtown. The Third District watch commander had made a critical error.

As long as no one attempted to enter the gate, the assigned cops paid no attention to what was going on in the streets beyond the boundaries of their area of responsibility. A couple of drag racers, peeling rubber, flew by the open gate at a few minutes before 8:00. There were a number of "in progress" calls within a short distance of the plant, but the watch commander had indeed assigned better-than-average officers to this detail, and they remained at their post.

The one problem that the watch commander failed to take into account was that the pair of veterans that he'd assigned to watch the South Chicago drug plant had no training or experience in security. They figured that their presence alone would be enough to discourage the average intruder from attempting an unauthorized entry. They were totally unprepared for an attack by experts.

At 9.00 P.M. a black Ford drove northbound on South Chicago Avenue and cruised slowly past the entrance. The cops both looked up and noticed that the vehicle had tinted windows, which were illegal. But they were not about to leave their assigned post to go after a traffic violator. About a minute later, what appeared to be the same car drove southbound on South Chicago. Only one of the cops noticed the Ford this time.

"Didn't that car just go by?"

Lazily, stifling a yawn his partner said, "So what? It's a free country. Probably just a couple of dumb-assed citizens, who saw what went down here earlier on television, and came to take a gander for themselves. I'm surprised there haven't been more."

So they returned to killing time and forgot about the Ford.

Actually, two identical black Fords had driven past the factory. Each had tinted windows, which were for function rather than illicit style.

The occupants of the twin black vehicles could see clearly through the exterior darkened glass, but anyone attempting to look inside would be unable to see them.

Two men were in each car. There was an eerie sameness about them, as if they were either all related or had been cloned. The latter would be a more accurate explanation for the pronounced resemblance, because they had been organizationally brainwashed and trained to the point of mindless obedience by the Central Intelligence Agency.

The black Fords rendezvoused with a third identical car a block from the factory. The street they parked on was deserted, with only abandoned buildings surrounded by vacant lots. The front-seat passengers of two of the cars got out and walked over to the third. The rear passenger side window was lowered to reveal the face of Alain Marcus Casimir von Rianocek.

"You know what to do," the assassin said quietly. "I don't want any mistakes."

Turning, the men, who were all dressed in black, gestured toward the vehicles that they had exited. The drivers got out and joined them. One of the men carried a long metal rod with a T-shaped tip. With the others following, he walked to the middle of the street, yanked off the heavy metal cover, and descended into the sewers beneath the street. The others vanished into the hole behind him.

62

Clevey Barksdale had spent the entire afternoon and most of the evening attempting to get in touch with Dickie Fagan. He had telephoned, faxed, E-mailed, and even sent a telegram to the deputy director's office at CIA headquarters in Langley, Virginia. Fagan had not responded.

At 10:00, the managing partner of Barksdale, Barksdale, and DeVito, P.C., left his office. A chauffeured limo transported him from the Loop to his grandfather's mansion. As he walked from the driveway up the stone walk at the side of the house, he remembered what had occurred here so many years ago, when he had bashed in the man's head who was going to kill his grandfather. At this moment, Clevey felt the same murderous rage that he had on that long-ago night. Only the head he would like to bash in now belonged to Dickie Fagan.

The day became even more bleak for the younger Barksdale when he walked into the study and found it filled with smoke from the cigarettes his grandfather had been chain-smoking since he'd gotten the news of the disaster at the plant.

Instead of chastising the older man, Clevey went to the bar and poured a snifter of brandy. He downed the fiery liquid in one long pull. It settled in his belly, keeping company with the cold fury simmering inside of him. He would drink nothing else alcoholic tonight.

Turning around, he went to sit across from his grandfather. The old man sat behind the desk, appearing as composed and serene as

Clevey had ever seen him. Of course, Barksdale, Sr. had been through many crises before and if it hadn't been for the accursed cigarettes that he was smoking, Clevey would have been inspired by his calm in the face of disaster.

"I haven't been able to get in touch with Fagan," Clevey said.

His grandfather's eyes rested on him, but Clevey noticed that there was something different in his gaze—a vacant, distant quality, as if the older man's mind was far away from the physical location of his body.

Clevey forged ahead. "We've got to figure that the police are going to want to question us about what was going on inside the plant. I think we're in pretty good shape, especially with Sly Merrill being dead. We can lay it all on him and, with a little help from Dickie Fagan, I think we'll be in the clear."

The only movement that came from his grandfather was the lit cigarette being raised to his lips, smoke billowing into the air, and then him lowering the butt to the desk surface, where an overflowing glass ashtray rested.

Deciding that a more decisive approach was required, Clevey got up, came around the desk, removed the cigarette from his grandfather's hand, and stubbed it out. He then opened one of the study windows to vent the smoke.

Returning to his seat, Clevey noticed that his grandfather's emotionless gaze had not altered. For the first time, the younger man was starting to become alarmed.

"I've retained Penny Josephson to represent us and she's already set up a—"

Cleve Barksdale cut his grandson off. "We'll have to go to the Intercessore."

"Grandfather?" Clevey said in confusion.

"Monsignor O'Keefe will take care of everything for us. We will go down into the basement of the church and pray. Then the Intercessore will make a decision. Don't worry, Clevey, it will be fine."

A fear gripped Clevey the likes of which he'd never experienced before in his life. Monsignor Maurice O'Keefe had been dead for years. The Barksdales had severed all contact with him and those for whom he mediated back in 1977. Now Clevey was being forced to come to grips with the very real possibility that his grandfather had suddenly become senile or had suffered a nervous breakdown. This couldn't be happening to them at a worse time.

"You don't have to go with us tomorrow," Clevey said, noticing a strange hollow quality in his voice. He recognized this as indecision, with which he had never been burdened before. "I can handle everything."

A silence ensued between the two men. It was an awkward period during which Cleve merely stared off vacantly into space, while Clevey attempted to collect his own thoughts and figure a way to somehow, some way turn this disaster around.

Then the phone on the desk rang. Like the line in Clevey's office, this one was a private, secure extension and only one person would be calling at this hour. The older man behind the desk made no move to answer it, and instead reached for another cigarette. Quickly, Clevey rose and grabbed the receiver.

"Is that you, Fagan?"

There was a short pause before the deputy director's nasal voice came across the line. *"I understand that you've been trying to get in touch with me, Barksdale."*

Clevey willed himself to remain calm, as he replied, "I think we need to talk about our operation out here in Chicago."

"I am going to take care of the problems you caused earlier. Or at least a portion of those problems."

"I don't understand what you mean." Clevey did not like the tone of the deputy director's voice.

"I am a very thorough man, Attorney Barksdale. What occurred this afternoon displayed terrible incompetence on your part. That I cannot tolerate; however, I'm sure we can come to some sort of accommodation."

Clevey Barksdale gripped the receiver tightly and stared at his near-comatose grandfather, who continued to sit peering off into space, while puffing continuously on a cigarette.

Something drove Larry Cole out of a sound sleep. He sat up in the bed and looked around his dark bedroom. He was alone. Slipping into his bathrobe, he checked the bathroom, which was empty. He went downstairs looking for Edna, but there was no one else in the house.

Obviously, after he'd gone to sleep a few hours ago, she had gotten up, dressed and left. An angry frown crossed his face. She was simply using him, and this had become extremely annoying. One minute she was remote and cold; the next she was like an octopus in heat.

Cole started for the telephone with the intention of calling her apartment and having it out with her once and for all. Her sister, who had been known as Eurydice Vaughn, was currently an inmate in the ward for the criminally insane at University Hospital. Edna had moved into her sister's spacious apartment, as it was only a short distance from the hospital. The apartment was in a building overlooking the National Science and Space Museum in Jackson Park. Then, just as he started to pick up the receiver, the entire house shook. It was as if a lightning bolt had struck very close by. But it wasn't even raining.

Cole went to the front window and peered out. The street was quiet; however, lights were coming on in houses up and down the block. Cole retraced his steps across the living room back to the phone. He dialed the Operations Command desk at police headquarters.

"This is Chief Cole," he said to the officer, who answered on the first ring. "Has there been some type of explosion on the South Side?"

"We're getting reports from out in the Third District of a massive explosion in the vicinity of that drug plant you busted yesterday,

Chief. It's being checked out, but I haven't got any word back yet."

When Larry Cole hung up the telephone, he knew what had happened with the certainty that would have been the case had he been a bona fide psychic. He rushed back to the bedroom to dress. By the time Operations Command called him back, Cole was less than one-half mile from the spot where the explosion had originated.

63

MARCH 23, 1999
6:17 A.M.

The crater where the drug-processing Barksdale Manufacturing plant had been was the length and width of a football field and twenty feet deep. As the explosion had originated in the sewers beneath city streets, the crater was filled with raw sewage to a depth of six feet. Nothing at all was left of the building that had been the Barksdale Manufacturing Company—including the tons of narcotics evidence that had been inside of it.

Larry Cole stood at the edge of the crater and, ignoring the stench coming up from below, began reconstructing in his mind what had occurred here.

At about 11:30 last night, the pair of police officers on duty had been attacked by two men dressed in black, wearing ski masks. The obviously embarrassed cops had told Cole that the only way that the assailants could have slipped up on them was to come from inside the plant. This indicated to the chief of detectives that there had been a secret entrance to the plant they had missed. From what Cole was looking at now, that entrance was from the sewer.

The Third District cops went on to explain that the black-clad pair had suddenly appeared on each side of the squad car displaying exotic large-bore, semiautomatic pistols. They had ordered the policemen out and removed their guns, walkie-talkies, and pepper spray before handcuffing them. The officers were then forced into the back of the police car, which was equipped with a Plexiglas shield to facilitate prisoner transports. One of the attackers then drove the captives to a deserted side street four blocks away. Parking in the shadows of a viaduct, the masked man in black had left them. The last they saw of him, he was running back in the direction of the factory. Approximately thirty minutes later, a massive explosion rocked the area. It possessed sufficient force to smash all of the windows within half a mile of its origin, and could be heard as far away as Calumet City.

Cole watched the filthy water at the bottom of the crater swirl and break in waves over the jagged sides. Now all of the evidence had literally gone up in smoke. The destruction was so complete as to initially seem impossible to have been accomplished by an explosion at all. But the bomb and arson investigators responding to the scene had assured Cole that indeed an explosive, or actually a number of strategically placed explosives, had been used. Yet nothing else in the area, other than the broken windows, had been damaged. One thing was obvious: No street gang had done this.

Cole turned away from the crater. There was no resulting fire, but a full squadron of firefighters was standing by. There were also six police cars, to include a supervisor, from the Third District. The chief frowned. If the watch commander had assigned this number of units to guard the factory last night, the place might have been saved. The superintendent would deal with the lieutenant who made the error; however, Cole didn't think that finger-pointing would do much good now. A whole army of cops might not have been able to prevent what had occurred here.

As Cole got into his car for the drive to headquarters, a thought occurred to him. Whoever had done this had gotten the policemen assigned to the guard detail out of harm's way before the explosion.

They had also displayed exotic handguns. Although the masks had concealed their faces, the guns might give the CPD a clue as to who was involved. He would have the cops from the Third District look at a book on firearms before they went off duty. If they couldn't identify anything on file, then Cole would have the police artist make a sketch from their description. He would then have the sketch run through the NCIC database to discover the firearm's origin. Although Cole might not be able to identify the individuals who had destroyed the factory, he might be able to find out who or what organization had employed them.

Cole shuddered from a combination of his exposure to the cold and lack of sleep. Turning on the heater, he added up what he had so far: high-tech explosives, sophisticated sidearms, and men dressed in black operating with military precision. Then there was the disarming of the officers guarding the plant and their being transported out of harm's way. Obviously, the destruction of the Barksdale Manufacturing Company had all the carmarks of an intelligence operation.

Putting the car in gear, he drove downtown. This investigation was not over yet.

At 7:30, Judy Daniels left her North Side apartment, on her way to headquarters. Today she had assumed her "young professional" look, which consisted of her wearing a red shoulder-length wig and green-tinted contact lenses. She was dressed in a dark blue, man-tailored business suit. She carried a black attaché case and walked toward her fire engine–red Toyota with long, confident strides.

A black Ford with tinted windows was parked a half block away. Cornelius Shade was seated behind the wheel; Hannah Spencer was in the front passenger seat.

After a four-hour, high-altitude flight from Europe across the North Pole and Canada into the United States, they had landed in Chicago. En route by air, Rianocek had been closeted in a private compartment in the spartan interior of the huge plane. He had been communicating with Dickie Fagan via a computerized satellite hookup.

When they landed, the assassins had been met by three more men, who were clones of the pair that had accompanied them from Munich. A dark van had transported them from the airfield to a parking lot across from the main terminal. In a guarded, secured area on the top level, a row of identical black Ford vehicles was parked. After making sure that there were no prying eyes or ears present, Rianocek had given them their assignments.

The men in black had accompanied Rianocek to the South Chicago Avenue location. There they had entered the sewers beneath the streets to set the small, but extremely potent explosive charges, which succeeded in completely obliterating the structure and everything in it.

Hannah Spencer and Cornelius Shade were incapable of this level of physical exertion; however, their assignment was just as important to the success of the operation as was that of the stony-faced men accompanying the assassin.

Now the deadly pair watched Judy get into her car. They had identified it and its owner forty-five minutes before the cop came out of the apartment building.

"That's not her!" Shade said in alarm.

Hannah Spencer consulted documents in a plastic folder she carried. She scanned the folder's contents quickly. Then she laughed. "That *is* her, even if she doesn't look anything like her official Chicago Police photo. It seems that Sergeant Daniels is something of a disguise artist. They call her the Mistress of Disguise/High Priestess of Mayhem."

Shade coughed noisily before saying, "This chick has probably got a screw loose."

"You know," Hannah responded, "in our line of work we could occasionally use a chameleon like her."

"I don't need disguises to function efficiently, Ms. Spencer."

Despite the many years they had lived in such close proximity to one another, he still maintained the formality when addressing her. "I have managed to hide in plain sight for many years *very* effectively."

Judy turned the car on and was about to put it in gear when she saw the brown paper envelope lying on the bucket seat beside her. At first, she was more curious than frightened. She kept her car very clean and didn't leave stuff lying around inside of it. And she was certain that this envelope had not been in her car when she left it last night.

For a long moment, she remained stock-still, with her hands gripping the steering wheel. She considered getting out of the car and putting as much distance as she could between herself and what was lying on the front seat. Then she rationalized that if this had been a bomb or something deadly, she would already be knocking at the Pearly Gates. Willing herself to relax, she pulled her hands from the steering wheel and slowly reached for the envelope.

The assassins could see what she was doing. Hannah Spencer said, "She's got the information. It's as good as in our old friend Larry Cole's hands right now."

64

Penelope Josephson entered the visitors' booth attached to the Area One Police Center detention facility at 5101 South Wentworth. She was flushed, and her pretty features revealed the pressure of a long, traumatic day. Penny was a good attorney and took tremendous pride in her ability in a courtroom. She had tried over two hundred criminal cases during her seven years as an attorney and had a success rate of over 90 percent. No matter how damning the evidence against her client or how great the presumption of guilt was prior to trial, Penny always thought that she had a chance. Now, for the first time in her career, she had a case she knew that she couldn't win.

Penelope Josephson's clients were Cleve and Clevey Barksdale.

The visitors' booth was a narrow, dimly lit cubicle with a Plexiglas shield separating the visitor from the prisoner, who would be ushered into the booth from the jail side by a guard. Penny had been waiting for less than five minutes when the door on the other side of the partition opened and Clevey Barksdale was led in by an unarmed jailer.

"This door will be locked," said the jailer, who was dressed in a dark blue police utility uniform. "When you're finished, press the button there on the wall, and I'll come for you."

Then the jailer left them alone.

Before Penny could say anything, Clevey said urgently, "How's my grandfather?"

Penny waved a wisp of hair out of her face and then said, "He's had a stroke. Right now he's in critical condition at University Hospital."

Clevey sank down heavily in the chair across from her and cradled his head in his hands.

Penelope Josephson looked with compassion on the man she had come close to marrying. In the past ten hours, he looked as if he had aged ten years.

At 8:30 that morning, Clevey and his grandfather had met Penelope Josephson at the state's attorney's office at 26th and California for their meeting with Gus Lindsay. The defense attorney had laid out her strategy beforehand for dealing with any charges the state might bring against her clients. She was prepared to obtain an emergency bond hearing in case Lindsay and the police department were hell-bent-for-leather on charging the Barksdales with a crime. But she figured she could legally finesse the drug plant issue by claiming that her clients were merely unknowing owners of a building in which the deceased Sylvester Merrill had operated a drug-processing plant. She was certain she could carry the day, as there was nothing linking her clients with the illegal operation. Clevey had given her assurances of this. But he had been very, very wrong.

Penelope Josephson didn't see any problem with having Larry Cole and Blackie Silvestri in the office when she arrived with her clients. After all, they were the cops who discovered that the Barksdales' factory was being used to mass-produce illegal narcotics. It would be better to know what Cole had up his sleeve right now.

She had faced Gus Lindsay in court before and knew him to be an excellent prosecutor, who tried cases with the cool, calculating manner of a Mississippi riverboat gambler. Sitting in his office on this spring morning, Penny Josephson remarked to herself that the assistant state's attorney looked as if he'd just drawn to a royal flush.

After they were seated and exchanged a few brief pleasantries, the Barksdales' attorney got right to the point. "Before an unnecessary, high-profile and harassing proceeding is mounted against my clients simply because they leased that factory to the late Sylvester Merrill, I want to begin by saying that they had nothing to do with what went on inside that building. Mr. Cleveland Emmett Barksdale, Sr., and Cleveland Emmett Barksdale III are prominent, upstanding attorneys. They own a number of properties in the continental United States, Canada, Hawaii, and Alaska. Each of those properties is leased by parties engaged in a number of enterprises, none of which is in the least bit illegal."

Gus Lindsay graced her with a Cheshire-cat smile. "Under the Nuisance Abatement Act of 1996, referenced in Chapter 720 of the Illinois Compiled Statutes, property owners can be held accountable for illegal acts perpetrated on rental property."

"Do you think that you can make such remote accountability relevant to a judge and jury in light of the factory's destruction and all the evidence being destroyed?"

Lindsay sat forward and steepled his hands under his chin. "The destruction of the plant was an overt act of criminal sabotage, which will be quite obvious to that same judge and jury, Counselor."

"But you still don't have one single, solitary shred of evidence connecting my clients with what happened out on South Chicago Avenue," Josephson shot back.

Again the state's attorney graced her with that clever feline smile. "But we do have evidence that your clients purchased the raw opiates, marijuana plants, and coca leaves in Colombia, paid for and accepted delivery of the computers and robotic equipment used to operate the plant and, last but not least, profited substantially from the operation."

This galvanized the so-far-confidently-complacent Clevey Barksdale into action. "That's absurd!" he shouted.

The only reaction the elder Barksdale had was a widening of his eyes. Then he began to tremble.

Remaining composed, Penelope Josephson said, "Stop fishing, Gus. Chief Cole himself said yesterday that there were no financial records in the plant nor any indication where the profits went."

Now Cole spoke up. Opening a brown envelope, he said, "That was then and this is now, Counselor."

Everything had gone wrong for the attractive young attorney and her clients. The documentation that Larry Cole possessed was so extensive that Penelope Josephson thought initially that it was forged. But everything was verifiable, and all of the evidence pointed to the Barksdales. Cole and Silvestri had placed them under arrest on the spot.

Penelope had rushed to court to obtain an immediate bond for them, but Gus Lindsay was right behind her. The defense attorney was horrified when bond was set at $5 million each. This was devastating for her clients because the state had frozen all of their assets, alleging that they were the proceeds of drug transactions. She had tried getting the bond reduced, but the judge would have none of it in light of the evidence presented by the state's attorney.

The Barksdales were being processed at the Area One Police Center when Cleve Barksdale collapsed and was rushed to the hospital.

Now, separated from her client and ex-fiancé by the Plexiglas barrier, Penelope Josephson was attempting to come up with a defensive strategy for the Barksdales; however, things were not looking good at all.

"Clevey"—she stared at him with compassion—"do you have anything that I can take to Gus Lindsay in exchange for a plea?"

He looked up at her through terribly fatigued eyes. "Just take care of my grandfather. Penny. The rest of it will work itself out."

"Clevey!" she exploded. "Don't you understand what's going on here? Larry Cole is going to send you away for twenty years."

"Then I might do ten. Maybe less. I don't want my grandfather to go to prison. You've got to guarantee me that won't happen."

She knew that he wasn't telling her everything. There was much more to this drug operation than the evidence Cole possessed indicated; but without Clevey cooperating, she had nothing to fight with in court. Now she was too weary to think about it any more tonight.

"I'll do what I can," she said, shoving her legal pad back into her attaché case. "I'll see you in court tomorrow."

"Good-bye, Penny," Barksdale said, as she exited the booth.

Clevey remained in his seat for a moment longer. There was nothing he could do about his predicament right now. Dickie Fagan had seen to that. But he would not forget this betrayal. Someday he would get his revenge.

Slowly, he raised his hand and rang the bell to summon the jailer.

65

Washington, D.C.
MARCH 24, 1999
DAWN

They met on the Mall, in the same location near the Smithsonian Institution's Air and Space Museum. However, this time Baron von Rianocek, Hannah Spencer, and Cornelius Shade had arrived at the public meeting place in a chauffeur-driven black Lincoln stretch limousine. Dickie Fagan, with his pair of stony-faced bodyguards, was in a standard, gray four-door sedan. The assassin remained in the limo until the CIA deputy director exited his car, walked over to a park bench and sat down.

When the assassin finally did come out of the Lincoln, Fagan noticed the changes in the baron since the last time they'd met. Yes, he was heavier and a bit grayer, but there was still an air of controlled fury about him. Rianocek wore a custom-tailored charcoal-gray suit of a fabric which seemed to adhere to the contours of his body like a second skin. When he reached the bench, he did not sit down, but placed one foot on the wooden surface and leaned down to study the deputy director.

Now Fagan noticed how much the assassin had indeed remained the same over the years. His shoes possessed a shine that was so brilliant they appeared to be made of patent leather. On the second finger of his left hand there was a gold ring bearing a diamond-studded eagle on a black onyx setting. Fagan accurately guessed that the ring bore the von Rianocek crest. The assassin looked rich and prosperous. After all he was European nobility. But except for his talents as a dispenser of death or controlled destruction, Fagan had no use for him.

"Do you remember the last time we were here, Richard?" the assassin asked.

Fagan looked around. It was daylight now; their last meeting had been at night. However, it was a night that the CIA deputy director hadn't forgotten. In response to Rianocek's question, Fagan said, "I remember it very well."

"Things went much better in Chicago yesterday than they did in New York ten years ago."

"I would say so," Fagan stated with a pronounced lack of emotion.

"I remember"—Rianocek straightened his trouser cuffs as he stood up—"on that night, you recommended I retire from the trade."

The assistant deputy director felt that some form of concession was called for. "I was apparently in error."

The full menace of the assassin's fury came through as he said, "Well, I am back, but my reputation needs to be repaired. I'm sure that you can take care of that for me, can't you, Dickie?"

Fagan looked up at the tall, well-dressed man standing over him. "Everything will be taken care of." He hesitated a heartbeat before adding, "Baron von Rianocek."

Without another word, the assassin turned around and retraced his steps back to the limousine.

As the Lincoln drove away, Dickie Fagan watched it go. The nefarious, criminally minded intelligence operative realized that the world was now a decidedly more dangerous place, all because of Baron Alain Marcus Casimir von Rianocek.

66

Chicago, Illinois
JULY 2, 1999
2:07 P.M.

The sentencing following the Chicago trials of Shelton "Bad Man" Booker, MacArthur Williams—the Peace Stones lieutenant who had been wounded during the shoot-out at the Barksdale Manufacturing Company—and Cleveland Emmett Barksdale III was scheduled for a hot midsummer day. Although the trial had attracted a great deal of media attention, there were few people present in the courtroom for the sentencing. Larry Cole, Blackie Silvestri, Judy Daniels, and Manny Sherlock were there.

The three defendants had been tried together on charges of murder, conspiracy to commit murder, criminal racketeering, and possession of controlled substances with the intent to distribute. There were a host of other charges to include aggravated assault, resisting arrest, and the attempted murders of Chief Larry Cole, Lieutenant Blackie Silvestri, Officer Thomas Becker, and Officer Michael Castigliano. The elected Cook County state's attorney, Gus Lindsay's boss, decided to exploit the newsworthy aspects of the case and try all of the defendants—the Peace Stones gang members and the Barksdales—together, so he held a press conference on the front steps of the Criminal Courts Building at 26th and California. No member of the Chicago Police Department was invited. At this media affair, the state's attorney condemned a criminal element, which ". . . extends from the corporate boardrooms of LaSalle Street to the glass-strewn, abandoned-building-lined ghetto streets, where these monstrous purveyors of poison fill their pockets. We will also aggressively and systematically, without prejudice or reservation, prosecute these manufacturers and dealers of drugs to the fullest extent of the law."

The Cook County state's attorney had his eyes set on the United States Senate or, if that bid failed, the Illinois governor's mansion. So he made a political—as opposed to a legal—decision.

The trial began in mid-May of 1999. By mutual agreement, the three defendants were represented by Penelope Josephson. "Bad Man" Booker and MacArthur Williams of the Peace Stones Street gang had their hair trimmed close and wore conservative suits to court, which matched their serious, but contrite expressions. Penny Josephson painted them skillfully as the victims of a racist, morally corrupt society, which had forced them onto the path of gang involvement and drug dealing. Gus Lindsay, the attorney of record for the State, countered with their lengthy police records, which detailed a litany of violent acts. This, coupled with the testimony of Larry Cole and his colleagues, led to the gang members' convictions on all counts.

The prosecution of the Barksdales was a great deal different.

During the trial, Cleve Barksdale remained in the hospital under police guard. On June 1, 1999, he lapsed into a coma and died less than forty-eight hours later. The trial was halted to allow a jailed Cleveland Emmett Barksdale III to attend his grandfather's wake and funeral. Penelope Josephson made sure that the media captured the handsome defendant kneeling in handcuffs beside his grandfather's grave.

When they returned to court, the defense attorney attempted in vain to destroy the State's case against Clevey Barksdale.

Gus Lindsay watched the legal assault with grudging admiration. Penelope Josephson attacked the murder, attempted murder, and conspiracy to commit murder charges against Barksdale. She used the State's own witness, Shelton Booker, to do this. On the stand, "Bad Man" admitted that he had never had a face-to-face meeting with or been able to identify the man who gave him orders on the telephone. Booker was able to state only that Barksdale's voice "sounded like" his phone contact's. As there were no records connecting Barksdale with Booker, that part of the Cook County state's attorney's case collapsed. However, the criminal racketeering and possession of controlled substances with the intent to distribute was a great deal stronger than any other aspect of the case against the sole surviving Barksdale.

The central part of the State's case against Clevey was the testimony and evidence presented by Larry Cole and Blackie Silvestri. Had it not been for the documentation connecting the Barksdales with the South Chicago drug plant, there would be no case against Clevey at all. A cloud of mystery surrounded the incriminating documents that had somehow gotten into police hands. Penelope Josephson realized that attacking the cops' credibility was out. They were above reproach professionally. So she would have to attack the evidence.

Gus Lindsay finished questioning Larry Cole, who was the State's main witness. The broad-shouldered, handsome chief of detectives had testified for three and a half hours as to the events of March 22 and 23, 1999. The contents of the factory had been admitted into evidence over the vociferous objections of the defense attorney. Cole's testimony as to what was in the factory prior to its mysterious destruction, along with the police reports made out on the day the place was discovered, was deemed sufficient to establish criminal intent. Then there was the mysterious documentation.

"Chief Cole," Gus Lindsay said on direct examination, "you

have described the contents of the Barksdale Manufacturing Company plant. Would you tell the court who profited from this illegal operation?"

"Our investigation revealed that Cleveland E. Barksdale, Sr. and his grandson, the defendant, benefited substantially from the narcotics manufactured inside the plant."

"Do you have any evidence to support this?"

"We have invoices, bank statements from the Cayman Islands and Switzerland, and a list of assets, which show a direct link between the South Chicago plant and the Barksdale, Barksdale, and DeVito, P.C., law firm."

"Your witness," Lindsay said to Penelope Josephson, as he returned to the prosecutor's table.

The defense attorney got to her feet slowly, paused a moment to collect her thoughts, and then walked with purposeful strides toward the witness box.

"Chief Cole, where did you uncover the information linking the defendant to the drug operation?"

Without flinching, Cole responded, "Sergeant Judy Daniels found it on the front seat of her car."

The attorney's eyes widened. "You say she 'found it'?"

"That's right."

"Is that how you generally obtain evidence in criminal cases?"

"Sometimes," Cole said. "Anonymous informants provide us with information that leads to solving crimes every day."

"But have you ever had an anonymous informant give you extensive financial information implicating anyone in one of the most monstrous criminal conspiracies in history?"

Cole answered honestly, "No."

"Would this strange and unusual method of providing the police with sensitive information possibly indicate that someone wished to frame my client?"

"Objection," Gus Lindsay said from the defense table. "Calls for the drawing of a conclusion by the witness."

"Sustained," the judge responded.

However, Penelope Josephson had planted the idea in the jurors' minds.

"Did you verify the 'anonymous' information that was left on the front seat of Sergeant Daniels' car?"

The unflappable cop said, "Yes, we did."

But this was as close as Penelope Josephson came to cracking the State's case against her client. The Peace Stones and Clevey Barksdale were found guilty.

For his sentencing hearing, Clevey Barksdale was escorted into the courtroom by a deputy sheriff. His hands and ankles were shackled, and the expensive blue suit he wore was wrinkled. When he saw the shocked look on Penelope Josephson's face, he realized that it was due to his haggard appearance. The formerly virile, robust attorney now looked twice his actual age. To say the least, prison did not agree with him.

The former managing partner of the now-defunct Barksdale, Barksdale, and DeVito, P.C., law firm had to admit to himself that things could have been a great deal worse for him. A great deal worse indeed.

On the night before Barksdale's arrest, Dickie Fagan had implied on the telephone that Clevey and his grandfather would have to bear the weight for the discovery of the drug plant. Barksdale had argued that they could lay all the blame on the dead Sylvester Merrill, but Fagan had deemed that option "unacceptable." The CIA deputy director had gone on to say that the police—or, more specifically, Larry Cole—would not accept such a simple explanation for the complex criminal operation. A higher-up would need to be identified and sacrificed. And Clevey had known that Fagan was talking about him. However, he had hoped to spare his grandfather.

After the arrest and during the subsequent trial, Clevey had considered telling all, but quickly rejected this. If he said one word about the CIA involvement in domestic drug dealing, he would get dead very quickly. So he had kept his mouth shut and to some extent had benefited from a remote form of official protection.

In the human jungle known as the Cook County Jail, a white, corporate type like Cleveland Emmett Barksdale, III would not have lasted five minutes without becoming the victim of gang violence and sexual assault. Barksdale had also run afoul of Shelton "Bad Man" Booker. There was a large contingent of Peace Stones inside the jail, so the attorney would not have been safe if he was placed with the general prison population. The instant he arrived at Cook County Jail, he was given special treatment. Privileged special treatment.

Barksdale was housed in a private room in the hospital wing of the jail. All of his meals were served to him there and he had a small private washroom. On the third day of the trial, when he was returned to his room, he found a portable telephone lying on the bed. He looked at the guard accompanying him, but the man showed no reaction at all to the unauthorized instrument. Five minutes after the guard left, the phone rang.

It was Dickie Fagan. Now a far more formal agreement was arranged to ensure Barksdale's silence. An accommodation that Clevey hated, but was unable to do anything about.

Despite the inmate being held in a protected environment, he deteriorated rapidly both physically and emotionally. The man who shuffled into the court room on that summer day was a mere shadow of what he had been four months before. He had lost forty pounds, his hair was thinning rapidly and, due to his shackles, he moved along with a slow shuffle. There was also something different about his eyes. Where there had once been the gleam of keen intelligence tinged with arrogance, there was now a malevolent glare which lingered on the brink of madness.

As he moved toward the defense table a concerned Penelope Josephson got to her feet. "Clevey . . . ," she managed to say, but the rest of the words caught in her throat.

Then Barksdale looked past her at the people seated on the

second bench in the courtroom. When he spied Larry Cole, Blackie Silvestri, Judy Daniels, and Manny Sherlock, his eyes filled with hatred. Silently, he vowed to get even with them. With not only the cops, but also Dickie Fagan. He owed all of them for what had happened to him and to his grandfather.

Shelton Booker and MacArthur Williams were sentenced to life imprisonment at a separate hearing earlier that day. Having his own personal sentencing hearing was another aspect of the former attorney's privileged incarceration.

A few minutes later, the judge called the proceeding to order and instructed Barksdale to stand. Penelope Josephson stood beside him.

"Cleveland Emmett Barksdale III, you are hereby sentenced to serve a term of no less than five years and no more than ten years in the Omaha Correctional Center."

Cole and Blackie exchanged questioning looks. The Omaha Correctional Center was a minimum-security facility in Nebraska. By rights, Barksdale should have been incarcerated in the Illinois State Penitentiary in Joliet. But the cops had done their job. How the judge did his was not their concern. The five-year sentence was also quite lenient. If Barksdale did three years in Omaha, Cole would be surprised. As Barksdale was escorted from the courtroom, he gave them one final look of hatred.

"I don't think he likes us very much, Boss," Judy said.

Cole shrugged. "Well, at least he'll have a few years to think about what he's done. Then he'll be back on the street, probably setting up another huge criminal enterprise."

Cole had no way of knowing how accurate his guess was.

P A R T

"I plan to avenge myself on you, Mr. Cole, for what you and your government did to me and my grandfather."
—Cleveland Emmett Barksdale III

67

Cleveland E. Barksdale III did an easy two years in the Omaha Correctional Center. From the instant that he set foot inside the facility in the summer of 1999, he led a luxurious (by prison standards) existence. He had a private cell, which was an eight-by-ten foot cubicle with an actual bed, as opposed to the traditional army cots prisoners throughout the Midwest were issued. He had his own television set and a small refrigerator in his cell. He was assigned to the prison library; however, he did little actual work. Most of his time was spent reading or doing research. Very special research.

Despite the relative luxury of his confinement, premature old age had settled on him like a terminal disease. This aging was caused by the terrible hatred eating away inside of him.

There was a small mirror on the wall above the table he used as a desk inside his cell. Occasionally, he would catch a glimpse of himself in this mirror and his reflection produced an odd reaction from him. The virile, robust young man he had been was erased by the image of a much older man, whose gray hair had thinned to the point of baldness on top. The fleshy cheeks were now sunken hollows under sharp cheekbones and the skin possessed a parchment-like, sickly gray pallor.

In the blink of an eye, his youth had vanished. He had believed initially that his legal ordeal had been the catalyst for the onset of some form of virulent disease. His prison-intake physical had revealed that he was more or less in fair physical condition. However, that physical condition was for a man twenty years older than Barksdale's chronological age. This was another devastating reversal for the man who had been born into such wealth and position. But there was a bright side—of a sort—to Cleveland E. Barksdale III's transformation. As each day passed, he began to look more and more like his dead grandfather, who was the only person that the Omaha Correctional Center's pampered prisoner had ever loved.

Time did not weigh heavily on Barksdale because he wouldn't let it. He was busy from dawn until midnight. He read, studied, did research, and even taught in the prison's college extension program sponsored by the University of Nebraska. He also served as a legal advisor for inmates using the law library to prepare appeals of their convictions or civil lawsuits against the legal system that had put them behind bars. Such civil suits were usually no more than nuisance actions without substance. The objective was to inconvenience the targeted officials as a form of revenge. Clevey Barksdale knew that these lawsuits were a waste of time, but he understood the motivation behind them. He possessed a similar reason to seek revenge against those who had placed him here. But when he finally did seek redress, it would have a great deal more effective result than a frivolous lawsuit. A devastating result for all parties concerned.

On the day that Barksdale was released from the Omaha Correctional Center, he was the guest of honor for lunch at the trustees' table in the prison cafeteria. The menu for the day was broiled chicken, baked beans, tossed salad, and a choice of nonalcoholic beverages. The warden ordered a special cinnamon-raisin sheet cake with vanilla icing to be baked by the prison bakery. All of the inmates received a slice of this cake, with Barksdale's being ornamented with a small wax candle in celebration of his release. This was an unheard-of practice, but Barksdale had been a very popular and well-behaved prisoner. After lunch, the warden escorted him to the gate and he was officially freed.

Wearing a new wash-and-wear suit and carrying a cheap suitcase containing all of his worldly belongings, Barksdale was transported via prison van to the Trailways bus station in downtown Omaha. There, with the $700 he had saved while in prison along with letters of recommendation from the correctional center warden and head librarian in his pocket, Cleve Barksdale III caught a bus for Chicago.

He had imposed a strict timetable on himself that would see all of his accounts settled in full within the next five years.

68

Munich, Germany
SEPTEMBER 13, 2002
3:45 P.M.

In Munich, Baron Alain Marcus Casimir von Rianocek was at the top of his game. Since returning to the assassin's trade in 1999, he had taken his chosen profession from being a dark, shadowy operation to an international corporate level. Besides high-cost murders for hire, he brokered illegal arms deals, and carried out acts of espionage against governments, private corporations, and individuals for the right price, which was always extremely high.

An entire wing of von Rianocek Castle had been turned into the corporate headquarters of RanCorp and Associates. The area was now an exotic state-of-the-art command center. A computer-aided map of the world was displayed on one wall, which indicated the locations and details on all of the operations RanCorp was currently engaged in.

A full-time staff of ten ran the complex. The six men and four women had been personally recruited by the assassin for their educational backgrounds, IQ, and psychological profiles. Primarily, Rianocek was interested in highly intelligent sociopaths, who were motivated by greed. They could be difficult to control, but the Bavarian assassin understood exactly how to do this. After all, he was exactly like them. Discipline was taken to extremes at RanCorp and could become physical to the point of death. This, along with constant supervision by Rianocek, Hannah Spencer, and Cornelius Shade, kept RanCorp employees extremely alert, focused, and in a constant state of anxiety. Also the pay was good and the work always fascinating.

Rianocek's office was connected to the command center by a heavy wooden door. This door was always closed and no one, with the exception of Hannah Spencer, Cornelius Shade, and the castle's director of business affairs, was allowed inside the office without Rianocek's express permission. There was a fifty-two-inch closed-circuit TV monitor next to the baron's huge ornate desk at the center of the room. The desk's history could be traced directly back to the personal ownership of Napoleon Bonaparte. The crest it bore was once adorned with the characteristic letter "N." With no regard for the desk's antique value, Rianocek had the "N" removed and replaced with an "R," along with the von Rianocek crest. After all Bavaria and France were traditional enemies.

The TV monitor was on at all times; however, when he was in the office, Rianocek seldom glanced at it. The people he employed would never behave in a manner contrary to the assassin's interests. If anyone was ever caught engaged in any conduct that he did not approve of, the recalcitrant would have their employment and their life terminated simultaneously.

On this afternoon, Rianocek was conducting his weekly business conference. Present were Hannah Spencer, Cornelius Shade, and the castle's business manager, who had been in Rianocek's employ for fifteen years. Nigel Armbruster's function was to keep the castle books, supervise the domestic staff, take notes of RanCorp business meetings, and keep his mouth shut. Armbruster, a stiff-upper-lip, very proper English gentleman, performed all the functions of his position to perfection.

Although she still walked with a slight limp due to the injuries she'd received in New York City in 1989, Hannah Spencer was still a strikingly beautiful woman. Her blond hair was now platinum, and she spent a great deal of time sunning herself, which had given her a golden tan. Now that they were back in the business of murder on an international/corporate level, she kept her body in top shape and her skills as an assassin honed to razor sharpness. Rianocek seldom called on her to go into the field to carry out an assignment. She was now considered managerial personnel. However, he realized that if he needed to use her, he could do so, and that she would perform any required task far above minimal expectations.

Cornelius Shade was a different story. The years and his chronic lung disease had taken their toll on him.

Rianocek had forced Shade to see a respiratory-disease specialist in Vienna. It was learned that Shade's lungs were operating at less than 20 percent efficiency. The doctor expressed open surprise that the condition of Shade's cardiopulmonary system had not led to a heart attack or at least fainting spells. A sanatorium was recommended, but Rianocek would have none of that. The asthmatic's quarters in the castle were outfitted with the appropriate breathing apparatus, oxygen tanks, and proper medication. A nurse was hired to oversee Shade's daily treatment, although her movement inside the castle was limited and she was required to leave the grounds at night. Still, Shade was not doing well. Nevertheless, he refused to limit his activities as far as RanCorp went.

Rianocek and his staff were in the process of reviewing the activities that RanCorp was involved in around the world. A $2 million fee had been charged to a crime family of New York City to fix a federal racketeering trial involving certain high-ranking members of the organization. Using a private-investigating firm in the New York/New Jersey area, a child-molesting charge from the presiding judge's early college years was discovered, and four jurors were secretly intimidated through vulnerable family members. The indicted mobsters would eventually be acquitted.

A high-ranking elected American official had problems with a number of allegations against him regarding unwanted sexual advances he had made toward women *and* men, particularly teenage boys. The tabloids referred to him as an "aggressive sexual predator" and compared this scandal to the one that Bill Clinton had experienced as a result of the Monica Lewinsky affair. But the current scandal brewing in Washington, D.C., made former president Clinton look like a Trappist monk.

RanCorp was retained for $3.5 million to make the elected official's problems go away. And they did. Each of the politician's accusers met with sudden mysterious deaths. Eight people were killed in auto accidents, by suicide, in plane wrecks, and through other violent misadventures. Official investigations into these deaths were mounted by the FBI, as a criminal conspiracy to engage in mass homicide in order to obstruct justice was suspected. These investigations were currently in progress. However, nothing was discovered to either link the elected official to any of the deaths or indicate that they were anything other than accidents. RanCorp had seen to that.

The collapse of the Soviet Union had led to a bumper crop of sophisticated weapons, including atomic bombs, becoming available on the international black market. RanCorp had initially gotten into this business as a broker for sales from corrupt Russian officials to terrorist groups and Third World dictatorships. But problems developed when the Russian Mafia became a competitor of RanCorp in the illegal arms business. There were threats of violence from the Russians, which could have led to war between the two criminal factions. This Rianocek would not allow. It was not because the Bavarian assassin was afraid of the Russian Mafia, but only because open warfare simply was bad for business.

RanCorp had an endless succession of lucrative deals going at any one time. They managed to avoid official scrutiny by maintaining a front as a consulting firm specializing in executive security, international public relations, and as advisors in matters of diplomatic protocol. They also had help from the CIA, with which Rian-ocek had maintained a close relationship since his second incarnation as a global assassin dating back to 1999. However, Dickie Fagan had retired.

To hire RanCorp, prospective clients didn't pick up the telephone and call long distance to Bavaria, nor did they come knocking at the von Rianocek castle gate. To employ the very special firm, it was necessary to first have a great deal of money and the proper "contacts." This had kept the assassin's murderous corporation from being compromised by a few clever law-enforcement officials, like Gordon Edwards of Scotland Yard, Larry Cole of the Chicago Police Department, and Joe E. Leak of the New York City Police Department.

Now the RanCorp executive staff came to the last item on the day's agenda: the new clients' list. This was Hannah Spencer's area of concentration.

"We have a Canadian cattle rancher, who is anticipating a costly, complicated divorce from his third wife. The rancher is requesting our intervention on his behalf," she said, reading from a computer printout. "Our prospective client has a net worth of eight million Canadian dollars. As his wife will receive at least half of that amount in a divorce action and her untimely death will also net him a tidy sum in a double-indemnity insurance settlement, I suggest that we demand a one-million-dollar fee for the job."

"Quote the price to him through our representative in Toronto," Rianocek said. "If he doesn't accept the deal, have our operative threaten to report his murder-for-hire conspiracy to the authorities. I assume we have the usual video and audio records of the transaction."

Hannah Spencer smiled. "That is standard procedure, Baron."

"Good," Rianocek said. "After our Canadian cowboy with marital problems realizes that he can't back out, increase our projected fee by twenty-five percent."

"Done," Spencer said, before turning to the next item. "We have a somewhat unusual request from a potential client in the United States."

"Different in what manner?" the assassin asked.

"He is asking for a personal meeting with you."

"You mean a personal meeting with the CEO of RanCorp?"

"No." She looked up from her notes. "He has asked for a personal meeting with Baron Alain Marcus Casimir von Rianocek. He explained to our representative in Chicago that he is calling in a debt that you owe him dating back to December 1977 and, I quote, ' . . . the aborted assassination of then-reigning Mafia Godfather Paul Arcadio.' "

Rianocek mumbled something that the others could barely hear, which sounded like "I owe you one." After hesitating a moment, he asked Hannah Spencer, "What is this client's name?"

"Cleveland Emmett Barksdale III."

69

Chicago, Illinois
SEPTEMBER 15, 2002
10:17 A.M.

The storefront was located in a remodeled building in the 7200 block of South Stony Island Avenue. The front of the business was painted white, and the plate-glass windows were tinted blue. An ornate silver border trimmed the edges of the window, and the business's name was painted in Old English script across it. Any passersby taking the time to glance inside would see a large showroom displaying a wide variety of tastefully displayed merchandise. However, despite the attractive facade and the artistic arrangement of the available product, most people avoided this place because the business was called the C. E. Barksdale Casket and Burial Insurance Company. The proprietor was in the death business.

On this morning, a woman approached the ornate storefront and entered. She was an elegantly dressed, stunningly built, platinum blonde. She walked with long, confident strides, but a close examination of her gait revealed the presence of a slight limp. Hannah Spencer was paying a visit to the C. E. Barksdale Casket and Burial Insurance Company.

A chime sounded when the door opened. It was a soft tinkling sound, but in this environment, it had an ominous ring of finality. Initially, the interior appeared empty. The female assassin stopped a few feet inside the entrance and waited. Thirty seconds passed before a gaunt, balding man stepped from behind a brass casket display against the far wall and walked toward her. Apparently, he had concealed himself behind the display to spy on anyone entering the store. And as he came closer, the very deadly female killer felt a surge of revulsion tinged by apprehension as an aura of death surrounded this man like a shroud.

"Good morning, madame. May I help you?"

She managed a smile. "Perhaps. I'd like to look at a casket and purchase some insurance."

The strange man graced her with a dazzling smile that altered his grim appearance and made him seem almost cheerful. Then the woman, who had spent her entire adult life as an assassin, recognized that it was not joy illuminating the proprietor of this parlor of death, but madness.

"Well, you certainly have come to the right place, dear lady." He extended a bony hand. "I am Cleveland Emmett Barksdale. This is my establishment."

She took the hand, which was cold and clammy. "My pleasure, sir." She made it a point of not giving him her name.

The smile froze on his face. "Permit me to show you around."

"Why don't we look into the burial insurance first?"

"If you'd like. Come right this way." He led her to a glass-partitioned office at the back of the store.

The office was austere to the point of being spartan. There was a metal desk and three folding chairs. No pictures or other ornamentation adorned the walls. But there was a bookcase containing a set of old law books. The proprietor of the casket and burial insurance business noticed his guest's scrutiny.

"The books belonged to a deceased relative of mine, who was a lawyer," he explained. "I keep them for purely sentimental reasons."

"How nice," she said, taking a seat.

Opening one of the desk drawers, he extracted three brochures, which he arranged in front of her. He leaned across the desk and she caught a whiff of his cologne, which possessed a strong, cloying, unpleasant odor. She slid her chair back a couple of inches.

Each of the brochures had a different color scheme: gold, red, or blue. Barksdale explained that the colors designated a different monetary value.

"The blue one we call our 'economy with dignity' plan. Although it is inexpensive, it can provide a loved one or, in some distant future, yourself, dear lady, with quite a nice casket, funeral service, and graveside interment. Plan Red, although costing substantially more than Plan Blue, will provide—"

The front-door chime sounded, interrupting the sales pitch. "Could you excuse me for a moment, madame? I'll be right back."

"Take your time." She picked up the gold folder. "I'll just make myself at home."

He left the office, leaving the door open behind him. She heard him say. "Good morning, Reverend Finney. I think I have what we talked about on the phone right over here."

He returned to the office exactly six minutes and twenty-seven seconds later to find her still seated, but with a law book open on top of his desk. He stiffened, but said nothing. Walking around the desk, he picked up the book and returned it to the bookcase. When he turned around, he found her smiling up at him.

"I noticed that the bookplate on the inside cover bore the name Cleveland Emmett Barksdale, Esquire."

The merchant, who dealt in the paraphernalia of death, had turned to stone. In a voice she could barely hear, he said, "I told you that the law books belonged to a relative."

"Would that be a relative who died a few years ago while under investigation by the police for drug trafficking? A prominent attorney of advanced age, who left a lone surviving relative, his grandson?"

This galvanized Barksdale into action. Crossing the office, he snatched the burial-plan brochures off the desk and shoved them back into a desk drawer. "Are you a reporter or something?"

She stood up and faced him from a distance of less than a foot. Her presence and manner made him nervous. "I'm an ' . . . or something.' " she said.

"I would appreciate it if you would leave my place of business right now, madame."

Defiantly, she returned to her seat. "Keep your shirt on, Clevey, I'm a friend. That is what they used to call you, isn't it? Clevey?"

He remained standing. A confusing mixture of outrage and fear warred within him, but he made no response to her question.

"So, Clevey," she said matter-of-factly, "what is it that you believe that Baron Alain Marcus Casimir von Rianocek owes you and your deceased grandfather?"

70

After the trial in the summer of 1999, the State of Illinois mounted a civil action against the estates of Cleveland Emmett Barksdale, Esquire (deceased) and Cleveland Emmett Barksdale, III under the Asset Forfeiture Act of the Controlled Substance Abuse with Intent for Sale or Profit Statute. Ordinarily, drug dealers, especially those who sold dope on the scale that the Barksdales were alleged to have done, would have had everything they owned— homes, cars, furniture, boats, airplanes, clothing and jewelry—confiscated. But Penelope Josephson had fought the proceeding with every ounce of legal skill that she possessed.

The billion-dollar Barksdale fortune was gone, as the state's attorney's team of civil lawyers, assisted by Gus Lindsay, revealed to the court that most of the money had been obtained illegally. However, Penny was able to show that there were certain Barksdale family assets of long standing, which had no connection to the drug business at all. The mansion in Beverly Hills, its furnishings, a couple of cars, and a trust fund, which Cleve, Sr. had set up at the time of his grandson's birth, were protected. The net worth of the Barksdale estate dropped from a June 1999 value of $1.2 billion to less than $500,000 in September 2002. The majority of this wealth was tied up in the mansion and external grounds. But at least Clevey Barksdale had a roof over his head after he got out of prison.

Because of his reduced circumstances, Clevey could no longer afford to maintain a staff of full-time servants. He was able to employ a part-time cleaning woman and a cooking service, which provided door-to-door breakfast and dinner deliveries to a number of residences in his neighborhood. Tonight the lone resident of the Barksdale mansion had ordered dinner for four.

As there were no servants, Clevey personally served the dinner of broiled whitefish, boiled potatoes, broccoli with hollandaise sauce, hot dinner rolls and apple pie with vanilla ice cream to his guests. Predinner cocktails were available with Barksdale serving as bartender, and a vintage white zinfadel wine was served during the meal. Brandy was available in the study after dinner. The dining-room tablecloth and the napkins were of white linen; the eating utensils were sterling silver; and the glasses were of gilt-edged crystal. Barksdale still possessed a sense of style.

The former attorney's guests were Baron Alain von Rianocek, Hannah Spencer, and Cornelius Shade. Business was not discussed during dinner. The conversation that passed between his guests and their host was polite, but inconsequential. Barksdale left the dishes on the dining-room table and led the dinner party into the study. Hannah Spencer offered to help with the drinks, but the host declined and did the honors himself. It was Barksdale's objective to place his guests in the best possible frame of mind for the proposal he was about to place before them.

The study had been preserved in the same condition that it had been in on that last night that he had met there with his grandfather before their arrest. The law books on the varnished wooden shelves, his grandfather's large desk, and the Persian carpet with the cigarette burn in it were all the same. Although he needed nothing to help him remember his grandfather, Barksdale always felt the dead man's strong spiritual presence whenever he was here.

Barksdale took a seat behind the desk, and his guests sat in easy chairs around the room. When they were settled comfortably, he leaned forward and said, "Shall we get down to business?"

The assassin, clad in a blue blazer with the von Rianocek crest embroidered over the left breast pocket, lifted a snifter of Hennessy cognac to his host and replied, "By all means."

When Clevey was the managing partner of Barksdale, Barksdale, and DeVito, P.C., he had seldom appeared in court on behalf of any client; and the last time he had been in a courtroom, he was the defendant. But he was a Harvard Law School graduate and had an excellent legal background as a result of being raised from childhood by one of the most clever attorneys ever to practice law in the state of Illinois. So he knew how to argue a case effectively. Now he called on everything he had ever learned to present the proposition to his three guests.

"In December of 1977, Baron von Rianocek, my grandfather, the late Cleveland Emmett Barksdale, hired you to kill Chicago Mafia Don Paul 'the Rabbit' Arcadio. You received a substantial down payment for the assassination, but the contract was never carried out."

"The fee was returned," Rianocek said softly; however, everyone noticed the strain in his voice. The assassin was not a man who accepted failure—even a decades-old failure—lightly.

"Yes, it was," Barksdale said, "but there was also, shall we call it a pledge, promise or guarantee made following the aborted contract." He picked up a age-yellowed sheet of paper from the surface of the desk and handed it to the assassin. Rianocek read the telegram. "Was unable to carry out the assignment. I owe you one." It was signed with the letter "A."

"It is my understanding," Barksdale continued, "that this was the only actual failure that you experienced during your illustrious career."

Rianocek stared at the telegram for a full minute longer before he tossed it back on the desk in front of their host. The baron said disdainfully, "That is ancient history."

Barksdale smiled. "Yes, nothing but a minor blemish in an otherwise-sterling career. But the failure really wasn't your fault, was it, Baron von Rianocek?"

The assassin placed his brandy glass down on an end table with an audible clink, crossed his legs, and said, "The reason that I sent that telegram to your grandfather was because then, as is the case now, I always guranteed my work regardless of any obstacles or difficulties. On that December night in 1977, I was in the house preparing to carry out the contract when the police arrived. They arrested Arcadio, which forced me to abort."

"Tell me, Baron von Rianocek," Barksdale said in a soft voice, "was that night the first time you ever encountered Larry Cole?"

Rianocek gave Barksdale a look that would have frightened most human beings. However, the former attorney absorbed the glare with an ease that succeeded in impressing even Hannah Spencer and Cornelius Shade. Then the assassin did the unexpected. He laughed.

"Mr. Cole and I have crossed paths more than once. But you are correct about one thing. The night of the aborted hit on Paul Arcadio was the first time I ever came in contact with him."

"So he was the reason that you were unable to carry out my grandfather's contract?"

"Let's say he was a contributing factor."

Barksdale cleared his throat. "He was also a contributing factor in what occurred with your operation in New York City in the fall of 1989. In fact, had it not been for Cole, the assassination in the M. D. Hines Building in Manhattan would have gone off without a hitch, and Ms. Spencer would not have been injured."

"How dare you?!" the female assassin flared.

Rianocek held up a hand, and she went silent instantly. However, she continued seething.

"You are very well informed, Mr. Barksdale, but exactly where is all this leading us?" There was a demanding tone of finality in Rianocek's voice. His patience was obviously wearing thin, as was the case with his companions.

Barksdale sat up a little straighter and his face became set in a furiously intense grimace. "Please bear with me a moment longer, Baron von Rianocek, and if I have offended you, Ms. Spencer, I apologize. As to where this is leading, let me say this. The three of you and I owe Chief Larry Cole a great deal. Whereas you suffered business setbacks because of him, I lost virtually everything I had, including the one human being on this Earth whom I ever truly loved." His eyes misted and he blinked away tears. When he again spoke, his voice was hoarse with emotion. "I propose that we settle with Cole, Baron von Rianocek. Settle with him for what he did to you"—he extended an index finger to take in the three people seated in the study with him—"and for what he did to me. I also propose that we do so in a spectacular fashion, which will go down in history."

For a long moment, no one spoke. Finally, Rianocek glanced at his companions before asking their host, "What are you suggesting, Mr. Barksdale?"

71

SEPTEMBER 16, 2002
2:15 P.M.

Detective Mike Castigliano, who had been wounded in the shoot-out at the Barksdale Manufacturing Company in 1999, was assigned to the Recruit Processing Section of the Chicago Police Department's Personnel Division. His job was to check the backgrounds of police applicants. After he had recovered from his gunshot wounds, the doctors told him that he would have only 50 percent use of his right arm. Because it was a line-of-duty injury, Castigliano was given a meritorious promotion to detective and assigned to the Personnel Division. It was a job which paid well and was not very demanding. In fact, Castigliano felt more like a clerk than a cop. But police work was still very much in his system.

Whenever he was out "in the field" conducting background investigations, he kept his police-band radio tuned to the frequency that the operational units were on. His former partner, Tommy Becker, had just been promoted to sergeant and had been assigned to the Gang Crimes North squad. From time to time, particularly when he'd had a beer or two too many, Castigliano wondered how things would have worked out if Becker had taken that bullet instead of him. But he realized that there was nothing he could do about his current situation, so he continued to monitor "real" police calls, respond occasionally to a crime-in-progress call, where he served in a backup-only role, and to dream about what could have been.

Then Detective Mike Castigliano of the Chicago Police Department Personnel Division caught a break. He discovered the C. E. Barksdale Casket and Burial Insurance Company.

He had driven up and down South Stony Island Avenue hundreds of times when he was a Gang Crimes Specialist and after his career-ending injury. He had seen the storefront a countless number of times prior to the current tenant moving in. He couldn't recall any of the businesses that had been at this location before, and he might have missed it completely had it not been for one of the assist calls that he responded to.

It was a "Man with a Gun" call at 7300 South Stony Island Avenue. The offender was reported by the Office of Emergency Communications operator as a black male wearing a Chicago Cubs baseball team jacket. Castigliano realized that this call was less than one-half mile from the location where the Barksdale Manufacturing plant had been.

To get to the scene at 73rd and South Stony Island, he had to travel a distance of ten city blocks. By the time he pulled up, a pair of Third District tactical cops had the offender in custody after recovering a .45 caliber Colt derringer from his belt. They waved the Personnel Division detective off, and Castigliano made a left turn to cross the Stony Island parkway and proceed north from 73rd Street when he saw the storefront with the blue-tinted windows.

The business's name—The C. E. Barksdale Casket and Burial Insurance Company—made the detective's mouth go dry. That was six months ago.

Castigliano had testified at the Peace Stones trial. He had been present for every moment of the proceedings and also attended the sentencing of Shelton Booker and MacArthur Williams, who had attempted to kill him, Cole, Silvestri, and Tommy Becker. Castigliano did not attend Barksdale's sentencing because he had a physical-therapy session that afternoon. However, he remained intensely interested in the man who had been the mastermind behind the drug plant. The fact that Barksdale had been released from prison so early angered the handicapped detective. Castigliano had lost the full use of his right arm because of this man, who had received a nominal prison sentence, at best.

Still stopped at the cross street, Mike Castigliano began doing some figuring in his head. Perhaps, he mused, this C. E. Barksdale on the sign was not *his* Barksdale. Then he realized that there weren't a lot of people with that name walking around Chicago.

A car pulled up behind him and blew its horn. Distracted, it took Castigliano a moment to pull across the intersection and park the police car in a tow-away zone. Before he realized what he was doing, he was out of the car and walking back toward the C. E. Barksdale Casket and Burial Insurance Company.

He decided not to enter the office, but instead looked through the front window at the casket showroom. He couldn't see anyone inside. The scar, caused by the bullet tearing through his forearm, began to throb. He was certain that this place was a front for some type of criminal activity, just as the South Chicago drug plant had been. And at that moment, Detective Mike Castigliano of the Personnel Division vowed to bust the C. E. Barksdale Casket and Burial Insurance Company's ex-con proprietor.

As Castigliano turned to go back to his squad car, a shadowy figure moved across the casket showroom to the window. Clevey Barksdale watched the policeman, whom he recognized. Clevey wondered what Detective Castigliano had in mind. Perhaps he was interested in purchasing a casket or some burial insurance. After all, Castigliano was in a hazardous line of work.

"Lieutenant Klein wants to see you, Mike," Sergeant Kenny informed Detective Castigliano, who was seated at his desk in the Personnel Division office complex at police headquarters.

Slowly, he got to his feet and went to the lieutenant's office at the far end of the office bay. After knocking once, he went inside.

Ten minutes later, he came out. The other officers present noticed Castigliano's pale, sweating face. Whatever had just gone down inside the CO's office had not been pleasant. However, the observers knew that this had been coming for a long time. Mike was a good guy and also a hero, because he'd been shot in the line of duty. But lately he hadn't been doing his job. He did report to work on time and most nights he stayed late, which made everything all the more puzzling, because his caseload was seriously delinquent. He hadn't completed a single police-applicant background investigation in six months. With a new class going into the academy in November, the entire Personnel Division was working overtime to get the processing done. Malingering by investigators could not be tolerated, even for a guy with Mike Castigliano's reputation. So the lieutenant in charge of the Recruit Processing section had called him on the carpet.

Now, as his coworkers looked on, Detective Castigliano picked up his briefcase with his good arm and headed for the door. To a man, they all hoped that Mike would take the lieutenant's tongue-lashing to heart. Because if he didn't, there was no other job for him in the department. If he lost his assignment in Personnel, he would be forced to retire and take a 50 percent disability pension.

And what the CO of Recruit Processing had said did indeed frighten Mike Castigliano. But not because he was afraid of losing his job. If what he was working on bore fruit, he would be in line for a meritorious promotion to the rank of sergeant, despite his injuries. He only hoped that his superiors in Personnel would give him enough time to put it all together.

After signing an unmarked car out of the garage at police headquarters, Detective Castigliano headed south for the C. E. Barksdale Casket and Burial Insurance Company on South Stony Island Avenue.

72

SEPTEMBER 17, 2002
4:05 P.M.

"Why did you select this type of business to go into?" Rianocek asked, looking out through the glass partition in Barksdale's office at the casket showroom.

The proprietor of the unusual business smiled. Rianocek remarked to himself that every time Barksdale did this, the insanity gripping him became quite evident. The assassin would ordinarily not have become involved with someone like him at all. However, what Barksdale was proposing was so intriguing that Rianocek could not pass up the opportunity. And it would also help the assassin settle a few old scores.

His smile still in place, Barksdale responded, "This is a rather lucrative endeavor, Baron von Rianocek. I have an endless stream of clients, a substantial profit margin and, you could say that I am performing a public service of a sort. And perhaps you haven't noticed"—he pointed through the glass out at the casket showroom—"few people ever come in here, and those who do don't stay very long."

"You seem to have thought of everything. I was definitely impressed by the plan you laid out for me last night."

Again Barksdale gave him that strange smile. "I thought you would be, but then everything depended on your acceptance of my proposal."

"Why?"

Barksdale shrugged. "Because I don't have the money to pay your fee."

The assassin laughed. "I guess you've got a point. After all, I do indeed owe you one." With that, he got to his feet and extended his hand. Barksdale took it and the two men shook like old friends. What they were planning had made them fast comrades overnight.

"I will work on things from my end," Rianocek said. "I don't think there will be any problems obtaining what we need for the operation."

"And my timetable?"

"I'll be ready by December," the assassin responded. "Don't worry about that."

Barksdale accompanied his guest to the front door. A misty rain was falling, and Cornelius Shade was waiting at the curb in a black Land Rover. Rianocek lowered his head and ran across the sidewalk to climb into the passenger seat.

Barksdale called after him, "Keep in touch."

Slamming the car door behind him, Rianocek waved. Shade put the Land Rover in gear and drove north on Stony Island Avenue.

Barksdale remained standing at the front door for a moment before retreating back into the casket showroom. In an instant he was no longer visible from the street.

A block away, near the corner of 74th Street and South Stony Island Avenue, Detective Mike Castigliano used a pair of binoculars to observe the Land Rover drive away from the C. E. Barksdale Casket and Burial Insurance Company. The detective had placed the storefront office and showroom under surveillance at 2:15 P.M. To keep Lieutenant Klein and Sergeant Kenny off his back, he had completed a couple of recruit background investigations that day. Using a Nikon camera equipped with a telescopic lens, Castigliano had taken a photograph of the tall, aristocratic man when he entered Barksdale's place. Instinctively, the cop had known that this guy wasn't an American. He was unable to see the driver of the Land Rover and it made him curious. He'd run the license plate and discovered that it was a rental. Castigliano figured that a car like that had to cost at least a C-note a day to rent. That seemed like an awful lot of money for a guy to spend to come to the South Side looking for a coffin or some burial insurance.

Castigliano's damaged arm began to ache due to the damp weather; however, his curiosity had gone into overdrive. Putting the squad car in gear, he abandoned his surveillance of the C. E. Barksdale Casket and Burial Insurance Company and followed the Land Rover.

Shade drove north and entered Jackson Park at 67th Street. The only sound in the car was the wheezing noise the Englishman made with each inhalation. They were traveling past the National Science and Space Museum when he broke the silence.

"Isn't that bloke Barksdale a bit mad, sir?"

Rianocek was studying the gray facade of the huge museum. Without turning around, he said, "There's a method to his madness, Mr. Shade. The plan he has devised to get even with our old friend Larry Cole is pure artistry."

"But we have the plan now. What do we still need with Barksdale?"

The assassin turned to look at Shade. "Because I made a promise to his grandfather years ago, and I plan to keep it."

"I understand, sir," Shade said contritely. "Will I have a role in this operation?"

They had pulled onto Lake Shore Drive and were speeding

north. "I want you to set up a command center in our hotel. There will be plenty of details to keep track of before we become operational in December."

"Begging your pardon, sir, but I'd rather be out in the field with you. Ms. Spencer can—"

"Are you questioning my orders, Mr. Shade?!"

"No, sir. Not at all, sir. The command post it will be, sir." Then he emitted a loud, racking cough.

Rianocek went back to observing the scenery. He commented quietly, "You can't stand up to fieldwork anymore. It would kill you."

Shade didn't comment.

73

SEPTEMBER 17, 2002
5:45 P.M.

The assassin was headquartered in the Drake Hotel on Michigan Avenue in downtown Chicago. As was the practice whenever they were outside of Germany, the suite of rooms was in Cornelius Shade's name. Hannah Spencer had remained at the Drake, while Shade drove Rianocek to visit Barksdale.

Now the assassin and his asthmatic assistant were on Lake Shore Drive approaching the Chicago Avenue exit when Shade again noticed the brown Chevrolet hanging four car lengths off the Land Rover's rear bumper. This was the third time he had seen this same car behind them since they'd left Barksdale's address. Shade was certain that it was the same car because there was a large rust spot on the hood. He was also able to see that there was only a lone driver in the car.

Shade was still smarting from the remark that the baron had made about him being unable to do fieldwork anymore. Maybe this situation with the mysterious car was just what he needed to prove that he could still function in the assassin's trade and do so effectively.

Shade pulled the Land Rover up to the south entrance of the hotel. A doorman leaped off the curb with an umbrella held high and snatched open the passenger door to escort Baron von Rianocek through the falling rain to the shelter of the canopied entrance. A parking attendant, wearing a yellow rain slicker, walked around to the driver's side to give Shade a ticket for valet parking the car in the hotel garage. The Baron's driver was considered a menial and did not rate the umbrella escort treatment.

Shade rolled down the window and said, "I'm going to keep the car for a while."

Rianocek had already entered the hotel lobby and didn't look back. Shade checked the rearview mirror. There were a lot of cars on this downtown street and most of them had their lights on because of the approach of twilight and the falling rain. Despite his thick glasses, he spotted the brown Chevy parked down the block.

Shade crossed his fingers as he pulled away from the entrance to the Drake and drove across Michigan Avenue. Driving past DeWitt Plaza, he looked back to find the rusty car following him.

Shade was fairly certain that the guy in the Chevy was a cop, but if he wasn't, his presence didn't mean him, Baron von Rianocek, or their operation any good. So Cornelius Shade decided to personally take care of this intruder and prove that he was still very good at dispensing violent death.

Mike Castigliano watched the Land Rover pull away from the Drake. Now it was decision time. The tall guy had entered the lobby. The detective had already taken a photograph, which would make it simple enough for Castigliano to ID him through hotel

security. However, the driver had remained unseen. Castigliano decided to tail the black Land Rover.

The rain was falling heavily now, but the big four-by-four vehicle was easy enough to follow. When they reached the dense
traffic of Rush Street, the detective cut the distance between
them. When the Land Rover turned north, Castigliano was right behind it.

They proceeded in this fashion up to Oak Street. The Land
Rover pulled into a public parking lot west of the intersection. Castigliano drove down the block to a red zone, where he pulled to the
curb and draped the police-radio microphone cord over the rearview
mirror. Getting out of the car and pulling up his collar against the
falling rain, he trotted back to the corner. He was forced to leave
his camera in the car because carrying it would make him too conspicuous.

Castigliano could see the entrance to the parking lot and the
passenger side of the Land Rover. The interior light went on when
the door opened, but the rain made it impossible to see the driver.
Then, as Castigliano looked on, a man took a ticket from the car
hiker and walked out of the lot. The detective followed.

The man was short and walked slowly with a stooped, hunched-
over shuffle. He wore a battered snap-brim hat, which he kept pulled
low on his forehead. His back was to the trailing detective, who
was still unable to see the suspect's face. Castigliano was able to
keep up with him easily because he walked at a snail's pace.

For a moment, the detective thought he was headed back for
the Drake Hotel. Then, in mid-block on Oak Street between Michigan and Rush, he crossed to the Esquire Theater. Castigliano
stopped and stepped into the doorway of a woman's clothing store.
The place was open for business and he was back lit by a neon
sign. The man he was following did not turn around. Apparently,
he was going to the movies, and Detective Mike Castigliano
planned to go with him.

Waiting until the man purchased his ticket and entered the lobby, Castigliano crossed the street and flashed his badge at the attendant inside the booth. As he did so, the pain in his bad arm because so intense that he almost groaned. But he had a job to do and wasn't about to let an old bullet wound stop him from doing it.

"What movie is the guy that just bought a ticket going to see?"

"You mean the man with asthma?" the young man behind the glass said, his eyes going wide in surprise. "He's going to see *Good Cop, Bad Cop* in theater three, but it started almost an hour ago. I told him, but he said he didn't care."

"What's that you said about him having asthma?"

The attendant shrugged. "My sister's got it, Officer, but she's nowhere near in as bad a shape as the guy that just went inside is. I didn't think he was going to make it at all, he was blowing so hard."

"Thanks," the detective said, entering the theater lobby.

Castigliano again flashed his badge at the female usher collecting tickets. "Did the man who just came in go into theater three?"

"No, sir," she said. "I think he's sick. I offered to call an ambulance, but he said he would be okay."

"Where is he now?"

"He went to the men's room." She pointed to a door at the far end of the lobby.

Castigliano looked around. There was no place where he could conceal himself, and if he entered the theater, the suspect could easily slip back out. Basically, all he wanted to do was eyeball this guy for future reference. So he decided to follow him into the men's room.

Pushing open the door, Castigliano entered a well-lighted, white-tiled room. There were two metal sinks beneath a mirror and a paper towel dispenser on the far wall, three urinals on the adjacent wall, and two toilet stalls against the wall opposite the mirror. The detective spied the man he had been tailing instantly. He was down on one knee with his head against one of the sinks. His back was to the door, but Castigliano could easily hear his ragged breathing. As the ticket taker in the lobby had said, this guy was in a bad way. Forgetting the surveillance, Castigliano crossed the washroom and stood over the kneeling man.

"Hey, buddy, are you okay?"

Detective Mike Castigliano was totally unprepared for Cornelius Shade's attack. The kneeling man spun toward the detective and jabbed the knuckles of his left hand into the cop's exposed throat. At this point, the detective was more surprised than in pain as his hands flew up to protect the injured area, but it was too late. His larynx had been shattered. In a matter of minutes, he would be dead from suffocation. However, Cornelius Shade was a great deal more efficient an assassin than that.

Getting quickly to his feet, showing no signs of the incapacitating lung ailment he had used to lure the detective into the trap, Shade struck Castigliano across the left temple with the edge of his right hand. The detective dropped to the floor and lay motionless.

Shade checked the detective's pulse and grunted with satisfaction when he discovered that the man who had tailed him was dead. Stepping around behind him, the assassin lifted the body into a sitting position and dragged it into one of the stalls. By the time he got the dead man seated on the stool, Shade was sweating profusely, and his lungs ached from the exertion.

Quickly, he searched his victim. Finding the badge and snub-nosed revolver made the assassin smile. Baron von Rianocek would be glad to know that the detective had been following them.

Pocketing the gun and badge, Shade removed an inhaler from his pocket and took a healthy gulp, which made him cough. A thick wad of phlegm came up into his throat, and he spit it out on the floor. Then he cracked open the door to make sure no one had entered the washroom. Finding the place vacant, he crossed to the emergency exit door and stepped into the alley behind the theater. A few minutes later he retrieved the Land Rover from the public parking lot and headed back to the Drake Hotel. To say the least, Cornelius Shade was very proud of himself.

74

SEPTEMBER 17, 2002
6:32 P.M.

Chief of Detectives Larry Cole was about to leave his office at the new police headquarters complex at 35th and Michigan when Sergeant Judy Daniels called to him. She was seated at a desk in the private office area reserved for the chief of detectives and his staff. The new police headquarters building was ultramodern, with lots of room. Cole was still getting used to it after the cramped space of the former HQ at 11th and State.

"What's up, Judy?" Cole said, walking over to her desk.

The Mistress of Disguise/High Priestess of Mayhem had adopted a look for the day that Manny Sherlock had dubbed "the Viking Princess." She was wearing a blond wig with two braids hanging down to the small of her back. She wore a milkmaid costume consisting of a white blouse, denim jumper, and a pair of brown clogs that appeared to be made of wood. Now, as Cole got a close-up view of her, he noticed that she had accomplished one of the most thorough transformations he had ever seen. And, in the eight years that she had worked for him, he had seen her adopt some very elaborate disguises.

To alter her appearance even further, she used body padding as well as pads inside her cheeks. Her false eyelashes and blue contact lenses caused Cole to double-check the nameplate on her desk.

She pointed to the multichannel Sabre portable radio next to the desk name plate. "There's a report from the Eighteenth District of a homicide victim in the men's room of the Esquire Theater on Oak Street."

Even her voice sounded different. Mentally scolding himself, he concentrated on what she was saying, as opposed to how she was saying it.

"One of the officers at the scene believes that the victim is a detective assigned to the Personnel Division," she said.

"Let's go." He said, turning to head for the door. "When we get to the car, radio Blackie and Manny to meet us there."

As she slipped on a red hooded, plastic raincoat, the image of a girl romping through the forest on the way to Grandma's house flashed through his mind. But as they left the office, Cole was forced to admit that if the Big Bad Wolf ever ran into the Mistress of Disguise/High Priestess of Mayhem, the poor canine would never survive the encounter.

By the time Cole and Judy arrived at the theater, Blackie and Manny were already there. The rain was still falling, and the forecast was for no letup in the next twenty-four hours. Blackie was waiting for Cole in the lobby. The chief took one look at his old friend's face and knew that the news wasn't good.

There were a number of cops, in and out of uniform, in the lobby. Exhibiting a mixture of fear and excitement, the theater employees, who had seen the dead detective and the man who was suspected of killing him, were standing near the candy counter.

As Blackie led Cole across the lobby he filled the chief in. "Detective Mike Castigliano, badge #24770, was the victim of a fatal assault in the men's room. His star and gun are missing."

Cole frowned. "Mike Castigliano? Where do I know that name from?"

"He was the Gang Crimes officer who was wounded in the gun battle at the Barksdale narcotics factory a few years back."

Cole's face fell. "I remember him now. He received a meritorious promotion to detective and was assigned to the Personnel Division on limited duty."

"That's him," Blackie said.

"What was he doing down here?"

They reached the men's washroom door, where a uniformed officer stood guard. Tipping his cap to the chief and the lieutenant, the officer said, "The crime lab is finished with the scene, sir. The wagon crew is standing by to remove the body."

Cole and Blackie entered. The crime-lab technicians were packing up their gear. They acknowledged the chief of detectives' presence and went back to their tasks. Blackie went over to confer with them while Cole examined the body in the stall.

Despite the severe bruising of the left temple and the grayish pallor of the skin, Mike Castigliano looked much the same as he had the last time Cole had seen him. It was obvious that his death had been very violent. Blackie stepped up beside Cole.

"It's not a pretty sight, Boss."

"Is it ever?" Cole said.

They went back into the lobby. Blackie continued to brief Cole on what they had so far. "I talked to the Personnel Division CO, Lieutenant John Klein, and he told me that all of the recruit-background investigations that Castigliano was assigned to conduct were out on the South Side. Klein also told me that he had to call Castigliano in and have a talk with him this morning, because all of his cases were delinquent. Klein said that for the past six months Castigliano had been preoccupied, but he wouldn't tell anyone what was wrong. He wasn't married, so Klein figured he had girlfriend problems, or some such. Castigliano was supposed to return the squad car and go off duty at five o'clock this afternoon. No one from his unit saw or heard from him since nine o'clock this morning."

"So what was he doing down here on Rush Street?" Cole asked.

"He was following a guy with a breathing problem, like he had emphysema or asthma, who entered the theater and went straight to the washroom. Castigliano went in after him and was killed. Our killer went out the fire exit, and the kid working the ticket booth found the detective's body."

Something about a killer with a breathing problem struck a chord of memory for Cole, but he couldn't focus on it right at that moment. "Did they find Castigliano's police car?"

At that moment Judy Daniels approached them. "The squad car is parked in a red zone around the corner. Manny is over there with the crime-lab guys, who are going through it. There's a camera and a pair of binoculars lying on the front seat. Detective Castigliano was working on something, Chief, and it didn't have anything to do with recruit-background investigations."

75

SEPTEMBER 18, 2002
8:45 A.M.

Larry Cole arrived at police headquarters and went to his office, which still smelled of a strong disinfecting solvent from having been cleaned during the night. Blackie, Manny, and Judy had not arrived yet and he was forced to make the first pot of coffee. Actually, Cole didn't mind doing this; he made better coffee than anyone else on the staff. Blackie's was always as strong as lye and possessed the consistency of mud; Judy's was so weak that it tasted more like brown hot water than coffee; and Manny's, whose brew probably came closest to Cole's, barely missed the mark, but still did not measure up.

With the pot percolating, Cole went to his desk to start the day's work. The city had hit a crime plateau since the beginning of the millennium. Of course there was still crime in the Windy City. However, the Chicago Police Department, particularly its investigative arm under Cole, dealt efficiently with the serial killers, drive-by gang shooters, and child murderers who preyed on the populace. The detective division had a phenomenal 80 percent clearance rate in cases where there were even the most remote leads. This 3,000-strong investigative force was held up as a national model for other big-city departments to emulate.

Cole picked up the summary of the felony reports that had come in during the last twenty-four hours. Then he noticed the interdepartmental correspondence envelope at the top of the stack of correspondence in his "In" box. It was addressed to him from Judy Daniels. Opening it, he found the results of the investigation into the murder of Detective Mike Castigliano the previous night. Judy had remained on the scene at the Esquire Theater to act as the liaison between Cole's office and the other assigned police units.

The chief of detectives found copies of all the documents that had been prepared detailing the investigation from the lengthy report of the assistant deputy superintendent to the terse case report of the beat officer assigned to do the preliminary investigation.

Cole scanned these reports, quickly finding little contained in them of which he wasn't aware. Then he came to the crime-laboratory report on the contents of Castigliano's police vehicle, which had been found parked in a red zone on Rush Street. Attached to this report was a pink inventory form, which listed a Nikon camera, a pair of Zeiss binoculars, and a roll of high-resolution color film. The lab had developed the film, and there was a smaller envelope inside the package containing the negatives and twelve photographs. Cole removed the photos from the envelope and spread them out on his desk blotter. He was still staring at them with concentrated absorption when Blackie Silvestri walked in ten minutes later.

*   *   *

"Mr. Shade and his party are no longer registered at the Drake, sir."

Clevey Barksdale replaced the receiver on its cradle and stood staring down at the instrument for a long time. Rianocek had told him to call this morning to set up a meeting to discuss some of the details of what they were planning for December. Barksdale knew that Rianocek didn't plan to remain in Chicago indefinitely. In fact, it would be necessary for the assassin and his crew to return to Europe sometime in the next few weeks to make the final arrangements. But suddenly Rianocek was gone, which meant that something unexpected had occurred.

Barksdale was not alarmed. Rianocek was resourceful and had proven himself capable of overcoming difficulties in the past skillfully. This was evidenced by the incident in New York City in 1989.

So he would just have to wait. If he had learned one thing in prison, it was patience.

The *Chicago Times-Herald* was rolled up in a protective sleeve on his desk. Barksdale had brought the newspaper with him from home, but hadn't opened it yet. As he had nothing else to do, he unwrapped the paper and sat down behind his desk to catch up on current events.

The front-page headline blared up at him: "Detective Slain In Magnificent Mile Movie Theater." There was a picture accompanying the story. Barksdale recognized Mike Castigliano instantly. The death merchant was just starting to read the story when the chime sounded, signaling the front door opening. Looking up through the glass partition, Barksdale immediately recognized the two visitors. This was the first time he had seen Larry Cole and Blackie Silvestri since his trial. The sight of them made his blood run cold. Slowly, he got to his feet and walked into the casket showroom to greet the two men who had caused him so much grief.

Cole and Blackie stood just inside the entrance to the showroom and waited for Barksdale to come to them. They could tell that their sudden appearance had badly shaken the proprietor of this uniquely gruesome establishment. However, he appeared to be recovering quickly.

"Good morning, gentlemen," he said with a slight tremble in his voice. "May I help you?"

The cops flashed their badges, but remained stonily silent.

"I have a very good memory, Chief Cole," Barksdale said. "I recognized you and Lieutenant Silvestri the instant you walked through the door. I assume you are interested in purchasing a casket or some burial insurance."

"No." Cole never took his eyes off Barksdale. "We want to ask you some questions."

Barksdale turned away and walked over to a silver casket ornamented with a gold crucifix. Opening the lid, he removed a pillow, fluffed it up a bit, and placed it back inside. Over his shoulder, he asked, "Questions about what?"

"The death of Detective Michael Castigliano," Blackie said in a tone that most people would term threatening.

Barksdale closed the casket and moved over to another model. This one was black with chrome handles. He repeated the same pillow-fluffing manuever. Finally, he turned around and said, "Who?"

Cole smiled. He realized that Barksdale was playing for time. Stalling in order to give himself the opportunity to calm down and perhaps place himself in a more advantageous position. The chief of detectives was also aware that Barksdale was a smart, well-educated man. But the former managing partner of the Barksdale, Barksdale and DeVito law firm was up against truly formidable opposition in Larry Cole and Blackie Silvestri.

"You've never heard the name Mike Castigliano before, Mr. Barksdale?" Cole asked.

"Can't say that I have," he responded.

From his trench-coat pocket, Cole removed the same edition of the *Times-Herald* that was on Barksdale's desk. Opening it to the front page, he showed it to the casket salesman. Cole watched Barksdale's eyes flicker momentarily toward the glass-partitioned office. The tabloid had struck a nerve.

Still holding up the newspaper, Cole said, "He was killed last night. You don't recognize his photograph?"

"No," Barksdale said without hesitation. "Should I?"

"Perhaps not." Cole returned the newspaper to his pocket. "But apparently he knew you."

"I don't understand what you mean?"

Blackie removed a brown envelope from inside his coat and walked over to the black coffin. "Maybe these will help explain what we're talking about."

The lieutenant began spreading photos on top of the casket. There were ten of them. Each was either of Barksdale or the front of the C. E. Barksdale Casket and Burial Insurance Company. There was also a photo of his house in Beverly Hills.

"What is this all about?" Barksdale said, swelling with outrage.

"We were hoping that you could tell us." Cole stepped up behind Barksdale on the opposite side from where Blackie was standing. Now the cops had their man flanked, which was done for a purpose. Cole continued, "Detective Castigliano took those pictures before he died. We thought you might be able to shed some light on the reason why."

Barksdale stepped away from them over to another casket; however, he didn't perform his pillow-fluffing act. Instead he turned to face them.

"Could I ask you gentlemen a question?"

"Certainly," Cole responded.

"What was Detective Castigliano's assignment?"

Cole smiled. "He worked in the Personnel Division."

"Doing what?"

"Background investigations of police applicants."

Barksdale walked over and picked up one of the photographs. The picture was of him coming out the front door of his business.

"As I am not currently, nor do I ever intend to be, a Chicago Police officer, your Detective Castigliano was engaged in an unauthorized investigation. As you gentlemen are both high-ranking members of the Chicago Police Department, I am quite sure that you are aware that such an action is a violation of my First Amendment rights and could result in my filing a lawsuit seeking substantial damages from the city."

Cole leaned against a casket. "You've got a point there, Mr. Barksdale. That is, if Detective Castigliano didn't establish probable cause for the investigation."

Barksdale folded his arms and waited.

"Show him the other pictures that Castigliano took, Blackie."

The lieutenant removed two more photos from the envelope and handed them to Barksdale. Cole described what they were.

"The first one is of a black Land Rover, which was rented under the name Cornelius Shade. As you can see, that vehicle was parked in front of this establishment. The other photo is of a gentleman named Baron Alain Marcus Casimir von Rianocek, who, the last time I had any contact with him, was an international assassin."

"Was he really?" Barksdale said nonchalantly.

"So he *was* here?" Cole asked.

"Obviously. Didn't you say that Detective . . . ?"

"Castigliano," Blackie said, maintaining the threatening tone.

"Well, if your Detective Castigliano photographed this man while he was here, then I would say that that should provide the police with documentary proof." Handing the photograph back to Blackie, he added, "But if you had simply asked me if a man fitting his description had come in to browse, I would have told you that indeed he had."

"When?" Cole asked.

Barksdale looked up at the ceiling and scratched his chin. "Let me see. It was fairly recent; either yesterday or the day before."

"Could you be more specific?"

Barksdale looked directly at Cole. "No, I can't."

"Then could you tell us what he wanted?" Blackie interjected.

Barksdale extended his arms to encompass the entire showroom and said expansively, "A casket, gentlemen, and let me assure you, I have quite a selection, as you can see."

"Which one was he interested in?" Cole asked.

"Actually, he didn't say. He looked around a bit, but I think he had something along the lines of a custom job in mind."

"Did he give you any specifics?"

When Barksdale answered this time his eyes swung over Cole as if he was measuring him for a coffin. "No. As I said, all he did was browse."

"What about an address?"

Barksdale laughed. "I didn't even get his name, much less an address. You did say he was some type of European nobleman, didn't you?"

"He claims to be a baron," Cole said.

"An international assassin? Now, that *is* interesting," Barksdale said, repeating the pillow fluffing of the black casket.

"If he visits you again or makes contact in any way, I want you to give us a call." Cole handed over a business card.

Before taking it, Barksdale extracted one of his own cards from the side pocket of his black suit jacket. "And should you ever require my unique, but inevitable services, please don't hesitate to call on me."

Cole and Blackie were heading for the door when Barksdale added, "And you both should consider some burial insurance. After all you are in a very hazardous line of work."

It was still raining when Cole and Blackie exited the C. E. Barksdale Casket and Burial Insurance Company. They got into Cole's car, but Blackie did not start the engine right away.

"What do you think, Boss?"

Cole stared at the blue-bordered window. "Well, for one thing, our boy there has a serious mental problem. I saw it coming during his trial, but now he is a one hundred-percent, full-blown madman."

"Did you notice how he's aged?" Blackie said. "He's supposed to be around forty, but he looks seventy."

"Yeah, he *does* look bad, and this casket and burial-insurance scam is nothing but a front. He's got something else up his sleeve. Now all we've got to figure out is how Rianocek is involved."

76

Paris, France
SEPTEMBER 18, 2002
8:10 P.M.

Hannah Spencer lounged in the sitting room of her suite in the Hotel Internationale in Paris. She wore a flimsy negligee beneath a silk dressing gown and a pair of slippers with pom-poms adorning the toes. She was staring at a television set, but was not paying any attention to what was being broadcast. The beautiful assassin was bored; however, she realized that there was nothing that she could do about it. There would be no lights of Paris, nor whirlwind visits to nightspots. Baron von Rianocek had decreed this after the unauthorized stunt Cornelius Shade had pulled in Chicago that had forced them to flee the United States.

Rianocek had become concerned when Shade had not returned to their suite at the Drake in Chicago. The assassin required that when they were engaged in a mission in the field, each of his operatives had to keep him informed of their whereabouts at all times. Although Shade had been missing for only a short time, Rianocek was becoming increasingly nervous. Hannah Spencer watched him stalk around the suite, going to the window to look down at the rain-swept streets below. This was very unlike him, and the female assassin understood why.

Over the years that the three of them had been together, a strong bond had been forged. She and Rianocek had moved from the sexual athletic stage into a more spiritual union. They still resorted to the periodic physical relationship, but having sex was no longer a necessity. They had become more like an old married couple, whose companionship and the constant presence of the other was like a comfortable, durable piece of clothing. Often they were able to communicate in a nonverbal manner by a glance, change of expression, or simple nod. Despite the close nature of this relationship, there was never any discussion or even mention of marriage. Individually, each of them knew that consecrating their relationship might be the one thing that would destroy it.

The affection that Hannah Spencer and Rianocek had for Cornelius Shade was different, but just as intense as what they felt for each other. His ailment and the way that he endured it silently made them admire him. Shade's competence in their chosen field also caused them to hold him in high esteem. And they were a team with each moving in concert with the others.

Shade's disappearance in Chicago broke a long-standing pattern.

Rianocek spun away from the window overlooking Michigan Avenue and crossed to the telephone. "This is suite 462. Give me the garage."

A few moments later, he hung up. She could tell by the expression on the assassin's face that he had not liked what he'd just been told.

"After Mr. Shade dropped me off downstairs, he drove away," Rianocek said quietly.

"Did he say anything to you about going someplace? Perhaps to visit someone?"

The assassin's anger flared. "Whom would he visit in Chicago,

Hannah? Where have we ever gone that Mr. Shade has known anyone other than us?"

She stared unemotionally back at him. He was losing his cool,
which was very rare. With the knowledge gleaned from their long-
term relationship, Hannah waited for him to come to the realization
that he was out of control. Alain Rianocek was definitely not a man
who did that. At least, not for long.

With a heavy sigh, he calmed down and muttered, "Mr. Shade's
disappearance could be my fault."

Before she could inquire as to what he meant by that comment,
Shade walked in.

Now they were in Paris, after making a hasty exit from Chicago via
their American intelligence community–sponsored escape route. Initially, Rianocek had exhibited icy fury when he learned what Shade
had done. But somehow Hannah had sensed that the assassin was
pleased. A Chicago police detective following them was a very
serious matter. The surveillance meant that Rianocek's legendary
security had been breached. That hadn't happened since the incident
involving Larry Cole in New York. This Detective Castigliano's
death had the potential of developing into a disaster similar to the
one that had occurred in 1989. However, Cornelius Shade apparently had taken care of everything.

They had not returned to Germany, but had come to Paris so that
Rianocek could conduct some business. Hannah's understanding
was that the assassin was shopping for equipment to use in the
operation they would mount later in the year in Chicago. That is,
if they ever returned to the United States.

Continuing to stare at the television screen, Hannah Spencer
brooded over the reason she was confined to this hotel suite. It was
because of Cornelius Shade.

Yes, Shade's elimination of the nosy cop had indeed been impressive. It had also succeeded in nearly killing the asthmatic British assassin. The exertion, excitement, and damp weather of Chicago had resulted in closing his bronchial tubes and flooding his lungs with fluid. When Shade managed to get back to the Drake Hotel, if Rianocek and Hannah Spencer had not been present to assist him, he surely would have died. His heart was racing and his face was sweaty and flushed with the effort it took for him to draw breath. With the aid of an oxygen tank and a series of injections, they had managed to stabilize him to an extent. But when Rianocek learned of what Shade had done at the nearby Esquire Theater, the assassin did not hesitate.

Rianocek made a call to Washington. In less than half an hour, a pair of official-looking types with broad shoulders, military haircuts, and dark suits arrived at the hotel. They were accompanied by a private ambulance crew and a doctor. Within minutes, the RanCorp operatives were being whisked to a private airfield outside Chicago.

The flight to Paris via chartered Learjet took off within the hour. The doctor accompanied them and attended to the ailing Mr. Shade.

Hannah got up and switched off the television set. While Rianocek was out, she had been pressed into service to play nurse. The doctor had returned to the United States, so there was no one to watch over the critically ill man. But despite her affection for the deadly little Englishman, Hannah didn't possess much of a maternal instinct.

She crossed the suite to Shade's room. When she opened the door, she was struck by the unpleasant medicinal odor present. Entering, she examined the oxygen tanks, heart monitor, and IV bottles that had turned the Paris Hotel Internationale suite into a hospital ward.

She walked over to the bed and looked down at the man lying there. He was either asleep or unconscious—she couldn't tell which. She knew how to kill people, not nurse them back to health. She glanced at the heart monitor. The beat indicator was bounding up and down like a runaway Ping-Pong ball. She didn't know whether this was good or bad.

Quietly, she turned around and made her way back into the sitting room. She went to the bar and poured herself a glass of champagne. As she sipped it she stared at the door to Shade's room. Yes, she *did* care for him, but didn't like him lingering on the edge of death like this. Hannah Spencer had an idea. It would be simple enough to go back in there and . . . ! No. She couldn't do it. If Rianocek ever found out, he would kill her without a second's hesitation.

So she poured herself another drink and went back to watching television.

77

SEPTEMBER 18, 2002
9:15 P.M.

The Hotel Internationale's limousine pulled up to the gate in the wrought-iron fence surrounding the massive estate outside Paris. An armed sentry first carefully scrutinized the vehicle before stepping out into the driveway and walking over to the back door. The window was rolled down to reveal the face of Baron Alain Marcus Casimir von Rianocek. The sentry recognized the passenger and nodded. Walking around to the driver, he said, "You will proceed through the gate up the driveway to the main house. After the baron gets out, you will drive to the rear and park by the garage. One of the servants will bring you a refreshment tray. Do you understand me?"

The Hotel Internationale's chauffeur looked from the hardened face of the sentry to the menacing automatic weapon he carried and said nervously, "Yes, sir."

The driveway wound for 150 yards along a blacktop road up to the entrance to the chateau. Along the way, Rianocek noticed two additional armed sentries and a closed circuit television camera mounted high up on a tree. The assassin smiled. Georgi Yakolevich, formerly a major general in the Soviet Army, was still as paranoid as ever. This paranoia and the sentries were the reasons the Russian was still alive.

There was a servant in a black tuxedo and another armed sentry waiting on the front steps of the chateau. The servant opened the door for Rianocek and led the guest inside. The entrance alcove was spacious, with a crystal chandelier hanging from the ceiling and a carpeted staircase leading to the upper floors.

"Right this way, sir," the servant said, leading Rianocek into a book-lined study. "General Yakolevich will be with you shortly. You may help yourself to a drink if you wish."

"Thank you," Rianocek said, merely glancing at the drink tray resting on an end table beside the couch, with a single unopened bottle of vodka and glasses. Despite the wealth he had managed to escape with after the collapse of the Soviet Union, Georgi Yako-levich maintained a number of common soldier traits. But that is where any resemblance ended between the former general and Rus-sia's lower classes.

Rianocek liked this room. There were floor-to-ceiling bookcases covering three of the walls and the fourth wall consisted of glass windows interspersed with doors that led into a garden, which Georgi cultivated faithfully with the skill of a dedicated horticul-turist. The furniture in the study was a deep burgundy leather and the general's desk was almost as impressive as Rianocek's back in Bavaria.

Left to his own devices as he waited for his host, Rianocek

walked over to the desk. There was a notepad, a couple of books, and two full-color photos on the desktop. The notes were written in Russian, but the books were in English. Rianocek looked at the photos. One was a classic pose of Adolf Hitler with a swastika armband adorning his brown uniform coat. The other was of a painting of Napoleon Bonaparte. Then the assassin read the book titles: Professor Leonard Clarkson's *Napoleon's Campaigns of 1812* and D'Orville's *Hitler: The Fall—1941–1945*.

"The two dictators had a great deal in common, Alain," Georgi Yakolevich said from the study entrance. "It is even believed by some religious purists that they were both incarnations of the Antichrist."

Rianocek turned as his host entered. "The son of the devil, so to speak."

"Quite right," Yakolevich replied. "And there is supposed to be a third incarnation of this Antichrist coming to Earth in this century. Perhaps he walks among us at this very moment."

"Are you looking to do a deal with the devil, Georgi?"

The Russian smiled. "You are here, aren't you, Baron von Rianocek?"

The two men laughed uproariously.

Former Major General Georgi Dimitrievich Yakolevich was a rotund man of below-medium height. He had squat, thick peasant's legs, and walked with such a bowlegged gait that he appeared deformed. His hair was a thinning, uncared for arrangement that was seldom combed. When he had worn his Soviet military uniform, he shaved his skull. He was dressed in a red silk smoking jacket, white scarf, black slacks, and brilliantly polished black loafers.

Going to the drink tray, he poured a water tumbler of vodka. Rianocek declined the offer of a drink, because he hated vodka. They took seats on the couch.

"So, Alain, what can I do for you?"

"Do you still maintain contacts with your former military colleagues in Russia?"

Yakolevich laughed. "Why do you think I surround this place with armed guards? I am trying to *avoid* any such contact. There is a death sentence hanging over my head and, needless to say, the Russian who carries that sentence out will be well rewarded."

"But for the right price someone from the current general staff might be persuaded to forget about your past transgressions, at least temporarily?" Rianocek pressed.

Yakolevich shrugged. "Such a price would be extremely high." He turned to look the assassin directly in the eye. "For me to make the contact and for them to listen to what I have to say."

"That is understood, Georgi," Rianocek said easily.

The Russian went back to his vodka. "What are you looking for in Russia, Alain?"

"I want to purchase a tactical nuclear weapon."

78

Chicago, Illinois
NOVEMBER 27, 2002
2:17 P.M.

It was the day after Thanksgiving. In Chicago, Larry Cole had decided to take the entire weekend off. However, as was the case with the chief of detectives during his usual daily routine, he found it impossible to simply remain idle. So as midafternoon approached, Cole had already completed a five-mile run along the lakefront, lifted weights at the police gym, and done some grocery shopping at the co-op pantry store in his apartment building overlooking Grant Park.

Now he had finished putting the food away and was about to watch the videotape of the Chicago Bears/Detroit Lions football game that he had been too busy to watch the day before. He had fixed a lunch of tossed salad with oil and vinegar dressing, a boneless breast of chicken patty, and a baked potato topped with salt and butter substitutes. Lately, he had been into low-calorie, high-protein, and high-fiber foods. This had not only made him feel better, but had given him a great deal more energy. His high level of nearly nonstop, full-speed-ahead activity had drawn a few complaining comments from his staff. Blackie had also argued that Cole had lost too much weight, although Cole considered the weight loss simply the shedding of unwanted fat.

Cole had been up all last night in command of an operation which had resulted in the surrender of a demented man who had taken a stewardess hostage on an American Airlines flight from New Orleans. Then he had joined Judy, Manny and Lauren Sherlock—Manny's wife—for dinner at the Silvestris'. By the time the turkey with all the fixings had been consumed, Cole had lasted just long enough for an after-dinner beer before he'd headed home to bed. Eight hours of sleep recharged his batteries and he planned to spend the day taking it easy. He should have realized beforehand that this wasn't going to work.

Before the first quarter of the football game was over, Cole's mind began drifting to some of the cases that were currently open in the detective division.

An armed robbery gang had been hitting Loop jewelry stores since late summer. Three to four men wearing stocking masks and armed with semiautomatic handguns, entered the stores at the end of the business day and made off with cash, expensive jewelry, and high-ticket watches. Despite the robberies occurring in daylight, the alarm systems in the stores operating efficiently, and the legion of cops patrolling the Windy City's downtown area, the CPD hadn't even come close to an apprehension.

Cole had assigned the detective division mission team—a sergeant and eight detectives—to random stakeouts inside jewelry stores, which were potential targets. But the presence of the police did no good, as the robbers simply hit shops that weren't covered. This bothered Cole. Three robberies had been committed while stakeouts were in place at other locations. Cole had been a cop too long not to recognize the obvious. The stickup men were receiving inside information. And the only way they could obtain such information would be from a cop.

This was not unprecedented in the history of the Chicago Police Department or, for that matter, in the history of any American big-city law-enforcement agency.

The Summerdale scandal in 1959 involved Chicago Police officers casing homes for a burglar. Just about every ten years or so, there was a major scandal within the CPD. There had been the Marquette Ten, ten tactical cops who took kickbacks from drug dealers to let them operate with impunity in certain areas of the Tenth Police District on the West Side. The Wentworth Thirteen, an entire tactical team in the Second District which had protected illegal gambling houses for payoffs. Then had come the diamond thieves, who robbed traveling jewelry salesmen. The information used by the gunman was provided by high-ranking members of the Chicago Police Department, including a former deputy chief from the detective division.

Cole had never been directly involved in any of the investigations of the accused officers, but he had followed the cases closely. Basically, it all came down to greed and stupidity. The crooked cops saw the opportunity to make an illegal buck by selling their badges. The results were ultimate disgrace and long prison sentences. However, this never seemed to deter future thieves with badges, and Larry Cole had a strong hunch that the Loop jewelry-store stickups could be a cop scandal waiting to happen.

The chief of detectives made a mental note to set up a surveillance of one of the stores, which wouldn't be disclosed to the mission team or any other cop. Only Blackie, Manny, Judy and, of course he himself would be involved, and Cole knew that he could trust them with his life.

Halftime of the football game had arrived. Cole was surprised to see that the score was Bears—17, Lions—10. He didn't recall either team scoring any points at all. He wasn't being a very good fan today.

After washing the lunch dishes, Cole poured himself a cup of coffee and returned to the dining-room table. The second half of the football game had started and the Bears had the ball. Cole managed to concentrate on the game for a full three-and-a-half minutes this time before his attention drifted back to police work.

Police corruption was only a small segment of the overall problem of official misconduct. Such criminality affected all branches of government from the local to the federal level. Ghost payrolling, fixing court cases, selling promotions and contracts were all illegal moneymaking schemes politicians engaged in. Some politicians felt that winning an election or being appointed to an official position gave them a license to steal.

Thinking of official misconduct made Cole remember another case. Deciding that the football game rerun was a waste of time, he shut off the TV and went to his PC. He opened a case of computer disks and searched through them until he found the one marked "Mysteries—1999."

Inserting it into the computer he booted up the disk menu. "The Barksdale Drug Plant—March 1999" came up.

Cole reviewed the data contained in the file. There were photos of the drug plant before and after it was destroyed. There were also analyses of the drugs found there and the transcripts of the trials of Barksdale and the two Peace Stones. The question still remained unanswered as to how Barksdale had managed to operate the plant without detection and then cause its complete destruction with all of its contents. The operation had been run with the efficiency of a

Fortune 500 company and had made just as much money. Barksdale had received a minimum sentence for his involvement and came out of prison to open up that strange mortuary business out on the South Side. Then there was Barksdale's involvement with Baron Alain Rianocek, the assassin.

Cole removed the disk and searched through the case for the one marked, "Mysteries—2002." After scanning the menu, he called up the program, "Detective Michael Castigliano Homicide."

Cole scanned quickly through the data to the last two documents in the file. One was the response to an inquiry from the Chicago Police Department to Interpol regarding a British national named Cornelius Shade.

FROM: Interpol
TO: Chief of Detectives
            Larry Cole
            Chicago Police Department
SUBJECT: Cornelius Shade
REFERENCE: Inquiry #145-02-39
    In response to your inquiry of 20 September 2002 in regards to an individual known as Cornelius Shade, aka "The Wheeze," possible alien resident of the German state of Bavaria. Records of the Munich municipal police indicate that this individual is deceased, circa May 2001.

Cole knew that Cornelius Shade was not only alive, but dangerously so, as he had killed Detective Mike Castigliano.

He went on to the next inquiry. Again this was a reply to an official request from the Chicago Police Department to the U.S. State Department. The chief of detectives didn't give any credence to this reply, either.

On official State Department stationery, the reply read:

November 21, 2002

Chief Larry Cole
Chicago Police Department
Detective Division Headquarters
3510 South Michigan
Chicago, Illinois 60608

Dear Chief Cole,

In response to your earlier inquiry, a check of the entry and exit records for foreign nationals to date in 2002 reveal that no one by the name of Baron Alain Marcus Casimir von Rianocek entered this country on a German passport or any other passport recognized by the United States Government.

Sincerely,
James A. Williamson
Undersecretary for Inquiries and Information

Cole didn't necessarily believe that the State Department had lied to him, but rather that someone from the United States intelligence community had deemed the information the CPD had requested as "contrary to the interests of national security."

This was what brought Larry Cole full circle with his thoughts about official corruption. When cops engaged in corruption at the local level, it was a crime. When the U.S. intelligence community—FBI, CIA, or the NSA—did it at a national or international level, it was called "in the interests of national security."

There was one other part of this equation that Cole had yet to figure out. He scrolled through the document to the photographs that Mike Castigliano had taken of Clevey Barksdale outside of the C. E. Barksdale Casket and Burial Insurance Company. The ex-con lawyer was the wild card in this game, but at this point, the hand had yet to be dealt.

79

The delivery truck drove up to the gate surrounding the former Soviet General Georgi Dimitrievich Yakolevich's chateau outside Paris. The sentry on duty came out carrying an automatic weapon. Although he had been alerted that the general was expecting a delivery at this time, the sentry approached the truck warily.

There were two men in the cab. Both were dark, rough-looking types with menacing expressions. The sentry, who had spent half his life in the Soviet Army, could tell that the occupants of the truck were dangerous.

The sentry gave them the same instructions he had given to the chauffeur from the Hotel Internationale. With a loud grinding of gears, the truck lurched through the gate. Thirty seconds later, it arrived at the front entrance to the chateau. Georgi Yakolevich and Alain Rianocek, accompanied by a sentry, were waiting for them.

"Good evening, gentlemen," Yakolevich said in Russian.

The men in the truck did not acknowledge the greeting.

"I assume you have the goods that we ordered?"

The passenger merely nodded.

"Please drive around to the coach house at the rear and I will have my people unload it for you," Yakolevich said.

The passenger responded gutturally, "We do it."

"Whatever you say." Yakolevich glanced quizzically at Rianocek.

The assassin merely stared at the man in the truck.

Yakolevich and Rianocek followed them on foot to the coach house. The eighteenth-century brick structure was adjacent to the main building. The doors to the coach house stood open and the truck was driven inside. The driver and the passenger were out of the cab and waiting at the canvas-covered rear gate. Their menacing manner had not decreased. These men were members of the Russian Mafia and cold-blooded killers. But they were butchers, not assassins, and not in the same league as the man to whom they were selling the merchandise contained in back of the truck.

"May we see the goods?" Yakolevich asked.

"We want see money," the spokesman said, while the other one continued to glare at them.

"It's inside," Rianocek said, nodding his head to the main building. "If one of you would like to accompany me, I will show it to you."

"I go," the spokesman said.

"We'll be right back, Georgi." With that, the assassin led the man across the courtyard to the rear door of the chateau.

Rianocek watched the Russian Mafia thug count the three million francs that was the agreed-upon sum. Despite his brutish appearance, which was accompanied by a pronounced body odor, he counted the money with a skillful dexterity. It took him less than fifteen minutes to go through the suitcase containing neat stacks of hundred-franc notes.

"Now, may I see the merchandise?" Rianocek spoke Russian like a native Muscovite.

With a grunt, the thug closed the case and was about to carry it out when the assassin stopped him. "You can pick that up after I see the merchandise."

The Russian attempted to stare Rianocek down, but the assassin's gaze was enough to make him reconsider a challenge. To save face, the gangster shrugged, uttered a curse and headed for the door leaving the money behind.

*   *   *

Rianocek knew that there was something wrong the instant he stepped away from the back door of the chateau. Besides the driver, there was another swarthy man who hadn't been there before, standing at the rear of the truck. Georgi Yakolevich and the sentry, who had accompanied them from the front of the house, had vanished. The assassin didn't have time to ponder the former Soviet general's fate—he had a more pressing problem on his hands.

The Russian who had counted the money inside the chateau was walking a short distance in front of Rianocek. When they stepped outside, the henchman stopped and turned to flank the assassin. In less than a second, Rianocek assessed the situation, decided on a course of action, and made his move. ·

The assassin stepped sideways toward the Russian. The man was six inches taller and outweighed Rianocek by fifty pounds. He possessed a pair of enormous hands with thick hair covering the backs and knuckles. Forming fists, he grinned, splitting his face into a leer, which revealed missing front teeth. The assassin recognized the type. He was a brute who enjoyed beating his victims to death. The Russian was a human club. The Bavarian baron was a walking, highly skilled instrument of death.

The Russian swung his right fist at Rianocek's head. The assassin stepped deftly under the blow and, keeping the Russian Mafia henchman's body between him and the two men standing behind the truck, jammed his elbow into the Russian's rib cage. Rianocek felt the bones break, as the air rushed from the big man's lungs. He began falling to the ground, but Rianocek held him up and spun him around to face the others. The henchman was coughing up blood from a punctured lung and was deadweight, but the assassin wouldn't need him as a human shield for very long.

From a shoulder holster beneath his suit jacket, Rianocek removed a silenced .45 caliber semiautomatic handgun. The gun had been custom made for the assassin and was equipped with laser

sights. As he took aim at the Russian Mafia goons across the courtyard, they raised machine pistols and opened fire.

Just like the big man the assassin had disabled, they didn't
attempt to finesse Rianocek's death. Instead they fired on full automatic, spraying the target area with bullets. They hit their former
colleague numerous times turning him into a sieve and finishing the
job of killing him that Rianocek had started. They also hit the wall
of the chateau and completely blew out a pair of ground-floor windows. The assassin, continuing to hold the dead henchman in front
of him, was not touched.

Rianocek lined up the laser sights on one henchman's face and
pulled the trigger. Before the Russian's head exploded in a pink
haze, he aimed at the second man. The round from the silenced .45
struck the Russian killer in the cleft of his unshaven chin. The
dynamic force of the powerful round decapitated him. In a matter
of seconds, it was all over.

Splattered with blood, the assassin dropped the remains of the
Russian to the ground. Still holding the gun, from which he had
fired only two rounds, Rianocek checked the bodies of the three
men. They were all dead. Then he went in search of Georgi Yakolevich.

He found the former general lying in front of the truck. Yakolevich's throat had been cut. The sentry, his automatic weapon
broken in two, was lying a short distance away with his head bashed
in. The assassin gazed unemotionally at the bodies. Georgi Yakolevich had been a friend; but now that he was dead, he meant nothing. After all, Rianocek was in the death business.

Turning away from the bodies, Rianocek climbed into the back
of the truck. He hoped that the Russians, despite their attempt at a
double cross, had brought the promised merchandise with them.

A metal footlocker beneath a tarpaulin was the lone cargo. Removing the cover, Rianocek undid the clasps securing the container
and looked down at a seven-foot-long, one-foot-diameter nickel-
cadmium cylinder. There was a warning in Russian printed in bright

red letters across its surface. The warning translated as "Danger—Radiation Exposure When Opened." Rianocek was not overly concerned about this admonition; he planned to have the case open for only a moment or two.

Unfastening the latches, he opened the case to reveal a cone-shaped gray metal device inside. It was live and lethal. It possessed the explosive potential of the atomic bomb that had been dropped on Hiroshima in 1945. However, this weapon was a great deal cleaner. Although it would destroy everything within two miles, the fallout would be minimal, with only a ten-square-mile area affected. This is exactly what the assassin needed to carry out Barksdale's act of revenge in the United States.

Rianocek had just resealed the protective nickel-cadmium cylinder when he heard gunshots coming from the front of the chateau. Pulling his automatic, he jumped to the ground and checked the driveway.

Hannah Spencer and Cornelius Shade, mouth open as he gasped for breath from the simple exertion of walking, were coming around the side of the chateau. Rianocek's anger flared when he saw the sick Englishman. He had not wanted Shade to leave the hotel at all, but he had relented after Hannah had intervened.

The assassin had only agreed to let Shade accompany them if he stayed in the car outside the chateau grounds. Anticipating trouble, Hannah had come along as Rianocek's backup. From the automatic weapons that both of them carried, it was apparent that the assassin had needed both Hannah and Shade.

Rianocek waited for them to come to him. Shade's breathing sounded like a tire with a bad leak. From the color in Hannah Spencer's face and the gleam in her eyes, Rianocek could tell that she had killed recently.

"The Russians had a six-member assassination team in two cars tailing the truck," she said. "After it entered the grounds, they took out the gate sentry. Four of them came up the driveway on foot, and the others remained down by the gate. We took them first. Then we drove onto the grounds and caught up with the others just after they eliminated Yakolevich's sentries."

Rianocek gave Shade a hard look, which prompted Hannah to add quickly, "Mr. Shade did the two at the gate by himself and one of the Russians in front of the chateau. I don't think I could have taken them all without him, Baron."

Rianocek's features softened slowly and he smiled. Clapping Shade on the shoulder, he said, "Good work, but you'd better go back to the car and use that oxygen tank before you pass out."

"Yes, sir," he gasped. "I could use . . . a . . . whiff of air."

As Shade started back down the driveway, Hannah asked, "Did they bring the device?"

He nodded.

"How are we going to get it into the States?"

The assassin patted the side of the truck. "That won't be a problem, Ms. Spencer. We'll just ask our old friends at the CIA for help."

80

Arlington, Virginia
DECEMBER 1, 2002
2:10 P.M.

Although Assistant Deputy Director Dickie Fagan had retired to Arlington, Virginia, he still kept in touch with personnel in his old section of the CIA. The intelligence community had enough on its hands to worry about, so illegal domestic operations had been completely abandoned. Or at least placed on the back burner. But there were still a lot of skeletons rattling around in the Agency closet, buried deep and monitored carefully by trusted operatives.

On this winter afternoon, one of the agents assigned to the monitoring of abandoned covert operations placed a call to Fagan's Arlington home.

With the money that he had socked away from his nefarious official activities during his years with the CIA, along with his government pension, Fagan, his wife, Melissa, and three of their five children now lived on a small estate less than a mile from the National Cemetery. The red-brick Colonial-style mansion had nine rooms, three baths, an indoor swimming pool, a Jacuzzi, and a two-car garage, in which were parked his wife's two-year-old white Jaguar and his own brand-new GMC sports wagon. His eighteen-year-old son's 1998 Camaro was relegated to a space on the street in front of the house.

Dickie and Melissa Fagan's children consisted of three boys: ages thirty, twenty-five, and eighteen; and two girls: ages seventeen and twelve. The two oldest were college graduates, working currently as field agents for the National Security Agency. The rest of the children were still attending private schools in northern Virginia.

The Fagans were an upper-middle-class, all-American family. Following a traditional Christmas, spent around an elaborately decorated natural evergreen tree, the entire family—including the eldest son's wife and the second-oldest son's girlfriend—planned to spend the first week of the New Year on vacation in the Bahamas. The former assistant deputy director could definitely afford the cost of the trip.

Melissa Bentley Fagan was a tenth-generation native Virginian, and reputedly a direct descendant of General Robert E. Lee, hero of the Confederate States of America. She had met Dickie while she was working as a secretary for a Virginia state senator and he was an up-and-coming CIA administrator. Despite her future husband's being a Yankee with a less-than-acceptable pedigree, the southern belle saw potential in him. A potential that did not disappoint her, at least in the income department, over the ensuing years.

"Yes," Melissa Fagan drawled into the telephone in the Virginia mansion's foyer. Then, "Just a moment, sir. I'll get him for you."

"Richard," she called. Melissa never referred to him as "Dickie" and would not have called out to him at all if he wasn't in the study directly adjacent to the foyer.

She frowned when she saw that he was clad in a red-and-black checked flannel shirt and soiled khaki trousers. With a tolerant expression, she said, "It's a Mr. Anderson for you, dear." What she didn't say was, "You can take the Yankee out of Indiana, but you can't take Indiana out of the Yankee."

Unaware of Melissa's disapproval, Fagan took the phone and said, "Hello," into the receiver, as she quietly left the room.

The operative on the other end of the line was named Eugene Anderson, and he had been recruited by Dickie Fagan twenty-five years ago. He was loyal to the former assistant deputy director, up to a point. In the near future this same Agent Anderson would testify before a Senate subcommittee investigating excesses in the covert operations of the American intelligence community. The principal targeted official at these proceedings would be Dickie Fagan.

"Is something called the Barksdale Network one of your old operations?" Anderson asked.

Fagan's brow furrowed; but other than that, he was only mildly curious by the inquiry. "Yeah, but it's been shut down since March of 1999."

"Well, it's been activated again using your old operational code."

Now, Fagan felt a surge of alarm. The "Barksdale Network" was the code name for the operation by which illegal raw narcotics had been smuggled into the country from South America via military aircraft, transported to Chicago for processing, and then distributed throughout the country.

"That's impossible!" Fagan felt his palms becoming slick with perspiration. When no response came from the operative at the other end of the line, Fagan added, "That network must be shut down at once."

"I already did that, but apparently a single shipment, which originated in Europe, managed to get through."

"Where did it come from?"

"Paris."

"What was its destination?"

"Chicago."

81

Chicago, Illinois
DECEMBER 1, 2002
4:45 P.M.

Blackie," Manny Sherlock said, "isn't that Sergeant Martin from Area Three?"

The lieutenant walked over and peered over Manny's shoulder at the closed-circuit TV monitor. They were in a storeroom on the ground floor of the Diamond Mart Building on South Wabash Avenue in the Chicago Loop. Without notifying any of the other officers assigned to the jewelry-store robbery detail, Chief Cole had set up electronic surveillances of four strategic areas of this twenty-story building. The Diamond Mart was home to the most exclusive jewelers in the Midwest. Despite this, none of the shops located there had been hit by the stocking-masked stickup men. So Larry Cole and his crew were playing the odds that after successfully pulling twelve jewelry robberies, the thieves would get around to the Diamond Mart. Also, Cole had told Blackie, Manny, and Judy to watch out for any cops loitering in the area as if they were casing one of the stores. This had drawn curious looks from the lieutenant and pair of sergeants, but it hadn't taken them long to understand what the chief of detectives was getting at. Although to Blackie,

Manny, and Judy, the possibility that cops could be involved was distasteful, the fact that such involvement was likely could not be ignored.

Now, looking down at the monitor, Blackie's jaw muscles rippled as he said, "That's Joe Martin, Manny. He's got thirty-two years on the job. Spent over twenty-five of those years on the citywide robbery detail. Requested a reassignment to Area Three about four years ago, when his wife contracted cancer. She died six months ago."

Manny turned to look up at the heavyset lieutenant. Blackie had just said it all. If any cop could have masterminded the recent string of holdups, Sergeant Joe Martin was the man. Hoping against hope that their suspicions were groundless, they watched the policeman casually studying the display windows of the Hurt and Sebastian Jewelry Store on the seventh floor of the Diamond Mart Building. This particular shop had been left uncovered by the Detective Division Mission Team. It would have been a simple matter for Joe Martin to find this out. Now Blackie and Manny sat back to watch an armed robbery unfold.

Behind the counter inside the Hurt and Sebastian Jewelry Store was a lone female clerk. She had short, dark hair, wore an enormous pair of black-framed glasses and possessed the somewhat-pinched features of the lifelong spinster. For the most part, she was unremarkable to the point that she was seldom given a second look by anyone. This was by design. The clerk, whose plastic name tag on the left breast of her white cotton blouse gave her name as Tanya, was actually Judy Daniels, the Mistress of Disguise/High Priestess of Mayhem.

She noticed the man standing outside looking at the display case. Her sixth sense began tingling at the base of her spine. She didn't recognize Sergeant Joe Martin, but she *did* know cops. And this guy was a cop.

Ignoring him, she walked over to a display case containing

emeralds. Opening it, she began reorganizing the display. Her fingers trembled. She whispered a sharp "Stop it, Judy!"

Instantly, her hands became dead steady.

Sergeant Joseph L. Martin stared in at the jewelry display, but was not paying any attention to the glittering items on the other side of the glass. At the age of sixty-one, Martin was white-haired, overweight, had a drug-treatable irregular heartbeat, and suffered periodic bouts of severe depression. He was also a thief and a traitor to the profession he had sworn an oath to remain faithful to over thirty years ago.

Yes, it had been due to his wife's illness. At least, that was the excuse he gave himself. Deep down in his heart, Joe Martin knew that he had been turning into a rogue cop for a long time. Perhaps he had been a crooked cop since the first day he put on the uniform. Even as a rookie, he had always been looking for a way to use his badge to make a quick buck. The five-dollar shakedown of the traffic violator; extorting money from licensed establishments because of minor municipal-code infractions; and stretching police discounts to the point of outright criminality were all acts that Joe Martin engaged in before he became a detective.

Somehow, after he was assigned to the detective division, Martin had experienced a career rejuvenation. With his police sergeant's salary and his wife's income as a registered nurse, money hadn't been a problem. Their marriage was childless.

For years he had worked the citywide robbery detail, sending bad guys to jail for stealing millions and millions of dollars. As a supervisor, he was responsible for counting seized contraband currency and never once had he ever had the inclination to palm a couple of hundred-dollar bills or drop a stack of twenties into his briefcase. This money would never have been missed.

Then his wife had gotten sick. Their insurance took care of most of the bills, but it was obvious very early on that she was not going to recover. And as her life ebbed away, she took some of his soul with her.

He was no longer able to take any pride or satisfaction in police work. When Larry Cole, whom Joe Martin remembered from the old Nineteenth District as a wet-behind-the-ears rookie, became chief of detectives, the sergeant had requested and received a transfer to Area Three. There he managed to get by using his wife's illness as an excuse to do as little as possible. Then she died, and he was left with nothing but an empty house and a tarnished tin badge that no longer meant anything to him.

How the idea came to him to form a cop robbery gang he couldn't really recall. Perhaps it was due to the decades he had spent catching stickup men. Martin knew their MOs as well as the mistakes that they had made. He knew the locations that were the most vulnerable, despite guards and sophisticated electronic-alarm systems. He also knew the cops he could approach to assist him in this illegal enterprise. Cops who were strapped for cash, desperate, sufficiently lacking in integrity, and who knew how to keep their mouths shut.

There were four members of the Loop jewelry store stickup gang now; Martin, a detective from Area Three, and two patrol officers from the Ninth Police District. This would be their thirteenth job, and although the gang's ringleader was not superstitious, the number did succeed in making him nervous.

Looking in through the glass window, Joe Martin's eyes flickered up at the lone clerk inside the Hurt and Sebastian Jewelry Store. Although he had never seen this particular woman before, from the information he had gleaned surreptitiously from Cole's detective division mission team, there was seldom more than a lone attendant inside the store at this time of the day. At a given signal, one of his men would cut all of the electrical power to this floor. This would disable the alarm system and deactivate the closed-circuit cameras. With military precision the stickup gang would be in and out of the jewelry store with a respectable haul of gems, cash and expensive watches in less than two-and-a-half minutes.

Sergeant Joe Martin of the Chicago Police Department's Area Three Detective Division turned away from the display window and walked down the corridor to the stairwell door. Before opening this door, he turned to look back down the corridor. It was deserted. Then he stepped into the stairwell.

In the ground-floor observation post, Blackie picked up a walkie-talkie and said into the speaker, "Boss?"

"Yes, Blackie," Cole responded.

"It's going down."

A heavy sigh came over the line. *"Okay, we're ready. In case something goes wrong, make sure the building is sealed off."*

"Ten-four." Then Blackie signed off.

On cue, the power to the seventh floor was cut. The stairwell door opened and three men wearing ski masks stepped out into the corridor. They carried high-powered, semiautomatic handguns, which so far they had used only for show during the previous robberies.

The female clerk was just closing the display case when the masked trio appeared at the door. Apparently unaware of their presence, she turned from the case and crossed the floor. As they entered, the telephone started ringing.

"Hurt and Sebastian," she said into the instrument. Waiting a tick, she turned around. "It's for you." She extended the telephone to the leader of the masked group.

None of them moved.

Then a man stepped from behind a curtain at the rear of the store. When the robbers saw him, they stiffened in alarm. It was Chief of Detectives Larry Cole.

"It's over, Joe," Cole said quietly. "That telephone call is from Officer Mickey Lepkowitz, who cut the power downstairs. He's in custody. Now it's up to you guys how we handle this: the easy way or the hard way."

As the stickup men looked on, the mousy-looking, pinched-faced female clerk raised a .45 caliber machine pistol from beneath the counter. Cole's hands remained empty, but from the wicked look of the weapon the woman wielded, he didn't need a gun.

Slowly, Joe Martin and his crew of crooked cops lowered their weapons and surrendered.

82

DECEMBER 2, 2002
DAWN

The arrest of Sergeant Joe Martin and his crew of cop felons was one of the biggest news stories of the year. A throng of media people was camped out in the lobby of the police headquarters complex at 35th and Michigan. They were hoping that the chief of detectives would hold a press conference releasing details of the arrests in time for the morning broadcasts and the midday tabloids. They had been waiting for a long time, but were certain that when Larry Cole did finally convene the press briefing, it would be thorough and to the point.

As the sky began brightening over the city on this winter morning, the reporters continued to wait.

In his private office, Cole was preparing for the press conference. All of the paperwork had been completed and the four crooked cops were scheduled for arraignment at 9:00 A.M. Cole scanned the written outline he would use at the press conference before he washed his face, put on a clean shirt, and left his private office.

Judy and Manny were working at their desks in the outer office. After looking around, Cole asked, "Where's Blackie?"

Manny nodded at the closed door to the lieutenant's office. Cole crossed to it and knocked. When there was no answer, he opened the door. He heard the snoring first. His former partner was leaning back in his desk chair sound asleep. Suddenly Cole realized that they'd been working this case for over twenty-four hours. Guilt swept over him. In his enthusiasm to make the arrests of the rogue cops, he'd forgotten about his staff. He hadn't even given them a meal break.

On the top of Blackie's desk was half a cup of cold coffee and a Snickers candy-bar wrapper. Cole owed his old friend a great deal better treatment than this.

Stepping around the desk, Cole gently shook the lieutenant's shoulder and said softly, "Blackie."

He came awake instantly. "Sorry, Boss. I was just resting my eyes."

"Why don't you go home, have Maria fix you a good breakfast, and get some sleep?"

Blackie rubbed his hands vigorously across his face. "I should be at the arraignment in case the state's attorney needs my testimony."

"Judy and I can take care of that. Let Manny drive you home."

The lieutenant looked about to protest the chief's suggestion, but he was too tired. Actually, Blackie didn't want to risk driving home because he was afraid he'd fall asleep at the wheel.

"You win, Larry," he conceded. "But if you need me, call the house. I'll leave word with Maria to wake me up."

After patting his oldest friend in the department on the back, Cole headed for the press conference.

At the Casket and Burial Insurance Company on South Stony Island Avenue, Clevey Barksdale had also been up all night. With the lights out, he had sat alone in the dark, remembering his grandfather. Today he was going to get retribution for the death of Cleveland Emmett Barksdale, Sr. His revenge would reverberate violently throughout the entire United States and result in repercussions worldwide that would continue for decades, perhaps even centuries.

As the sun came up, Barksdale vowed that this day would be the last of Larry Cole's life.

The cold morning air revived Blackie Silvestri, but he still decided to let Manny drive him home. As the two cops stepped into the parking lot on 35th Street, snow flurries blew out of a low-ceiling, menacing gray sky.

"What's the date today, Manny?"

The sergeant pushed a button on the digital sports watch he wore. "It's the second of December, Blackie. You have twenty-two shopping days left until Christmas."

Blackie touched his left side self-consciously. "It's been twenty-five years."

Manny frowned. "Twenty-five years since what?"

"Twenty-five years ago today I got shot by a low-life scumbag named Frankie Arcadio."

"Didn't you and the boss blow this Arcadio away?"

Blackie chuckled. "Yeah, we nailed his ass seven times. After I ended up in the hospital, Larry got into a second gun battle with the Mob. Rabbit Arcadio's chief lieutenant, Sal Marino, led an assassination crew to whack our then-chief of dicks, John T. Ryan. They *did* kill Ryan, but Larry took out two of the Mafia goons and arrested Marino, who spent twenty years in the joint on a murder and murder-conspiracy beef. Last I heard, he's out on the West Coast up to his old extortion and racketeering tricks.

"After what went down on that night in 1977, me and Larry ended up making detective before Christmas and the rest is history."

"Sounds like a good career move," Manny said as they reached the new silver unmarked Ford squad car that had been recently assigned to the chief of detectives' office.

"Getting shot is never a good career move, Manny," Blackie said. "In fact, a bullet has probably ended more cops' careers than anything else." Examining the sleek lines of the new car, he added, "Nice wheels."

"Yeah. I picked it up yesterday before we went to the Diamond Mart."

Once inside, Blackie took in a deep breath. "You know there's nothing like the smell of a new car."

Manny sneezed. "Yeah. It's great." Then he blew his nose loudly. "But I'll be glad when the smell wears off, because I think I'm allergic to it."

Blackie laughed.

Rianocek watched them pull out of the police parking lot. The assassin was seated in a plain white panel truck, which was parked in the McDonald's parking lot at 35th and State. Utilizing a compact cellular phone, he pressed a single digit on the keypad, which connected him with Hannah Spencer. Rianocek frowned when Cornelius Shade answered the phone.

"I thought you were to remain at 'Ground Zero'!" The assassin's voice held an angry tone.

"Everything is in readiness there, sir." He paused to draw a breath. *"And I will stay out of the way unless I'm needed, as was the case in Paris."*

"You don't have to bring Paris up every time you want to prove your competence to me, Mr. Shade." Rianocek sighed. "But it will be necessary for you to remain acutely aware of your physical limitations. Now let me speak to Ms. Spencer."

"Yes, sir."

When she came on, he said, "Silvestri and Sherlock are in a late-model gray Ford traveling westbound on 35th Street approaching the expressway."

"We're waiting in front of the baseball stadium," she said. *"It should be a simple matter to take them."*

The assassin's hand tightened around the small phone until the exterior housing was in danger of cracking. "Ms. Spencer, have you forgotten the problem you had in New York City with a pair of cops?!"

"I haven't forgotten." she said softly.

"Then govern yourself accordingly. I don't want anything to go wrong with this operation."

With that he terminated the connection.

For a long moment he remained sitting behind the wheel of the panel truck staring out through the windshield at the Illinois Institute of Technology building on the other side of 35th Street. What he hadn't said to Hannah Spencer was that he wanted this assignment to go off without a hitch because it was going to be at once the most spectacular of his career. It was also going to be his last.

83

DECEMBER 2, 2002
8:30 A.M.

Blackie Silvestri fought his way up out of the black hole of a drugged sleep. He was not quite fully conscious when he attempted to open his eyes, but he was so dizzy that he was unable to do so. There was a dull ache originating somewhere in the area of his temples and a sour metallic taste in his mouth. Finally, with no little degree of effort, he sat up straight and looked around.

He was in a dark, high-ceiling storeroom, which was dank, cold, and reeked of mildew. There were dusty boxes stacked along the walls, which reached almost to the ceiling and a metal staircase leading up to a door approximately twenty feet above the floor.

The detective lieutenant had no idea where he was, but it was apparent that *they* were in trouble. *They* were himself and Manny Sherlock. Like Blackie, the sergeant was tied securely to a chair a short distance away. Manny was still unconscious.

Shaking his head and wincing from the effort, Blackie was forced to remain motionless for a full minute. When the pain in his head had subsided to a more bearable level, he opened his eyes again. Manny had still not awakened, but Blackie could tell that he was alive because he was struggling weakly against the restraints and moaning softly.

Then the lieutenant remembered how they got here.

Manny had pulled the car out of the headquarters complex lot and driven west toward the Dan Ryan Expressway at 35th Street. Blackie remembered commenting about the vehicle and laughing when Manny said he was allergic to the "new car" smell. The lieutenant also remembered mentioning that he had called Maria before they left headquarters and asked her to fix Italian sausage, peppers, and scrambled eggs for breakfast. He was just about to invite Manny to join them when the blond woman, who had been standing in front of White Sox Park, stepped into the street and flagged them down with frantic hand gestures.

"What's her problem?" Blackie said, as Manny pulled to the curb.

She came up to the driver's window. Blackie could tell that she was a looker, maybe a couple of years past her prime. There was a slight but noticeable hitch in her walk, which indicated an old injury to one of her legs. And she had her right hand in the pocket of her expensive leather coat.

Manny, ever the good cop, began rolling his window down, as Blackie shouted, "Manny, don't!"

But it was too late. Or at least almost.

The blonde pulled a green metal aerosol canister from her pocket. Sherlock's window was halfway down when the woman pointed the canister and sprayed the inside of the car with knockout gas. As the world began to dissolve around him, Blackie became aware of the Ford moving forward. The last memory he had before waking up in this storage room was of a dull thump originating somewhere outside the squad car.

"Blackie," Manny said hoarsely. The young sergeant had regained consciousness and was staring around at their strange surroundings with confusion. "Where in the hell are we?"

Before answering, Blackie looked past Manny at the nickel-cadmium circular container sitting on the stone floor. The lieutenant could not read Russian, but he did recognize the international symbol for radiation.

Finally, in response to Manny's question, Blackie responded, "I think we're in deep trouble, kid. Very deep trouble."

The thump that Blackie heard just before he lost consciousness was the police car knocking Hannah Spencer to the ground. She was not struck hard, but the car was still rolling when she sprayed the knock-out gas at the two cops. She was forced into an awkward position with the canister in one hand and a specially treated protective cloth to keep her from succumbing to the gas in the other hand. She actually bounced off the side of the vehicle as opposed to being hit; however, when she fell, she reinjured the leg that had sustained the gunshot wound in New York City back in 1989. The police vehicle had traveled six more feet before rolling over the curb and coming to a stop with the front wheels on the sidewalk.

Cornelius Shade was driving a white van identical to Riano-cek's. He had watched Hannah Spencer disable the policemen before she fell. He had pulled the van up to where she was lying on the ground, got out, and helped her to her feet. She was in obvious pain.

"Is your leg broken?" he asked.

"No," she managed, "but it hurts like hell. We've got to get them out of that car and into the van."

"I'll do it." He took a deep, ragged breath and hurried toward the stopped police car.

As she looked on, he pulled Silvestri out of the front seat and hefted the unconscious man's body over his shoulder. Struggling under the burden, he carried the cop to the back door of the van. Limping badly, she opened the door and helped Shade dump the body inside. Then they went back for Sherlock.

The female assassin kept a watchful eye out for any curious passersby or a cruising police car. Their luck held, the street remained vacant while they completed the operation. The police car was left with its engine running outside of Comiskey Park.

Now Shade and Hannah Spencer were in a room above the storage area where Silvestri and Sherlock were being held captive. Shade had kept an oxygen mask clamped over his face from the instant they left 35th Street until they reached the location which Rianocek had designated as "Ground Zero." Although she had managed to drive, she was obviously in a great deal of pain.

Shade recovered gradually from the exertion of carrying the two cops' bodies. Hannah Spencer had removed her pantyhose and pulled up her skirt to expose her left leg, which was swollen and inflamed from knee to ankle. From a first-aid kit the assassination team always had available when they were in the field, she injected herself with morphine. This made her marginally more comfortable. However, it was obvious that she was in a bad way.

"We're supposed to go after the lady cop next," Shade said, after managing to stay off the oxygen mask for a full five minutes.

"And so we shall, Mr. Shade." She paused and massaged her knee. "But I think you can handle Sergeant Daniels by yourself."

For a brief instant, he was dumbfounded. Then his face split into a very broad grin.

84

The assassin approached the killing of Larry Cole as if it were a work of exquisite art. Rianocek wanted this sanction to be as perfect an act as was humanly possible. And he intended to enjoy every second of that perfection.

He had begun working on the plan that would culminate today since he had been given the original idea by Clevey Barksdale weeks ago. And although it was indeed Barksdale's idea, it had been Baron Alain Marcus Casimir von Rianocek who had put it all together. From obtaining the device and smuggling it into the United States, to kidnapping the three cops closest to Cole, it had all been planned and then carried out to perfection by the assassin.

Except for the nuclear device, the minor details of the plot had been left to Hannah and Shade. Now the assassin was going to savor the last hours of Cole's life with the relish he would employ if he were sitting down to a fine meal in a four-star European restaurant.

Rianocek followed Cole from police headquarters to the Criminal Courts Building at 26th and California. The arrests that the chief of detectives and his people had made yesterday were being covered by every major media outlet from coast to coast. Once more Larry Cole was the hero, front-page-headline cop. But Rianocek vowed that it would all come to an end by midnight.

Unlike the Mistress of Disguise/High Priestess of Mayhem, who had accompanied Cole from police headquarters and would later join Silvestri and Sherlock, Rianocek did not employ elaborate disguises to conceal his identity. A pair of wire-rimmed glasses, a gray homburg, matching custom-tailored overcoat, and a false goatee were enough to sufficiently alter the assassin's appearance. However, he didn't think that anyone in Chicago, other than Cole, would recognize him.

Rianocek entered the front entrance of the Criminal Courts Building and, without incident, passed through the metal detectors manned by Cook County Sheriff's deputies. It was then a simple matter to follow the noise made by the media throng covering the story of the cop stickup men. He managed to squeeze into the back row of the huge, high ceiling courtroom. There was a squad of stern-faced bailiffs attempting to keep order and the black-robed judge banged her wooden gavel continuously on the surface of the wooden bench. However, the throng of spectators continued to emit a monotonous drone, which was just a few decibels below a roar. Then Chief of Detectives Larry Cole was called to the witness stand. The instant hush that fell over the courtroom impressed the assassin. Rianocek leaned against the back wall and settled in to listen to the testimony of the man he planned to kill.

Gus Lindsay was the state's attorney prosecuting the cop jewelry-store robbers. As this was merely a preliminary hearing, Lindsay had only to establish probable cause for the arrests and he needed only one witness to do this. That witness was Larry Cole.

"And after their arrests, Chief Cole, you were able to identify the armed men wearing stocking masks as members of the Chicago Police Department?"

"That is correct," Cole responded from the witness box.

"Are those officers in court this morning?"

"They are seated at the defense table."

Lindsay turned to the portly white-haired attorney who was representing the crooked cops. He had a reputation for being clever, but not always ethical in defending his clients. The instant the attorney saw the evidence that Cole had accumulated against his clients, he knew that he couldn't win this case. So before he agreed to represent the crooked cops he had demanded that half of his $100,000 retainer be paid. The defendants had come up with the money in cash.

Now, with the questioning of Chief Larry Cole completed, the defense attorney said, "I have no questions for this witness."

The black-robed female judge said, "You may step down, Chief Cole."

As Cole got up to leave the witness box, he caught a brief glimpse of a tall, bearded man standing at the back of the jam-packed courtroom. The instant that their eyes locked, the bearded man lowered his head. To Cole he looked vaguely familiar, but the policeman couldn't place him. However, there were more pressing matters the chief of detectives was concerned about at that moment.

Cole returned to the front bench in the courtroom, which was reserved for police officers. Judy Daniels—who was again wearing her long blond braid, Little Red Riding Hood look—was the only police officer there. Gus Lindsay and the defense attorney were arguing over the setting of bond. Once seated, Cole felt a heavy malaise drop over him. He hadn't slept in over thirty hours, and he couldn't remember the last time he'd sat down at a table to eat a meal. He had indeed solved the series of Loop jewelry store robbers, but at a very high price.

He looked over at the defense table where Sergeant Joe Martin and his accomplices were seated. Their police careers were over and they all faced long prison terms. Cole was sorry for this but he realized that they had brought this situation upon themselves. He had merely been the instrument of their downfall.

Finally, the proceeding came to an end. The bonds for the four robbers were set at $250,000 apiece. Cole was too tired to ponder the possiblities of their making bail. As the preliminary hearing was adjourned, he got slowly to his feet. It was at this point that a strange unease gripped him. He looked around the still-crowded courtroom, but didn't notice anything out of the ordinary. He tried to see the spot where the bearded man had been standing, but Cole's view was obstructed.

"Something wrong, Boss?" Judy asked, noticing the strange expression on his face.

Cole rubbed his eyes. "I guess not. I'm just tired, which has a tendency to make me jumpy. Let's get out of here."

85

DECEMBER 2, 2002
11:42 A.M.

When Judy Daniels left Larry Cole in the parking lot of the Criminal Courts Building, she noticed that he appeared totally exhausted. Respectfully, she suggested that he go home, get something to eat, and sack out for at least twelve hours. He gave her a weak smile and got into his squad car. She watched him drive out of the garage and realized that he would probably get only a couple of hours of sleep before returning to the office. She planned to talk to Blackie and figure out a strategy to make Cole begin taking it easier.

However, right now she was too charged with energy herself to go home and turn in. She had been on the job as many consecutive hours as Cole, Blackie, and Manny. But there was something in either her physical makeup, her metabolism, or both that kept her wired at times like this. She always thought that this peculiarity in her personality was a contributing factor to her initially joining the police department, then becoming an undercover narcotics officer, and, finally, developing the reputation as the infamous Mistress of Disguise/High Priestess of Mayhem. So it was, after leaving the

Criminal Courts Building garage, that she headed for the Area One Police Center Range in the basement of the station at 51st and Wentworth.

The range master was Police Officer Elvin Boone, whom Judy had known since she was in the academy.

"Hi, Elvin," she said, entering the range office and placing her attaché case on a gun-cleaning table.

"I assume that it's you behind that milkmaid disguise, Judy," said Boone, an exceptionally tall black man, who had been an All-American basketball player in college.

She curtsied and replied, "None other than the Mistress of Disguise/High Priestess of Mayhem at your service. Do you think I could shoot off a few rounds?"

He glanced at the wall clock over his desk. "You're going to have to be quick about it. I've got a recruit class coming in at twelve-thirty."

"I'll be fast," she said, opening her attaché case. "I only want to fire off thirty re-loads."

When the range master saw the gun she pulled from the case, he gasped and said, "Judy, what are you going to do with that?"

She hefted the stainless-steel, six-and-a-half-inch barrel, .454 caliber Taurus revolver. "You never can tell when a girl will need the extra protection."

Judy Daniels had no way of knowing how soon she would be needing that extra protection.

The white panel truck pulled up in front of the West Rogers Park six-flat apartment building. The occupant of apartment Two-South in this building was Chicago Police Detective Sergeant Judy Daniels. The van parked down the block, but the engine remained on with faint exhaust fumes coming out of the tailpipe. The driver of the van rolled the window down and adjusted the side-view mirror to reflect the entrance to the building.

Cornelius Shade was behind the wheel and Hannah Spencer was

in the passenger seat. Her face was a mask of intense pain. The morphine injection had worn off, and she didn't want to take another one until they got back to "Ground Zero." She had come along to back up Shade on his mission to kidnap Judy Daniels, but Hannah didn't think she would be of much use to him. And she was also very concerned about Shade's physical condition.

The deadly Englishman with the bad lungs was actually gasping to take in each breath.

"Are you sure you can make it?" she asked with concern.

"This . . . will . . . be simple . . . enough," he managed with great difficulty. "She's . . . just . . . another . . . frigging cop." With that, he got out of the van and slowly made his way to the entrance of the apartment building.

The pair of teenagers had not intended to cut their junior-high-school morning classes to steal a car, but they couldn't resist the temptation. The brand-new gray Ford with its doors open and engine running had been too much to pass up. The oldest had just turned fifteen and had taken two driver's-ed classes. So, after a brief debate, they decided to take the car for a spin. After all, they rationalized, they weren't actually stealing the Ford; it was kind of being offered to them. When they were finished, they would park it right back where they found it. In fact, they would close the doors and leave the keys over the visor, which would be doing the owner a favor.

They tuned the radio to a rock station, turned the volume up as high as it would go, and took off. The Ford drove like a dream, and the short trip they had planned became a bit longer until the morning was gone and it was approaching noon. But the teenagers weren't overly concerned because the gas tank was full.

Then the passenger got curious and opened the glove compartment.

"Wow!" he exclaimed, picking up one of the two compact Motorola portable radios.

"That's neat," the driver chimed in. "Turn it on."

He did.

The car was filled immediately with voice traffic on the frequency the Chicago Police Department Detective Division transmitted on. The teenagers were too stunned to speak. At that exact instant, a marked police cruiser pulled up beside them. The lone cop inside turned to stare at the occupants of the unmarked police vehicle. The pair of young auto thieves turned pale.

86

DECEMBER 2, 2002
12:45 P.M.

Judy Daniels was starting to feel the effects of the long hours as she pulled up in front of her Rogers Park apartment building. But she was in a good mood because she had shot a perfect score with the .454 caliber Taurus and then some. Officer Elvin Boone, the range master, had been dumbfounded.

"Where did you learn to shoot like that, Judy?" Boone asked.

She ejected the spent cartridges from the shiny gun and reloaded with a speed loader before returning the gun to its holster. Turning to the range master, she said, "Do you want to see me do a neat trick, Elvin?"

He was still staring in awe at the pair of targets she had fired thirty rounds into. The "X" ring at the center of each target had been obliterated by the tightest shot group he had ever seen. And she had fired all of her rounds in rapid succession from a distance of twenty-five yards.

"What are you going to do next?" he said, looking up. "Turn

your back to the target and use a mirror to sight in on the silhouette?"

"No," she said with a smile. "I'm going to show you a little something I learned at that combat training course I took last summer."

Recruits attending the 12:30 shooting class had begun drifting into the range office. They were staring through the partition into the shooting area at the oddly dressed blond woman with the large gun strapped to her waist and the range master.

The Mistress of Disguise/High Priestess of Mayhem loved an audience.

"You got a coin, Elvin?"

He reached into the pocket of his uniform trousers and removed a quarter.

"That's too big. A penny or a dime will do."

He came up with a penny.

"Give me a fresh target."

He did.

"Now tape the penny anywhere on the torso of the target outside of the 'X' ring. Don't let me see it."

She turned her back as he taped the penny over the right breast of the silhouette.

"Now send it down to the twenty-five-yard line."

He did.

When the target was in place, she kept her back turned to it. She noticed that the recruits on the other side of the partition were staring at her with wide-eyed interest. If they didn't know who the Mistress of Disguise/High Priestess of Mayhem was before, they certainly would after what she was about to do.

"Is the target in place?" She was forced to shout, because they were wearing ear protectors.

"It's ready, Judy."

"Give me a count of three."

"One."

She took another glance at the recruits. Their eyes bulged as wide as saucers.

"Two."

She forced herself to go limp. The image of the target floated through her mind. As she had been taught at the police combat-shooting school, she reached out with her inner self to touch the target spiritually. She was ready.

"Three."

In one fluid motion, she spun around, drew the .454 Taurus, raised it to shoulder level, and fired.

Judy parked her car and lugged her attaché case with her as she entered the lobby. She checked her mailbox before climbing the two flights to her apartment. Despite her fatigue, there was a sly smile of satisfaction on her face.

Back at the range, after she had fired a single round, Elvin Boone had wheeled in the target. The recruits were plastered to the partition like bugs on the windshield of a speeding car. Judy stood placidly by with the formidable pistol down at her side.

Placing her key in the front door lock, she repeated the Range Master's words. "You hit the penny dead center, Judy."

"You're damn right I did," she said, opening the door to her apartment and stepping inside.

Her place was small, but nicely furnished. The living room furniture was of white leather, and there was a circular, glass-topped cocktail table with a clockface with Roman numerals etched on its surface. Thick floor-to-ceiling drapes covered the windows. When these drapes were drawn, all light from the outside was cut off. This made it easier for Judy to sleep when she had been up all night on a case. Then there were the plants.

The entire one-bedroom apartment was alive with lush greenery, which Judy tended with a watchful, loving eye. She made sure they received plenty of light, were properly watered, received a nourishing plant food supplement periodically, and their leaves were kept bright by applying a leaf shine substance. Now, despite the fatigue dragging at her like a physical entity, she checked a palm plant, which she had repotted recently.

The leaf shine was in an aerosol bottle inside a wooden armoire next to the living-room windows. After examining the plant, Judy removed the spray bottle and first checked to make sure that the nozzle was pointed away from her face. Although the substance was not toxic, there was a warning on the bottle prohibiting consumption or spraying directly into the face. She began applying the liquid sparingly to each leaf.

Then she heard a noise behind her.

At first Judy thought that what she heard was air blowing through the central heating ducts. But when the sound grew louder, she turned around to check it more out of curiosity than alarm. Then Cornelius Shade was there with Judy Daniels in the living room of her apartment. Breathing heavily, he pointed a small, but wicked-looking semiautomatic handgun at her chest.

"Now let's . . . be . . . the good little . . . girl and . . . come along . . . quietly."

The .454 Taurus was in her briefcase over by the front door. She carried a snub-nosed .38 caliber Smith & Wesson revolver in a holster under her sweater. But she would have to be a great deal more clever a magician to get to it than had been the case with that shoot-the-penny-off-the-target trick back on the Area One Range.

"I can . . . see . . . your mind working, darling," he rasped. "You think . . . that I'm . . . just a . . . sick old man. Maybe . . . you think . . . I . . . won't." He had to pause to take in a long, ragged breath. "That I . . . won't shoot . . . because you're . . . a copper. Well—"

Judy Daniels sprayed Cornelius Shade in the face with her bottle of leaf shine and dropped facedown on the hardwood floor. A bullet from the assassin's weapon went off over her head and embedded itself in the wall. But there was only the single round fired.

Without looking up, she rolled away from him, clawing simultaneously at her holstered revolver. She rammed into the television console across the room and twisted her body to swing her gun up. She expected to see the armed intruder standing over her. But he was not there. With her gun extended, she swung the barrel in an arc in front of her as she searched for him.

Her search didn't take long. The intruder had collapsed back onto her couch. The gun he had fired at her was lying on the floor in front of the palm plant she had been spraying with leaf shine. Keeping the .38 trained on him, Judy got slowly to her feet. She felt a dull pain originating somewhere in the vicinity of her right hip. But, other than that, she was unhurt. She couldn't say the same for the armed intruder.

She walked over and picked up his gun. She noticed the laser sights and the extended round bullet clip. Then she checked the man.

He was lying on her couch with his eyes and mouth wide open. He was fighting to draw breath without success and, as she looked on, his skin went from a bright pink to a dull purple. Then, with a final strangled exhalation, his eyes glazed over in death. She checked his pulse quickly, but found none. She considered applying mouth-to-mouth resuscitation, but it was obvious that he was too far gone for it to be effective.

He had apparently died of a massive heart attack. Then she picked up the bottle of leaf shine. She could only surmise that his already-impaired breathing was unable to withstand the nontoxic, but potent plant spray. She looked down at the dead man once more, and then back at the aerosol bottle.

"Who needs a .454 magnum?" she said with a shrug.

87

Despite the long hours, Larry Cole was wide awake when he got to his condo overlooking Grant Park. He was still very tired, but he was too uptight to sleep. He decided that a short run, maybe two miles but no more than three, would take the edge off and allow him to get some rest, which he knew he needed very badly.

Dressed in a hooded sweatsuit and a dark blue CPD wind-breaker, Cole stepped outside and looked up at the overcast sky. Snow flurries were blowing, and it was a degree or two below freezing. After five minutes of stretching, he started off at a slow pace, running south on Lake Shore Drive. The harbor was empty and the icy lake reflected the color of the dark midday sky. Off in the distance, approximately a mile from his apartment building, was the Museum Park complex, which was made up of the Shedd Aquarium, the Field Museum of Natural History—of which Cole had less-than-fond memories—and the Adler Planetarium. This was where the chief of detectives was headed. Crossing the Museum Park complex, jogging completely around the planetarium, and re-turning to the condo building would give Cole the desired distance for his run.

As he ran down the east walkway of Lake Shore Drive, he breathed in the cold, fresh air and felt himself beginning to revive. It was on a day much like this one that he and Blackie had become involved in the incident that had led to the Mafia assassination of John T. Ryan, the former CPD chief of detectives. In fact, Cole consulted the Rolex Submariner on his wrist, today was December 2. It was exactly twenty-five years ago. Cole grinned at the thought. The memory of that day and ensuing night was as vivid to him as the arrests of Sergeant Joe Martin and his band of crooked cops yesterday. Continuing to run, Cole recalled other cases that had followed after that first big headline case in the winter of 1977.

The assassin was seated in the white panel truck in the parking lot of the Chicago Yacht Club a block south of the point where Cole had started his run. Through a pair of binoculars, Rianocek was able to see Cole smile, as he ran past the lot. The assassin had no way of knowing that the memory prompting that smile was directly related to the odd twenty-five year relationship that he had had with this cop.

Rianocek had not expected Cole to come out of the building so soon. From the way the cop had looked in court this morning, he was obviously exhausted and looked to be headed home and straight to bed. Then, in an hour or two, after everything was in place, he would make a call that would wake the cop from a deep sleep and plunge him into a waking nightmare which he would never survive.

Rianocek watched the jogging figure recede into the distance. The assassin checked his watch. By now he should have heard from Hannah and Shade. Picking up the mobile phone, he punched the button on the keypad that would connect him with them.

"Yes, Baron?" she answered after one ring.

He noticed the strain in her voice. "How is everything proceeding at your end?"

"We expect to have achieved our final objective shortly."

Rianocek didn't like the sound of her voice. He could tell that something was wrong, but he was not about to demand a detailed explanation on this unsecured line. But he did ask, "Do you have everything under control?"

"Yes, Baron," she said flatly. *"We are just fine. I had a slight*

problem with my leg during the initial phase of the operation, but it is not serious."

"Are you okay?"

"I will be able to complete the task satisfactorily."

Then she broke the connection.

For a brief moment, he considered abandoning Cole and going to check on their progress. But that would alter his meticulously planned timetable. He had promised Barksdale that the act of vengence would be carried out today; December 2.

Rianocek would remain with Cole. Hannah and Shade knew what they were doing. And who were Blackie Silvestri, Manny Sherlock, and Judy Daniels compared to them?

As he waited for Cole to return from his run, the assassin looked west at the Chicago skyline. He studied the maze of skyscrapers in the downtown area. A dangerous look came over the assassin's face. It was the look he always displayed just before he killed. But he had never killed an entire city before. Of course, there was a first time for everything.

After breaking the connection with Rianocek, Hannah Spencer chewed on her bottom lip so hard that she broke the skin and blood flowed into her mouth.

"Damn!" she swore, snatching a tissue from her purse and dabbing at the cut. It wasn't a bad wound, and the pain, compared to the throbbing in her leg, was minor. But even the injury to her leg could not diminish her rising concern and anxiety for Cornelius Shade.

She checked the front of the apartment building where the female cop lived once more. Hannah had watched the woman with the long blond braids get out of the same car in which they had planted the incriminating evidence against the Barksdales several years ago. The female assassin remarked to herself that the lady cop kept pretty good care of the red mid-sized Toyota. However, it wouldn't be necessary for Shade to identify this so-called "Mistress of Disguise/High Priestess of Mayhem"—he had already picked the locks to her apartment and gained access.

Judy Daniels should have been easy for Shade to kidnap. All he had to do was get the drop on her at gunpoint and force her out to the van. But now Hannah Spencer was aware that he was critically overdue.

Deciding that this was the time for action, she gritted her teeth against the pain, checked the small SIG P225 pistol she carried in her coat pocket and got out of the van. It was beginning to snow heavily now, and the ground was becoming slippery. The pain in her leg had settled into a dull throb, which she managed to ignore as she made her way to the entrance to Judy Daniels's apartment building.

88

DECEMBER 2, 2002
1:15 P.M.

Lake effect" snow occurs in winter, when cold air blows across the warmer waters of Lake Michigan. This results in blizzard-like conditions of such density that visibility is often reduced to zero. Such a meteorological phenomenon occurred in Museum Park as Larry Cole was on the return leg of his run.

The lone jogger trudged along through the accumulating snow with his head down against the elements. There was not a single pedestrian in sight, and the cars on Lake Shore Drive were an indistinct blur. He felt as if he was running through glue because his shoes stuck to the ground with each step. His exertion had increased remarkably and he was beginning to regret having come out on such a wretched day.

The portable radio in his windbreaker pocket beeped, indicating that he was being paged. This granted Cole a brief respite from his battle with the elements.

He moved over to a tree next to the Field Museum of Natural History to get out of the wind and pulled the instrument from his pocket. The Motorola radio was compact, but provided the user access to all fifty-eight radio frequencies utilized by the Chicago Police Department. It was also equipped with a cellular telephone. Only a select few members of the department were issued this equipment. The staff of the chief of detectives were among them.

"Cole."

"Boss, it's Judy."

"Yeah, Judy." He turned his back against the icy storm to enhance the clarity of the transmission.

"I've got a bit of a problem. There's a dead man in my living room. I think it's the English assassin Cornelius Shade."

Stunned, Cole completely forgot that he was standing on the lakefront in a blizzard.

"What happened?"

She told him.

"He was obviously attempting to kidnap you, and I don't think that he's working alone. Get some backup right away. I'll contact Blackie and Manny. I've got a funny feeling about this. Call me back when you get some uniforms there with you."

"Roger, Boss."

Cole decided to dial Blackie's home instead of contacting him by radio. Maria Silvestri answered the phone.

"Hi, Maria. Is Blackie still asleep?"

Then the elements seemed to resume their ferocity with a fury that chilled Larry Cole to the marrow of his being. Blackie had not arrived home that morning. Before Maria could become alarmed,

Cole told her that he was probably still at the office, which was something that the chief of detectives sincerely hoped was true.

Cole contacted detective division headquarters; then he spoke briefly with Lauren Sherlock. Blackie had not been at the office since Cole had left for court, and Manny had not been home, either. Finally, he tried their radios. There was no response.

Slowly, still standing in the blowing snow on the western shore of Lake Michigan, Cole returned the combination radio/telephone to his windbreaker pocket. Something mysterious and equally dangerous was happening here. He was about to leave the shelter of the tree when his radio beeped once more. It was Judy again.

"The Twenty-fourth District is sending a couple of cars and a patrol sergeant over here, but it's going to take them a while in this weather," she said in a whisper. *"But somebody was trying to get in my front door a little while ago. I think they're still out there."*

"Where are you?"

"I slipped out the back door. I have the key to my next-door-neighbor's apartment. I'm there now. I'm going to take a look through her peephole and see who's out there."

"Do it, Judy! I'll keep the frequency open."

Again he settled in to wait in the cold. After what seemed like an eternity, she was back.

She whispered, *"It's a woman with short blond hair. She's favoring her right leg. She just used a set of lock picks to get inside my place."*

"That's Hannah Spencer," Cole said. "And she's just as dangerous as Shade, or their boss, Alain Rianocek."

"I've got an idea."

"Judy," he said with urgency, "just wait for your backup units."

There was a pause. Then she said, *"They're here."*

Hannah Spencer stood in the living room of Judy Daniel's apartment and stared down at Cornelius Shade. Dead bodies were not an alien sight to a woman who had been a homicidal maniac since she was sixteen years old. But somehow Shade's death touched a secret place in the blackness of her killer's soul.

She did not sob, nor did her eyes brighten with tears. But she was indeed moved. It was as if a part of her had died with him. Then she realized that she would have to inform Baron von Rianocek that their old colleague was dead.

She was reaching into her pocket for the telephone when she became aware that she was no longer alone.

Hannah still held the automatic in her hand, but it hung limply down at her side with the barrel pointed at the floor. The exertion of her journey through the falling snow to the lady cop's second-floor apartment, followed by the shock of finding Cornelius Shade dead, had placed her in a state of mild shock. She hadn't even checked the apartment for Judy Daniels, whom she and Shade had come here to kidnap.

Now she turned around to find six Chicago police officers surrounding her. Five of these officers were in uniform. The sixth was the blond ponytailed Mistress of Disguise/High Priestess of Mayhem. And each of the cops had a gun pointed at her.

For a brief moment, she considered making a fight of it. But, although she was insane, as manifested by the number of people she had murdered over the years, she still possessed a regard for her own safety.

She allowed the weapon to slip from her hand and fall to the floor. Then she raised her arms slowly.

A smile spread across her face. Hannah Spencer had been in police custody before. Despite her arrest now, these people and their leader, Larry Cole, would still have to deal eventually with Baron Alain von Rianocek.

89

Blackie!" Manny shouted.

The lieutenant jerked himself awake. Still bound to the chair in the cold subterranean storage room, he had dozed off. He was unaware that he had been asleep for two hours.

"Damn!" Blackie twisted in his seat. "My left hand has gone numb."

Trapped a few feet away, Manny said, "And I have to go to the bathroom."

Before Blackie could make a comment, they heard footsteps in the corridor at the top of the wooden staircase. The cops looked up just as a tall bearded man wearing a beige overcoat and matching homburg strode into view. The man stopped and stared down at them for a long moment, which succeeded in making the captives uneasy. Then he started down toward them.

Cole stepped out of the shower and began toweling himself dry. He was still chilled after being caught in the lakefront blizzard which was going to drop four to six inches of snow on the Chicago area before nightfall.

The chief of detectives brushed his teeth, combed his hair and was about to dress when the telephone on his bedside table rang.

"Hello."

There was a long pause before Cleveland Emmett Barksdale, Ill's voice came over the line. *"Good afternoon, Mr. Cole."*

Cole sat down on the edge of the bed. "Good day to you also,

Mr. Barksdale. To what do I owe the honor of this unexpected call?"

"We're playing the gallant law-enforcement-professional role to the hilt on this frosty winter's day, aren't we?" he said with barely controlled anger.

"We do whatever the job demands."

After another pause, Barksdale said, *"Do you know what today is, Cole?"*

"Your birthday?"

The sound of the former lawyer's teeth grinding together became audible. When he again spoke, there was very real menace in his voice. *"I never knew that cops possessed such a remarkable sense of humor. Before this day is over, Cole, you're going to need it."*

The cordial tone was gone from Cole's voice as well. "Now that we've got the idle chitchat out of the way, are you ready to get down to business?"

"I want you to take an automobile ride with me this afternoon, Mr. Cole. I'll even do the driving."

"Would we be riding in a hearse, Mr. Barksdale?"

There was a chuckle from Barksdale's end, which sounded to Cole like a strangled cough. *"That's an excellent idea. Do you have any aversion to being a passenger in such a vehicle, sir?"*

Cole was growing tired of this game of cat and mouse. "Suppose I do?"

"Then you will never again see Blackie Silvestri, Manny Sherlock, or Judy Daniels alive."

"I'm surprised at you, Barksdale. As a former attorney and inmate of a penal institution, you should know that as of right now you have committed the crimes of aggravated kidnapping, aggravated battery, unlawful restraint, and extortion, all of which are felonies."

"The risk is acceptable to me, Mr. Cole. Now I will collect you from the front of your Grant Park apartment building in exactly thirty minutes. I'm quite sure you'll have us placed under some form of official surveillance, which I have no objection to; however, if

we are stopped or interfered with in any way by any of your cop
buddies, then I promise you'll never see your friends again."

"What are you hoping to get out of this farce, Barksdale?"

The laugh that echoed across the telephone line sounded as if
it came out of a mausoleum. *"I plan to avenge myself on you, Mr.*
Cole, for what you and your government did to me and my grand-
father." Then he hung up.

Cole replaced the telephone on its cradle and stared at the instrument for a moment. Now the chief of detectives had another
piece of the puzzle. Cole also knew that Barksdale was unaware
that the attempt to kidnap Judy had failed. This gave the cop an
advantage, but Cole still had no idea what kind of game Clevey
Barksdale and Baron von Rianocek were playing. And although the
assassin had yet to show himself, Cole knew that he was here in
Chicago and deeply involved in the strange events that had occurred
on this day. His adversaries might have the advantage, but the game
was just beginning.

The watch commander at the police headquarters detention facility
where Hannah Spencer was to be incarcerated ordered her to be
examined by a doctor. This was due to the preincarceration screen-
ing procedure uncovering the injury to her left leg.

The female assassin was in pain, but she forced herself to think
through the agony she was experiencing. With Shade dead, it was
up to her to help Baron von Rianocek carry out the sanction for
Barksdale. So she would have to accomplish the escape from police
custody on her own.

She recalled her brief detention in New York's Bellevue jail
ward. On that occasion, Baron von Rianocek had arranged her escape through the infamous, but now dead, criminal mastermind,
Karl Steiger. Now she could not wait for assistance from the outside
because time was rapidly running out. And her best bet to carry out
the escape would be while she was being treated at the hospital.

The snow was still falling and there was at least a three-inch accumulation on the ground. She had been transported from police headquarters to the hospital in the back of a police van. She was shackled securely to a foul-smelling padded seat, which prevented her from moving while the vehicle was in motion. She was alone in the rear of the prisoner transport vehicle, which helped her to think better. But she was unable to come up with a clear-cut plan of action. She would have to react, rather than act.

The pair of burly police officers unlocked the back door and helped her climb out. Her shackled hands and the injury to her leg made it difficult to walk through the accumulating snow. One of the cops held her arm as they moved from the parking lot into the emergency room. She had expected Judy Daniels to be there, but the dangerous lady cop was nowhere in sight.

Inside the ultramodern, but crowded emergency room, Hannah Spencer was led over to the admittance desk. One of the policeman handed the harried-looking nurse seated there a form, which she merely glanced at before handing it back to him and saying, "Cubicle three. I'll be back there in a couple of minutes."

They took Hannah through a swinging door into a large oblong room, which reeked of alcohol and was lined with curtained cubicles. The second curtain on the left bore the number 3. The cops led her there.

Although she concealed it effectively behind a mask of intense discomfort, Hannah Spencer was conducting a fierce inspection of the men accompanying her and the treatment area. The police-van operators were veteran cops, who looked to have been around for quite a few years. She noticed that they exhibited mild boredom and appeared to be simply going through the motions. But there was no way that she could take them physically, so she would have to use her wits.

The cubicle was sparsely furnished with a paper-covered bed on rollers, and a table containing miscellaneous medical supplies, such as gauze, bandages, tongue depressors, alcohol swabs, and Q-Tips. There were also a couple of drawers built into the tabletop.

The female assassin was speculating as to what was in those drawers when the nurse from the front desk entered. Now Hannah Spencer was able to get a better look at her.

The nurse was thin, with lank gray hair and skin that still bore the scars of severe acne suffered during adolescence. She possessed the attitude of the overworked, underpaid public servant. A clipboard in her hand, she began questioning, "So what seems to be your problem, Ms. Spencer?"

"I suffered a gunshot wound years ago, which I aggravated in a fall earlier today."

"Where is this wound?"

She pointed to the general area.

"Are you in pain?" the nurse demanded officiously.

Hannah Spencer glared at the ugly woman. "I've felt better."

"Are you currently taking any medication?"

She looked down at the puddles of melting snow on the tile floor. "I gave myself a shot of morphine about five hours ago."

"Are you allergic to any medication?"

"No."

"Okay," the nurse said, "the doctor will be in to see you shortly. I want you to strip from the waist down." She turned to the pair of cops. "I need you gentleman to remove those handcuffs and take a seat out in the waiting room."

"Now hold on a minute," one of them protested. "This woman is under arrest for committing a felony."

Defiantly, the nurse responded, "I don't care if she just shot the Pope. You gentlemen cannot remain in this area while she undresses and is being treated. It is *strictly* against hospital rules. Now, if you want this woman to receive care at this facility, you will have to follow those rules."

The policemen exchanged puzzled looks. Then the one who had spoken before said, "Would it be okay if we cuffed her to the bed?"

The nurse frowned her disapproval, but finally acquiesced.

"That will be acceptable as long as it does not impede the doctor's examination."

Coming forward, he unlocked the right bracelet and relocked it to one of the bed railings.

"Will you be able to undress?" the nurse asked Hannah.

Concealing the raging excitement coursing through her, the female assassin responded, "I'll manage."

Then the nurse escorted the policemen out of the cubicle and closed the curtain leaving Hannah Spencer alone.

She waited until their footsteps had receded before she sprang into action. Utilizing her free left hand, she tried the drawers in the utility table and found them locked. Frantically, her mind raced. There had to be something in here that she could use. She again scanned the table. Then she saw what she had missed the first time.

It was wedged between the containers for the tongue depressors and Q-Tips. Possibly one of the doctors, or even the ill-tempered nurse, had left it there. It could have been from a patient's file or used to hold a stack of forms together. It was an innocent-enough item, which had a simple function. However, in the hands of Hannah Spencer, the stray paper clip became a handcuff key.

She managed to unlatch the bracelet in less than thirty seconds. Once free, she got to her feet. The pain and stiffness in her leg made movement difficult; however, the adrenaline flowing into her system erased the discomfort temporarily.

She peered out from behind the concealment of the curtain. There was a great deal of activity taking place in the treatment area. In cubicle 2, a team of medical personnel were attempting to restart a cardiac arrest patient's heart using electric shock. A man with a bloodstained towel wrapped around his head was lying on the bed in cubicle 4. The other cubicle curtains were drawn.

She checked the entrance to the treatment area. Neither the cops nor the nurse were visible. But there was no way she would attempt an escape that way. She looked around for an alternative.

Between cubicles 4 and 6, there was an emergency-exit door. All she had to do was cross the treatment area and go through that door. She didn't hesitate.

It seemed that everyone in the treatment area was staring at her, but none of them said a word as she made her way across the wet floor. She expected to hear one of the cops shout, "Halt!" Then she could very well end up with an additional wound in her body to keep company with the one she'd received back in New York.

She concentrated on the door, which seemed miles away. Then she found herself six feet away, then four, then two, and . . . She pressed the release bar and a cold blast of snowy air hit her in the face. She didn't take time to reconnoiter where she was, but kept going straight ahead putting as much distance between herself and the emergency-room treatment area as possible.

She stepped around a corner of the brick hospital building and found herself on a street running in front of the main entrance. She glanced back the way she had come. The door she had made her escape through was barely visible through the falling snow, but there were no signs of pursuit. She kept going.

Then she saw the taxi stand.

As she limped toward the line of cabs, she felt the first glimmer of hope that she would indeed make it. Although the cops had taken her gun when they searched her, the matron had allowed her to keep all of her other belongings, including her money and, after a brief examination, even her cell phone. All of her personal items would be taken from her before she was placed inside a cell. But they had been unable to do that until she was checked out by a doctor.

Hannah Spencer got in the backseat of a Yellow Cab. After giving the driver a downtown location, she activated her telephone and called Baron von Rianocek.

90

Langley, Virginia
DECEMBER 2, 2002
3:18 P.M.

The temperature in northern Virginia was 60 degrees, under clear skies. At CIA headquarters in Langley, business was proceeding as usual with no hint of the potential storm brewing inside the building's gray stone walls.

In the top-floor executive wing, the presidential appointed Agency Director was conferring in an emergency session with the Deputy Director of Field Operations and the Assistant Deputy Director for Special Operations. Prior to his appointment, the director had been a federal judge. The deputy director and the assistant deputy director were intelligence community professionals, who had been with the Agency for nearly twenty years. In the face of the disaster the director had just been informed of, he had gone pale and his hands had developed a noticeable tremble. By contrast, the pair of Agency veterans seated across from him were relaxed to the point of serenity.

Falling back on his former legal career, the director attempted to get a handle on this situation by examining it thoroughly and analytically.

"Now, what you gentlemen are telling me," he said in the same solemn tones that had pronounced many a severe sentence in a court of law, "a Russian-made nuclear device has been smuggled into this country with the cooperation of the United States Government?"

The deputy director—a gaunt man with white hair—responded

matter-of-factly, "That's pretty much the case, sir, but I don't believe there's any cause for alarm."

The director said incredulously, "I don't understand what you're talking about!"

The assistant deputy director—an aging Ivy League type—quipped, "Director, we have done this type of thing in the past. As long as we maintain the integrity of the mission, there won't be a problem."

The former judge looked at the men seated across from him as if they were from another world. "What 'mission' are you talking about? Engaging in any form of domestic intelligence operation by this Agency is against the law."

The deputy director and the assistant deputy director exchanged amused glances that were not lost on the director. Before he could explode, his intercom buzzed.

"Yes!" he barked.

"There's an Agent Anderson here to see you, sir," his secretary, another agency veteran, announced.

"Excuse me, Director," the deputy director said, "but we invited Agent Anderson to attend this meeting. He supervised the shipment from Paris to its final destination in Chicago."

The assistant deputy director added, "We assumed you would want to speak directly to him, sir."

Swelling with outrage, the CIA director shouted, "You're damn right I want to speak directly to him! Send him in!"

But as he sat behind his desk fuming, the politically appointed head of the most powerful intelligence organization in the world, began getting a sinking feeling in the pit of his gut. It was as if he was about to leap into a bottomless pit. Then, when Special Agent Anderson walked into the office, the director knew that he was in trouble.

Special Agent Anderson's first name was Eugene, but he seldom used it after he joined the Agency. He preferred, in all of his dealings both official and unofficial, to be known as either Agent Anderson or simply Anderson. He was middle-aged, overweight, stoic, and cynical. He was an avid disciple of the Dickie Fagan school of intelligence operations. Now, wearing a rumpled brown suit and unshined black oxford shoes, he stood before the director of the Central Intelligence Agency. This was not a first for him; he had been with the Agency longer than any of the men present.

The assistant deputy director turned in his seat to look at Agent Anderson. "The Director would like the details concerning the shipment that we transported from Paris to Chicago utilizing the Barksdale Network."

Agent Anderson looked confused momentarily. Then he said, "May I ask the reason for this inquiry, sir?" He addressed his question to the assistant deputy director.

The deputy director exploded. "Because, Agent Anderson, I am your boss!"

The outburst didn't faze the agent. "Then I must ask, sir, if you are aware of the Nixon Protocol?"

"The what?"

The deputy director cleared his throat before interjecting, "The protocol was named for Richard M. Nixon, Director. It was established to give not only the President, but also the occupant of this office, plausible deniability in the case of a public disclosure. Had Mr. Nixon had such deniability, he might not have been forced to resign. In fact, Ronald Reagan used it. . . ."

"I don't want to hear about any protocols, gentlemen. I want to know about this nuclear device."

The assistant deputy director first shrugged, and then nodded to Agent Anderson.

"Very well, sir," the agent said. "The Barksdale Network was reactivated on November 28 of this year. This network had been inoperative since March 23, 1999. A shipment was placed into the network in Paris and transported via normal channels to Chicago. En route it was inspected routinely, and the Russian-made tactical nuclear device was discovered."

The director was now staring at Agent Anderson with an expression approaching total awe. Now he managed to say, "And who activated this network?"

"It was done by operational code, sir. The origin of such information is on a 'need to know' basis." Anderson paused a moment. "As the code was correct, I didn't have a 'need to know.' "

"And you permitted this . . ." The director had to swallow before he could complete the statement. ". . . shipment to continue on to its delivery point in Chicago?"

The agent first glanced at his fellow intelligence professionals seated across from the director before replying, "Of course."

91

Chicago, Illinois
DECEMBER 2, 2002
TWILIGHT

In Chicago, the snow stopped after dumping a five-inch accumulation on the city. The temperature dropped into the twenties, and there was barely any wind in a town noted for it. In Grant Park, the snow covered the trees and the ground, giving the area a Christmas-card appearance.

The streetlights had just come on when Larry Cole stepped outside of his apartment building, but the beauty of the winter scene was lost on him. He took in a breath of the arctic air and exhaled a thick vapor cloud. He was ready, but he had no idea what awaited him at the conclusion of his ride with Barksdale.

Cole was dressed in a black turtleneck, black slacks, and a fur-lined black leather waist-length jacket. A pair of black boots with a mirror shine completed his grim ensemble. Beneath the jacket he wore a Kevlar bulletproof vest. He carried a stainless steel .44 caliber Beretta semiautomatic pistol in a shoulder holster. He carried two extra fourteen-round clips for this weapon. In the small of his back, hidden beneath the turtleneck, was the nickel-plated .45 Colt Commander he had carried twenty-five ago on the day of the shoot-out with the Mafia. He felt that this gun brought him good luck, and tonight he needed all the luck he could get. But he also realized that he would need more than random good fortune to rescue Blackie and Manny from Alain von Rianocek. To this end, he had taped a .25 caliber Browning automatic to his right ankle. A flash-light, a Swiss Army knife, and a set of handcuffs were attached to his belt. He also carried his compact radio.

As he stood in the cold, Cole felt a familiar feeling descend on him. As he looked off across the park at the lights of the Chicago Loop, the years fell away. He remembered the feel of the .45 in his hand and the violence of the recoil when he fired at the Mafia soldiers. He recalled the heavy, cloying stench of cordite and the taste of gunpowder in his mouth. But most of all he remembered the giddy sense of dangerous excitement that had coursed through him on that night so many years ago. An excitement that he had felt many times over the ensuing years. An excitement that was with him right now.

Now he watched the black Cadillac hearse pull off Lake Shore Drive. Cole noticed that the car was spotlessly clean and shone with the brilliance of a recent wax job. It was equipped with tinted win-dows, so Cole was unable to see the driver. But he had no doubt as to his identity.

With the frozen snow crunching beneath its tires, the hearse pulled to a stop at the curb directly in front of Larry Cole. No movement was visible inside, nor were the windows lowered or any of the doors opened. Finally, Cole stepped forward and opened the door. As if he were descending into Hell, he got into the hearse.

The Sears Tower in downtown Chicago is one of the tallest build-ings in the world. The structure has 110 stories, and the highest occupied floor is 1,431 feet above the ground. The twin antennas provide an additional 19 feet, giving the building a total height of 1,450 feet from base to apex. The building has a multiple-tube design, was completed in two-and-a-half years, and was topped off in 1973. To support the massive edifice, excavation of the site had to be taken to depths up to 50 feet below street level down to limestone rock with a load-bearing capacity of 100 tons per square foot. The 65-foot caissons anchored in the bedrock are connected by a 54-inch concrete slab that covers the entire floor area of the structure.

Because the building was built in the "Windy City" it was designed with two wind-load factors: "design level," with a normal safety factor and a "limit level" for extreme wind velocities. So at times, when there are extreme weather conditions in Chicago, occupants of the upper floors feel a definite sway, which a few have compared to being on the deck of a ship at sea.

There were four subbasements built into the foundation of the tower. Each of them served various functions: heating and air conditioning, building maintenance, and storage areas for building tenants.

Access to these areas was prohibited to the general public. Building security maintained excellent control over access and egress to the building, and very few crimes had ever been reported inside the tower. However, authorization could be obtained by a simple process: leasing floor space in the Sears Tower.

The German firm of RanCorp and Associates had entered into an agreement with the real-estate firm that managed the tower. RanCorp had leased a suite on the ninety-second floor for a period of one year. Exclusive access was also provided for RanCorp personnel to sublevel storage area 4. This storage area was at the lowest level of the 1,450-foot building, where the assassin was now holding Blackie Silvestri and Manny Sherlock captive.

The policemen were still confined, but not in the painfully restrictive manner of before. In fact, under the circumstances, they were being treated very well.

When the tall, bearded man arrived, he held them at gunpoint, removed their tight rope restraints, and used a single set of cuffs to handcuff them together. He had allowed them to use a basement washroom and then produced a bag containing sandwiches and bottled water. Then he moved to the opposite end of the storage area, some thirty feet away from Blackie and Manny, where he removed his hat and took a seat on a wooden crate. Removing a paperback book from his pocket, he began to read.

Manny chewed listlessly on half a dry ham-and-cheese sandwich. Finally, he turned to the lieutenant. "What in the hell is going on here, Blackie?" he whispered.

Blackie had already consumed a turkey sandwich on white bread. Now he sipped from a bottle of Evian water. "I've been working on this all day, Manny," he responded softly. "And it doesn't look too good for us. You see that metal container over there?"

Manny nodded.

"The writing on the outside is in Russian, but that symbol on the side is a radiation warning."

"That's a nuclear device?!"

The sharp tone made their bearded captor look in their direction, but he made no move toward them. After a moment, he returned to his book.

"Keep your voice down, kid," Blackie cautioned. "We don't want to get that gentleman riled up."

"Who is he?"

"I'm not 100 percent certain, but I believe he's a European assassin named Baron Alain von Rianocek. The boss had a run-in with him in New York twelve or thirteen years ago. I did a profile on Rianocek. That woman, who sprayed us with the knockout gas, and the guy who had trouble breathing are his associates. They are Hannah Spencer and Cornelius Shade."

Manny managed to finish his sandwich. "But why did they kidnap us?"

Blackie looked from the assassin, to the metal cylinder, and then back at the sergeant. "If I don't miss my bet, we're bait, Manny."

Rianocek was reading the novel *The First Deadly Sin* by Lawrence Sanders, which he had picked up in a used bookstore. While he was actively engaged in an operation, losing a portion of his mind in a work of fiction helped him to maintain his emotional equilibrium. He was aware that the kidnapped policemen were talking, but he didn't care. They weren't going anywhere. Barksdale would be collecting Larry Cole shortly, and then it would all begin. The assassin corrected his thinking! Then it would all *end*.

But at the moment, he was more concerned about Hannah Spencer and Cornelius Shade. They were seriously overdue on the quest to kidnap Judy Daniels. He hoped that this delay was due to the weather. He was just about to call them again when his phone rang. Placing his book down on the wooden crate beside him, he answered it. It was Hannah Spencer.

92

DECEMBER 2, 2002
5:17 P.M.

The interior of the hearse reeked with the stench of rotted flowers. Barksdale, dressed in a black suit, white shirt, black tie and hat, sat behind the wheel. His complexion had developed a ghostly pallor that made him resemble a corpse.

When Larry Cole got into the front seat beside him, Barksdale put the hearse in gear and drove slowly across the snow-covered ground.

"Where are we going?" the policeman asked, when they halted for a red light at Lake Shore Drive.

"To see your colleagues. Lieutenant Silvestri, Sergeant Sherlock, and Sergeant Daniels."

"Where are they?"

The light changed and Barksdale turned south on the drive. "Not very far."

At Monroe Street, he turned right to travel west toward the Chicago Loop. The traffic became heavier due to a combination of the weather and the raging rush hour. Barksdale was a cautious, tentative driver, and their progress was maddeningly slow.

"You said that you were looking for revenge against us for what happened to you and your grandfather," Cole said as they crept across Columbus Drive. "The implication is that you feel that what we did, as far as the prosecution of the two of you for wholesale drug trafficking, was wrong."

Barksdale's face remained cast in stone. "During the time I spent in prison, I thought about you quite a bit, Mr. Cole. I analyzed everything that happened to me and my grandfather going back to that first time you became involved in our affairs twenty-five years ago.

"You see, my grandfather was the chief counsel for Don Paolo Arcadio's Family. It was my grandfather who discovered that one of your predecessors, Chief of Detectives John T. Ryan, had coerced the Don's bookkeeper into testifying against the Arcadio Organization. It would have been a simple matter for Frankie Arcadio and Tony Lima to eliminate 'Big Numbers' Albanese. Then you and Silvestri showed up, and everything went wrong."

The hearse exited Grant Park and turned north from Monroe Street. As far as the eye could see, the entire boulevard was decorated with Christmas ornaments. The beauty of the decorations was lost on the occupants of the black vehicle. After a short wait for the light to change at Madison Street, the hearse turned left and headed for the heart of the Chicago Loop.

Staring stonily through the windshield like an upright corpse, Barksdale continued, "That's when my grandfather suffered the first setback of his brilliant legal career. Don Paolo was a strong, practical man, who was singularly lacking in imagination and suspicious to the point of paranoia. So when he heard about the death of his nephew Frankie at the hands of you two cops, he was certain that my grandfather was somehow involved."

For a moment Barksdale took his eyes off the street and studied his palms. Cole stiffened at seeing this, but the hearse driver returned his hands to the wheel quickly. As they crossed the intersection of State and Madison, Barksdale said, "It was because of you that I was forced to kill Tony Lima to protect my grandfather. I still have the ugly little man's blood on my hands."

"How tragic that must be for you," Cole said sarcastically.

Barksdale continued as if the policeman had not spoken.

"Because of what you did on that December night, my grandfather was forced out of the Arcadio Family and prohibited from doing any business with them ever again. It took years for us to regain our firm's prominence."

"Is that when you went into the drug business?" Cole interjected.

"No," Barksdale responded, as they picked up speed on Wacker Drive. "That's when the United States government became our principal client."

Above them loomed the gigantic Sears Tower.

The electronic monitoring computer had been developed by the FBI. It was utilized primarily to track criminals, who availed themselves of twenty-first-century technology. Basically, after the proper information was placed into the data bank, it was possible to trace the origin of computer transmissions or use a cellular telephone as a homing device. Now the FBI monitoring computer was homing in simultaneously on a police radio and a cellular telephone.

The Chicago Police Department's eight-member SWAT team

were hunched around the computer console watching the screen. A female sergeant sat at the keyboard. They were in a police van parked on Jackson Boulevard at Canal Street on the southeast side of the Sears Tower. The SWAT team was ready to mount a mission at the command of the sergeant. But they would not make a move until she gave the order.

Now there were two signals being broadcast as bright circles of light on the screen. One of them represented the signal being broadcast by the radio carried by Chief of Detectives Larry Cole. This signal was moving steadily toward the second signal. This one had been identified as the cellular telephone which Hannah Spencer had called after she escaped from custody. The screen revealed that this signal was stationary somewhere inside the immense building.

Then, as the sergeant and the black-clad SWAT team watched, the two signals merged.

Rianocek was having difficulty coming to grips with the death of Cornelius Shade. When Hannah informed him of the sick Englishman's death, the assassin had been so overwhelmed that his brain refused to process the rest of what she had told him. At least, momentarily.

The assassin had never been close to anyone before in his life. He had never known his parents, he had no brothers or sisters, and the lovers in his life were merely sex objects. He had never really had anyone he could call a "friend" and, in fact, he had not considered Cornelius Shade a friend. He was a "colleague." Perhaps he could even be called a "close acquaintance." Now he was dead, and Rianocek was having a problem dealing with it. Then he considered the rest of Hannah Spencer's message. She had managed to single-handedly escape from police custody. Despite his absorption with Shade's death, this had surprised him.

"Where are you now?" he asked.

"In a taxi heading for the downtown area, but it is snowing heavily and our progress is slow."

"Return to 'Ground Zero' at once."

Slowly, as his killer instinct began reasserting itself, danger signals began going off in his mind.

He hadn't questioned Hannah in depth about her escape. Yes, she was undoubtedly one of the most dangerous and cunning human beings he had ever encountered. But she was also quite human, as the incident in New York City when she was wounded and subsequently captured, demonstrated. Perhaps it had simply been negligence on the part of the Chicago Police Department. However, Alain von Rianocek had learned long ago to respect the law-enforcement agencies of the world with a particularly high regard for New York and Chicago cops. After all, these agencies had produced Larry Cole and Joe Leak.

The assassin snapped himself out of his hypnotic trance and rejoined the world. If Hannah's escape from custody had been orchestrated by Cole, she was indeed free. Once Barksdale and Cole arrived, he and Hannah would leave so smoothly and quickly that there would be little the famed cops of the Windy City could do about it. Then, in short order, as Barksdale had requested months ago, there would be no more Windy City.

"Hey, Rianocek!" Silvestri called.

The assassin looked across the storage area at the bound policemen. He didn't respond. Then he noticed the reason the lieutenant had called to him. Sherlock was violently ill.

The assassin crossed to them, but stopped seven feet away. When the sergeant vomited, he had managed to twist in his chair so that the contents of his stomach were deposited on the cement floor. Sherlock was still heaving, his face was flushed a beet red, and he was sweating profusely.

Rianocek checked Silvestri. The heavyset cop was pale and also looked ill. Then an alarming thought jolted the assassin. His eyes flickered to the metal cylinder. Before they left Paris he had used a Geiger counter to check for possible radiation leakage and found nothing that exceeded normal levels. However, something could have occurred in transport, which was causing the cops to suffer the effects of radiation poisoning.

Rianocek was just about to check the container when the sound of a loud bell ringing resounded through the lower level. This was the signal that someone was on the way down.

The assassin prepared to receive guests.

93

DECEMBER 2, 2002
5:35 P.M.

Traffic around the Sears Tower, both foot and vehicular, was extremely heavy due to a combination of the business day coming to an end and the recent snowfall. The entrance to the underground parking garage was on the northeast side of the building. Barksdale drove up to the ramp and stopped at a key-card terminal. From his inside coat pocket he removed a piece of plastic, which he inserted into the access port. The wooden barrier swung upward and the hearse entered the garage.

Cole was alert for any wrong moves coming from either the inside or the outside of the hearse, but nothing threatening occurred. Barksdale drove from the public parking area into the reserved parking section. He proceeded to a freight elevator and stopped with the front bumper less than a foot from the elevator door. He flicked on the high-beam headlights and a sensor opened the door automatically. He drove into the elevator, which was big enough to accommodate three normal-sized vehicles or four to five compact cars. Barksdale maneuvered the hearse to a control panel and rolled his window down and inserted a key attached to the access card into a lock on the panel. Then he pressed the bottom button.

With a lurch, the elevator began to descend into the subbasements beneath the Sears Tower.

The taxi pulled to the curb at the west entrance to the building. A woman with short blond hair paid the driver and got out. Slowly, walking with a pronounced limp, she crossed the sidewalk, climbed the steps to the lobby and made her way inside the building. She went to the elevators servicing the lower-level garage and the storage areas. A moment later, she was en route to sublevel 4.

The ride in the freight elevator ended and the doors opened. Barksdale drove the hearse onto a winding ramp that wound down even farther beneath the Tower. Finally, they came to a halt at a cinderblock wall into which a single metal door was set. On this door was stenciled "Sublevel 4 Storage Area" in white paint.

"We have arrived, Mr. Cole," Barksdale said.

Now the policeman pulled the .44 caliber Beretta. "Okay, now we're going to get some ground rules straight before this charade goes any further. You will stay in front of me at all times. If you try anything funny, I'm going to put a bullet in the back of your head. And if anyone else tries anything, you're going to get it first. Do I make myself clear, Barksdale?"

The disbarred lawyer sat rigidly behind the wheel staring stonily through the windshield. He replied, "I have no intention of doing anything to provoke you, Mr. Cole."

"Lead the way."

They got out of the hearse and crossed to the metal door. Barksdale opened it and, followed closely by Cole, proceeded through it. They entered a long corridor illuminated by frosted glass covered ceiling lights. Barksdale walked at a steady, unhurried pace. At the end of the corridor they stepped out onto a landing above the area where Blackie Silvestri and Manny Sherlock were being held. Alain Rianocek stood over the captives with a gun pointed at their heads.

The assassin shouted, "Cole, give Mr. Barksdale your gun or I will kill your friends."

Cole looked down at Blackie and Manny for a moment before handing over the Beretta.

"You'd better check him for additional weapons, Barksdale," Rianocek instructed. The assassin added, "You've been to prison, so you should know the drill."

Cole surrendered the Beretta and submitted to the search. Barksdale was indeed good, but he had been on the receiving end of frisk searches and had never been taught to do one thoroughly. So he missed the .45 Colt Commander anchored at the small of the cop's back.

"I want to see about my friends," Cole said.

"He wants to come down," Barksdale called to Rianocek.

"Come on." The assassin continued to hold the weapon on his captives.

Cole took the lead as they descended the stairs into the storage area. The policeman was aware that Barksdale was not covering him, but rather holding the confiscated weapons down at his sides. Perhaps, before this was over, he could exploit that advantage.

When they reached the bottom of the steps, Cole came face to face with Alain Rianocek for the first time in years. Now the cop recognized the assassin as the bearded man he had seen standing in the rear of the courtroom this morning. Then Cole noticed that Blackie and Manny were ill. He rushed over to help them.

When Cole approached, Rianocek, still holding the gun, backed away. Moving over to the place where Barksdale was standing at the foot of the steps, he said, "It is time for me to depart, my friend. My debt to your family has been paid in full. You can handle everything from here."

Barksdale's bloodless complexion became a shade or two paler. "Have you armed the device?"

The assassin began displaying a marked degree of menace.

"That will be simple enough for you to do after I'm gone. After all, it was you who selected this place to be your tomb."

When Barksdale had laid out the plan for Rianocek, the part that had particularly intrigued the assassin was that the act of destroying Cole and the city the cop had protected for so many years would be the last of Barksdale's life. In committing suicide in this manner, the assassin perceived a level of nobility in Barksdale that he found quite admirable. However, at this point, Rianocek's job was done. It was time for him to leave.

Another bell sounded, indicating that someone else was on the way down to the subterranean storage area. Rianocek knew that this would be Hannah Spencer. Indeed, time was getting short.

"How are you going to ensure that Cole and the others won't try to escape after you leave?" Barksdale said.

"You've got his guns. You should be able to keep them here until the detonation."

The irregular tapping of heels on the stone floor of the corridor at the top of the stairs could be heard. A moment later, a woman appeared. Rianocek merely glanced at her before saying to Barksdale, "I'm going to show you how to arm the device. Then we're leaving."

The assassin kept an eye on the cops, as he led Barksdale over to the case.

"Undo the clasps and pull it open," Rianocek instructed.

Barksdale opened the cylinder.

"There are three triggers to arm the bomb. There is one on the left, one at the center, and the last one—"

Barksdale began to laugh. Annoyed, the assassin turned around to find out what was so funny. Then he saw what was inside the case he had shipped via the Barksdale Network from Paris to Chicago. Instead of a nuclear device, it contained kilo-sized cellophane packages of white powder. Rianocek guessed accurately that this powder was either heroin or cocaine.

Now Barksdale's laughter became wildly hysterical. He ripped open one of the packages and began tossing its contents into the air. The powder floated down to cover his head, face, and clothing. All the while, he continued his insane laughter.

94

DECEMBER 2, 2002
5:45 P.M.

Cole moved Blackie and Manny away from the area where they had been confined, and Manny had become ill, over to a spot against the far wall. At the moment, he was more concerned about them than for his own safety. But he figured he had an ace up his sleeve of which Rianocek was unaware.

Then Barksdale went mad.

The assassin was momentarily distracted and even appeared amused at the hysterical antics of the man who was covering himself with white powder. But there was no way Cole could make a move against Rianocek because he was too far away. Also, the policeman would have to be careful in reaching for the .45 anchored at the small of his back. If a gun battle broke out, an unarmed Blackie and Manny would be caught in the cross fire.

Now Rianocek began moving toward the stairs. Cole watched him carefully. The moment of truth was near.

The blond woman remained standing at the top of the stairs. Since her arrival, she had not moved.

So this—the assassin's last job—had failed. And again Larry Cole was involved. Somehow the Russian tactical nuclear weapon had

been removed from the metal canister and replaced with . . . Rianocek saw his error. He had activated the Barksdale Network to
smuggle the device into the United States. As the network was
created to smuggle drugs into the country, some idiot along the way
had figured that was what it had been reactivated to do. Rianocek
wondered what they had done with the bomb. That was really of
little consequence to him right now. It was time to leave. Other than
the operation's failure, the only regret he had was Cornelius Shade's
death. However, Rianocek rationalized, no one lives forever. Before
leaving, he planned to kill Cole to balance the scales for Shade.

Keeping an eye on the cops, the assassin climbed the stairs. He
was not worried about their interfering with his escape. They probably had the entire Sears Tower cordoned off, but he and Hannah
would get out. This was because they would be going by a route
that the police would never think to cover.

He glanced at the top of the stairs, where Hannah still stood in
shadow. Even in the dim lighting, her appearance was very familiar—as familiar as Cornelius Shade's had been. Suddenly he realized that something was wrong. She was standing as she always
did, with her weight on her good leg. But she was favoring the
wrong leg.

The assassin stopped. Barksdale's insane, hysterical laughter
continued to echo through the storage area. Rianocek studied the
woman more closely. She looked like Hannah, but then it was not
Hannah, which meant—

He turned around and looked at the trio of cops against the far
wall. Because Silvestri and Sherlock were handcuffed together, Cole
was standing over them holding the sick cop's head. Rianocek
raised his gun and pointed it at them.

"Chief Cole, I want you to tell Officer Daniels to come down
here with her hands up. If she doesn't, then I'm going to kill you.
And I can assure you that I possess deadly accurate aim."

Cole faced the assassin's gun. "I don't know what you're talking about, Rianocek. I came here alone with Barksdale."

"Baron," the woman said. "What's wrong?"

The sound of Hannah Spencer's voice stunned him. He swung around to look at her once more just as the bell went off, signaling that the sublevel elevator was descending from the lobby. This was followed immediately by the alarm indicating that someone was coming in from the garage. Adding to this confusion was Barksdale's continuous laughter. Rianocek swung his gun barrel away from Cole and shot Barksdale in the back. He collapsed facedown inside the canister and lay motionless.

Then Cole shouted, "Freeze, Rianocek!"

This was followed by the woman pulling a six-inch-barrel pistol, pointing it at him and yelling in a voice the assassin had never heard before, "One move and you're dead!"

The assassin was trapped between them, but he didn't believe that they possessed his skill with a firearm. Cole had a .45 automatic trained on him. Rianocek doubted if the cop could get off an accurate shot with that weapon at this distance. So his game plan was to deal with the woman first, then turn on Cole. Then he would take on whoever was coming down in the elevator and entering through the garage. The odds against him were high, but he was an extremely capable dispenser of death.

In one smooth motion, he swung his pistol in the direction of the woman and fired. A continuous volley of shots echoed through the sublevel storage area beneath the Sears Tower.

EPILOGUE

The traffic around the Sears Tower was still quite dense as the Chicago rush hour ebbed. The Chicago Police SWAT van and a pair of marked squad cars parked on the Upper Wacker Drive side of the Tower received scant notice from the passersby on the street. An unmarked olive-drab Huey helicopter circled high above the Sears Tower and took up a position parallel to the sixtieth floor on the south face. A pair of bos'n's chairs were lowered to the sixtieth-floor roof, which ran at right angles to the main tower. Despite the fierce wind blowing, the helicopter, which was capable of accomplishing rescues on the high seas, hovered in a virtually stationary position above the ground.

A man and a woman appeared on the lower roof of the building. Fighting the wind, the couple made it to the bos'n's chairs and strapped themselves in. Then they were lifted off the roof and pulled into the belly of the aircraft.

A man in a black flight suit and crash helmet assisted them out of the chairs before calling the pilot on the shipboard intercom to inform him that their passengers were on board. With that, the helicopter gained altitude and flew off in a north-by-northwest direction. Less than fifteen minutes later, it landed at O'Hare Airport's military airfield.

The plane taxied to a hangar in a restricted area. A black Chevy Blazer with tinted windows drove from the shadows of the hangar and pulled up to the aft side door of the helicopter. Special Agent

Anderson got out of the front seat of the Blazer and approached the helicopter. A ramp was extended to the tarmac and the man and woman, who had been airlifted from the roof of the Sears Tower, exited the aircraft.

The helicopter's engines had been shut off, but the noise was still quite loud, forcing Anderson to shout, "Your exit route out of the United States has been prepared as instructed, sir. The flight will leave from this location in forty-five minutes. I have arranged a Learjet, which will fly you nonstop to Paris."

The man stepped forward. "Do you know who I am?"

Anderson squinted at him for a moment. "No. Should I?"

"Then you've never seen me before?"

"No."

"Why did you arrange the escape route?" the woman asked.

Anderson became annoyed. "I prefer the term 'extraction,' ma'am."

"I have a term that I prefer as well," the man said.

"What's that?"

"You are under arrest," Larry Cole said.

DECEMBER 24, 2002
3:40 P.M.

The press had a field day with the arrest of the CIA agent in Chicago on narcotics-trafficking charges. The story was covered by local, national, and international media outlets. Although he stood mute and refused to even speak to a court-appointed attorney, the front pages of newspapers and the lead stories of all newscasts featured photos of the handcuffed CIA agent being escorted from the Criminal Courts Building by Chicago cops.

Accompanying each story were interviews with CPD chief of detectives Larry Cole. Interviews containing some very damaging information about the intelligence community in the United States.

At the center of this raging controversy was the Russian-made metal cylinder, which was smuggled into Chicago containing twenty kilos of cocaine. A physicist at the University of Chicago examined the container and discovered traces of excessive radiation. Although the scientist refused to speculate as to what the case had contained prior to the cocaine being placed inside of it, Cole filled in the blanks: a Russian-made tactical nuclear device, which was indicated by the markings on the outside of the case.

But despite the evidence, the government, or more specifically the CIA, denied any knowledge of what had occurred in Chicago on December 2, 2002. Then the official disinformation process began.

Special Agent Anderson was portrayed as a rogue intelligence operative, who had a long history of erratic and bizarre behavior. When questioned by the media as to whether any of this alleged "erratic" behavior had been criminal or conducted within the boundaries of the United States, the CIA spokesman replied a diplomatic, "No comment."

Then, as quickly as the story had blossomed to national prominence, it vanished from the news. No follow-up stories, editorials, or commentaries were forthcoming. It was old news. However, Larry Cole was still very much interested in the events that had led to the kidnapping of Blackie Silvestri and Manny Sherlock and the attempted kidnapping of Judy Daniels. Events that had also resulted in the deaths of Cleveland Emmett Barksdale III and the international assassin Baron Alain Marcus Casimir von Rianocek.

The staff had been given the afternoon off on this Christmas Eve and Cole was alone in his office with only a desk lamp on to provide illumination. A light snow was falling on the city, but there was no noticeable accumulation and none was anticipated. Judy and Manny had decorated the chief of detectives' office, and Christmas lights twinkled and blinked in the semidarkness.

Cole was using the dim, quiet atmosphere to enhance his perception and thinking processes. There were a number of loose ends connected with this case and he planned to tie all of them up. Everything including finding out what the still-in-custody Agent Anderson knew.

Judy had done a masterful job of getting Hannah Spencer to make a call to Rianocek on her cell phone. The female assassin's escape from police custody had been artistically staged by the Mistress of Disguise/High Priestess of Mayhem. After Hannah made the call to the assassin she was quickly recaptured and never outside of police surveillance at any time.

The sickness Blackie and Manny had succumbed to in the sublevel storage area of the Sears Tower was not caused by radiation. The canister had been hermetically sealed and would not have emitted dangerous levels of radiation even if the nuclear device had been inside. A check-up at the hospital revealed that the violent sickness Manny suffered was due to a combination of excessive fatigue, stress, and gastrointestinal irritation.

Another problem solved.

But that canister bore the markings in Russian for a tactical nuclear device and the U. of C. physicist had speculated that such a device could have indeed been contained inside the canister prior to the narcotics being placed inside. So, Cole asked himself, where was the bomb?

Agent Anderson wouldn't talk even under the most stressful interrogation that Cole could legally conduct. Then there was Hannah Spencer, who had been just as uncooperative as Anderson. Perhaps Cole could come up with a strategy to crack the female assassin's shield of unyielding silence. He was starting to work on this problem when his intercom buzzed. It was Blackie.

"I thought you'd gone home."

"I've got a couple of things to finish up first. But I thought you'd like to know that they've found the bomb."

"Where?"

"What used to be a mountain in Colombia, South America."

CHRISTMAS DAY, 2002
11:00 A.M.

Hannah Spencer was alone in her cell in the Federal Correctional Facility on South Clark Street in Chicago. She had been there for three weeks. The only times that she was removed from this overheated gray-steel vault was for two court appearances, during which she had entered the pleas of "not guilty" to a plethora of felony charges. Each time she left the cell her hands and feet had been secured with steel bracelets attached to a heavy chain. Her meals were served to her three times a day by a pair of matrons, who were both younger and more fit than the prisoner. A librarian provided a catalogue of reading material—paperback novels and magazines—and there was a television set mounted in the wall of her cell. By notifying one of the on-duty guards, Hannah could choose to watch one of four stations—HBO, CNN, WGN, or NBC—from nine A.M. until midnight.

Although she had been arrested before, this time the incarceration wore more heavily on her. This was because there would be no rescue now. Baron von Rianocek and Cornelius Shade were dead. To some extent, she considered her own life over as well. There was no way she could beat the charges, and it was likely that she would spend the rest of her life in prison. This caused her to go into a deep depression. On top of everything else, it was Christmas and she felt terribly alone.

The door to her cell was unlocked and two matrons entered. It was too early for lunch and there were no court proceedings conducted on Christmas Day, so the inmate wondered what they wanted.

"Come on, Spencer," one of the matrons said. "You've got a visitor."

Surprised and more than a little curious, Hannah was led to a narrow telephone-equipped visitor's booth. She instantly recognized the woman in the milkmaid costume with the long blond braid.

"Well, Sergeant Daniels," the inmate said, "what do you plan to give me for Christmas? Cancer?"

DECEMBER 26, 2002
9:00 A.M.

There had not been a nontest demolition of an atomic device anywhere on Earth since the end of World War II. As a result, the explosion in South America attracted worldwide attention. The United Nations sent an inspection team to the site, which had been previously known as a criminal haven for the Colombian drug cartel. Now there was nothing left but an enormous crater nearly two miles in diameter.

A wave of fear spread around the world. Nuclear terror was once more a threat to human existence, and there was a demand for answers as to what had occurred.

The day after Christmas, Larry Cole asked for an emergency meeting with Carolyn Falk, the United States Attorney for the Northern District of Illinois. The attractive attorney with the severe manner was far from pleased at being called into the office during the week that she planned to take off before the New Year. That was until Cole laid out his plan for her.

"I can guarantee that Hannah Spencer will testify before the grand jury concerning the atomic detonation in South America. She can give you dates, times, and places as to where the bomb was obtained and how it was first smuggled into this country before ending up in Colombia. That should give you some leverage to use against the stonewalling Agent Anderson."

And it did.

JANUARY 9, 2003
1:45 P.M.

Agent Anderson testified before the U.S. Senate Intelligence Oversight Committee in Washington, D.C., for three days. The hearings were held behind closed doors, and none of the participants would make any comment to the press during the course of or at the conclusion of the proceedings. However, there were leaks.

It was rumored that a retired CIA deputy director named Richard "Dickie" Fagan had engaged in illegal domestic intelligence operations, which had a connection to the Colombian drug cartel. During the course of the hearings, Dickie Fagan went into the study of his Arlington, Virginia, mansion on a frosty winter afternoon, placed a loaded .38 caliber revolver in his mouth, and pulled the trigger.

At the end of January the Senate Intelligence Committee sent an "Eyes Only" report to the president. By March 1 a number of sweeping changes were made in the American intelligence community, including a complete overhaul of the CIA and the NSA. It was rumored that this housecleaning was due to the Agency having a connection to the nuclear detonation in South America, which virtually destroyed every vestige of the Colombian drug cartel. Nothing was mentioned about the CIA engaging in drug trafficking. Agent Anderson admitting to the senate committee that he had followed the Barksdale Protocol by removing the Russian-made tactical nuclear device from the metal canister and replacing it with narcotics provided by the Colombians was never mentioned. However, the secret protocol also dictated that the device be shipped to the Colombians as payment for the drugs, where the wrong person tampered with it and . . .

JANUARY 10, 2003
3:50 P.M.

Cole and Blackie arrived at the Chicago Medical Examiner's office. They were met by Assistant Medical Examiner Darlene Johnson, a dark-haired woman with a winning smile that belied her profession. "Thank you for responding so quickly, Chief Cole. The gentleman's papers were quite in order, and I can't hold Alain Rianocek and Cornelius Shade any longer."

"Where is this 'gentleman?' " Cole asked.

"In my office."

The M.E. led them there.

He was seated at her desk smoking a cigarette in violation of the morgue's somewhat ambiguous "Clean Air" policy. When the M.E. and the cops entered, he turned around.

Cole and Blackie sized him up.

Tall, thin, and impeccably dressed in a brown pin-striped Savile Row suit with accessories that were worth a king's ransom and a cashmere overcoat that would cost Blackie a week's salary. His hair was light brown and worn shoulder-length. There was a three-carat diamond ring on the pinky finger of his left hand, which sparkled in the overhead lights. The cigarette he was smoking was inserted in an ivory holder.

"There is no smoking in the morgue, sir," the M.E. announced.

He possessed pinched features, a narrow pointed chin, and eyes of such a light shade of gray as to appear opaque. With a disdainful snort, he detached the smoldering cigarette from the holder and dropped it to the floor. He ground it out with the heel of a polished brown shoe.

"So sorry," he said with a noticeable British accent. "I forgot I was in America, where death by violence is the highest in the world, yet you still attempt to regulate personal choice."

"Chief Larry Cole and Lieutenant Blackie Silvestri of the Chicago Police Department," Dr. Johnson said, "this is Mr. Ian Jellicoe. He has come to claim the bodies we talked about."

"Were you a relative of either Alain Rianocek or Cornelius Shade?" Cole asked.

"No," Jellicoe responded, remaining seated and placing the empty ivory cigarette holder back in his mouth.

"Then what was your relationship to the deceased?" Blackie demanded.

"That is none of your concern, gentlemen," the Englishman said, stifling a yawn. "I have obtained the appropriate documents from your State Department and have arranged for transportation to Europe for Baron von Rianocek and Mr. Shade. There they will be buried following an appropriate ceremony."

"Are you aware that Alain Rianocek was an international assassin, Mr. Jellicoe?" Cole said.

The Englishman stood up. "I am aware of many things, Chief Cole. Now if you don't mind, I'll collect the bodies and be on my way."

Darlene Johneon hesitated until Cole nodded. Then she said, "The coffins will be loaded in the hearse parked at the south loading dock for transport to the airport."

"Very good, Dr. Johnson. And a good day to you all," Jellicoe said with a bow. Then he draped his overcoat over his shoulders, clenched the empty cigarette holder in his teeth, and walked out.

When he was gone, Blackie said, "What do you think of this guy, Boss?"

Cole smiled. "Someday he's going to be trouble for us, Blackie. Big trouble."